DANGEROUS
GIFTS

First published 2013 by Solaris
an imprint of Rebellion Publishing Ltd,
Riverside House, Osney Mead,
Oxford, OX2 0ES, UK

www.solarisbooks.com

ISBN: 978 1 78108 079 5

10 9 8 7 6 5 4 3 2 1

A CIP catalogue record for this book is available
from the British Library.

Designed & typeset by Rebellion Publishing

Printed in Denmark

DANGEROUS GIFTS

A BABYLON STEEL NOVEL

GAIE SEBOLD

SOLARIS

To Dave. My constant star.

CHAPTER
ONE

I WALKED INTO the humid, faintly citrus-tinged air of The Swamp, an Ikinchli hangout run by my friend Kittack, looking for a chat and maybe a sip of one of the few things he serves that don't dissolve the top off my tongue.

The minute I was through the door my shoulder-blades started to itch. There were a lot of hunched shoulders, a lot of people looking at me out of the corners of their eyes, and that sharp silence of conversations that have finished in mid-air. Several of the males' cranial crests were up; not a good sign in a normally laid-back bunch of lizards.

Kittack's customers are mostly, like him, expatriate Ikinchli from Incandress, their home country, where the self-appointed master race, the Gudain, are in the habit of giving them a pretty wretched time.

I glanced around for Kittack, but he must have been down in the cellar. The barmaid, Talia, was looking worried. Being a lamia, she can normally calm down punters just by giving them the eye till their knees buckle, but nobody seemed to be in the mood.

I walked up to the bar as though I hadn't a care in the world, but I kept my hands free. "Hey, Talia. Kittack around?"

"Hey, Babylon. He's just..."

I felt the Ikinchli come up behind me. He was a big lad; only half a head shorter than me, with dark chestnut scales on his head and arms fading to creamy yellow on the chest and belly; solidly muscled. Pretty, but unfortunately he didn't look friendly. He stood a foot or so along the bar, leaning on one elbow and looking me over. "When you start serving Gudain in here, Talia?" he said, without taking his eyes off me.

Oh, dear.

"I told Kittack this place needs better lighting," I said. "I'm human, not Gudain."

"Oh?" the Ikinchli said. "Funny. Look like Gudain to me; darker, maybe. Maybe you got dirty doing Gudain's dirty work."

"Excuse me?"

"She called you Babylon, right? Only one person I know called Babylon in this town. Someone who messed in our business. Someone who helped the Gudain pull one big trick on my people."

"I don't know what you think I've done, mate, but..."

He leaned forward and hissed, "The *Itnunnacklish*. There *is* no Itnunnacklish."

Ah.

The Itnunnacklish was a girl born, to all appearances, Gudain, who, if mated at the right time to both an Ikinchli and a Gudain male, became a fusion of the two species, proof that they had once, as Ikinchli legend had it, been one and the same. She'd been in Scalentine for her transformation, and I'd been sent to find her, not knowing, at the time, who or what she was.

She was still here, under the eye of the Diplomatic Section, but she was due to go home and take up her role as one of the ruling council of Incandress. And I had agreed, for reasons that seemed more ill-considered by the minute, to think about going with her.

Right now, though, that wasn't my problem; getting this guy out of my face without a fight, *that* was a problem.

"What she is or isn't is no business of mine," I said.

"She is *Gudain*. Only thing any Gudain wants is to live high on our sweat. She is a fraud, and you..."

I saw the fist coming in and got my arm up before it connected with my argumentative friend's head. The hitter – another Ikinchli lad, taller, skinnier and with paler colouring – looked shocked when my forearm connected with his. Lucky for him I wasn't wearing studded bracers; those are strictly for when you *want* to rip someone's arms up. Even so, there was a loud slap, and he winced.

"You want to hit someone, why don't you take it outside?" I said.

He hissed something in Ikinchli. The other hissed back. What little Ikinchli I know mostly means something on the lines of "bring it on, big boy"; this conversation sounded similar in meaning, but rather less friendly in intent.

People were watching, some were pushing back their chairs, as if about to join in.

The cellar door swung open and Kittack walked into the room and swore. At least, I think he swore. It can be hard to tell in Ikinchli. "Babylon?" he said. "You for hire today?"

"You think this is the time?" I said, still holding my arm up between the two angry customers.

"I think this is a fine time for me to hire someone who can rip off heads and spit down necks," he said. "You want to start with these two?"

"Now, Kittack, you *know* I don't rip off heads. Generally. Fingers, perhaps. Even arms, if necessary. But no heads. And no spitting. Spitting is vulgar."

"I will pay you very much money. Maybe all the money they will never be spending in here again because *they will have no arms left to lift a drink with*."

The two had stopped arguing and were looking at me uncertainly.

Talia slid out from behind the bar with a pot, and I heard a rattle as she dropped in a couple of coins.

"Talia," I said, "what are you doing?"

It really isn't possible for a lamia to look innocent, but she tried. "I just thought maybe I'd see if anyone wanted to, perhaps, place a little wager..."

"No bets, Talia. Besides, I don't want to fight anyone. I just came in for a nice quiet drink and a chat."

"Yes," Kittack said. "Like most people. Anyone who wants to have a big argument, they can get out of my bar, now, and not come back until they can act like respectable citizens, and leave the political stupids at home where they belong, okay?"

The first Ikinchli hissed disgustedly and turned away. "I have no home, not any more. You know why? Taken for Gudain taxes." He snatched up his coat, catching the chair and knocking it over. "You believe Gudain lies if you want. Gudain and human, I don't see no difference; humans beat up on us too. Me, I got better things to do. No pretenses, no One who is Both. When our land is cleansed of all the Gudain, *then* we can go home."

He slammed his way out, pulling a puff of cold air into the warm moist atmosphere.

His opponent let out a breath, and his crest sank. He sat down and put his hands to the sides of his head, as though it hurt, and muttered something. One of his friends reached over and slapped him on the shoulder. "More drink, hey?" he said.

Kittack signalled Talia, and turned to the lad. "You going to be any more trouble?" he said.

"No."

"Ah, is stupid peoples everywhere," Kittack said. "You drink up now, don't talk any more politics, okay?"

A few other people got up and left quietly; but I didn't like the way they were looking at me.

"Kittack, can I have a quick word?"

"Sure." He looked around, sighed, and said, "You come on in back. Talia, get Babylon a drink. On the house. And one for me."

Once she had done so, he shut the door behind us, shaking his head.

I know Kittack pretty well. We've been friends and occasional lovers for a while. "You all right, Kittack?"

"What I just did, maybe that wasn't so smart."

"How do you mean?"

"Never mind. What you need?"

"Advice," I said, watching his face. "I'm thinking about taking up a job guarding the Itnunnacklish, for a few days."

He looked away from me, fidgeting with his glass. "Why you got such a thing for her, Babylon? You done her one pretty big favour. Now you want to walk into a pile of *guak* for her?"

"I haven't said I will, yet."

"Thinking about it."

"Yeah," I said.

Why *was* I thinking about it? Sure, I needed money, I always seem to. Besides, I know what it's like to be a symbol of something important. Been there, done that, got the screaming nightmares. She needed friends.

But already this job was putting my back hairs up, and I hadn't even spoken to her.

"I haven't said yes, Kittack. But I'd be grateful for some pointers about Incandress. So long as you don't mind..."

"Mind? No. Some of them talk about home all the time: 'oh, so wonderful, why we ever leave,' you know? Sometimes I say, if it was all so wonderful, what you doing here, wailing all over my bar?" He shook his head. "Me, I don't talk so much. But okay. Incandress, she is warmer than here. Lots of hot pools, too." He looked mournful for a moment. "Very good for the blood, hot pools."

"I'm sure they are. But I really meant the people."

"Ah, okay. Well, you know, Gudain, some are maybe decent. Treat you okay. But to many, anyone who is not Gudain is a beast, made to work, and just waiting to sacrifice Gudain maidens to the Old. The Old don't want sacrifice maidens, what good is a Gudain girl to some Ikinchli who is dead for two hundred years? But some Gudain, they believe this, or maybe they just want to."

"I remember you told me." The Maiden Sacrifice legend got dragged out whenever someone wanted an excuse to beat the Ikinchli up, it seemed like.

"Oh, and the Gudain, they are very..." He paused. "They don't like to talk about bouncy. Or think. Or do, much."

"What? They don't talk about sex?"

He grinned at me. "All this bouncy is very animal, you know? The Gudain, they are most superior and have no animal needs."

"They must *do* it, otherwise where do little Gudain come from?"

"Not many little Gudain. Also, just don't *mention*. For Gudain bouncy is only to happen with the one person, after much delicate ceremony, and in private, and never, ever to speak of. Not even jokes."

"You're kidding."

He shook his head, still grinning. Bloody lizard; *he* wasn't the one who was going to have to weld his mouth shut if he went to Incandress.

"And religion?" I said.

"They worship the Great Artificer. Who is like big super-Gudain who raise Gudain up from rolling around in hot mud with the rest of us, and make them all special. They go to a special house and burn smelly smoke to talk to him."

"All right. So what about your people, Kittack? Anything I need to not mention?"

"The Itnunnacklish, she is a good subject to stay off."

"Since, *if* I take the job, I'm going to be standing right next to her most of the damn time, I'm hardly going to be talking about her. Like that's going to help. And Ikinchli religion?"

Kittack's tail shuddered; it took me a moment to realise he was actually embarrassed. It's not a state he visits very often.

"They say, every Ikinchli who dies has all the wisdom of their life, and all those bits of wisdom, they are the Old. So gods and ancestors, they are pretty much the same thing, for Ikinchli." He gave a long, hissing sigh. "You don't accuse anyone of kidnapping maidens for sacrifice, probably you be fine. Me, I don't go to ancestor ceremonies in a long time. The older I am, the more it seems is all smoke and mirrors, you know? And I see people get treated like *guak* all the time, what are the Old doing? Nothing. Is no surprise some Ikinchli get tired waiting for the Old, and start fighting back. You sit on someone long enough, one day they will bite your bottom."

"Are we talking civil war here?"

"War, I don't know. Big mess and lots of people dead, maybe."

"Sounds pretty much like war to me," I said. "Enthemmerlee wants to prevent that, doesn't she?"

"Wants, yes. But you going to have your work cut, Babylon, to keep her safe. Plenty of Gudain want her dead, for what she is. Ikinchli too. The ones who hate Gudain and think she is a trick they are playing, but also, some of the ones that believe she is real. Because, there is a big difference between you believe in something, and it turns up, you know? Sometimes a thing looks better when it is still a long way away."

Yes. The Avatars on my home plane had looked a lot better (or at least, more impressive) before I'd become one of them.

Kittack stared into his glass.

"Kittack?"

"I got family, back home. Tried to make them come here, but they won't."

"I didn't know."

"I said to them, Scalentine is a bit crazy, but at least you got a chance here. But, 'Oh, no, can't leave, got to look after the ancestors, got to keep the family farm,' why? This farm? It is some mud, some rocks, lucky if you get half a crop. If you do, the *guak* come and say, 'Oh, look, you got some food, now you owe us big taxes, thank you so much.'"

"*Guak*? I thought that meant shit?"

"Also is a word for the Fenac. They are like the Militia here, only mostly not so decent. What can I do? I send the family some money." He swallowed the rest of his drink, and blew out air through his nostrils.

"If I go," I said, "you want me to try and get in touch with your people while I'm there?"

He turned his cup around in his hands, the webbing between his fingers flexing. "They are old," he said. "Change, new things, these frighten them. Gudain, too. And you, maybe." Okay, maybe I look a little like a Gudain. Unlike Ikinchli I don't have scales, a tail or a long blue tongue. But I'm more of a bronze colour; Gudain skin is green-tinged.

"So the Ikinchli won't trust me because I look like a Gudain and the Gudain won't trust me because I'm *not*. Great. Well, thanks." I got up.

"Babylon."

"What is it?"

"I got to ask *you* a favour now." He was looking at his glass again, not that there was anything in it.

"What would that be, Kittack?"

"You got your foot into politics, with this. Politics and religion both. Me, I got a bar to run, you know? Best, maybe, you don't come in here for a while."

"Ah. Right. So you don't want to hire me after all."

He tried to smile. "Can't pay what you're worth anyway. I'm sorry, okay?"

"Yeah," I said. "Me too."

THAT LITTLE ENCOUNTER had put me in a grim mood. I needed to get my head freshened, as I had a couple of clients that afternoon, and a party to prepare for. I headed home through the smart part of town; by the good hotels and the Exchange hall. There's a little park there where, in summer, people walk about and lie on the grass, and listen to musicians or strolling players, or get themselves a little loving. Too cold for much of that, now; one draggled lutist stamping and blowing on his fingers, and a meaty chunk of a man standing on an upturned crate. He had two chins and thick black hair, and had a little symbol sewn onto his coat: it looked like a square with a triangle on top. Standing with their hands clasped behind them, either side, were a skinny big-eyed boy no older than sixteen, who, in contrast to the speaker, lacked any chin at all, giving him a chickenish look, and an older, more solid lad who seemed faintly familiar.

They'd already drawn a bit of a crowd: the lute-player, obviously hopeful that he'd get a bit of attention when the speaker was done; a handful of delivery-boys taking time off their bosses wouldn't approve; a couple of the freelance whores, underdressed for the weather. A mostly human crowd, for a wonder. The good people of Scalentine, eager for a moment's amusement.

"Fellow citizens! Look around you!" The chunky man invited, gesturing in case they hadn't understood his instructions. "What do you see?" he said. "The best hotels, the best eating-houses, shops full of finery and gold. But for ordinary citizens, the price of grain is rising by the day. The bread is being torn from the mouths of children. Can *you* afford these places? No." I wondered if he meant the tall, human exquisite about two feet in front of him, who was wearing a year's worth of a dockworker's earnings, and a hairstyle so fantastically elaborate it looked as though it were designed by a clockmaker. "And why are these things beyond your reach? Because other forces are pushing you aside. Forces that do not belong here, and the people who encourage them, and befriend them, and ride side-by-side with them over the rights of those who built this city." I wondered whose rights were being violated, exactly. As far as I was aware, no one knew who had built Scalentine. I should have left; this was doing nothing for my mood. But the speaker had an oddly hypnotic quality.

"Friends, I – Angrifon Filchis, a son of the city through ten generations – am here to tell you that our time is coming." He leaned forward, encompassing the crowd with his pale brown, slightly bulbous eyes. "Rightful citizens are weary. They see other people getting the biggest slice of a loaf their forefathers ground the grain for. We know what is due to us. We are the Builders."

"Who's *us*?" Someone said.

"Why, *humans*, friend. People like you and me."

Oh, great, one of *those*. I thought they'd gone back under their rock, but maybe it was getting crowded under there.

"Why is the price of grain so high? Why is it so hard for decent people to find work? Because there are too many people who have come here to leech off what our fathers built. People who only help their own, always giving each other a hand up, selling to each other at a discount, creating their own cabals and secret gatherings within *our* city. And our rulers, what are they doing? They're ignoring the problem. They're saying it *isn't* a problem. Now why is that, friends? Why do you suppose that's happening?

"I'll tell you why. Because in the *very midst* of our rulers these people have friends and supporters. Some of them even have high positions of their own; and you can't always tell, can you? Because not all of them are obvious, oh, no. You can spot Dra-ay or Monishish or Barraklé. But can you spot weres? Not unless it's a full moon, you can't. And I say it's time we fought back. It's time we rooted out these weeds" – he made a yanking gesture with one pudgy hand – "before they can grow and spread. Root them out, I say, before they strangle all our futures! Root them out and let the good crops grow!"

"Root them out!" the chicken-necked boy yelled, with squawky enthusiasm, jerking his fist. "Root them out!"

"Root them out!" someone in the crowd yelled. "Root them out!"

Failing to be picked up by the crowd, this rousing cry whimpered out. "What do you mean, exactly?" someone else said. "Are you saying, you know, that people should, like, attack people? Because the Millies'd have something to say about that."

"No, of course I'm not saying any such thing!" Filchis said. "Why, that would be incitement, and I wouldn't dream of it. All I'm saying is that maybe those who don't belong here should be encouraged to leave. Although I will say to you: ask yourselves what happens when someone breaks the law. Someone who, perhaps, is supported by those very forces I speak of. Is justice done?"

He leaned forward. "Let me tell you about something that happened recently. A friend of mine was walking home, minding his own business, and he was *set upon,* because he was in some part of the city the Dra-ay consider theirs! *In our own city!* He was beaten bloody! And when he went to the Militia, what did they do? Why, they gave *him* a warning. And you know why? Because the Militia itself, the Militia that's supposed to protect our interests, has been infiltrated. So ask yourselves how you feel about a law that is biased against you."

"This friend of yours," I said, "where was he?"

"A district that is being overwhelmed by the Dra-ay," Filchis said. "The point is, it was in *Scalentine.* Our own city!"

"Only I've been in a Dra-ay district, and I didn't get beaten up."

He looked me over, then smiled with a sort of greasy gallantry. "But you, madam, carry a sword, and look as though you could use it. Perhaps they felt it was easier to set on a man walking alone and unarmed."

"Your friend was walking around unarmed?" someone else said. "Daft, is he?"

There were a few snickers, and Filchis shot the speaker a flat, ugly look. "And shouldn't the Militia be doing something about that?" he said. "What sort of city is it where everyone needs to carry weapons? Besides, what right have the Dra-ay to tell us where we can't go in our own city?"

"Well, I can't walk into your house any time I please," I said. "That's called the law, I believe."

Another voice rose, if that was the word for a bass rumble like someone rattling gravel in a drum. "You know what I heard? I heard some human tried to get into one of the sacred spaces, where they keeps their gods. 'Cos that, that really annoys 'em. They tend to be real specific about it, too. They have signs up in like eighteen languages telling people to piss off out of it, and if you can't read, they'll tell you, in yer own language. Smart bastards, the Dra-ay. So either this friend of yours is a bit soft in the head, or he was looking to cause trouble. That's what it sounds like to me."

Filchis was peering over the crowd. "Would you trust the propaganda and rumour-mongering of Dra-ay over the words of an honest human?"

The crowd was shifting back and I finally got a glimpse of the speaker. "Depends," she said. "Show me an honest human, first."

She was short – as in, she came up to just above my waist. Her skin was a deep green-brown, the colour of river water under trees, and she had small sharp tusks, a shortsword tucked into a battered leather scabbard, and the easy, flexed stance of a professional fighter.

"Well," Filchis said. "I see. So you've been listening in. Perhaps you've been sent to infiltrate our ranks, hmm? To act as a spy?"

"A spy?" She grinned a grin that looked as though it might have been a few people's last sight. "And me so carefully disguised, eh?"

There was more laughter.

"But if you were," Filchis said, "and you went before the authorities and accused the humans here of attacking you, of causing trouble, who would be believed?"

"If I accused *you* of attacking *me*?" She looked him up and down, and snorted. "They'd ask me how much cloud I'd smoked."

"Shut up, greenie," the older of Filchis' two companions said.

I had definitely seen him before. And there was something familiar about his idiocy, too; although, let's face it, it's not exactly rare.

"Greenie? *Greenie?* That's the best insult you can come up with? Bloody hells, mate, my son can do better'n that and he's only just got his first sword. My name's Gornack, if you want it. What's yours?"

"Brendrin Klate. A proper *human* name."

I caught Gornack's eye as she briefly sought, and gave up on finding, any sort of response to that. Considering some of the human names I've encountered, which you had to practically knot your own vocal chords to pronounce, it made about as much sense as anything else.

"Of course, at least with her sort you can *tell*," someone in the crowd said, a female voice, soft and cultured. "Not like those weres, now. They hide. They *sneak*."

"My sort? Now you want to explain exactly what you mean by 'my sort'?" Gornack said. "'Cos I'd like to know. Really."

Filchis said, "We honest citizens have nothing against people who go about their business *openly*. But what about those who pretend to be other than they are, who turn into uncontrollable animals every full moon? Even *their* laws insist they be restrained. That tells you something, doesn't it?"

"Oh, so I'm all right because you can *tell* I'm a savage? That's real forgiving of you," Gornack said.

"*You* said savage," Klate said. "No one *else* said savage."

"Now," Filchis said, "we don't want any trouble. It doesn't take much for others to accuse us of *starting* things, of being the source of disturbance, so let's keep it calm, shall we?" His voice was smoothly, eminently reasonable, his gaze moving over the crowd, pausing briefly, moving on.

Then something hit him high on one well-padded cheek. The sudden jag of red on his pallid skin was startling in the grey winter light. He yelped and clapped his hand to his face.

"Bastards! They're throwing rocks!" The older bully-boy started forward, and I saw the glint of a dagger. I dropped my shoulder ready to shove into the crowd, to get between him and whoever he was aiming for.

A child screamed, ear-drillingly high.

Crap. People were pushing forward to see, pushing back trying to get out of the way. A figure in a blue cloak ducked out of the crowd and skittered away, a flicker of pale green about her feet; someone deciding they liked their politics less physical. Gornack roared, "Get those cubs out of here!" She grabbed the children and pushed them towards their mother, who was standing, her hands up, looking wide-eyed and helpless.

"She's attacking the children!" Klate was aiming his blade for Gornack; I got in front of him and kicked him in the crotch. He gaped and buckled, bringing his head conveniently close to be grabbed and firmly introduced to my knee. He dropped. I glanced up at Filchis, who was wiping his face, and watching with remarkable calm. Then there was the drum of boots, and a battlefield yell: "Militia! Break it up, break it up *now!*"

About time. No one else seemed in immediate danger of death, so I decided to make my exit before I got arrested. I didn't have time, and it always irritated the Chief something rotten. Making up with him was fun, but I generally preferred not to have anything to make up for.

Gornack was also making a hasty exit. She nodded at me as she went past, as though we knew each other, and I felt a little pang. There was something about her that reminded me of my friend Previous.

Filchis was wiping juice from his face – it had been some sort of fruit, not a rock – and ranting at the Militia. 'This is *none* of my doing. I was stating my opinion, as the laws and ordinances of the city entitle me to do, and I was viciously attacked by some thug...of course they've disappeared. That sort isn't going to stand around and face the consequences. No, I did no such thing. It's because of what I was saying, isn't it? There are forces in this city... oh, I could be a babe in arms, and somehow this would be made to be *my* fault...' and so forth. Well, he did bear some resemblance to a baby, I suppose – babbling nonsense and creating shit. I didn't wait to hear the rest.

I walked home with my insides all of an itch. And it might have been my imagination, but I couldn't help feeling that there were more sideways looks, more mutterings, more people huddled in groups like nervy sheep who've smelled a wolf, than was normal for Scalentine.

This city's not the safest in the planes. But generally, it's an accepting sort of place. If you're willing to rub along with your fellow creatures and don't cause more trouble than you can help, it'll welcome you with open arms, at least one of which won't be holding a dagger because it needs to be free to take your money.

Seemed like Filchis and his friends wanted to change that.

CHAPTER
TWO

I FOUND LANEY in the hall, hands on her hips, staring at the curtains with such fine Fey disdain they should really have crumbled to dust out of sheer shame.

"I think we should have yellow," Laney said. "They'd make everything look so much brighter." The old curtains, their once rich crimson velvet now faded in stripes, drooped mournfully, as though aware they were about to be retired.

"The only thing is, Laney," I said, "not all our clients want it that bright, you know? Especially the new ones. Some of them prefer things a little more... discreet."

"Hmm. True. I must *think*." She pushed her blonde curls back behind her elegantly pointed little ears and frowned fiercely.

"Try not to think of anything too expensive, there's a love. I've already had Flower moaning at me about food prices. Bread keeps rising, he said. I thought that was a good thing, but apparently I was wrong."

"Babylon. We have to do things properly, or what's the point?"

"The point is spending money faster than we make it. Look what happened the last time. How many clients do you think we can take on?"

The knocker boomed. "Speaking of clients..." I said, and went to open the door.

The doorway was full of furry muscles. I looked up; masses of shaggy hair, moustaches as long as my arm, eyebrows you could lose a dog in.

"*Flossy!*" Laney sped past me, and caught our visitor by the hand.

"That is a very disrespectful name," he complained, as she tugged him into the hall. Well, she pretended to, and he allowed it, despite the complaints.

"But you're my own dear Flossy," Laney said. "Stay and talk to Babylon, darling, I won't be a moment. I must change." She sped away up the stairs.

"Why must she change?" Flosgrim said, frowning. He was wearing embroidered linen trousers with a hole for his tail, and his own tawny fur. That's practically overdressed, for a Nederan not actually on the battlefield.

"Beats me," I said. Laney was, as usual, wearing about two hints and a shimmer; I always had a problem telling the difference between her bedroom clothes and her casual-lounging-around clothes. "Come into the parlour a moment, she won't be long."

Flower was putting out some fresh pastries on the sideboard. "Afternoon," he said. Flosgrim nodded, a little stiffly. Flower is even bigger than a Nederan, has four-inch tusks, muscles in competition with his other muscles, and some serious battle-scars lacing his smooth green hide – all things a Nederan can respect. But he also wears an apron, and cooks. Very well, as it happens.

"Anything for you?" I said.

Flosgrim swallowed and looked away. "No." I could swear, the bits of his face that weren't covered in hair were actually blushing. It was almost sweet. I picked up one of the pastries, like a little gold cloud laced with honey, and took a bite just as Laney reappeared. She shook her head at me and led her prize away to her room.

Flower growled. "Sometimes I wonder why I bother."

"You haven't been to Nederan, have you?" I said. "Know much about it?"

"I know they like fighting and very long poems."

"Well, you know how the Vessels of Purity regard sex?"

"Yes?"

"The Nederans are kind of that way about food. Decent food, anyway."

Flower looked at me with horror all over his big tusky face. "What?"

"Anything that's too much pleasure to eat is a bit dodgy. Corrupting. They take their food as plain and indigestible as they can get it."

"That's..." Flower shook his head. "No wonder they fight all the time."

I HAD TWO clients that afternoon; one a rollicking wine-merchant of generous dimensions and roaring laugh who was hairy enough to be a were in change and as enthusiastic and easily pleased as a puppy; the other a rather stately and subtle lady from Third Turning, whose profession I hadn't yet discovered but whose shimmering skin, graceful snakelike appendages and liking for taking things extremely slowly made for a pleasing contrast. They managed to keep my mind mostly off the morning's events, until it was time to bathe and get ready for my last client of the day.

An hour later I was perfumed, silk-clad from the skin out and leaning against one of the exquisitely gilded columns in the main ballroom of the Roundhouse Tower, Scalentine's most expensive place to throw a party. The wine, I'd bet a fair sum, had cost more than its taste would suggest, and the crowd had the heft and sheen of the elite. An orchestra played something fashionably forgettable, just loud enough so as not to drown out the light chatter. Talk of styles and scandals, deal-making that could reshape countries and more rivalries than a deer-wood in rutting season. There were a handful of children, too; some racing about, shrieking with laughter, others trying to look grown-up and sneak drinks off the server's trays.

I'd been paid for my time, but the gentleman who had hired me to accompany him had gone off into a side room with some other people of serious and moneyed aspect. It's always a little delicate in these situations; one must remain available to one's client, without looking abandoned. For the moment I contented myself with watching the floorshow.

A lean, pale creature in full Perindi Empire court dress, high embroidered collar standing halfway up his face, glided across the room as though on wheels, the motion of his feet invisible under the stiff brocade of his gown. A pair of carefully matched and extremely handsome human bodyservants strode after him. They wore loose silk trousers and nothing else but jewellery, oiled torsos gleaming in the lamplight, bearing his writing implements, paper, and personal spice-box. Servers in the Roundhouse Tower's gold-trimmed grey satin livery moved among the crowds with trays; the drinks brimming in small glasses, the food piled high on small platters. Three silver-skinned beings with smooth domed heads, wearing what looked like armour in shades of blue and green, hovered over a spread of delicacies, pointing them out to each other and making a low hooting noise.

I thought for a moment I saw Enthemmerlee over the shoulder of one of the silver-skins; a slight female with pale hair and humanlike, faintly green-tinged features. *Why, she hasn't changed much at all,* I thought; but when I looked closer it wasn't Enthemmerlee. This woman was not unlike Enthemmerlee as I'd last seen her, but older; dressed in an odd garment like a tube of cloth hanging from some kind of internal ruff below the neck. Definitely Gudain. Whoever she was, she was smiling and seemed to be enjoying herself despite the Gudain reputation for xenophobia. Perhaps she was stunned into enjoyment by the sheer expense of her surroundings.

A very small child with a mop of bright silver hair, dancing solemnly by herself, stamping her feet carefully in time to the music.

A tiny glimmering Fey, in a vast gauzy puff of a dress that made her resemble a glittering beetle in the heart of a chrysanthemum, her slender arms waving like feelers, chattering up at someone I couldn't see.

The crowd parted, revealing her companion; shoulders broad and flat in his bright red uniform and long greying hair pulled back behind his head, bending low in order to hear her. Hargur, doing the polite. I hadn't even known he was going to be here. She gestured to the small girl, who stopped her dancing long enough to trot over to them and raise her arms imperiously at the Chief. He bowed gravely, took her hands, and danced a measure with her, bent almost double.

"Ah, now, that's better," said a voice beside me. "A lovely woman should always smile."

My new friend was a tall, solid fella in understated but expensive tailoring. He had sleekly cut grey hair, a full-lipped mouth and blue, assessing eyes. "Now, I wonder what *made* you smile, and whether I can make it happen again?"

"I'm at a party in the Roundhouse Tower, drinking *very* expensive wine, and watching the powerful at play. Why wouldn't I be smiling?" I said.

He held out his hand. I put mine in it. He had soft, well-kept hands; when he bent and kissed my fingers, his mouth felt, somehow, slightly too warm. "Thasado Heimarl."

"Babylon Steel."

"Ah, indeed? I *am* privileged," he said.

"You have me at a disadvantage, Mr Heimarl."

"I have nothing like your reputation, Madam Steel. I am merely a trader, you know."

"Oh? And what do you trade in?"

"This and that. There's no reason at all why you should have heard of me," he said, with a self-deprecating shrug.

"But without trade, no country survives, Mr Heimarl."

"I am sure Scalentine would manage adequately without my meagre services," he said. "I'm only attending this very glittering occasion because of a lucky deal or two and the hope of making more of the same. One must, as they say, spend money to make it."

"So I'm told," I said, looking down at my gown. Not as extravagant as one of Laney's, but it hadn't been cheap.

"Speaking of spending money," he looked around, and lowered his voice, "I wondered if I might put a proposition to you."

I wondered what good he thought lowering his voice would do, since anyone in the room interested in such things would already have assumed he was trying to book me.

"I'm afraid my books are rather full at the moment." The words were out before I could stop them. He seemed pleasant enough, and I had space for another client; but it's a gut thing. That overwarm touch of his lips on my hand had been enough to tell me we wouldn't suit.

"Oh, no, I apologise, you mistake me," he said. "Not that I wouldn't be delighted, but it would be an unwarranted extravagance in these difficult times. No, I just wondered... some of your clientele must talk about their business. You could turn such knowledge to your advantage."

I thought I knew where this was going, but I'd give him the benefit of the doubt. "Oh, certainly, sometimes they can put me on to a good bargain," I said. "Knowing when a fresh shipment of rare fruits is coming in always pleases my cook."

"I was thinking more of knowledge they might let slip, about the turn of the market, or perhaps new customs laws that a man might find useful to know about before they were implemented... there are those who would be willing to pay for such information, you know."

"Ah." I smiled. Not the first time I've received such a proposition. "I'm afraid, Mr Heimarl, that I have no memory at all for such things. I concentrate on the matter in hand, as it were, and after that, I can barely remember a thing my clients might have said. I'd never retain any information of the slightest use to anyone."

He looked down at his glass and sighed. "A pity. A good memory is so useful. But discretion, of course, is also a quality to be greatly valued, and is no doubt essential to building a reputation such as yours."

"I see you understand my position."

"Oh, indeed. You can't blame a man for trying, I hope. With things as they are, we're all struggling, you know, all looking for that extra edge."

"I most certainly don't blame you for trying," I said.

"Well, I suppose I had better tear myself away and go talk to the rich and powerful, who will no doubt turn me down with far less courtesy." He bowed, smiled, and walked away. He had a certain charm, no doubt of it. And I really didn't blame him; but passing on pillow-confidences is very bad business. I have been known to do it, but only in cases of serious crime or danger to others in the profession. That's not betrayal of confidence, it's more of a civic duty.

I glanced around for Hargur, and found him leaning against the wall, surrounded by a gaggle of youngsters. He took off his helmet and perched it on the head of a small boy, who – despite looking like a toadstool as a result (a toadstool that couldn't see) – was instantly the object of envy. Hargur laughed, as the rest of the children clamoured for some equal sign of favour, and held his hands up helplessly.

I felt my heart contract.

As though he'd heard something, he looked over the children's heads right at me, and smiled, the long lines of his face tilting up. I smiled back, then turned away before we became completely obvious.

Those who knew about us, knew. But we didn't make our liaison too public. Some people don't think the Chief of the City Militia should be associating with a whore, even though whoring is legal in Scalentine. Anyway, it was no one else's business.

But that wasn't the only reason I turned away. Seeing Hargur with the children got me thinking about things I didn't want to think about, and I didn't want him to see something in my face. He was too sharp.

It was absurd, anyway, I told myself; we hadn't even been seeing each other for that long.

The music changed, to a patter of applause. People recognised *The Lady of the Greenlands*, and started to line up down the long, gleaming room, ready to dance.

My client appeared, waving to a server; I noticed he chose a drink without alcohol in it. "Babylon, my dear, I do apologise. Unforgivable to leave you standing about. But since I have just begun what may be a very profitable, but undoubtedly *long* conversation, may I release you for the rest of the evening? With a little bonus?" He pressed a small but pleasingly heavy sack of coin into my hand.

"Well, I shall be sorry not to have your company, of course, but thank you. I hope your conversation goes very well."

"You bring me luck. Now find yourself someone to dance with." He kissed my hand, and hurried off.

Unfortunately it was too late to find someone to dance with, at least for this tune. Figures met and parted, spun, stepped across, moved down, met someone else, parted again. Between the whirling bodies I caught a glimpse of Hargur, talking to someone I couldn't see; then there was a sudden flurry as one of the servers appeared at his elbow. In the doorway I saw the crimson of another Militia uniform. Hargur nodded stiffly to the man he'd been talking to and left.

I moved around the dancers and managed to collar the server who'd brought the news. "What was all that about?"

She was a thin, pasty, anxious little woman. "Oh, I don't know, madam. Nothing to worry about, I'm sure."

"Listen, love." I pushed back my sleeve to show her the long white scar that twisted down my forearm. "See this? I'm a professional soldier, I'm not going to scream and faint at the thought of trouble. Just tell me. Smooth?"

"Yes, ma'am. Been a murder, ma'am. Down in Lacemakers."

Lacemakers – a quiet area; not rich, not desperately poor. Small traders and clerks; respectable and struggling.

"That's all I know, ma'am."

"Right, thank you."

She scurried off.

I didn't feel like dancing. Or like trying to pick up another client, either. Suddenly the room seemed oppressive; there was too much glitter, too much perfume, too many people who would get home safe tonight, largely because of Hargur, while he was out chasing murderers.

I got my cloak and went home, where I could worry about him in peace.

THERE WAS A piece of paper on my desk with a note in Cruel's swooping handwriting.

Bad Boy, 73 Upper Griffon Street, opposite the chandler's. I grinned, hoping Bad Boy was enjoying his evening. Cruel and Unusual were building an impressive roster of clients, these days, and those who liked something a little out of the way were usually prepared to pay plenty for it. We should be rolling in cash – funny how it all got spent.

Or not, I thought, realising that the bit of paper next to it was a bill from the silk merchant. Laney, I'd bet money on it – if I had any.

I was used to extravagant invoices for Laney's wardrobe, but the figure made me stretch my eyes. I looked again. *1 bolt Tesserane silk in Dragon's Eye. 1 bolt Tesserane silk in Dawn Smoke.*

Two *bolts* of silk? And Tesserane at that, the most expensive silk money could buy? That would make about forty dresses, and we didn't have that many crew, even counting the ones who didn't habitually wear dresses. I had a brief vision of Flower in a silk ball-gown, which was disconcerting.

I walked downstairs. Laney was kissing her latest client goodbye; he wandered out with the usual jelly-kneed walk and dreamy grin. She was an asset, no doubt about it – if only she could understand that the money she brought in didn't actually cover things like two bolts of Tesserane silk.

"Laney!"

"Oh, you're back! Did you have a nice evening?"

"Ish. Laney..."

"Yes, darling?"

"I know you have fabulous taste."

"Well, of course I do."

"But, Laney, two *bolts* of Tesserane? What in all the planes were you planning to do with it?"

"New curtains, of course!"

"Wh..."

"The hall. Dawn Smoke, which is... well... smoky, lined with Dragon's Eye – it's a gorgeous flame-colour shot with blue, you'll love it. It will look like fire opals. Too perfect."

"Laney. Honey. No one makes *curtains* out of Tesserane silk! We can't afford it! I don't think the Perindi Emperor could afford it!"

"We can. I checked. Now we have that new accountant, I can tell," she said, proudly.

That was Laney all over. Once she'd been brought to understand that money was required, in order to buy things (*not* an easy concept to get into a Fey head), she'd pushed me into getting the accounts sorted out. Now, she thought she understood how money worked. I knew exactly what she'd done. She'd seen how much was in the kitty, and decided there was exactly enough to buy two bolts of silk. The fact that that would leave us with no money for food, or coal, or laundry, simply wouldn't have occurred to her. There was enough to buy silk, so of course, that was what she'd done.

"Laney, no. I'm sorry. It's a lovely idea, but we need money for other things, as well. Cancel the order, there's a dove."

She frowned. "Well, if you say so, but I think it's a terrible shame."

I'd have to check that she actually had cancelled it; she could be wilfully absent-minded.

Mind you, I couldn't really blame her. Fey didn't use money, so she'd never had to deal with it before she came to

Scalentine. I'd gone from a caravan-guard who thought two coins to clink together was riches, to an Avatar with the best of everything handed to me without the need for money, to a freelancing whore and sellsword who often had little more than a few coppers (or palinth shells, or scented wooden *briant*, or whatever the local currency was) between me and starvation. I did know the value of money. But somehow, it just ran away through my fingers. A little perfume here, a new bracelet or a pair of dress daggers there... well, perfume and jewellery were part of the job, and the daggers were so beautifully made. Perfect for when a sword was inappropriate wear; practically an investment, in fact. Only a rather expensive one.

"How was *your* client?" she said.

"Generous. Why? You're changing the subject."

"Yes, I am," she said, in a way that indicated it wasn't going to change back, whatever I did. "You look tired, and you came home early."

"He found something else to occupy him, that's all."

She gave me a disconcertingly sharp look. "Is Hargur coming over tonight?"

"I don't know. I doubt it, there's been a murder. He'll probably be busy most of the night."

"You're worried."

"There's been some... stuff going on. Laney, have you had any trouble? I don't mean here. Outside. Anyone giving you lip?"

Not that it was likely, unless the lip-giver was unusually dim. Fey can't wield enough magic to kill you, not on Scalentine, but they can still make your life extraordinarily unpleasant. And both in and outside Scalentine Laney has friends. Family. *Influence.* Mess with her and you'd almost certainly meet a variety of interesting and memorable fates, either one after another, or all at once.

"It's not the Vessels of Purity again, is it?" she said.

"No. Some bunch who think humans are better than everyone else. If we get any new clients, I want to check them out. I know you can look after yourself, but..."

"Of course. Come into the kitchen; Flower's been keeping some soup hot for you."

I'd had nothing but bits and fripperies at the Roundhouse Tower, and the thought of some of Flower's soup was too good to resist.

"Did I see Flosgrim earlier?" Jivrais poked his head around the door. The little horns on his forehead, legacy of his faun blood, were shedding. He rubbed them furiously against the frame. Velvety skin peeled away.

"Ouch, don't *do* that," I said. "And yes, you did. Stay out of his way, please."

"It doesn't hurt, it's just an itch. I'll get him one day, you know."

Laney snorted. Only Fey can make a snort sound as delicate as a snowdrop taking snuff.

"Jivrais..." I said.

"Oh, go on. He'd love it."

"Jivrais, I don't want him offended, and even more do I *not* want you getting your neck broken because you tried to seduce someone who thinks it's a huge insult to his masculinity."

"*Some* people would be flattered."

"He's a *Nederan*. The only way to flatter a Nederan is to tell him he's death incarnate on the battlefield or capable of fathering a thousand offspring."

"Or a good poet?" Flower said, ladling another spoonful into my bowl.

"That too. Jivrais, why can't you get a crush on someone actually obtainable, for a change?"

"Where's the fun in that?"

CHAPTER
THREE

THE BED FELT too big without Hargur in it, and I didn't get to sleep until dawn was silvering the sky. I finally woke to a knock on the door.

"Who is it?"

"Ireq. I brought tea."

I groaned. "Come in. How late is it?"

Ireq's an ex-soldier, a quiet, solid type; he has a short-muzzled face, grey fur and one arm missing below the elbow.

"You've got a client in an hour and a half," he said. "I thought you might want time to digest your breakfast."

"What would I do without you?" I said, taking the cup.

"Get indigestion. Belch at the clients."

"Some of them might like it. Ireq, were you ever in Incandress?"

He tilted his head. "Incandress... might have been. Worked the silk route once."

I knew Incandress was an Empire satrapy, but I'd forgotten it was on the silk route. "Remember anything about it?"

"Not much. Good roads. Quiet."

"That's it?"

He shrugged. "Sorry. Long time ago, and no one chopped anything off I wanted to keep."

"Right. Thanks for the tea, sweetie."

He smiled and closed the door.

* * *

MY LAST CUSTOMER of the morning was Jonek. Nice enough bloke, if a bit of a misery. I'd done my best to cheer him up, but he always spent at least half his allotted time moaning about his business, a bakery. It always struck me funny that a baker should be so thin; I suppose it was the worry. I thought, myself, that if he spent a little more time using his body and a little less in his head, he'd be happier, but there you go. It's up to the client how they want to spend the hour, after all.

"The business is on its last legs, I swear," he said, hauling his skinny self upright and sitting slumped with his feet flat on the floor, looking like something washed up on a beach. "I don't know if I can afford this next month."

I patted his shoulder. "You make good stuff," I said. "Every time I pass your place there are people queuing up."

"I just wish I could get reliable suppliers. Nothing but trouble. Flour, butter, spices, everything. The minute you think you've got it sorted, it's, 'Sorry, Jonek, can't fill the order this month, got a big new contract.' 'Sorry, Jonek, price of grain's gone up.' Then they say they can't even *get* the grain. Who can't get grain? We've one of the biggest trading ports in the planes! It's an excuse. They don't care, wave a big bag of money in their face, and you can forget the small guys like me."

"You're not a small guy," I said, but he wasn't listening.

"And the prices... they keep going up. Three different traders, I've tried now. I'd swear they were all working together to put prices up."

"Isn't price-fixing against the law?"

He tapped the side of his nose. "So they say."

He was still grumbling as he pulled his clothes on and left. Oh, well, I thought, I did my best.

I heard a knock at the front door. I waited for Previous to get it.

Then I remembered.

Flower and I got there at the second knock, him in apron and spoon, me in dressing-gown and sword. We glanced at each other, and he took a deep breath. "Damn," he said. "I should be used to it by now."

"Yeah, me too."

He put one big hand on my shoulder for a moment and then opened the door.

The human woman standing outside was high-browed, fair-skinned, and swathed in a heavy woollen cloak of deep blue lined with pale green. It had been expensive, but was now a little worn at the hem, and the lining was torn.

One eyebrow flicked up at the sight of my dishabille and I wondered how exactly she was expecting to be met at the door of a whorehouse. The sword was standard wear for anyone in Scalentine who could use one and had any sense, and for quite a few to whom neither applied.

"Can I help?" I said.

"I'm looking for... well. Could I come inside?"

"Let me take your cloak," Flower said, and whipped it neatly away as she stepped in. She had long straight blonde hair, like heavy silk. She was carrying a pretty little dagger that looked more like jewellery than weaponry, and she looked nervous. Often the case with new clients, especially women. I led her through to the blue parlour and closed the door, in case she was the sort to be disconcerted by the sight of others wandering in and out.

She stood looking around at the fixtures and fittings, fidgeting with the pouch at her belt, her collar, her hair. "Would you like some tea?" I said.

"I... no. No thank you. I wanted to ask... do you... it says on the door..."

"'All tastes, all species, all forms of currency.' Yes, ma'am. No permanent injury, no death, no children or animals. Anyone taking part has to be old enough, sharp enough to know what they're doing – and willing. Apart from that..."

"I see."

Jivrais chose that moment to pop his head round the door. "Did I leave my – oh, sorry, don't mind me." He came in and started rummaging about for something.

"So, was there something you had in mind?" I gave the woman a reassuring smile. Not too big, just a calm, matter-of-fact sort of smile.

"Only... well. You see, I'm... I like..." I gave her plenty of time, not looking at her directly. Often, the ones who are most nervous aren't really asking for anything that outrageous; they just *think* they are.

She took a deep breath, and said, finally, "I like weres. Shifters."

Damn. "I'm very sorry. I'm afraid we don't have a were on the staff at the moment."

"Never did persuade the Chief, did we?" Jivrais said, emerging with a long silk scarf in one hand. "Pity, they'd line up."

I glared at him; but domestic arguments in front of clients are not good for business, unless staged on request. He grinned at us both and slipped back out of the door.

I turned back to the woman. "If it's the fur you like, we do have someone who's furry? No? Or we can arrange for a convincing imitation of a were in change. Some of my crew are very talented actors, and a glamour..."

"No," she said, "No, thank you." I saw her shoulders drop. I felt briefly sorry for her, wondering how long she'd spent nerving herself up for this, and whether she'd get up the courage to do it again any time soon. Even on Scalentine, it can be tougher for a woman to indulge her personal tastes, although it's better here than elsewhere. "In that case," I said, "why not try the Midnight Rose, on Upper River Street? They've got at least three weres on staff, and it's a nice place." I knew Sometimes Betty, who ran the place; we often referred clients. I know we say 'all tastes' and we do our best, but we couldn't possibly cover them all, not even with a crew of several hundred. People can come up with more variations on a fairly basic theme than I would have thought possible when I started out.

"Yes, I... thank you." Having made the effort to get here, and been balked, she seemed to be finding it hard to move. I wondered what sort of culture she came from; whether having an interest in weres or simply being sexual at all was the problem. Humans turn up all over the place, and cultures vary so widely – but they do seem to have a tendency to be *twitchy* about sex, one way or another.

Well, not my lot, obviously. Tiresana was a place with a lot of problems, but disapproving of sex wasn't generally one of them.

"I can escort you to the Midnight Rose, if you like," I said. "I'm going past there."

"Oh, no, that won't be necessary," she said. "Thank you." Paralysis finally broken, she scurried for the hall and was out of the door before I could even open it for her.

I couldn't help a faint sense of relief, although the All knew we needed all the clients we could fit in at the moment. Those rampant nerves, the way she'd kept looking around all the time, made my back hairs tickle.

Anyway, she was gone and it was time I was likewise. "Jivrais, you've got a client at three, and *please* make your room nice, it was appalling last time I looked."

"We need someone to come in."

"We need you to hang your clothes up and make your bed. I have to go."

"Will you be back for supper?" Flower said.

"I hope so." I was on my way to talk with High Panjandrums. That sort of thing makes me nervous. And hungry.

Not long ago, we'd run out of money close on tax time and I'd ended up, out of fear of poverty (and, admittedly, a few other motives), working for Darask Fain, socialite, gaming-house owner and unofficial member of the semi-official government of Scalentine: the Diplomatic Section. Fain was the man I was about to see, together with the girl he'd asked me to look for, her being missing at the time.

Although I supposed "girl" was no longer appropriate, now she was the Itnunnacklish.

I HADN'T VISITED one of Scalentine's government buildings since I'd first been to get my papers, along with a hundred or so, other new arrivals down near the docks, by Portal Bealach; a permanent portal and the main trade route into and out of Scalentine. The doorway Fain had directed me to was as discreet as a good servant, so it took me a while to find it, which meant I was even later than I was going to be anyway. I decided not to worry about it. I didn't exactly want to offend Fain, but I didn't want him thinking I was at his beck and call, either.

I knocked.

Above the door was an odd little brass bump, like the boss of a shield. It split open, and with a scratchy, ratcheting sound spilled out a tube made of overlapping metal rings, with a round glass globule fixed in the end. It swung around in the air for a bit, then pointed at me. It was disconcerting. Imagine lifting a rock, and the slimy inhabitants of its underside rearing up and staring at you instead of skittering away.

Then – ratchety-slurp – the thing withdrew back to a lump. Some moments later, the door opened. "Madam Steel," Darask Fain said. His black hair gleamed, his chocolatey eyes glowed, his skin was gold and smooth as butter over elegant cheekbones.

My hand instinctively went to the pocket where I was carrying one of Laney's lust-damping potions. His eyes followed the move, and something that wasn't quite a smile touched the edges of his beautifully sculpted mouth.

"Do come in."

I didn't need the potion; yet. Fain had an odd personal trait, a form of sexual charisma so powerful it was positively dangerous, and usually under his control, except around full moon. I carried the lust-damper as a precaution. I might fancy the arse off the man, but trusting him was another matter. Not that I thought he'd ever use it to bed someone against their will; he seemed – genuinely, I thought – horrified by the idea. But he wasn't above using it to try and nudge someone into agreeing to something he wanted done, simply because they were too busy drooling to think.

I could tell he wasn't using it at the moment, though; it was just him. Damn the man, it wasn't even as though he *needed* anything to make him more attractive.

He led me down an anonymous white-painted corridor, which at least gave me the opportunity to appreciate his deliciously well-muscled rear and the feline grace of his walk.

Eventually he stopped and opened a door. A very *thick* door. And there was a certain silvery smudging around the frame, as though someone had been brushing it with the dust you get when you sharpen a blade.

Seated around a table of dark wood, so highly polished it looked like something you could drown in, were a number of people, all looking at me. I heard a *snick* behind me as Fain locked the door.

I knew three of those at the table; two Ikinchli, and one Gudain. The fourth... "You know Enthemmerlee Defarlane Lathrit en Scona Entaire, of course," Fain said.

"Enthemmerlee?" I tried, and failed, to keep the question out of my voice.

I'd thought I was prepared for a radical change in the girl, but I wouldn't have recognised her. The long pale silver-gilt hair was gone; her skull was smoothly overlaid with pearly green scales, delicate as a baby's fingernails. Her nose had flattened, her jaw drawn back. She was still, in her own unique way, beautiful; but she was no longer the lovely girl I'd first met in the sewers under Scalentine.

She was the Itnunnacklish, the One who is Both.

"Madam Steel. It is very good to see you again." She got up, and held out a hand. The way she moved had changed, become something easier, more fluid. She was dressed in a robe of deep green silk, with puffed sleeves, a high, embroidered collar, and a rigid ruff about the neck under the cloth, so that the robe hung in a stiff curtain several inches from her skin. The tiny webs I'd noticed between her fingers were larger now, the skin had a greener tinge; but her hand still seemed very small and fragile when I took it in my own. Her eyes, too, were just the same: golden, with that straight, serious gaze. *Fated,* was what I'd first thought, when I'd seen those eyes.

I hadn't changed my mind.

"Also Malleay Devinclane Solit en Scona Mariess." The young Gudain man rose and bowed, a little stiffly. He had pearly-green skin and short, very curly hair the colour of wet moss. He was dressed in a high-collared jacket of some thick, stiff material, and the wide loose trousers I was used to seeing on Ikinchli. He was actually rather edible, despite his sulky expression, but that costume wasn't the happiest of combinations. It made him look as though he'd borrowed the bottom half of his body from someone else.

He was one of the two males required for Enthemmerlee's transformation. I wondered, privately, exactly how that had gone; he looked like the kind of lad to lose his nerve at the wrong moment, but obviously he'd managed his part adequately.

"Lobik Kraneel." Enthemmerlee's Ikinchli mate. Taller than average, for an Ikinchli, which meant he came higher than my chin, with rich reddish-brown scales like good leather shading to buttery yellow on the throat. He had a quiet confidence about him and a certain spark to his smile. In that odd little ménage, I doubted *he'd* suffered any nerves between the sheets. As he took my hand in a strong warm grip, I thought I wouldn't have minded finding out for myself.

"The Ikinchli Ambassador to Scalentine, Rikkinnet Dree." A female Ikinchli, Enthemmerlee's friend and bodyguard.

She had bronze scales, broad shoulders, and sharp, pale green eyes.

I held up my hand, but instead of taking it, she slapped palms with me and grinned. I grinned back. "Ambassador?"

"Yes. Good, no?"

"Very good. I'm glad to see you all."

"Please, sit down," Fain said. "And has everyone tea?" I was glad to see the pot, and filled myself a good steaming cup, although something a little more solid wouldn't have gone amiss, either.

"Good. Now," Fain said. "Madam Steel, you have agreed to escort Madam Defarlane back to her home plane, and act as her bodyguard. Is that correct?"

That wasn't quite how he had originally put it to me. "Unofficial envoy" was the phrase he'd used. "Spy," was my word for it.

"I haven't agreed to anything yet," I said. "I agreed to come to this meeting, that's all. I wanted to see how Enthemmerlee was getting on."

"You shouldn't call her that," Malleay said.

"Sorry?"

"It is disrespectful. She is Madam Defarlane Lathrit en Scona Entaire the Itnunnacklish, even to a foreigner."

If I had to call everyone by their full titles, this meeting was going to take a very long time. "Excuse me, Madam Defarlane, if I was rude."

"Not at all," Enthemmerlee said. "You are a friend, or at least, I hope you will allow me to consider you a friend. I am glad that you were kind enough to agree to this meeting, at least. Please, call me Enthemmerlee. There are few enough left who will." She laid a hand on Malleay's arm. His mouth twitched; not quite a flinch, but almost. Enthemmerlee did not appear to notice. "Actually my formal title is a good deal longer," she said. "But fortunately foreigners" – she gave Fain and myself an apologetic look – "are not generally expected to learn them."

"Being barbarians and all," I said. That was a relief, at least. "What should I call you in public?"

"Oh, Madam Enthemmerlee will do. Or Itnunnacklish."

"Now, to business," Fain said. "The appearance of the Itnunnacklish has not been greeted with unmitigated joy on Incandress. Madam Defarlane is at some risk."

"I get that," I said. "But why me? You can hire a dozen competent bodyguards from Bressler's in Southside; you could send half the Militia, if you wanted." I shut my mouth abruptly. The Chief wouldn't thank me for that, he was always complaining about being short of warm bodies who could actually be relied on to stay in that condition.

"The Militia are needed here," Fain said.

"I'm just not sure I'm the person for the job."

"I would be most grateful," Enthemmerlee said, "if you would at least consider it. I plan to return to Incandress in three days. There will be a ball, held at the Palace, which I must attend. Then there is an Ikinchli ceremony, the Enkantishak, that recognises me as the Itnunnacklish, then, finally, the Patinarai, at the Advisory Hall. This is when I become Patinate: the head of my family and one of the Advisors to the Crown. Then I will have the power to change many things, and, I hope, begin to bring Incandress' two peoples together. However, I regret that there may be those who do not wish me to survive Patinarai."

"So I gather. But again, why me?"

"Because I have seen what you can do, and also, you are outside the politics of Incandress."

"I'm not so sure of that," I said, thinking of Kittack. "I look too much like a Gudain for some and not enough for others. Plenty of people are going to be suspicious of me."

"But I am not," Enthemmerlee said.

"Yes, well, you wouldn't be the one hiring me," I said. "The Diplomatic Section would. And Mr Fain told me my role wouldn't just be that of bodyguard." I kept an eye on Fain as I said it.

"Of course. Mr Fain has told me that you would be expected to keep him informed about the situation on Incandress," Enthemmerlee said.

"You're happy with this idea, are you?"

She lifted her hands. "I am very much aware of the obligations I owe to the government of Scalentine. Without their help, my transformation might not have been completed. And in troubled times, friends are always of value." She smiled. It was a calm, knowing smile.

She'd been idealistic enough to risk her life and who knew what else for this transformation, but it seemed the girl was also a realist when it came to politics.

"How do we know you're even capable of protecting her?" Malleay said.

"Tell me," Fain said, leaning forward, "if you *were* to take up this offer, what would you do?"

I thought about it. "First, I'd need a good look around wherever Enthemmerlee would be staying. If I could get drawings, *detailed* drawings, of the layout, even better. I don't just mean, 'there's a guard tower here,' I mean, 'just south of the postern gate there's a stair leading up to the interior of the wall, there's a window here big enough for a well-aimed arrow, there's a place here where a dog once got in...' everything. The same for anywhere she'd be spending time, particularly where the ceremonies take place."

Malleay said, "But there will be the family guard."

Rikkinnet snorted loudly enough that Malleay glared at her. "*And*," he went on, "at the ceremonies there will be the guards of the other families, and the Palace's own guard, that's at *least* a hundred guards. Maybe more."

"And who commands the loyalty of the Palace guard, and the guards of the rest of the Ten Families?" I said. "And what about the Ikinchli ceremony, the Enkantishak? Besides, I've dealt with political assassination before. Sometimes it's done on the quiet, a knife in the bedchamber. Sometimes, it's done in a big noticeable public way, to make a point. It's the possibility you don't think of that comes back to bite you. Also, I'd want to know exactly who would have access to her. Everyone. Family, friends, servants. Down to her old nurse."

"Is that truly necessary?" Malleay said.

"People can be bribed. People can be threatened. And sometimes, people just change sides."

Enthemmerlee's hand rose, and touched her jaw, an odd, unhappy little gesture.

"I'm sorry," I said. "But the less trusting you are, the safer you'll be. I'd need to know if anyone new had come into the household recently, too."

Fain, damn him, was smiling smugly to himself. I began to wish I'd kept my mouth shut.

"Your overview seems comprehensive, Madam Steel," Fain said. "And may I ask where you learned these skills?"

"A number of places, over a number of years. And I lost my first charge to a sneak attack. Not only did I not get paid, I nearly got killed as a result. And I had a soft spot for the gentleman. I regretted failing him. I learned."

"I see. And did you lose any more?"

"Two." I shrugged. "Advancement by assassination is hardly uncommon, whatever the plane."

"How... how did you lose them?" Malleay said. Enthemmerlee simply watched me with those wide gold eyes.

"One in battle, when nothing I could say would prevent her riding out at the head of her troops, wearing extremely recognisable armour, and protocol prevented me from knocking her out and tying her up until she got some sense. Another... well. You know what I said about watching those closest to you? His brother. Close companion, trusted friend, just happened to have a much-loved wife who'd fallen into enemy hands. They promised they'd free her if he did the deed. They lied. Everyone died. A mess."

"But you escaped," Malleay said.

"Barely." I'd exited via the garderobe with nothing but a short sword and the clothes I stood in, and spent too long running, stinking, scavenging and starving, until I was out of that unhappy kingdom. *Not* one of my pleasanter memories.

They looked at each other.

"Look," I said, "even if I was to take the job, one can't foresee everything. And it's been a long time since I did this kind of work. *And* I don't speak the language."

"But mainly we speak Lithan, as you do here," Enthemmerlee said. "The influence of the Perindi Empire."

Damn.

"What about the Empire?" I said. "Do they have a finger in this pie?"

"They have a finger, but they don't want to risk shoving their whole hand in," Malleay said. "The Empire's overstretched. So long as Incandress keeps the roads open, they'll be happy enough to leave us be; Incandress may nominally be a satrapy, but the Empire hasn't the resources to waste on forcing the issue. They'll only do so if it seems a war might spill past our borders, and even then, they'd be pushed. They've got troops out in Belasia, the uprising in Lorf and the difficulties they're facing with the Sanz-Rubolt Convocation. We could see a massive power-shift over the next three years. Imperator Locreint made a mistake naming a successor at this stage."

He looked up, and blinked, as though surprised by his own sudden eloquence. "I keep my ears open," he said.

"Malleay knows the international situation far better than the Advisors to the Crown," Enthemmerlee said.

"The Crown. You have a... what, a king? A queen?" I said.

"Not for many decades. The Patineshi are known as Advisors to the Crown, that is all."

Not that it mattered. What mattered was I wanted out of this more with every passing moment. I grasped at another straw. "What about magic? Can't help you there."

"Magic?" Enthemmerlee said.

"Magic. Do you have it on your plane? Does it work? If so, do you have anyone who can protect you from it? If not, you'd need to hire someone who can. That is, not me."

"The magic on our plane is not dangerous," Enthemmerlee said. "The Gudain cannot use it, and the magics used by the Ikinchli are..." She looked at Lobik. "Quiet ones."

"Yes." Lobik nodded. "Magic to fill the net and find safe passage. Not killing magic."

"If there had been," Rikkinnet said, "the history of Incandress would be a very different one."

Fain broke the silence that followed. "Since there *are* working sorceries, someone determined enough might be able to use them. Many Fey magics work on a number of planes, for example. Don't worry; we have someone we can make available to you."

I glanced at Enthemmerlee. She smiled. "That is most kind," she said. "Though I doubt it will be necessary."

"Better to take the precaution, don't you think?" Fain said.

I wasn't so sure. I didn't like the idea of someone whose first loyalty was to the Diplomatic Section being so close to Enthemmerlee; part, in fact, of her protection. However, I could hardly object, since I was the one who'd pointed out that *I* couldn't protect her from magic. Oh, hells.

"Someone mentioned your family guard," I said.

"They are useless," Rikkinnet said. "And..." She looked at Enthemmerlee. "You *know* what I think."

"Then perhaps Madam Steel should hear it too," Enthemmerlee said.

"Very well. They are, mostly, dregs, captained by a drunk. Worse than useless, maybe dangerous. Gudain and Ikinchli both."

"But they are the Entaire guard." Enthemmerlee turned to me. "Among the Ten Families, one's family guard are different from other servants. Guards are never dismissed, they receive a pension, they are part of the family. It is a tradition with the force of law."

Lobik said, "Enthemmerlee, Rikkinnet is right. Maybe once they were not so bad, but you yourself have noticed the changes, hey?"

"Why not stay here, at least until the Patinarai?" I said. "You should be safe enough." Fain, at least, wouldn't be able to harm Enthemmerlee – I'd pushed him into taking an oath to that effect. In the normal way of things, you can trust an oath as much as any other promise from a politician, but this was a Fey oath. Once sworn, they insist on being fulfilled, one way or another. I doubted he'd forgiven me for that yet.

"The ball is officially a social occasion, but in fact, it is politically necessary. It is vital I attend the Ikinchli Enkantishak – not to do so would be a dreadful insult – and even after Patinarai, I will still need a guard."

"You will not hire others?" Lobik said.

"No. I will not," Enthemmerlee said. "I will not dishonour those who have done no wrong, who have, by all custom and tradition, the right to a decent living and an honourable retirement under the protection of my house."

"Enthemmerlee..." Malleay said.

"I have told you my decision," Enthemmerlee said.

Her three companions exchanged glances. Rikkinnet gave a small, sinuous shrug. "You are the Itnunnacklish," she said.

"Yes. I am also about to become the head of my household, and in this respect, that is more important. This is what I would ask of you, Madam Steel: that you would try to improve my guard to the point where my friends will cease worrying me on this subject."

"Wait," I said. "You want me to train the guard from useless to the point where they can protect you from assassination, *while* looking after you, in, what, a few days? Sorry, but that's not possible." It might have been, once, but I'd been an Avatar then. I could turn a man into a potential general with a few rousing words. Not any more.

And, of course, I'd have to be doing whatever other duties Fain required of me in the spying line. Something for which I simply could not fathom why he seemed to think I was qualified.

Fain sat back and steepled his hands under his chin. "You will, of course, be adequately compensated, Madam Steel."

"How adequately?" I said.

"Very," said Fain. "Very adequately."

"This is no time to be coy, Mr Fain."

He named a sum that was a substantial amount more than I could usually make whoring in the same time. Enough to be tempting. I wondered how carefully he'd calculated it. To the last penny, knowing him. He had an unpleasant habit of knowing exactly what state my finances were in, and of course he knew what my rates were – not that he'd ever indulged.

Pity, that.

But still, it felt... wrong.

You sell sword long enough, and survive, and you get some sense for a bad job. It may be nothing much: the way the patron stands, or the way their subordinates look when they walk into a room, or a certain quiet among the guards. It may be no more than a feel in the air.

That feel was draping itself around my shoulders like a chilly fog. And there was that silvery powder around the doorframe.

Enthemmerlee leaned forward and fixed me with those beautiful eyes. "The Itnunnacklish is a symbol, yes. But it is an important one. If I become Patinate, I will represent the union of two peoples who are in danger of tearing each other apart. It is only a start – there is a great deal of work to be done – but if I can survive long enough to begin the work, long enough, even, for people to see what my existence actually means, to see the possibilities for their own futures, then..." She leaned back in her chair. "Then, perhaps, there is hope." She suddenly sounded very young, and very tired.

"I'm sorry," I said. "I wish I could help you. But you need more than me. You need at least one dedicated bodyguard, *and* a trainer, and if your own guards are not merely bad, but, as it sounds, possibly untrustworthy..." I left it there.

"If it is money," Fain said, "more can be found."

"No. No, it isn't."

"You will not reconsider?" Enthemmerlee said. "Please."

"I'm sorry. I really am." I didn't want to look at her, or at any of them. I pushed myself to my feet. "I wish you the best, but I'm not the person you need. I hope you find people. Try Bressler."

I saw their faces despite myself. Malleay looked vindicated; Lobik was leaning towards Enthemmerlee with concern; Enthemmerlee herself had lowered her head, as though she was too tired even to keep it steady on her neck. The one who seemed most upset by my decision was Rikkinnet, who was glaring. Then she shrugged and turned away, which was worse.

Fain, unreadable as ever, stood up with swift grace and said, "Would you excuse us for just a moment?"

He unlocked the door and ushered me ahead of him. I clamped my fingers around the little bottle of anti-lust potion in my pocket, just in case he was planning to try a bit of extra persuasion.

He ushered me into another room with a very thick door, and locked this one too; I saw the same faint dusty shimmer around the frame as I'd seen on the meeting room door.

There was a delicately pretty desk of some rich reddish wood, a matching armchair and couch upholstered in worn green velvet, a low table with a rather lovely tea set in scarlet and gold porcelain.

Fain gestured me to take a seat.

"No. I'm not staying."

"Why the change of heart?"

"It isn't a change of heart. I never promised anything other than to listen."

"True."

"If you're planning to try that little trick of yours..."

"Since you have already proved yourself immune to my charms, Babylon, I have no intention of trying any such thing."

"Who says I'm immune to your charms?" He blinked, and I felt a brief triumph that I had, for once, managed to surprise him. "I just don't like them artificially enhanced for the purpose of messing with my ability to think. Look, this isn't getting us anywhere. I don't want to take this job, however much money you throw at me."

"Why not?"

"Because my gut doesn't like it. And I have a lot of respect for my gut, it's in the habit of keeping me alive."

"I hope that your gut is, on this occasion, overanxious."

"I don't think so. Something's wrong, isn't it? In the Section."

His gaze sharpened as though on a whetstone. "Now what would give you that idea?"

"The fact that you're after me, an outsider, and no damn diplomat, to do this. *Again*. The fact that you're locking every door in what's probably the most secure building in Scalentine, and there were what looked like wards on the meeting room door as well. This does not bode well for anyone you've hired, Mr Fain. I don't need arrows aimed at my back as well as my front."

He looked down and straightened one of the cups on the tray. "I can say that I need someone on Incandress that I trust."

"I thought you had a magician?"

"The Scholar in question would not have been my first choice, had circumstances allowed, and he is not excessively experienced. You are."

"I'm experienced at surviving. I'd prefer to continue doing so. It sounds to me like there's a civil war brewing in Incandress; in a situation like that, *anything* can happen. I doubt that one person can make much difference to the outcome. Especially if there are other influences trying to mess things up."

"That's not what Enthemmerlee believes."

"I admire her. I'm *not* her. Why is the Diplomatic Section suddenly so interested in Incandress anyway?"

"It's on a major trade route. Our situation on Scalentine makes the free flow of goods uniquely important; civil war would disrupt that. And an unstable situation anywhere close to the portals by which we connect to the other planes is something on which we wish to keep a very close eye indeed."

"But it's not as though anything really dodgy could get through, is it?"

The portals to Scalentine prevent anyone coming through with big armies or really powerful magic, and they stop the worst infectious diseases. It makes it a good place to run a whorehouse. It also makes it the ultimate in buffer states, and extremely useful as neutral ground on which to trade and conduct the kind of political negotiations better done outside all parties' home territories. But they've learned not to send negotiators who have a case of the sniffles.

"Unpleasant things getting through the portals is not the point," Fain said. "The point is that we, like any other country, must be aware of what happens near our borders. And I believe that if Enthemmerlee survives to become Patinate she is the best hope for stability that Incandress has. Symbols are powerful; she understands this, and so do those who want to destroy her. But if your mind is made up..."

"It is." I looked at him with some apprehension, but he only sighed, which I found rather worrying.

"You need not be anxious, Madam Steel. I do not intend to try and force you into this." He gave a slightly twisted smile. "A willing participant is almost always more effective than one under duress. I ask only for your discretion regarding any suspicions you might have about what is going on in the Section."

"You have it."

"Thank you." He stood up and gestured me towards the door. We walked in silence down the corridors, and he whisked me out of yet another small, discreet door. "Babylon?" he said.

"Yes."

"You don't think one person could make a difference. But one did, on Tiresana."

I turned, but the door had closed behind me.

Damn the man. Again. Tiresana was *different*. I hadn't had a choice, I was the only person who could do what needed to be done.

As I walked away, there was no denying my gut was suddenly easier. The backs of my thighs, on the other hand, were not. For some reason, that's where guilt makes itself felt for me; a kind of stabbing ache that's not so much in the flesh as in some hollow place inside it. I wandered around for a while, trying to shake off the memory of Enthemmerlee's weary eyes, and ended up on the outskirts, watching Carnival open. A line of purple-red light showed against the swirling, dark not-quite-nothing of Scalentine's borders, broadening, pulsing, then spreading open, emerald and vermillion coruscating along its edges, and beyond the opening, a strange, heavy, grey-yellow light, like the look of clouds before snow.

My gut turned over again.

I realised it wasn't just Incandress that had my insides all of a roil; it was the thought of leaving Scalentine. It made me feel like a turtle about to be stripped of its shell.

CHAPTER
FOUR

IT WAS GETTING on for evening. There were a scattering of Ikinchli in the streets, heavily bundled against the chill, as I headed home; fewer than usual, even for the cold weather. I remembered what the touchy fella in Kittack's had said about humans beating them up. Was it the Builders? Filchis had made a big thing about not starting trouble, but maybe some of his followers weren't so careful.

There weren't many freelancers about, either, human or otherwise. Not many people at all. I whipped around at a scratchy sound behind me, only to see a piece of paper tumbling along the paving stones, before it was trapped by a murky puddle, where it stained brown and turned limp.

When I got home, I went round back, to the garden.

There was a small grey headstone there. *Previous. Brave warrior; best of friends.*

A couple of weeds had pushed their way up through the gravel. I tugged them out. "Hey, Previous," I said. "Getting cold." I crouched down next to the grave, sitting back on my heels. "I've turned into a right homebody. Funny, isn't it? All those years we spent wandering about, and now, I don't want to leave.

"Some of it's you, probably; but, I mean, I wasn't planning on taking anyone with me on this job and still... I don't know. The gut's a funny thing. What would you do, Previous?"

I knew the answer, of course. That's how she'd got her name, and quite a few scars; belting in ahead of the line, taking the fight to the enemy.

But now I wasn't even sure who the enemy was. All I knew was, I didn't want to be in this fight, and I felt bad about *not* being in it. I sighed and pushed myself to my feet. "Well, this won't pay the rent."

"Stay where you are, in the name of the law," a voice growled behind me.

I spun around. "Whatever the charge, I'm innocent."

"Mmm-hmm." Chief Bitternut shook his head at me. "I really doubt it, Babylon."

"I'm hurt," I said. "You're so suspicious."

"That's my job," he said, putting an arm around my waist and kissing me. "So. What have you been up to?"

He looked desperately tired. I wanted to feed him, and get him into a hot bath, and into bed. Not necessarily in that order.

I wrapped my fingers in his long hair, and tugged, gently. "Oh, the usual. Trying to stay out of trouble. You?"

"Much the same," he said. "What's that nice smell?"

"Stew, I think."

"Good. Am I invited to supper?"

"You're *ordered* to supper."

"You can't order me, I'm the Chief of the Militia. I do the ordering about. It's written down somewhere."

"Then you're invited to a good supper and a decent night's sleep, and if you don't accept, I'll force you at sword point. How's that?"

"I look that bad?"

I hooked my arm through his. "A little weary."

He sighed. "We've had another murder, and it isn't even full moon."

"Ouch."

I unlocked the door and waved him in. The Twins were on their way up from the basement. "Hey, Chief," Cruel said.

"Hi, Cruel. Unusual."

The Twins smiled and disappeared into the dining room. Hargur shook his head. "How can two people wear that much leather and metal and still look so... naked?"

"Talent?"

I got a jug of hot water from the kitchen and we went upstairs to wash up. Hargur cheered up enough to put his arms around me while I was splashing my face; a certain amount of wrestling ensued, and it was only because we were both very hungry that we actually made it to supper at all. Even then we were a bit damp and the last to arrive, and got a severe glowering from Flower as we slid into our seats.

"You have no idea of the trouble I've had getting this lot to leave you any," he said. "I had to take it back out to the kitchen. Sit there, don't move."

"Yessir," Hargur said. Flower went out, muttering.

"I'm surprised you're here, Chief," Jivrais said, bouncing up and down in his seat. "After that party at the Roundhouse, we must look *very* dull."

"Trust me, I'd rather be here."

"You can't mean it," Jivrais said. He sighed. "All those rich people, all that wonderful food."

Flower came back in with a pot and ladled aromatic red-brown stew – dotted, I was happy to see, with fat fluffy little dumplings – onto our plates.

"Thanks, Flower," I said.

"Hmph."

"It looks gorgeous."

"Three hours, that took me, so it had better be," Flower growled. "And the food at the Roundhouse isn't *that* good."

"How would you know?" Jivrais said.

"I used to work there. Note the 'used to.'"

"And they serve stingy portions," I said.

Jivrais held out his plate for more stew. "But isn't the main ballroom completely gilded? With mirrors everywhere? Come on, Chief. Babylon didn't tell us *anything*."

"It was glittery," the Chief said. "Mainly I had to stand around and be talked at, when I had work to do. But they tell me it's part of the job."

"Who was there?"

"Lot of rich people."

"There must have been someone important doing something they shouldn't? *That's* always fun."

"How about letting the Chief have his supper in peace, before I drop you out of a window on your head?" I said. "Maybe those new horns of yours will stick in the ground, and we can hang things to dry on your legs."

Jivrais pouted. "Only *asking*."

"Tell you what," Hargur said, "Next time, you can go. We'll dress you in my uniform, I'm sure no one will know the difference."

Jivrais, nearly two feet shorter than the Chief and about the width of a twig, yelped with laughter. "Ooh, yes, let's! All right, then, have there been any good murders?"

The lines either side of Hargur's mouth deepened.

"Jivrais," I said. "Shut it."

"Oh. Sorry."

"There have been murders, yes," Hargur said. "I'm surprised you haven't heard. You probably will, in a day or so; these things never stay quiet for long. A shopkeeper in King of Stone, a young man in Bethalia Street. You lot been keeping up your training?"

"I see to it," I said.

"Good." He lifted his fork, and paused. "Anyone new on the staff?"

"Not since you were here last," I said. "You know all the crew, don't you?"

"Yes." He looked around the table, paused, then shook his head. "Well, so long as you're careful."

"After that last business?" I said. "We're careful." We'd had a madman who didn't like whores break into the house and make a pretty serious attempt to kill me, not long ago. He'd attacked Cruel, too, and she still had a scar on her forehead. He was no longer a problem, having been taken care of in no uncertain terms by the religious order, the Vessels of Purity (the very ones who'd helped create the raving scrote). But it had made us all a little more wary.

"You need a door guard," he said.

"I know." I just hadn't been able to face the idea of replacing Previous. Seeing someone else in her place at the door was something I couldn't quite bear. Not yet. "Now eat," I said. "Or Flower's going to be very sad."

"Can't have that," Hargur said. "I don't like people being sad." He put his hand on my leg and squeezed gently.

I laid a hand over his, and squeezed back.

WE WERE ALL sitting in the Blue Parlour, having eaten ourselves to temporary immobility. No more clients, an evening to ourselves, for once. Laney strolled in last, unfastening her necklace and tossing it onto a table. "Oh, what a relief."

"Why?" Jivrais said, picking up the silver chain. "It's splendid."

"Well, look at it, darling. You could anchor a boat with that thing. But you have to wear a client's present when you see them, otherwise it's just rude."

"New client?" I said. "Is that where you've been?"

"Yes, in Little Copper Row. I did tell Ireq."

"What's he like?" Jivrais said.

Laney wrinkled her nose. "All right, I suppose. Not very interesting. Fairly generous, though I don't think much of his taste. And he wants more than he's saying, but I don't think he's going to tell me what it is. Still, he did give me some good advice."

"Oh?" I said. "About what?"

She waved a hand, her eyes sparkling with mischief. "You'll see, darling. You'll see. I promise you'll like it."

"So long as it isn't going to cause trouble. Speaking of which... hey, Chief?" I said.

"Hmm."

"I saw a speechifier the other day. One of those 'Scalentine for the humans' lot. There was a bit of a ruckus." I looked at him, but he wasn't giving me his growly look. Which meant I hadn't been spotted getting involved, or he hadn't heard about it yet.

"Oh, them – that was the Builders. I'm keeping an eye on them, but they haven't got themselves in anything more than minor trouble yet. Too concerned for their own skins. Noisy and unpleasant, but generally harmless, we think."

"Not that harmless," I said. "One of them tried to stab somebody."

"Yeah, we know. Brendrin Klate. We scraped him up and stuck him in the cells and waited for him to wake up. Somehow, he seems to have fallen and hit his head, or something like that."

"Shame," I said.

"Dreadful shame, yes. Could have damaged the pavement." That was unusually sharp, for the Chief.

"Sounds like you don't like him."

"No, I don't. He's an irredeemable little shite who's constantly looking for an excuse to pulp someone and feel self-righteous about it. Obviously the Builders make him feel right at home."

"You've met him before, then?" I said.

"Yeah. So have you. Little barney at Gallock's last year?"

"I *thought* I knew him from somewhere." He and some friends had tried to cause trouble and I'd smacked his arse and taken his sword off him. Some people shouldn't be allowed weapons. Some people shouldn't be allowed out, frankly. "Brendrin Klate, eh? Did he ever turn up and collect his sword? I'm sure I left it at the barracks."

"Surprisingly, no."

"Is it me, or are there more of that sort around lately?"

"Hah. Wouldn't surprise me, the Brendrin Klates always seem to breed faster'n the good ones."

I patted his arm. "I mean, the 'Scalentine for the Humans' lot, specifically."

"Maybe."

"So what's their thing, the Builders? Apart from humans being better than other people," Unusual said.

"They think that humans built Scalentine," Hargur said.

Laney perched on the arm of his chair, filing her nails and frowning. "But that's silly. No one knows who built Scalentine."

"No. But we're not really dealing with knowing, here, as in, actually knowing something because it's a proven fact. We're dealing with people who really, really want to believe something." Hargur sighed, stretching his legs out towards the fire. The flames threw a warm light over the blue velvet upholstered chairs, and the crew. Flower and Unusual were bent over the chess board. Chess and the tarot are two things that seem to turn up on every plane, in some form. Of course, so does stupidity.

"So they want everyone else to leave?" Laney said.

"Yes. Apparently this will make everything better."

"And how exactly will it do that?"

"Because, it seems, all the problems that happen in Scalentine are caused by there being other races here. And if they all buggered off, the natural superiority of humans would assert itself, and there would be a golden age." He shrugged. "Don't look at me, I'm a were."

"Natural superiority." Laney gave a delicate snort. Fey, admittedly, tend to assume they're superior to everyone else, as a matter of course – but the ones I've met generally still *like* other species, if only because they find them entertaining.

"Sounds like another bunch of idiots to me," I said. "But nasty ones. If anyone's worried, just find someone else to team up with when you go out, all right?"

There were some thoughtful looks, but no one seemed too bothered.

"Too long since the last Migration, that's what it is," Flower said. "You get funny ideas building up when the place starts to get crowded, and too many people too close together... well, they get itchy."

Migration's another of Scalentine's odd little attributes. About every seven years, a whole lot of people get restless. You can feel it in the air for months; a heady, unnerving sense of change. People mostly find good reasons to leave; they reconnect with family members on their home plane, they spot a business opportunity, they need a bigger place and property is cheaper elsewhere... but some just up and go, leaving behind whatever won't fit in a knapsack.

And Scalentine empties out. Not completely, never completely; just enough to make the place feel a little thin and quiet for a few months. And gradually it fills up again.

But it had been a while. Maybe Flower was right.

"What do you think, Chief?"

A faint snore was all the answer I got.

"Hargur?" I nudged him.

"Mmm."

"Bed."

"Huh? Oh, right." He got to his feet. "'Night, all."

I ushered him upstairs to a chorus of "'Night, Chief's.

"Long day?" I said.

"They all are." He fumbled at his buttons, and I helped him out of his shirt.

"Sorry," he said on a yawn. "I..."

"Shh. I can tell you're exhausted. No demands tonight."

He gave me a tired grin. "Wish everyone was as straightforward as you, beautiful."

"Oh?"

"That party... I was being sounded out." He rubbed a hand down his face. "It's not the first time. But it always leaves me feeling as though... I dunno. Smeary."

"If everyone doesn't know you're as honest as the day is long by now, Chief, it's their own fault. Hope you smacked him down."

"It wasn't obvious enough for that," he said.

"If it's any comfort, someone was doing the same to me."

Hargur mumbled something. I slid in next to him, and he wrapped around me.

"Don't let m'oversleep," he muttered. "M'on duty tomorr'."

Next minute, he was asleep. Well, he was nice to snuggle even when he was unconscious. And I most certainly was *not* letting him oversleep. We had unfinished business from before supper.

IN FACT, HARGUR was the one who woke me, sliding a hand around my breast and another between my legs, while I was still struggling my way out of a dream.

"You're feeling better," I said, reaching around behind me. "I have evidence."

He laughed and gave a little gasp of pleasure as I grasped the evidence.

I slid around to face him, took hold of his cock again and ran the other hand over his chest. It wasn't close enough to full moon for him to be completely furry, and when it got that close, we wouldn't be bedding. But he was pleasantly hairy. I liked him whatever state he was in; I was rather afraid I loved him. A little scary, after all this time. I nibbled his shoulder and pinched one of his nipples lightly; his cock, warm and solid in my hand, jumped.

He started to stroke my neck, his gentle, nearly reverent touches somehow making it feel longer, more graceful; he touched my breasts and nipples as though they were something precious he'd just discovered. *The best gift of a pleasing lover is to make one feel desirable.* My first teacher in the sensual arts had said that, long ago. All the way down, he stroked, sliding his fingers over me, into me.

I loved his body, broad-shouldered and lean and long in the limb; I loved the way we seemed to interlock so neatly; I loved the way he felt so warm.

We paused, briefly, while he reached for a preventive. I drew a breath; should I tell him it wasn't needed? But it wasn't the time. Somehow, it never seemed to be. I rolled it on, bit by tiny bit, until he laughed with impatience and pushed me down.

I lay back and guided him inside me, loving the feel and fit of him, his hair brushing my shoulders, his hand on my breast, the deep delicious rub of him, the way he watched my face, serious, until pleasure started to take him and he threw his head back and growled deep in his throat. The way he wouldn't let me up until he'd stroked me to a liquid quiver, warm lapping pleasure spreading out from his fingers.

The only things I didn't love were that he was on duty, I had a job to do, and we couldn't lie there all morning.

"Hargur?"

"Mmm, what time is it?"

"You've got time" – I poked him gently in the side – "*if* you don't go back to sleep."

"By the way, when are you going to Incandress?"

"Oh. I'm not."

He propped himself on one elbow, looking at me. "You decided against it?"

"Yes."

"Why?"

"Why? What, you *wanted* me to go?" It came out sounding more hurt than I intended.

"Of course not, woman, don't be idiotic," he said, tugging on a lock of my hair gently. "It's just that you said you were. What changed your mind?"

I shrugged. "Combination of things, I suppose. It wasn't just bodyguarding; Enthemmerlee's guard need training up, too. I couldn't see how to do both. Not in time. And... well. Things here... I just wasn't happy about leaving."

"You worried about the Builders?"

"Some."

"We're watching them. Is that all?"

"No. But nothing I could put my finger on. It feels hinky, that's all."

He frowned at the lock of hair, twisting it around his finger.

"Sometimes you have to trust your gut," I said, not liking the note of pleading I could hear in my voice, but not able to stop it. "Don't you?"

"Of course," he said.

"But?"

"But nothing. It's your decision, Babylon."

"Yes," I said.

He thought I was wrong. He thought I was breaking a promise. The fact that I agreed with him, and so did that hollow place in the back of my thighs, didn't make me feel any better.

"So. Never mind Enthemmerlee, Babylon." He leaned back, and put his arm round me, so that I rested against his shoulder. He was tall enough that I could do that; it was one of the things I liked so much. Just one. Of course, it also meant he wasn't looking me in the eye when he said, "What about me?"

"What about you?" I said.

"Is there something I'm doing, that you don't like?"

"I don't... what? No!"

"You sure?"

"Of course I'm sure." I pushed myself upright so I could look at him properly. "Hargur, why would you think that? You think I wouldn't *tell* you?"

He glanced at me, and looked away. "No, 'course not."

He's good at hiding his thoughts. That's part of his job. But he can't hide all of them, not from me.

Of course he thought I wouldn't tell him. Because convincing a man he's pleased you is part of *my* job.

"Hargur..."

There was a flurry of knocks on the door. "Chief? Chief?" Jivrais.

"What?" Hargur growled.

"There's a guard at the door, he says there's been another one."

"I'll be right there." He pushed himself out of bed and was halfway into his uniform before I could catch my breath. Just for a minute, I hated both our jobs.

I threw on a robe and followed him down the stairs, where a guard, a middle-aged man with a face like a chewed boot, was flirting with Essie. The grin fell off his face as soon as he saw Hargur. "Chief, there's..."

"Tell me on the way," Hargur said.

"Chief."

"Be careful," I said.

He kissed me on the nose. "I'm always careful."

I watched them walk off, deep in conversation. Whatever had been bothering him had already been put aside.

I wished I could put it aside as easily. It wasn't like Hargur to worry that way; he'd not seemed like someone who needs constant reassurance that his performance is up to scratch. I went upstairs and dressed, half glad I had no client for a couple of hours, half wishing I did, in order to take my mind off things. I decided to go to Bressler's instead, and train. With Previous gone, there wasn't anyone at the Lantern, other than Flower, who could push me; and Flower didn't fight for practice. I'd asked him. Once.

I GOT BACK bruised and sweating, walked into the kitchen for water, and found the whole crew gathered around the table, looking dishevelled and shocked as though they'd been blown there by a storm. The minute I walked in, everyone started talking at once, and it took me several minutes to work out what was going on.

Once I had... "You did *what?*" I stared at Laney in utter disbelief.

"But I thought you'd be *pleased!*" she wailed.

"Laney..." I turned to Ireq.

"How bad is it?" I said.

"Everything we had in the kitty. You hadn't been to the bank for two weeks."

"I was going to take it in this week."

"I'm not," Ireq said, "going to say I told you the takings should be banked daily. This is me, not saying I told you. That's not the worst of it, though."

"No, I know."

"She mortgaged the Lantern. She mortgaged our *home*."

"I know. Flower?" I said. He sighed, and folded his arms with massive patience. The chopper he'd been using for the meat spilled slow drops of blood onto the floor. "Oh, don't ask me; all I know is I can extend our lines of credit with the butcher and the grocers only so far. After that..." He shrugged. "Basically, we can feed ourselves and the punters well for about a week. Or" – he closed his eyes and shuddered – "I can feed the *punters* well for two weeks while we eat whatever I can scrape in the last half hour of the markets. Then we stop feeding the punters, because I *will* not ruin my reputation, even for you."

"I wouldn't ask it."

"Don't forget the laundry bill," Ireq said. "And the bill for coal. And the bill for..."

"All right," I said. "I need to get the accountant over here. In the meantime, Laney, you need to sit down with Ireq and make a list of everyone you borrowed from, and at what rates of interest."

Her perfect, pearly brow furrowed. "Interest? Oh... yes, a few of them mentioned interest. I thought that meant they were, you know, *interested*."

I let my head drop until it hit the table. I lay there for a moment, with my eyes closed. It was nice like that. Peaceful.

"Babylon?" Laney said. "Babylon, darling, it'll be all right. I mean, it's Tesserane silk. Everyone *knows* it's the best. That's why everyone was willing to give me money, to buy lots of it. I don't understand why you're all so *cross*."

"Because, Laney, investing money like that is for people who *understand* money. And markets, and trade, and things like that. Which you don't. And neither do I. And now," I said. "We not only have no money, we owe an awful lot of it to an awful lot of people who are going to be very, very unhappy if they don't get it back."

"Do you have any idea how many things can happen to a cargo of silk that has to come so far?" Ireq said. "Fire. Rats. Moth. Bandits. Civil war."

Something at the back of my mind tolled an ominous little bell. At the same time, my gut, already clenched, clenched tighter.

"Oh," Laney said. She looked at her nails, then sighed heavily. "Well, then. I shall have to talk to the family, I suppose. Daddy will..."

"*No.*" The chorus was unanimous, even from Jivrais. Laney looked up, startled.

"Laney," I said, as gently as possible. "You don't want to do that."

"Well, no, I don't, but..."

"Laney. Listen. I know things are... tricky, between you and your family. But that's only part of it." I was trying to think of a tactful way to put things when Jivrais forestalled me, only somewhat missing the tactful part.

"Laney, sweetie. You borrowed money from people who can walk through King of Stone at three in the morning, unarmed, and out the other end because even the Kingsters don't dare touch them. And the only thing worse than being in debt to *them* is being in debt to Fey." He shuddered theatrically. "At least your standard loan-shark only cuts bits off if you can't pay. They don't make them grow back a completely different *shape*."

"Oh," Laney said.

"Or fill your eyes with bees. Or make you serve them for the next two hundred years, wearing your pants on your head. Or someone *else's* pants. Or..."

"Jivrais," I said. "That's enough."

Laney's eyes were glimmering with tears. "I'm *sorry*," she said. "I thought it would solve everything."

"I know, Laney. But next time you want to help, just... ask one of us first if it's a good idea, all right?" That little warning bell at the back of my head was now ringing a loud, persistent alarm.

Civil war. I looked at Ireq. *Silk route.*

Fain's voice. *'Enthemmerlee... is the best hope for stability that Incandress has.'*

"Oh, buggery crap," I said.

"What?" Flower said.

"I think I'm going to Incandress."

CHAPTER
FIVE

"YOU CHANGED YOUR mind," Enthemmerlee said.

It was a different room, but I could see the silvery dust of wards on the windows this time, as well as the door. Obviously things in the Section had got no better, as far as Fain was concerned.

"Yes," I said. "I changed my mind."

They were all looking at me; their faces were unreadable apart from Malleay, who was scowling fiercely. "Why?" he said.

"I have my reasons. If you still want me."

I tried not to look at Fain, wondering if he knew about the mess Laney had got us in, and if not, how long it would be before he did.

"Enthemmerlee," Malleay said.

"Yes?"

"'I have my reasons?' How do we know what those reasons are? If we can buy her loyalty, so can someone else."

He had, although I hated to admit it, a point. Over the years I had developed my own set of rules about who I sold my sword to and exactly what loyalty that bought, but a sellsword I had been, and now was again. There's a reason "mercenary" is an insult.

I shrugged. "What can I say? I don't want to see a civil war in Incandress."

"You *wouldn't* see it if you stayed here," Malleay said.

I looked at Enthemmerlee. What was I going to do if they

turned me down? I would have to travel to Incandress myself, try to find the trade caravan... even if I could catch up with it, the chances of getting hired as a guard, if I simply turned up, with no references... if I did get hired, that didn't bode well for the security of the caravan. If I didn't...

My stomach clenched on acid emptiness. I could lose the Lantern; and where would my crew go?

"Rikkinnet?" Enthemmerlee said.

Rikkinnet looked at me for a long time, cold-eyed. "And if the stability of our country suddenly does not look so attractive, then where will your loyalty lie?"

"I can assure you," Fain said, "I have every reason to believe that Madam Steel has at heart the best interests of the Lady Enthemmerlee the Itnunnacklish." He gave me a sharp look; no, he hadn't forgotten the oath I'd made him take.

"Lobik?" Malleay said.

They all turned to look at the Ikinchli, even Fain.

Lobik was leaning back in his chair, watching me. He rested his hand along his jaw, thumb pressing against the corner of his mouth. His eyes were calm. "I think we should remember that Madam Steel helped Enthemmerlee before, when she did not know who she was. Yes, firstly for money, but then, when she realised the situation, she did her best to provide protection even though she could have lost by it. I believe she was, and is, a person of honour."

I looked at Enthemmerlee. She frowned down at the table, then up at me. "I will trust you."

"I don't know if I can do everything you want of me," I said. "I don't know about training up your guard. I don't know if I *can* keep you safe. I can promise I will try my best."

"That is all that can be asked of any of us, is it not?" She smiled then, brilliant as the sun coming out, and despite everything, I couldn't help but smile back. It wasn't all relief, either. I *liked* the girl.

"So what else do I need to know?" I said.

Lobik said, "What is your feeling about snakes?"

"Snakes? How do you mean, how do I feel about them? I've never had a lot to do with them. Why?"

"I understand some humans find them disturbing."

"I'd find one disturbing if it bit me, otherwise, I'm happy to leave them alone if they leave me alone. Again, why?"

"They are, in a manner of speaking, pets among the Gudain."

"Pets," Rikkinnet said, and snorted. "That is one word for it." She flicked her long blue tongue out through her teeth.

Lobik shook his head at her, but was fighting a grin.

"Fine," I said, wondering what was funny. Snakes I didn't mind. Beetles, on the other hand... "But are there other things I need to know? Rules of behaviour? Things that must or mustn't be done?" I'd spent enough time in various courts that I knew how easy it was to trip over the etiquette.

"Life among the Ten Families is generally quite formal," Enthemmerlee said.

"Not 'quite,'" Malleay snapped. "Ridiculously. Degrees of this, degrees of that. Depth of the bow. Forms of address. Given my way..."

"Given your way you would sweep it all aside," Enthemmerlee said, smiling at him. "And I would no longer be Enthemmerlee Defarlane Lathrit en Scona Entaire the Itnunnacklish. Which would be a relief for those who have to learn our names, I am sure."

"Is easy," Rikkinnet said, snapping the words out like the cracks of a whip. "Do as we Ikinchli have always done. Smile, say 'sir' and 'madam,' bow. Treat every Gudain as superior. Then, if you are lucky, no one beats you because they have had a bad day or someone's spilled their drink."

There was a silence, then Lobik said, "I don't think anyone is going to try and beat Madam Steel over a spilled drink. Though I think would be fun to watch them try, no?" He turned to Rikkinnet, and said something softly in Ikinchli.

She hissed.

He said something else.

She turned to the rest of us, and said, her voice tight, "Lobik reminds me that those here are not responsible for the past, and that we look to the future."

"The past leaves scars," I said, and didn't realise until I saw Fain's eyes following the move that I was rubbing my own scar, the one on my jaw, symbol of the Goddess Babaska.

"Yes," Lobik said. "And we will not deny the injuries that caused them. But if all we can see is scars, we will never see anything but the past, and the future will slip away while we lick over old wounds."

"True enough," I said. However, they *are* supposed to fade with time. They're not supposed to do what mine had, which was disappear and then come back.

And sometimes, it itched. And sometimes, when it itched, I felt a buzz in the back of my head, as though an insect were trying to gnaw its way in.

I had been the Goddess Babaska's Avatar. It had been a stolen power, and I'd given it up willingly; but I wasn't quite sure she'd given *me* up.

I pushed it out of my mind, as I was in the habit of doing. "So, what else do I need to know?"

"There are certain formalities to social occasions," Enthemmerlee said. "But as a..." She broke off. "You will not be expected to know them all."

"Ah, well, I won't be eating with you. Not at the same time. I shall be on guard."

"You'll need to watch out for the Fenac," Malleay said. "Though you look enough like Gudain that they might not haul you in just for the sake of it."

"They're your Militia, yes?"

"In a manner of speaking," Enthemmerlee said. "They are in need of reform. Like so much else." She sighed. "Almost all Fenac are Gudain. If there is trouble, they look at the Ikinchli first."

Which didn't mean they wouldn't look at a handy foreigner,

such as me, if there *was* trouble. I hoped I could keep out of their way.

"The few Ikinchli Fenac, most of them are *tic dricancai*," Rikkinnet muttered. Malleay looked slightly horrified; his mouth opened, but he shut it again.

Before I had a chance to ask what *tic dricancai* meant, Lobik said, "The uniform is a dark brown tunic, brown leggings, and a low round helmet. You will hear them called *guak*, but this is not wise to say if they can hear."

"Not if it means what I think it means," I said. "Gotcha."

"There is one other thing. The way we dress, normally, is quite covered," Enthemmerlee said. She glanced down at my cleavage and away, quickly.

"I will be more covered," I assured her. Exposed flesh is strictly for non-lethal situations. I have worn chain-mail underwear and nothing else but boots, but only in the bedroom. What can I say? Some people have funny ideas about armour.

"There is a reason the clothing is very covering," Lobik said. Malleay stared at the table. Enthemmerlee had a faint pearly-green flush along her cheekbones. Lobik went on. "The Gudain... they do not touch, in public. And" – he glanced apologetically at Enthemmerlee – "Sex, this is not spoken of, you understand?"

"Yes, I've been told," I said.

"I need to be clear," Lobik said. "They do not mention, *ever*. Even to speak of marriage except in the most formalised way, this is disapproved, because it implies that the sex will be had. Pregnancy is not mentioned. Nothing with any connection whatever. There are many, many laws governing behaviour, and they are enforced by the Moral Statutes. They do not usually apply to Ikinchli, because in law, we are still largely considered animals, and therefore beyond moral reform, but for the purposes of your visit you would have many of the privileges of a Gudain, and it would be wise to be... circumspect."

"Oookay. I assume I shouldn't mention my profession, then?"

"Your profession?" Enthemmerlee said.

Hoo, boy.

"Er..." I said. "I sort of thought you knew."

"It has something to do with..." She stopped.

If it was difficult for her to even *say* the word, I wondered just how she had brought herself to do the deed with two men of different species. And if neither Enthemmerlee nor Malleay could actually bring themselves to mention what it was they were supposed to be doing, how had they done it at all?

"Yes. It has to do with that," I said. "For money. That's how I make my living, generally. You understand?"

"Oh." Her blush deepened until it was a glowing jade. It made her look very pretty. "I see. Yes, it would be best that it was not mentioned."

"Well," Fain said, into the echoing silence that followed. "I believe that concludes the business for now. Is everyone happy?"

I wasn't sure "happy" was the word, but no one seemed to have anything else to say. Lobik and Rikkinnet seemed amused but unfazed, but Malleay's eyes and mouth had gone completely circular; I looked at him and, perhaps unfairly, smiled. His mouth snapped shut, his own deep green blush rising up his neck as though he were drowning. He really was cute. Oversensitive, touchy, and sulky as a wet cat, but cute, nonetheless. I wondered idly what he'd look like out of those dreadful clothes.

"In that case," Fain said. "If you would come with me, Madam Steel?" He pointed towards his office. "I need a few words with you."

"You're the client," I said.

He led the way and locked the door behind us. "Well, are you going to tell me why you changed your mind?"

"You'll probably find out soon enough. Let's just say I really, really don't want to see Incandress descend into civil war, especially within the next week or so. Will that do?"

He looked me over. "It will. For now. However" – his eyes

were cold – "I do not have a Fey oath to put on you, Madam Steel, but rest assured that I do have every expectation you will do your best to fulfil your part of this bargain."

"I intend to."

"I do hope so."

"So what exactly do you want from me, Mr Fain?"

"Firstly, the ship is the *Delaney's Promise*, leaving through Bealach, two days from now on the afternoon tide."

"I'll be there."

"Once you arrive on Incandress, I want you to keep your ears open. Everyone knows the situation is volatile; most people who do not *have* to stay will have left, or be leaving. Unless they have serious investments in the area or are clinging on there for other reasons. I want you to watch for unusual alliances; unexpected encouragement for one side or the other to push things to open confrontation."

"You mean you think there are people who *want* it to come to war? Why?"

"There have been some unusual trading patterns."

"*Trading* patterns?"

"Yes. I believe there may be people with an interest in the outcome of the situation on Incandress, an interest that may not be to the best advantage of its people."

"Can you forget you're in the Diplomatic Section long enough for you to tell me, in plain language, what you're actually talking about?"

He smiled a little. "I'm sorry. Very well. Someone is buying grain; a great deal of it. I'm not sure who; a conglomerate, perhaps, or a single person acting through intermediaries. But they may be planning to profiteer: to sell at inflated prices to desperate people with few crops or stores of their own after a civil war. And it is not unknown, in these situations, for people to *nudge* things."

"War could make someone a profit."

"Indeed."

"Oh, great." The little couch creaked in protest as I sat down. I knew how it felt. "Has this anything to do with why you've got wards slapped up all over the place?"

"I am merely taking precautions."

"As if things weren't bad enough. Fain, I don't see how I'm supposed to do this as well as look after Enthemmerlee." Not to mention finding the silk cargo. "I don't even know anything about grain trading."

"You know about war. And you have a capacity for engaging people which could be extremely useful."

"You did *hear* what Lobik said, I take it?"

"It would be insulting to assume that your ability to make friends is confined to the bedroom, Madam Steel. After all, Enthemmerlee regards you as a friend, and you have not slept with her." He looked at me, one eyebrow raised. "Or so I assume."

I coughed. "Point taken."

"All I want you to do is listen," Fain said.

Well, if I couldn't do that, I'd be out of a job. "So what do I do if I find out anything?"

"Get a message to me. We have arrangements with the Empire's courier service." He gave me instructions. I was to write to him (not, obviously, under his own name), as though discussing arrangements for an exotic party, with several of my crew providing entertainment and Flower doing the cooking.

That level of deception I thought I could manage.

"Now. You haven't met any of Enthemmerlee's family, have you?" Fain said.

"No. I didn't get the impression they were terribly happy about her transformation, though."

"Would you expect them to be?"

I shrugged. "I suppose not."

"Her father is Lord Enboryay. He is one of the Advisors to the Crown; the eldest of each generation of the Ten Families undergoes Patinarai and becomes an Advisor, unless there are exceptional circumstances which render them unsuitable.

Enboryay is not one for great intrigue, so far as I have been able to discover; he is mainly concerned with his estates, and likes things the way they are. He breeds racing beasts. I would say the turn of events has left him largely bewildered."

"The others?"

"Selinecree, the aunt. She seemed even more bewildered than her brother, but despite the circumstances, she appeared to enjoy her time on Scalentine; even after the transformation had taken place, I saw her at some social functions before they returned to Incandress."

"Oh, yes, I think I may have seen her at the Roundhouse Tower. I thought Gudain didn't like foreigners?"

"They may not, but they do receive foreign traders. They are on a major Perindi Empire trade route, so they could hardly do otherwise."

"Who else?" I said.

"A child. Chitherlee. The daughter of Enthemmerlee's dead brother, brought up as one of the household."

"That's all?"

"There are no other surviving family. There are, of course, the Defraish, the family into which Enthemmerlee was supposed to marry. Tovanay Moth en Laslain Defraish and his mother Daryellee. The boy I have not met, though it would be wise to assume that he is upset and angry. The mother was somewhat icy."

"Capable of vengeance for the insult?"

"Only if it could be done in a way that did not exacerbate the appalling scandal."

"And the rest of the Ten Families?"

He rummaged in the desk, and handed me a sheaf of paper. "This is what we know."

I took the papers. "And the Council itself? What's the feeling of the Gudain government?"

"There are those who see the Itnunnacklish as a plot by the Ikinchli, those who see her as a ghastly family embarrassment, and those who see her as a clever move which may help to calm an increasingly volatile situation."

"And what about the Ikinchli? I don't even know their system of government."

"Officially, the ruling power still lies with the priests, but it seems their role has become increasingly ceremonial. There are a number of local leaders of varying degrees of influence. Some are in favour of the Itnunnacklish, some are actively hostile, many are waiting to see which way the wind blows."

"Wonderful." I hate politics. At least on a battlefield it's usually pretty damn obvious who your enemy is; they're the one trying to remove your head.

"Don't look so down in the mouth, Babylon, I have every faith in your abilities."

I wished I did, but I wasn't going to say so, in case he decided not to hire me after all.

"Now, if there's nothing else," he said, "I'll show you out."

He turned away for a moment, and a door I hadn't known was there opened silently behind the pretty couch, revealing a low archway leading onto the street.

"Always useful to have a way out," I said.

"Indeed." He smiled, and kissed my hand, which sent the usual little shiver down my spine. "I hope you are not having second thoughts."

"I am having second thoughts. And third, and probably fourth. But I'll be there."

It could be worse. All I had to do was keep Enthemmerlee from getting assassinated, train her household guard up to scratch, track down our silk and get it safely to the border, find out if some mysterious person was trying to make a bad situation worse, and not mention nookie.

I was probably buggered six ways to sunset, but at least that ugly feeling of guilt in the back of my thighs had disappeared.

*　　*　　*

FAIN HAD TOLD me nothing about the magician he was sending; but then Fain always dealt out information as though it was his life's blood. There wasn't much I could do about it.

I wondered briefly if I should take someone with me. There was Laney, but even if I had wanted to take her away from the business for that long, she could be a bit of a liability, and not just financially. Like most High Court Fey, she's extremely good at certain forms of diplomacy, but only when she feels like it; she's also *very* easily bored, she enjoys the sensual arts and if she wants to bed someone she'll do it. Considering how the Gudain felt about such things, taking Laney was probably not a great idea.

Besides, I didn't really want to take any of the crew. Scalentine's not the safest city in the planes, but there are a lot worse places, and a country potentially on the verge of war was one of them.

I only knew a couple of other really powerful magical practitioners. I'd known more, but several of them had moved on in the last Migration. There was Mokraine, but he wouldn't be interested. Or suitable. He was an addict, disturbing company and a fair day's walk from sane. Mattie Longsides could no longer find sane with a good map.

But Mokraine might, perhaps, be able to give me some information, if I caught him in a communicative mood.

To settle my unhappy stomach, I went to Gallock's to get some food.

Gallock was, as usual, cooking, yelling at hir staff and gossiping with customers in hir raucous, master-sergeant's voice all at once. "Hey, Babylon." Ze waved a spatula at me as I sat down, and a few minutes later came out from behind the counter to serve me hirself.

Watching hir move was quite something. Barraklé are always pretty impressive; they tend to be broad, with a four-armed, four-breasted torso melding into the thick-furred muscular tail that propels them along; but Gallock was massively pregnant, too. Hir stomach went ahead of hir like an aggressive herald; threatening to knock people off their chairs.

"By the All, Gallock, how many have you got in there?"

Ze laughed. "Maybe just one big one. One is enough. What I get you, Babylon?"

"You got that fish soup on? The one with the crunchy bits?"

"For you, always."

"That, then. Oh, you haven't seen Mokraine, have you?"

Hir face darkened. "No. And please do not bring him in here. That familiar he got put everyone off their food. Waste my good cooking."

"Ah, come on, Gallock, the man's got to eat."

"Not here, he not."

As I was waiting for my soup amid the crowd of dancers, actors and whores joking and laughing and arguing and shovelling in Gallock's excellent food, I became conscious of a faint breeze on my cheek, blowing through the rich-smelling fug. I looked round to see that one of the small round window-panes was broken.

As ze set the soup down, I said, "Gallock? What happened to your window?"

"Oh, that. Builders, they call themselves. Wreckers, is more like. Pity you not here, eh? Smash their heads in for me."

"Seems like everyone wants me to smash someone's head in," I muttered into my soup. "Is it me, Gallock, or is there more of that sort of thing recently?"

Gallock scowled. "Some, yes." Ze nodded at a skinny dark-furred lad with a wide grin who had plates in each hand and another gripped in his tail, who was flirting with a tableful of actors. "The boy there, he get chased home, after his shift. Lucky he can climb good, got out of their way." Ze shook hir head, and moved ponderously away, pressing one hand to the small of hir back. Gallock was big, and strong; but that far advanced in pregnancy, ze was also slow, and vulnerable. I hoped ze had someone to see *hir* home.

The soup was, as always, excellent, but neither that nor a particularly nicely put-together dancer with a lush mouth and buttocks as tight and inviting as a freshly-made bed could distract my thoughts. I finished the soup, so as not to insult Gallock, but it was a struggle.

When I left, I put my head into a few of Mokraine's haunts; gambling dens, the small elegant squares where lawyers' offices clustered. Nothing. His addiction to the powerful emotions of others had taken him somewhere else today.

I'd almost given up when I found him down at the docks, sitting on an old crate, watching the ships. Portal Bealach flamed and roared, painting fine craft, grand warehouses, heaped litter and rat-corpses alike with shifting blue and gold.

Silence puddled around Mokraine: a man in a ragged robe leached by time to a dim absence of colour. Tangled grey hair spilled down his back. One hand hovered over the head of his familiar; of all the ugly creatures I'd seen in my travels, possibly the ugliest. A mouthless clot of a thing, with three blood-coloured eyes and three splayed, toadish legs, its flesh a slimy grey that seemed out of place on anything living. Though whether the thing was actually alive was moot. Even Mokraine seldom touched it, and most people went out of their way to avoid getting anywhere near it.

A ship came through the portal, the creak of wood, crackle of sail and voices of the crew all drowned in the portal's roar. A small crowd waited on the dockside: stevedores and freelance doxies hoping for trade, merchants waiting for cargo, families waiting for the return of their kin, people waiting to leave. I saw a couple of the blank, dimmed faces that meant Mokraine had been feeding. It was hard to say that what he did was harmful, as such; he drained strong emotions from people, and it left them, for a few moments, emptied out. They came back to themselves swiftly enough, though I'd never met anyone who enjoyed the experience. He also drew out, along with the emotions, a handful of memories, often to do with whatever had caused the emotion. Which meant that he was casually pickpocketing people's private thoughts. Mokraine had never shown any interest in blackmail, but word got about. One day someone he'd fed on was going to have something they *really* wanted to hide, and then they'd try and kill him.

Which could be very bad, and not just for Mokraine.

Today, I thought he was looking a little better than usual – he had shaved within a day or so, and looked fractionally less cadaverous than the last time I'd seen him.

"Mokraine," I said, sitting down on a wrapped bale.

"Babylon," he said. "How odd."

"Odd?"

"You are seeking me out."

"I was, yes."

"It seems to me that you did so not long ago, too – though I admit my sense of time is a little... vagrant, these days." He watched the ship come into dock, the swoop of ropes through the air, hands reaching up to haul her into safety. "And now you have found me."

"What's odd about me looking up an old friend?" I said.

"You consider me a friend? I seem to have lost the knack for friendship. Or perhaps I never had it. It's hard to tell, sometimes."

He'd been a powerful warlock, once. Probably he still was, somewhere in the mess that his last experiment had left of his mind.

"I wanted to ask you something."

"Yes," he said.

"Is there an amulet, a spell, anything that will protect someone against all forms of magic?"

"All forms?" He turned his head to look full at me; his eyes, deep-sunk and pouched, were weary, but amused. "My dear Babylon!"

"What's funny?"

"Magic is not one thing. There are a thousand different systems; things which work on one plane and not on another, things which use physical objects, or will, or the intervention of a god. Magics of cooking-pot and consciousness. But there are the magics that simply *are*. Magics of breath and birth. If one could find one thing that would stop them all, why, it would probably stop *everything*. The turning of the planes would falter and cease, and all would fall away into the abyss."

Something walked down my spine on bony little feet.

"Well, then," I said. "Something that would help? Against whatever magics work on a particular plane?"

"Which plane?"

"Whichever one Incandress is on."

"Incandress."

"Where the Ikinchli come from? Satrapy of the Perindi Empire?"

"Perindi... I was there, once, I think. The court. Yes. What did you ask me, Babylon?"

"Protective amulets? Shielding against magic?"

"What sort of magic?"

"The type that kills people."

"There are many magics that kill. Are you planning to destroy some more gods?"

"They weren't gods. And how did you...? I never told you about that."

He waved a hand. "I... acquire things. Titbits. Fragments. You returned to your home plane, and there you destroyed those who were acting as gods." He picked up a fragment of crab shell that was lying at his feet, and turned it in his fingers. "Interesting."

"You 'acquire' things."

"Things leak. People leak. Thoughts, memories, emotions; it was much in your mind. And out of it. You were not, yourself, inclined to become a god?"

"I'd *been* Tiresana's version of a god, thank you. I had absolutely no desire to do it again."

He dropped the shell. "Desire. Yes. That was you, too. And something remains." He traced a finger down his jaw, following on his own face the line of my scar, his eyes on mine, rapt. "You have rejected power, but power has not yet let go of you, Babylon."

"What do you mean?"

"Portals," he said. "Portals and planes and powers, all linked. Sometimes I get a glimpse... like a net of silver, woven through the darkness. Be careful when you tug at the threads of the universe."

"I'm not planning to do any such thing," I said.

"Neither was I... At least, I don't think so. It's hard to remember. But I created a portal where there was not a portal, didn't I?"

"Yes, you did. What has that to do with me? I'm no warlock. I leave messing with the universe to you lot."

He laughed. "You are linked to something, now; as am I. Creating a portal tied me into that silver net, and speaking with gods... speaking with gods has done the same to you."

"I placed an order! What am I supposed to use?"

The words, furiously spoken, pulled Mokraine's gaze away from me. I shuddered with relief. I might, once, have spoken with gods... *a* goddess, anyway. But so far as I was concerned, the conversation was over.

I turned towards the argument that had attracted Mokraine. A red-faced man was yelling at a solid-looking Edleskasin woman bundled in the traditional red-leather-fringed, thick, quilted coat, with elaborately embroidered red cloths draped over her large, fragile ears. Two muscular young men loomed behind her. Her sons, by their looks. I knew her by sight; one of the grain merchants, with a big warehouse nearby.

"You were outbid," she said. "It's business."

The red-faced man was getting redder, and his face was swollen in a worrying way. I could clearly see a vein in his temple that I was pretty sure shouldn't be standing out like that. It brought back unhappy memories of a client I'd lost when his heart gave out on him.

Mokraine, helplessly drawn, got to his feet.

"Mokraine!" Should I actually try to stop him, though? It did go through my mind that having his emotions drained at this juncture might just save red-face from collapsing lifeless on the dirty cobbles.

"We had a contract! I'm beginning to think the Builders are right about you lot!" Red-face said.

One of the sons moved forward, growling.

Red-face, for whom I'd just lost most of my sympathy, spat, and walked off. Mokraine sat back down. "Oh, well," he said. "Rather a meaty dish, that, in any case. Too heavy for a delicate palate."

"Mokraine? Do you know of any magicians who work for the Section? Someone called a Scholar?"

"No. Why would I? Scholar is only a few steps above Initiate. Those lacking sufficient imagination remain Scholars all their lives."

"Unlike you."

"As you say."

"But why would someone choose a Scholar for an important mission?"

Mokraine shrugged. "Perhaps because they require someone without imagination. Why do you ask me?"

"Because you know things. Because you're a First Adept."

He looked at me, and I caught a glimpse of the man he'd been. The First Adept Doctor of the Arcane, famous across a dozen planes; arrogant as an eagle on a crag, and just as touchy. Then the arrogance was gone, as swiftly as it came, and a sort of bleakness took its place. "I don't know what I am," he said. "Go away, Babylon."

I felt myself sweating slightly with relief.

"All right. Try and take care of yourself, Mokraine."

He only waved his hand impatiently, staring out to sea again, his ravaged face and dimmed robes bathed in portal light, his gaze fixed on something far out of reach.

CHAPTER
SIX

IT WAS A dim, foggy evening, smelling of woodsmoke and wet wool. I walked back via Glimmering Lane, which is packed with tiny shops, the sort known as 'exclusive'; that is, they'll only let you in if you happen to be in possession of a ridiculous amount of money. Even when I'm solvent I can't afford to shop there. There was a woman there who ran a magical shop who had provided me with useful information before, but the place was closed.

I looked in a few windows. A jewellery shop caught my eye – not because of the merchandise, most of which was of the vanishingly discreet sort (I've never understood the point of jewellery that's so tasteful you can hardly see it, myself), but because of the neatly lettered notice tucked into the corner of the window. *Excellent prices offered. Every discretion applied.* Next to it was a tray of rings, more striking and varied stuff than further up in the window; some were fairly new, others had that smooth gloss of things that have been long-worn.

So they bought old, as well as new. I ran my finger over one of my rings, a square-cut emerald in a setting of that iridescent black gold that only comes from Disla, in the far eastern quadrant of the Perindi Empire. It was a present from a client. Lovely, and unfortunately instantly recognisable, should the client happen to wander down here, which they might.

And even pawning all my rings wasn't going to get us out of Laney's mess.

There was a woman at the counter with long blonde hair spilling out of the hood of her cloak, showing something to the proprietor. I caught a glimpse of gold before he shook his head. She shoved whatever it was back in her pouch and turned, pulling up her hood, tucking her hair away, pale against the pale-green lining. I felt I'd seen her before, somewhere, but Scalentine's like that, full of half-known faces.

Then something truly horrible in the next shop caught my eye.

It was probably meant to be a couch. It was hard to tell under the gilding, flags, fruit, furbelows and cherubs. It looked like one of the most uncomfortable things I'd ever seen, as well as being quite astonishingly ugly. I was tempted to go in and ask the price, just so I could laugh.

A customer emerged from the back of the shop, and ran a hand over one of the gilded swags. Now him, I knew. Trader Heimarl. 'Difficult times.' Obviously not *too* difficult. The way the Dra-ay proprietor was twisting his brow-feelers together, he'd not had to slash the price.

I heard hasty footsteps behind me, and turned; but it was only the woman with the hood of her cloak pulled around to hide her face, hiding all but a crescent of skin.

She hovered outside the shop. Heimarl caught sight of her, and the sides of his full mouth pulled tight for a moment with irritation, quickly smoothed over.

He said something to the proprietor, who flickered his feelers outwards in a quivering fan – translated into human, it would be a greasy, hand-rubbing bow.

I slid around the corner of the building, not wanting to be spotted. It's always embarrassing meeting someone you've turned down. Behind me I heard the door of the shop close, and Heimarl's voice. "Did you finish your business, my dear?"

"No. Thasado, you *promised*. I've done everything..." Her voice was a peculiar and ugly combination of arrogance and whine.

"Soon, Suli, dear. We'll have our justice, I promise you. Now, look at this stain on your cloak. What is that, fruit? You've not been taking care of yourself."

"I shouldn't *have* to."

"Let me walk you home."

THE FOLLOWING DAY was busy. The sheets were barely on before they were off again. We got through more laundry... but I'm fastidious that way. It was one of the reasons I'd chosen this site; there was a wash-house just around the corner, and we gave them enough business to get a discount.

Laney kept, rather unnervingly, *doing* things for the rest of us; my dressing-gown whisked itself to the hook almost before it was off, I found a cup of tea on my dresser with enough golden in it that if I'd drunk it I'd have been unconscious. Very good golden, too, by the smell, maybe even Levantish, which was the worst of it. Golden like that you don't put in tea, at most you wed it to a very small amount of pure spring-water, after making the proper introductions. Wincing, I poured the dreadful concoction away. I heard a yelp of horror that had me belting downstairs, only to discover Flower holding up his favourite chopping knife, which now had a solid gold handle.

He looked at me. "It's ruined the balance," he said.

"I'll talk to her."

He opened his mouth, then closed it, shaking his head. "No, don't. She's just trying to make up. And besides, it's gold; it'll be back to normal tomorrow."

Laney, in typical Fey fashion, can't actually make gold that lasts. If she could, we wouldn't be in this mess. Although the All knows what it would do to Scalentine's economy.

I heard Jivrais wail, "My hair! It's gone purple!"

We looked at each other. "When are you going to Incandress?" Flower said.

"Tomorrow."

"Can I come?"

* * *

I TOOK A shortcut to the Midnight Rose through the Sleeping Gardens. They're at their best at night in summer, but even now, with winter getting a grip on the city, they have a sparse sort of charm. Stone nymphs doze with silvery webs in their hair. The stream mutters to itself like a small child happily absorbed in some quiet game. Berries, chalky blue and blood red, cluster on the bare-stemmed bushes, and the dried grasses, leached pale gold by the chill, rustle and whisper. But all the little moths that dance there in the summer sleep in cocoons underground, waiting for spring.

The Midnight Rose is in a prime site, on a hill near the centre of Scalentine, close enough to the gardens that in summer the scents drift in through the open windows. A nice looking house, although very pink. There was a laughing stone cherub perched on the steps. Jillifai was on the door: a slim, pretty, fragile fella with brilliant green and scarlet feathers on his head that marked him as a Thrail, one of the Perindi Empire races. I could lift him in one hand, but I wouldn't try it. I've seen those long slender legs of his pop a rib with a kick.

"Babylon."

"Jillifai. How's it going?"

He tilted his head and made a clicking noise. "Much as usual."

"Betty around?"

"She is." He bowed me in.

I blinked, as always, and waited for my eyes to adjust.

Sometimes Betty likes pink. A *lot*. And not just any pink. The sort of pink that plants a big loud sloppy kiss right smack on your eyeballs. She also likes sequins. And feathers. And just about anything that sparkles, or glitters, or is fluffy. Walking into the Midnight Rose is a bit like being inside a giant cupcake on its wedding day.

One of her girls appeared out of a side door, a dark-skinned lass in soft green. She'd have been easy on the eyes in any setting; in this one she was like a cool drink of water.

"Hi, I'm here to see Betty?"

She smiled and motioned me through to Betty's parlour. Heat and pinkness enveloped me like a big sugary blanket.

In the middle of a room like an exploded carnation, Betty was lounging on the coral satin sofa, dressed in a raspberry velvet concoction adorned with shrimp coloured lace, drinking from a cherry-blossom-and-gold cup and contemplating the tarot hand lying on a table the colour of a highly polished pig. Until I met Betty, I didn't even know you could *get* wood in that colour. I wondered if the forest it grew in looked like Betty's parlour.

"Babylon." She waved at me without looking up. "Have a look, see what you think."

"I'm no tarot reader." I squeezed in next to her. She was currently built on generous lines.

"Oh, come on, have a go."

I stared at the cards. The layout wasn't familiar to me, but then, as I said, I'm no expert. The Jester, with his little dog, and wide-eyed grin. The Gravida, heavily pregnant, with a shawl over her head, and a cup in each hand. The Double-Headed axe.

"Um... You're going to be fooled into thinking you're pregnant with twins?"

"Hmm..." She stared down at the cards, then swept them away decisively. "No, I don't think so. What can I do for you, Babylon?"

She brushed long bronze hair out of her face and smiled at me. Her eyes were both brown, at the moment.

"You got any space over the next couple of days?"

"You overbooked?"

"I'm away for a bit." We chatted about the clients. Not all of mine would want to be referred: but it was good to have something set up for those who did.

There was always the risk, of course, that they'd find someone they preferred, and not come back – but that's the business. Mostly they just seemed to appreciate the courtesy.

"Oh, I referred someone else to you. Lady who likes weres. Anxious type, so I don't know if she'll turn up." I described her.

Betty nodded. "I'll keep an eye out for her. Now, I really *must* change – I've a client due."

A tide of yellow poured over her hair, as though someone were standing overhead with a bottle of gold ink, and kept flowing as it grew down over her shoulders. Her skin paled to ice-white, her eyes elongated and became sky-blue with dark rims around the iris. Her ears shifted and grew points, and her voluptuous frame straightened. Standing in front of me now was a slender male Fey, with straight blond hair flowing back from a widow's peak, and a finely-drawn mouth.

"You like?" he said.

"Wow. Very pretty."

"*Very* popular," he said, grinning. He glanced down at the wrap. "I'd better change. This one likes woodsy colours. Subtle. Dull, in fact. More Fey, you know."

"They haven't *met* Laney, I take it," I said.

"Oh, darling Laney, I haven't seen her in a dozen moons! Tell her to come to tea."

"If you meet her looking like that, you're not going to have time for tea."

"Does she *do* Fey? I thought they bored her."

I laughed and turned to go, and my sword in its sheath caught the tarot pack, tumbling them on the floor. I bent to help Sometimes pick them up, and one slender white hand clamped my wrist so hard I almost hit him.

"What the..."

"Babylon." He pointed at the cards. Four had fallen face up. The High King, the Empress, the Masked One, and the Five of Cups.

"What?" I said.

"Have you been playing with the powerful, Babylon?"

"What makes you say that?"

"Please. There's a *reason* why they're called the High King and the Empress, you know."

"Sometimes you sound just like a real Fey," I said. "Full of yourself."

"This isn't a joke, Babylon."

"They're just *cards*."

"The High King. A man of great power and influence, reversed. The Empress: a great power, a creator power. The Five of Cups, difficult decisions, a choice to be made, regarding those you care for. The Masked One: change, a chance to choose the right road. Great matters are about to intersect in your life."

I thought of what Mokraine had been saying, on the docks. I rubbed the scar on my jawline, realised I was doing it, and snatched my hand away.

"I don't want great powers intersecting in my life, thank you. I've got enough problems."

"The cards aren't about immutable fate, Babylon," Sometimes Betty said. "They're about the paths open to us, the decisions we choose to take. That's all."

"That's more than enough for me for one day. Go have fun with your client."

"Tell Laney about tea. And Babylon?"

"Yes?"

"Be careful."

I walked out into a low, chilly drizzle.

I PULLED UP the hood of my cloak. I was high enough up, here, to see a good portion of Scalentine. I stood for a moment, watching the rain make everything glimmer. I could see the glow above the open portals: it looked as though Carnival was still open, carmine and emerald flaring up suddenly to shocking pink and the vivid green of new leaves.

Spirita, over to the north, was a low bloom of grey that shivered like moonlight on water. Spirita's one of the fixed portals, like Bealach: it's always there and always open, but the plane on the other side of Spirita isn't fixed. Not much comes through, and no one in their right mind would go through it from here, since you can't tell what's going to be on the other side if you do. It's where Sometimes Betty turned up.

Whether she remembers anything of where she was before, I've never asked. She was very ill for a while. Out of her mind, and flipping shape randomly. She got better.

Nightwind wasn't open tonight: when it was, its light was murky green and bruise purple. Nor was Crowns, with its brassy yellow. Throat portal, which links to Nederan among other places, was hidden from view by the buildings behind me; it's the loudest of the portals. They all hum, but Throat roars. Its light is a cold steady blue. Eventide, over to my left, the portal to the Fey lands, casts intertwining colours of dawn at sea and dusky woods, silvered with magic, and its hum shivers with distant bells and faint far singing.

Bealach, the largest, and the one I'd be going through to reach Incandress, painted the low cloud with gold and lapis, imperial colours.

Have you been playing with the powerful, Babylon?

I had a sudden urge to head for the Barracks. I knew Hargur would be on duty, but I wanted to see him, even if there was no time to talk.

As soon as I got there I knew Hargur wouldn't have time for me today. Under all the usual racket of note-taking and accusations and disclaimers and weeping, there was a silence like a stretched fiddlestring. The only person I recognised was a young officer called Roflet. His handsome face was set grim, and he was deep in conversation with a tall, pale young woman in a plain dark green cloak, her face shocked to stillness. Seated next to her, with the girl's hand on her shoulder, was a middle-aged woman with her handkerchief pressed to her mouth, her whole body rocking with stifled, wretched sobs.

Roflet nodded to the girl, bent down and said something to the woman. She hardly seemed to register his presence. He moved away, stopping near me to collar a young Ikinchli officer. "I told that lump Venchlen to get them tea. Of all the useless – get them some, will you? Strong. And tell Venchlen I want to see him." He caught sight of me and said, "Madam Steel. Is there something...?"

"No, sorry, I was just passing, thought I'd see if the Chief was around, but this looks like a bad time."

"It is a bad time, I'm afraid." He sighed. "The Chief's not about, he's off checking the scene..." He shrugged.

"Anything I can do?"

"Not unless you're inclined to sign up."

"I already have a job. Two, actually, at the moment."

"Have your crew had any trouble from these human primacist... idiots?"

"These who?"

"They're the ones who prove the superiority of the human race by behaving like thugs."

"What did they do?"

"Pounded that poor woman's son to splinters. He may not make it."

"What? Why? She isn't human?"

"Her son's a were. He and the girl – she's not – were seeing each other, and some of the so-called Builders objected."

"You know, sometimes I loathe humans. And I am one."

"I know the feeling." Roflet shook his head. "If he dies, that'll be the third in a moon."

"The third..."

The noise level in another part of the room suddenly escalated; a very tall, beaked creature draped with greyish folds of skin was yelping like a trodden-on dog. It was also waving a disturbing number of limbs around. I hoped they all belonged to it.

"I'm sorry, Madam Steel, but..."

"Of course. Let the Chief know I called in, would you, if you get the chance? Tell him... tell him I'm going after all."

"'You're going after all.' Will do."

AND THEN IT was the day. I went over the list of stuff I was taking: mostly armour and weapons (with some slightly smarter versions for special occasions). One or two useful items, like my blue jug.

Little as there was, I couldn't seem to finish packing; I kept going over it, feeling as though I'd forgotten something vital.

I realised I was listening for the door; for Hargur. Waiting for him to come and tell me I was doing the right thing; waiting for him to come and tell me not to go.

Or just waiting for a chance to sort out whatever was on his mind, about us. But he didn't turn up, and soon I was out of time.

Jivrais, Ireq and Flower were the only ones about. It was sort of a relief Laney wasn't there, since I didn't need any of my luggage turned into something inappropriate. "Watch out for those Builders idiots," I said. "If you get any trouble, deal as needed, but try not to break any bits of them that won't heal. Keep up your training..."

"Eat your greens and wash behind your ears..." Jivrais said, hanging over the bannister. "Baby*lon*."

"It's a crime to worry about you?"

"We can survive without you, Babylon," Flower said. "It's barely more than a week. I'll keep 'em in line."

There was an audible snort from Jivrais.

"If anyone causes trouble I'll just ban them from the supper table," Flower said.

"Ooh, you wouldn't!" Jivrais leaned further over and tried to untie Flower's apron.

Flower picked him off the banisters as though he were a kitten and held him squeaking and wriggling in mid-air, and looked at me with monumental patience. "Just don't be gone too long," he said. "Please."

"Ten days, no more, I promise. And if it looks like real trouble, get in touch with the Chief."

"We will," Flower said. "Go, go. You'll miss the tide."

I gave him a quick hug, poked the still-dangling Jivrais in the ribs, and left.

I MADE MY way to the docks through more of that dim, penetrating drizzle. I was scratchy-eyed from lack of sleep, with a kitbag over my shoulder (the amount of food Flower had insisted on packing for me almost weighed more than the weapons), and wearing a heavy, dark red coat of oiled wool with the hood pulled up.

The *Delaney's Promise,* when I finally found her, was a trim little rig; she had polished sides and neat blue sails, and looked, to my untrained eye, seaworthy and fast. Sailors were dotted about, doing whatever it is they do, or at least, looking as if they were waiting to be told to do it.

Rikkinnet was on deck, and raised a hand as I approached. "You hurry, eh?" She called down to me. "I think, the captain, he wants to go now."

"Damn right. You the last?" The captain, presumably, glared over the side at me. He was a lean brown muscular fella with dark hair in a hundred tiny plaits and thick gold bracelets on his arms and his long brush-tipped tail, which was whipping with irritation. "Get aboard before we miss the tide!"

I ran for the gangplank.

I'd barely got my feet on deck before someone was dragging the plank out of the way, and the captain started yelling at people to haul things and splice things and for all I knew fillet them.

"Hold up!" someone shouted. "Ship! Lower the plank!"

Rikkinnet and I both whipped around; she had her sling to hand, a stone already in the cup.

Darask Fain was belting along the dock, dodging around bales and crates, leaping what he couldn't dodge.

The captain said, "Another one? He's too late." The water, thick and brown and bobbing with rubbish, widened between the ship and the dock.

"What is he doing?" Rikkinnet said. "He was not supposed to be joining us."

"I have *no* idea." The man could run, I'd give him that; but there was no way in the planes he was going to make it.

"What's wrong?" I yelled. "What's going on?"

He didn't answer, just put on a burst of speed I wouldn't have thought possible.

There was a small boat edging under our nose, between us and the dockside. Some fisher, desperate to get their catch in before the market turned, caution thrown aside for commerce. They threw their rope, and snagged a bollard just in front of Fain. They pulled it taut.

Fain ran along it. Right up the damn rope, neat as a dancer, the fisher-folk yelling in surprise, then, using someone's shoulder as a step, he flung himself with a superhuman surge at the side of the ship. Acting on impulse, as with so many things I've later regretted, I flung myself flat and *just* managed to catch his hand.

This left him hanging by my hand from the side of the ship, my other arm clutched around one of the guardrails to try and stop myself sliding into the water under Fain's weight. "Could I have a little *help* here?"

The captain yelled an order and a length of rope with a loop in it was thrown over the rail and dropped down to Fain. He got his head and arm through the loop, and let go of my hand, which was some relief. He was no lightweight.

I rolled over and stood, nursing my shoulder, and glared at Fain as he was hauled up to the rail. He managed to swing himself onto the deck as elegantly as though he were climbing a stile on a country walk.

Before I could speak, the captain planted himself in front of Fain, looked him up and down, and said, "Money. For inconvenience, suspicious behaviour and general pratting about, you pay extra, you understand?"

"Yes, of course, that will be arranged," Fain said. His eyes were not on the captain, however, but on me. And he didn't look happy, for all that I'd saved him from a dunking.

"Arranged? Arranged? I don't like arranged. Things happening now, on the nail, that's what I like," the captain said.

"As soon as you can get me back to shore..."

"Not going back to shore. We're on the tide, my chummy, and we stop at Calanesk Port. Then, you can find a ship to take you home."

Fain dragged his gaze back to the captain. "Calanesk Port? How far..."

"Eight hours. You're lucky. Our last trip, we were crossing the Bresillian Sea, no port for thirty days. So. Payment, please."

"How much?"

"Forty silver."

It was an outrageous price. Fain sighed, and said, "You will have to accept scrip, I don't carry that kind of coin on me."

"For payment in scrip, forty-five."

"Very well." He pulled out several lengths of highly-coloured paper, handed them to the captain, turned to me, and took me forcefully by the arm, the grip of those slender fingers startlingly strong. "Babylon?" He said. His voice was so low I could only just hear it under the growing roar of the portal. "A word, if you please. *Now.*"

"Mr Fain, please remove your hand." He was obviously upset; normally he was pretty aware of my feelings about who was allowed to touch me, and under what circumstances.

"My apologies, Madam Steel." You could have chilled wine with his voice. He let go, and we moved along the deck to a space where we could have some privacy. The shouts and swearing, the plash of oars and the whipshot cracks of the sails filling surrounded us.

"What's going on?" I said. "Why are you here?"

"I strongly suspect I am here because of you," he said. "I found myself suffering an irresistible compulsion, when I should have been doing other things, to come to the port. And then to get on this ship. An *irresistible* compulsion, you understand? I was in acute discomfort until I set foot on the deck, and now I am not."

"Mr Fain, I don't know what you're thinking, but I assure you I had nothing to do with any odd impulses you may have had."

"Oh, really? I suppose you *do* remember that you made me take an oath? A *Fey* oath? To protect Enthemmerlee?"

I had, at that. My only trump card where Fain was concerned, and I'd already played it. "But what... oh."

"'Oh' is inadequate to describe the situation, Madam Steel. I have been dragged from my post at a time of great delicacy. I am now, at the very least, going to be away for several hours until I can get a ship home."

"Oh. I am sorry. Really. I had no idea it would do that. I thought it would just work while Enthemmerlee was on Scalentine."

"In the clutches of the Diplomatic Section. You really don't trust me at all, do you?"

"Look, I *am* sorry."

"Perhaps next time you will hesitate before using a magic with which you are obviously completely unfamiliar."

"Well, quite," I said. "You're right."

"Now would you get on with removing it?"

"Ah. Well, the thing is..."

"The thing is what?"

"I don't know how to take it off. To undo the oath. Laney never showed me."

"You don't..." I could see a muscle twitching in Fain's jaw, and his long fingers clenched.

"I'm sorry, I just don't."

"You have no idea what you may have done, Madam Steel." If I'd thought his voice was cold before, it was arctic now.

"What do you mean?"

"I mean that the situation on Incandress is not the only one that is extremely volatile."

I glanced back at the rapidly disappearing shoreline. We were getting close to Portal Bealach, and its voice was filling the air.

"Portal ho!" The captain yelled, and I grabbed the handrail.

The ship juddered, the roar of the portal turned to thunder, and before I closed my eyes I saw halos of blue and gold shuddering around every surface. My insides did their usual trick of jolting to the left, bouncing off my outsides and returning unhappily to their usual position. Something hissed in my ears. I opened my eyes, leaned over the handrail and threw up.

I could hear a few other people doing the same.

Fain, who – apart from the obvious irritation – looked completely fine, damn him, was waiting for me with his arms folded.

I rinsed my mouth with water from the barrel and spat over the side. "You don't get portal sick, then."

"Apparently not."

"Apparently? This can't be your first time through a portal..." I hesitated, and turned away, not sure whether I was about to throw up again, but the nausea had backed off for the moment. "Is it?"

He didn't answer, just stood there giving me the cold eye.

"Look, I'm sorry," I said. "But I don't know what else you want from me."

"A solution, preferably. Failing that, at least an acknowledgement of the damned awkward position you've put me in!"

"I've never had a chance to put you in any position," I muttered.

"Excuse me?"

"Well, what about the magician fella you've hired, he should be here, maybe he can help?"

"Let us hope so," he said, and turned away.

Dammit. Dammit, dammit, *dammit*. I kicked at a coil of rope lying on the deck, and hurt my foot.

CHAPTER
SEVEN

"BABYLON, HOW ARE you?" Enthemmerlee said, coming forward beside me.

"Better, thank you. And you?" As I watched her move around the deck, even in that stiff, ugly robe, the new ease of her motion was obvious. I wondered how the other Gudain would react to it.

"I like the sea," Enthemmerlee said, tilting her face up into the breeze. "Although the portal was not comfortable. But it is good to travel, and good to go home, too. Oh, dear." She glanced to where poor Malleay was still clutching the handrail like his last hope and making the desperate yacking yawns of someone who has emptied himself out but whose stomach doesn't believe it yet. "He does feel it so badly. I wish I could help."

"Could I suggest pretending it's not happening?" I said. "I think his dignity's probably at least as upset as his stomach."

"Ah." She sighed. "Yes."

We stood in the bow, watching the ship cut its way through the water, the foam rushing away. Ahead of us, the water stretched out wide and blue. The breeze pressed Enthemmerlee's gown against her, so that you could almost make out her shape.

"Mr Fain decided to join us," she said.

"So it seems."

"I wonder what made him change his mind?"

I hesitated: Fain was sufficiently angry with me as it was. "He isn't a man to explain all his reasons," I said.

"No." She frowned at the sea. "Do you trust him?"

"Where your best interests are concerned? Actually, yes, I do." *At least until he finds someone to take the spell off.* "I would say you can rest easy on that. For the moment."

"Good." She gave me a sideways look. "You have much experience with... with men, yes?"

And women, and a surprisingly wide variety of alternatives. "Some," I said.

"I have not. Until..." She glanced over her shoulder; Malleay had managed to drag himself upright and was rinsing his mouth.

"I am handling things badly," she said, in a rush. "There was so much I did not know. I thought... I thought so much, and felt so little, and now, now it is as though I had never had a body before. Everything is different. And I would like to talk to you, please. Not here," she said hastily, as Malleay moved towards us. "But later."

"Of course. Anything you want to ask me, please do. I'm pretty damned hard to embarrass, all right? And try not to be too hard on yourself. Any great change... Well, I've been through a few, and I never came out the other side quite the same person I went in. How could you possibly know what all the consequences would be? It's not as if you had another Itnunnacklish around to give you advice."

"No." She looked down at her hands, and spread her fingers; the webs thinned, translucent yellow-green in the clear sea light. "It is hard. To be the only one." She snapped her hand closed. "But I chose this. I must live with my choice, or die with it. What is hardest, sometimes, is that others must, too."

"Enthemmerlee." Lobik was coming along the deck with his smooth easy stride. Enthemmerlee turned towards him, her face lifting into a smile, like a flower turning towards the sun.

Malleay turned away, his shoulders hunched.

*   *   *

THE CAPTAIN SENT sailors to usher us below; I think we were getting in the way. The cabin was spacious and well-lit, and smelled pleasantly of sea-salt and cured wood. A long table took up one side of it, with padded benches running alongside and a high-backed chair at either end. Grey sea-light filtered in through the portholes, and a rather fine wrought-iron lamp swung from a hook in the ceiling.

Unfortunately the chill radiating in my direction from Darask Fain was enough to put paid to any possible cosiness. He stalked up to me, putting me very much in mind of a cat whose dignity has been offended and is waiting its moment to get its revenge. Unfortunately, I doubted he'd content himself with peeing in my boots.

Following in his wake was a young man I didn't know.

"Scholar Bergast? I don't believe you have met Madam Steel."

Bergast took my hand in a cool clasp, and bowed. "You will be dealing with the more direct physical threats, yes?"

"That's the idea," I said, looking him over. Probably human or mainly human; fine-boned, about twenty, with a high-bridged nose which was likely to get beaky as he aged. Brown eyes that flicked to meet mine and then away. Hair in a careful plait, bound with silk; a robe of rich brocade in subtle greens and browns; a heavy silver ring with a green stone. A tasteful scent that I recognised, popular with my more moneyed clients. He might be a low-grade wizard, but he certainly wasn't short of cash.

"Is he able to..." I broke off, not sure how much Fain might have said.

"Scholar Bergast was not able to provide assistance."

"It really isn't my area," Bergast said. "Fey magic is a somewhat specialised subject."

"Indeed." I looked at Fain, who refused to meet my eye. He had once used that sexual trait of his to try and get me to do what he wanted; not by actually seducing me, like any decent person, but by drenching the air with enough rampant personal alchemy that I'd had trouble keeping my mind straight. I'd realised what was going on and not really trusted him since, which is why I'd made him take the damned oath in the first place.

"Well, maybe we can find someone in Incandress to take it off," I said.

"I can only hope you have had the sense not to mention this situation to anyone else?" Fain said.

I shook my head.

"That, at least, is a relief. Scholar Bergast, the same applies to you. I do not want this mentioned. Should anyone ask, I am Darask Fain, gambling house owner, on my way to look for sites for new houses, possibly in Incandress."

"Has Darask Fain, gambling house owner, any idea that the place is on the verge of civil war?"

"He does own a *gambling* house," Fain said, with a little flicker of humour that died before it could catch. "Now, if you will excuse me." He nodded to both of us, straightened the sleeves of his beautifully cut, dark blue coat (still immaculate despite all the running and charging up ropes), and strode off to inform the others who they were travelling with.

"So," I said. "Scholar Bergast. Have you been to Incandress before?"

"No. I'm looking forward to seeing it."

"Were you pleased to get this assignment, then?" I turned, leaning my back on the panelling, so I could see his face better.

"Oh, yes," he said, his eyes, for once, meeting mine. "I've been waiting for the opportunity to travel. It's important, you know, in the Diplomatic Section, to gain as much experience as possible. I understand there is not a great deal of local magic, which is a shame; I was hoping for the chance to do some original research." He shrugged. "This should prove more interesting than my last assignment, anyway."

"Are you allowed to tell me what that was?"

"I don't see why not, since any half-trained street-magician could have done it. I had to check something like three hundred identical wards on three hundred identical rooms in preparation for something-or-other to be stored in them."

"Sounds like fun."

"I was told it was vital. I'm sure someone thought it was," he said. "Bureaucracy, you know."

"Well, this will be a bit different, all right. Assassination attempts, an entire country in danger of boiling over. Much more exciting. You've dealt with this sort of thing before?"

"I've been fully briefed, I assure you," he said, though his eyes flicked away from mine again and I saw him swallow. Not excessively experienced, Fain had said? I'd bet money, if I damn well had any, that he had never dealt with anything life-threatening in his entire fledgling career. He looked as if he'd never dealt with anything that would threaten so much as a broken nail. What had Fain been thinking?

"Do you know Mr Fain?" I asked.

"Oh, well, yes, he's taken a very kind interest in my career."

Perhaps that was why. Fain thought Bergast's loyalties were safe. Politics within politics, and we'd ended up with a magician I wouldn't trust not to wet himself the first time some nutcase with a grudge came screaming out of the crowd.

"Well, Scholar Bergast, I think we ought to talk strategy, don't you?"

He bowed.

We joined Rikkinnet and roughed out the basic principles (*very* rough, since until we'd had a chance to look over the board and the players I really didn't know what sort of game I was getting into).

"Rikkinnet, now you're an ambassador..."

"The title is of convenience. It allows me to accompany Enthemmerlee in places that otherwise Ikinchli would not be permitted. I will share her protection with you."

"Good." That was a relief; at least that would give me a chance to get on with some of the other stuff. Including eating and sleeping, with luck.

The first occasion, the ball, would take place in one of the minor rooms of the Palace, the second in the Ikinchli Ancestor Caves, then we'd be at the Palace for the Patinarai, and out in the open, which had its advantages and disadvantages.

"I need to check the layouts. What about the Palace? I don't suppose there's a nice set of architect's plans or something?"

Rikkinnet grinned. "No. Too easy, no? Also, the Palace is very old, built and rebuilt many times, any plans would be very much out of date. But we have something better. My cousin Inshinnik. He has been serving in the Palace since he was a child. He knows every brick, every tile. And every way to get out quiet and go have a little fun."

"Sounds like a venturesome lad. And useful. I have to ask, though; what's his feeling on the Itnunnacklish?"

"I think he probably wonders what she is like in the cushions. Nice boy, but most of his thinking he don't do with his head."

"Ah."

AFTERWARDS I WENT back on deck. The ship was pitching gently, but it didn't bother me; I don't get seasick, just portal sick. The portal was a blue-gold arc falling away behind us, Scalentine no longer visible. I felt that clench of unease again. Well, I was committed now.

I distracted myself with watching the sailors. An interesting bunch. At least six different races, some more humanlike than others, and all hung about with weapons, amulets, fetishes, and the feet, tails or pizzles of various creatures considered to be lucky. Personally I felt that if an essential part of you ended up hanging off someone else's belt, you weren't *that* lucky, but maybe I'm cynical.

Regular portal travellers are all a little crazy, if not when they start out then pretty soon after. It's not just the danger of what you might find on the other side. The very act of travelling through portals does *something*. I generally just get sick, but there are some... like poor Bliss, one of my crew. We call them Fades. People who got some essential part of themselves stripped away, and ended up like half-embodied ghosts. And I've heard of worse things. Cross portals on a regular basis, and even if you do survive overtly intact, it's likely to drive you more than a little sideways in the head.

The sight of Bealach portal fading over the horizon began to depress me, so I went back below, wandering about the ship, trying not to get in anyone's way. I passed a big cabin, with hammocks strung from the beams, and amused myself with remembering a voyage I'd taken some years ago, where I'd had some fun in a hammock – though the fun had got too enthusiastic at one point, and resulted in a quick and somewhat bruising trip to the floor.

The ship really wasn't that big. She was designed for both cargo and passengers; I stuck my head in the cargo space, but apart from a lot of stuff in barrels and boxes, and a small cat who was more interested in something hiding under a bale of cloth than in my friendly overtures, there was nothing of interest. I wandered back towards the main cabin, passing several small, polished doors. Private cabins, presumably, for the captain and his richer passengers.

Passing one, I felt a sudden chill, and paused, rubbing my arms. This bit of the corridor seemed darker, somehow. Then I heard Fain's voice.

"...No, *stuck*," he said. "...No, I do not! ...There may be..." He must have been moving towards the door, because one phrase came through loud and clear. "I want Chief Bitternut *watched*. Constantly, you understand?"

What? I moved as fast and quietly as I could around the nearest corner, my heart pounding. I only just made it out of sight before the door opened. I risked a glance; Fain was walking away, back towards the companionway, shoving something into his pocket.

I waited for whoever had been in there with him to appear, but the cabin door stayed stubbornly shut. I was trying to think of an excuse for knocking on it, when someone behind me said, "Hey, you Babylon Steel, yah?"

It was one of the sailors, a skinny type who looked a little like a rather handsome ferret, with sleek golden fur and a long nose. "Who wants to know?"

"You don't remember me? I come to your place last shore leave, I save up. Had a real good time."

"Well, that's good to know," I said, giving him a smile while desperately wishing he'd go away so I could keep an eye on the cabin.

"So," he said, leaning against the wall of the corridor and grinning, "I'm off duty, I was thinking, maybe... I got some money, huh?"

"Sorry, friend. I'm on other duties right now, but you come see us when you're next in Scalentine, all right?"

"Okay." He gave me a cheery wave and walked off.

I made up my mind and walked up to the cabin Fain had come out of, and pulled the door open.

No one there. Damn. Whoever it was must have left while I was talking to the sailor.

What was Fain up to? Who had he told to watch the Chief, and why? The only person who seemed to make sense was the Scholar, but how could Bergast watch anyone when he was here, and the Chief was back on Scalentine? Unless there hadn't been anyone there at all. I've heard of people who can mindspeak, though I didn't think they did it out loud. I'd not heard of someone – or something – that could do it across planes, but it was exactly the sort of thing Fain might have up his sleeve. Still, I thought I'd check on the Scholar in any case.

When I got back to the main cabin, Bergast was still tucked up in his chair, reading and scratching notes with a quill pen, not looking as though he'd moved. Still, he *was* a wizard.

I went over to the porthole nearest to him, and pretended to look out, all the time trying to sneak glances over his shoulder. I couldn't make head nor tail of the book, it was all squirmy symbols and tiny cramped handwriting, and if he was using it to watch what was happening on Scalentine, he was doing a damn good job of disguising it. A notebook lay next to it; as I watched, Bergast copied one of the symbols into the notebook, then cursed quietly as the end of his quill splayed and blotted the page.

"Can I help you with something?" he said, looking up.

"Is that part of what you're planning to use?"

"This? No. I'm studying for the next stage of Service exams." He glanced up at me and looked away, flushing slightly. I wondered why; there's no shame in study. Quite the reverse. Unless he was doing something else. If he *was* involved in some plot against the Chief, he'd do more than blush. He'd bleed.

"It looks complicated," I said.

Bergast glared at the book. "It is. And considering the last known speakers of this language died out a thousand years ago, and no one who wasn't of their race could work any of these spells in any case, I really don't know why it's considered useful to memorise pages of them."

"I suppose the Service has its reasons."

"Oddly enough," he said, "it's one of the old languages of the Thralian continent." I must have looked bemused. "Where we're going?" he said, in a somewhat patronising tone. "It shares some root words with Old Andretic, which was one of the major Gudain tongues on Incandress until the Perindi Empire spread Lithan through the planes. A country's history is drawn in its languages, you know."

Enthemmerlee walked over to us. "You study very hard, Scholar Bergast. I hope that assisting me will not interfere too much with your learning." She looked at me. "He has not moved in an hour at least!"

Bergast smiled. "Oh, no, not at all. I'm happy to be of service. Travelling to your country will provide me with new opportunities for study. In fact, I was hoping to ask you about some of the wording of religious rituals."

At least an hour? In that case, he wasn't the one Fain was talking to. But *something* was going on, and I didn't like it.

I want him watched. Why? What did Fain think Hargur was up to? I *knew* the Chief, in and out of bed; and he was as straight-line decent as anyone in the planes. Why would the Diplomatic Section suspect him of being up to something? Had they been given false information? Was someone out to cause him trouble?

But the Diplomatic Section had its own agenda, its own ways and means, and a habit of keeping its cards so close to its chest they were practically inside its skin. Maybe someone, maybe Fain, thought the Chief was onto something the Diplomatic Section didn't want him to know. And that could be worse.

Either way, it seemed as though Hargur was in a very nasty situation, he didn't know it, and I was stuck several hours' journey from Scalentine, for ten bloody days, and couldn't even warn him.

Or could I?

I found the ferret-fella in the middle of losing at cards down on the lower decks. "Hey," I said, as other members of the crew stared and commented. "Got a minute?"

"Got two hours," he said, throwing in his hand and grinning. "Then we coming into port."

He followed me into the corridor, and gestured hopefully at one of the empty cabins.

"I need a favour," I said. "Payment in kind, a freebie, once it's done."

He paused in the act of undoing his trousers. "Not now?"

"Sorry." Enthemmerlee was probably safe enough for the moment, but I really wasn't in the mood. "I'll give you a password, for the Lantern, and you get to have whatever you want – within our rules – next time you're in Scalentine, all right?"

He sighed, and did his trousers back up. "So much for thinking it's my lucky day for once."

"It will be – but first I need a message taken back to Scalentine, soon's we hit port."

His mouth turned down. "Ship's going out along the coast, not back to Scalentine."

"Can you get me a message from the port? On another ship?"

"Oh sure. Cost, though."

"Right. How much?"

"For Scalentine? Three, four silver maybe."

I dug out the coin; then struggled with the words.

Hargur. I *had* to warn him, but what could I say? And how to get a message to him without tipping off the Section? If Fain was having Hargur watched, there was every chance he was having the Lantern watched too.

Laney. Laney was a Court Fey. They lived on intrigue; I'd have to take the risk she'd get what I was talking about. I scribbled a note.

Laney. Remember the fella who likes to gamble? Not been a client yet but might be – he seems to be interested in our dear Millie. You might warn her that he's keeping an eye on her – it could be to her advantage to be very *careful.*

I sealed it with my ring, and gave it to the ferret-man. It wasn't much; I just hoped it was enough. He promised to get it on the fastest ship he could find. "Anything I want?" he said, tucking it away.

"Anything. Within the rules."

I went back up on deck and stared, trying to make out the glow of Bealach portal. There was a faint bluish smudge on the horizon that might have been it, or might just have been wishful thinking.

CHAPTER
EIGHT

WE FINALLY REACHED Calanesk as the evening was falling. It's huge, noisy, and reeks of its trade in some sea-crawling thing known as purple thepalia. They're a delicacy, apparently, but having seen them (and smelled them) I'd have to be paid a fairly substantial sum to actually eat them.

The sun was going down, smoky and red.

Coaches, sedans, and riding animals were lined up at the quay, from the very fancy, all gilding and sleek-looking matched beasts (the favoured animal was something like a fat snake with two big muscular legs), to little rickshaws that looked as though they'd fall to grimy matchsticks if anyone actually sat in them. There were a few Gudain and Ikinchli at the port, along with a number of other species, milling, shouting, buying, selling. You could spot the Gudain at a distance by their clothing: wide-ruffed, straight-falling robes, the cloth pressed into rigid little pleats, so it looked as if each person were moving about inside a small, stiff column of material. So designed, I realised, as to give almost no hint that there was a body beneath at all. The width of the ruff varied. As with most fashions, only the leisured dressed in the most exaggerated version, the material hanging at least a foot from the body, the sleeves huge puffed things, out of which their hands protruded like stranded starfish. If everyone around Enthemmerlee dressed like that, it really wasn't going to make my job any easier; you could hide half an armoury under the damn things.

Mind you, extracting a weapon from all that cloth probably wasn't easy.

"Where is our transport?" Malleay said. "It was supposed to be waiting."

"You can't see it?" I glanced at Rikkinnet. She shrugged, but I noticed she was holding her sling in one hand. So was Lobik.

Bergast stood calmly, his hands loosely clasped in front of him. I hoped he had something ready if there was trouble.

"Who was arranging this transport?" I said.

"The family," Rikkinnet said. "Ah, there..."

She shaded her eyes, looking at the road leading into the docks. There were two carriages, drawn by pairs of those long-legged snake things. Several outriders and twenty or so figures in dark blue trotting alongside.

"The ones in blue?" I said.

"Family guard," Rikkinnet said. "One in the helmet with the tall crest, you see him? That's the captain. Tantris."

"Got him."

Another, much smaller coach followed. Rikkinnet hissed something.

"What is it?"

"See the other coach, close behind, with the bird symbols around the top?"

I peered, and could just make out the little shimmering figures; carved pieces of metal raised above the sides of the coach. Birds, in flight, leaping for the air. Pretty.

"Is the Defraish family carriage," Rikkinnet said. "The betrothed."

Enthemmerlee came up beside me. "So, the Defraish are here. That is unexpectedly courteous."

"Wait," Lobik said. "The Defraish have come with no guard, and only one driver?"

Enthemmerlee shaded her eyes with her hand, watching a figure descend from the coach. "That is... oh."

"What is it?" Malleay said.

"Tovanay."

The former betrothed himself. Alone, by the look of it, except for his driver.

I suspected his motives. But then, a good bodyguard suspects everyone's motives.

His hands were at his sides. Wound around his wrist, below the huge puffed sleeve, was a thick, gleaming bracelet. I kept him in my vision, while scanning the rest of the crowd for a tell-tale movement, a lift of the hand, the glint of metal.

"Well," Enthemmerlee drew a deep breath, and lifted her chin. The gangplank was in place. She reached out her hands to either side. Lobik clasped her left. Malleay looked at her hand a moment, then took it. She squeezed them gently, let go and stepped forward, putting on dignity like a cloak.

SECURITY THEY MIGHT be, but I could have wished the family had brought a smaller escort. Every sailor, stevedore, lounger, pickpocket and passer-by was now watching us with great interest, wondering who the disembarking figures were to have so many people come to meet them.

The family guard – whose uniforms, thankfully, were a tunic with only a small ruff, and trousers – were a mixed bunch: roughly half and half Ikinchli and Gudain. Most of them carried their weapons like something they'd picked up by accident, and many of their uniforms were a disgrace. It's possible to make a worn uniform neat and mended at least, and keep the buttons polished, but a lot of them had failed to manage even that much. Those that had, I noticed, were mostly Ikinchli.

Of the Gudain, some kept flicking their glances to Enthemmerlee, and away, as though embarrassed. A couple sneered when they thought no one was looking. Most of the Ikinchli watched her with fixed, avid expressions; one stared straight ahead as though determined *not* to see her, and at least two were weeping. I remembered something Kittack had said, when he first met Enthemmerlee. *Is not often a legend is walk out of the story and say, hello.*

Two Gudain got out of the family carriage. Enthemmerlee greeted them with what I assumed was the Gudain equivalent of a bow, a sort of sideways sweep of the head and hands; a graceful gesture which her new physique turned into something like a move in a dance.

They dipped sideways in return, looking, in those strange stiff gowns, like bottles on the verge of tipping over. The male had one of those bracelets wrapped around his arm. It wasn't until it lifted its head and stared at me that I realised it was, in fact, a live snake. Rather a beautiful one, too, with scales patterned in reds and corals.

"Father," Enthemmerlee said.

"Enthemmerlee." Although he had been back on Scalentine when his daughter had changed, and had seen her since, he seemed unable to take it in. His gaze went from Enthemmerlee, to Lobik, to Rikkinnet, to Malleay and back to his daughter. He had been handsome, once. Now he was jowled and suety. His gown was rumpled, and muddy around the hem.

"Selinecree."

The aunt. She was still handsome, with a long slender nose and dark gold hair in a jewelled net. And if I remembered rightly, she was definitely the woman I'd seen at the Roundhouse Tower party.

"Enthemmerlee, darling, introduce us to your friends!" she said.

"This is Babylon Steel. She is here as my friend, and my consultant on matters of security," Enthemmerlee said. I bowed.

"Ah," Enboryay said. He made that sideways sweep of head and hands, though in a fashion so perfunctory he looked as though he were shaking a broom free of dust. "Security."

Selinecree made, much more gracefully, the same gesture. "Of course, I know who you are. You found our poor girl when... oh, well, yes."

"And this is Scholar Bergast, a distinguished magical expert, who is here at the most kind offer of the government of Scalentine, to help ensure that everything goes smoothly in the run-up to the Investment." Bergast bowed, briefly. His gaze was darting about, skimming the guard and the passing crowd. I was glad to see him keeping his eyes open, but he looked twitchier than I'd have liked.

"And this gentleman is Darask Fain. Mr Fain sees Incandress as a possible area for financial investment, and perhaps may be persuaded to stay and see the Patinarai ceremony."

Fain bowed and smiled, every inch the merchant. "It sounds most intriguing," he said.

"Finance, eh?" Enboryay said. "What sort of finance would that be, Mr Fain?"

"Entertainment. Gambling. Tredecta, the Seven-Pointed-Star, Chasing the Leaf... Such games are permitted in this country, are they not?"

Enboryay's face lightened. "Oh, indeed. Though if you plan to gamble with Gudain, I hope you have deep pockets. We have some notable players."

"Perhaps this is something we should discuss at home?" Selinecree said. "Mr Fain, if you have not yet arranged accommodations, maybe you would do us the honour of staying with us? We are very close to Lincacheni, where the ceremonies will take place."

"The Gudain ceremonies, at least," Enthemmerlee said.

"That is a most generous offer," Fain said, "Though I am not sure if I will be able to stay. Excuse me a moment."

He strode off, down the quay. I saw him approach someone, reaching for his pouch; I supposed he was looking for a ride home.

"Ah, that reminds me. Enboryay, look after our guests. I ordered a little something special for our dinner and I simply *can't* trust the servants not to fling things about and bruise the fruit. You'd really think they'd know by now..." Selinecree sighed like a woman burdened by massive responsibilities and hurried off down the quay, in the opposite direction to Fain. Though there were a few other Gudain about, none were wearing quite such wide-ruffed, huge-sleeved gowns. Ugly as the thing was, it stamped her as upper-class Gudain as clearly as a brand. I hoped no one would take it into their heads to rob her or, worse, kidnap her; we could do without those kind of complications.

I caught movement out of the corner of my eye. Tovanay, the rejected suitor. I shifted my stance, and realised that Bergast had gone off, like Fain, along the dock. Dammit.

As Tovanay approached, the guard shuffled and glanced around. An aura of awkwardness rose like heat.

Enthemmerlee stepped forward. "Tovanay. How kind of you to come and greet me."

The guard shifted aside, and I watched Tovanay's hands. The green and gold scaled snake he wore appeared to watch me in return, its tongue flickering in and out.

He kept his gaze rigidly fixed on her. "Is it true, then?" he said. "You are Enthemmerlee?"

"I am."

"And these..." He looked at Malleay and Lobik, then back at Enthemmerlee. "I see. This, then, is what you have chosen."

"Tovanay..." she said. "I..."

Tovanay turned away; walked back to his coach, climbed in, and called out to the driver. The coach bowled away, the flat slap of the beasts' feet and the rattle of the wheels loud in a sudden silence.

"Was that Tovanay?" Selinecree reappeared, with a little parcel in her hands, wrapped in white satin and tied with bright yellow ribbon, and a much larger basket borne by a young Ikinchli behind her. "Is he not staying?"

"No, Aunt. He's not staying," Enthemmerlee said.

"Oh, a pity, he could have joined us for dinner. Or perhaps... No, well, just as well. Oh, dear. Shall we? Oh, Mr Fain, did you find what you were looking for?"

"It seems," Fain said, "that I am unable to continue my journey at the moment. There's not a berth to be had. A number of ships have developed leaks, or been delayed for one reason or another... or the captains all become strangely deaf as I approach them. So if I may still take you up on your very kind offer?"

He wasn't actually looking at me, but I could feel his fury scorching my skin. "Where's Scholar Bergast?" he said.

"Here!" Bergast darted through the guards. "Just wanted to..." He waved, vaguely. "A long journey." He gave me a high-nosed look when I glared at him. There had been a perfectly good place for that on the ship; they even had a kind of wall around them, for privacy. If he was too fussy to hang his bum over the water like everyone else, he'd not last long in the field.

We headed for the coaches, and their odd beasts. I stared at one, as it murmured and rubbed its flat snaky head against its side, and realised they had no forelegs. The elongated body was smoothly uninterrupted between the head and the great muscular legs.

I stuck to Enthemmerlee as though glued. Fain chatted with Enboryay; I could see him creating a persona, a little sleek, a little self-satisfied, but with a businesslike edge. I had to admire him. The man could put on a role like a new robe, as expertly as any whore I've known.

The coach bore a symbol at each side of its roof, done in silvery metal. A little lizard, caught in the act of reaching out with one front foot for something to cling to, nicely carved, with a jaunty vitality. Selinecree got into the coach with me, Enthemmerlee and Lobik. She smiled brightly. "Mr Kraneel, we have had only the briefest of meetings, but I'm sure we shall be great friends." The falseness of the statement rang in the air, but at least the woman was making an effort.

Lobik smiled. "Thank you, madam, for your kindness."

"Well, Enthemmerlee." Selinecree looked her over. "You look better, dear."

"Yes, Aunt, I feel better."

*   *   *

WE LEFT THE stench of Calanesk port behind us and rolled out across the country. It was a reasonably smooth road, at least; well-paved and well-maintained. Well, it would be, being one of the Perindi Empire trade routes. But going at the pace of the foot soldiers, it would still take us until the following morning to reach the Incandress border.

Hills jagged the horizon, and the sun, smoking red, dropped below heavy purple cloud to paint their sides bloody. Mist pooled in the fields either side of the road. The air was moist, almost warm.

I dropped into a waking doze, one ear open for anything untoward. The sound of the booted feet of the guard, the rumble of our own wheels and those of the coach behind, the dap-dap-dap of the beasts' feet, the creaks and shifts of the coach, the occasional murmured remark or low laugh from one of the guard.

Selinecree slept. Enthemmerlee stared out of the window, her hands clenching and unclenching in her lap, until Lobik reached over and clasped them.

Damn, I missed the Chief.

EVEN BEFORE THE coach halted, I could feel it. A change in the air. I strained my ears, and caught something that might have been only the wind, rising with the dawn, whispering across the empty land.

Then the coach came to a stop. The Ikinchli driver leant down and said, "Ma'am, we have reached the border. I think maybe you should look."

I glanced at Enthemmerlee, who nodded.

I leaned out.

It was a grey dawn, with a thin penetrating rain; I could smell something half-sweet, half-alchemical. The border was marked by a stone archway across the road, a guardhouse either side. There were two guards, in dull grey uniforms that made them hardly more than sketches against the stone of the archway.

Behind them, lining the road four and five deep on either side, were hundreds of Ikinchli.

They were almost completely silent, patient as rocks. I wondered how they'd known when Enthemmerlee would be arriving. Perhaps they hadn't, perhaps they had been waiting all night, or longer.

True believers, come to worship the Itnunnacklish, the one who would free them from servitude? True believers who thought Enthemmerlee was a heretic? Assassins? The merely curious? A mix of the lot?

I could really have done with more sleep before dealing with this.

"You have an audience," I said. "All Ikinchli, by the look of it, and a lot of 'em."

Enthemmerlee took a deep breath. "Ah. I should perhaps have expected this."

"What is it?" Selinecree said, blinking. "What's happening?"

"We have reached the border, aunt. There are people who want to see me."

"People?"

"Yes. I think... Kotenik?"

The driver leaned in again. "Ma'am?"

"I think I should come up there. Will you have room?"

"Plenty enough room, ma'am, but... is raining."

Enthemmerlee smiled. "Thank you, Kotenik, a little water won't hurt me."

Unlike an arrow, or a stone. Unhappily, the driver glanced at the rest of us.

"You must do what you think is best," Lobik said. "Kotenik, there is room for another, yes?" He looked at me.

"There will be, if I have to stand on the driver," I said.

"Is room without that," the driver said.

"Enthemmerlee, wait," Selinecree said. "You shouldn't do this!"

"I have a bodyguard, Aunt."

"That's all very well, but you can't make your first public appearance this way! After such a journey, and in that... garment! Besides, I am sure they wouldn't expect it. They'll be happy to wait and see you in a more proper..."

"Selinecree. 'They' have waited centuries for someone to take their side. Whatever 'They' may think of me, 'They' should not have to wait one moment more to see whether I actually exist." She put her hand on the door of the carriage.

"If I may," I said, "I'd like to have a quick word with the household guard, first. Would you permit?"

"Why?"

"Because this is a potentially difficult situation, and it would be better if it wasn't allowed to become more so."

"If you think it wise," she said. "But I do intend to let them see me."

"Of course," I said. "Absolutely."

I scrambled out – somewhat gracelessly, having been cramped up for several hours – and swung myself up the steps at the rear of the carriage. The guard were looking extremely twitchy; I could see this all going very wrong. It didn't even need someone to try something. All it would take was a guard to see, or think they saw, or decide they saw, a raised hand. Someone would send an arrow into the crowd, and one way or another things would get nasty fast.

The other coach had stopped behind us, and I could see Rikkinnet on the roof with the driver, Fain and Enboryay craning out of the windows. "What's the delay?" Enboryay said.

"Lot of people waiting to see your daughter, sir," I said.

"What? Who are they?"

"Just people," I said. I caught the eye of the guard captain. His crested helmet, worn low, couldn't conceal his disgruntlement. "If I could have your attention for a moment," I said. "You don't know me, but I've been hired as personal bodyguard to Madam Defarlane Lathrit en Scona Entaire the Itnunnacklish. We're about to drive through a big crowd of people. They look inclined to be peaceable; I think they're just here to have a bit of a gawp. Now I'm only responsible for Madam Defarlane, and you, I know, need to watch over the whole family. I'm sure you realise that with these kind of numbers, if anything kicks off, everyone is at risk. You look a professional bunch," I lied. "And I'm sure you don't need me to tell you to stay alert, but I'd take it kindly, and I'm sure the family would too, if you weren't overly quick to see an assassin where there's maybe someone just scratching their arse. Right?"

The captain looked me in the eye, then very deliberately turned his head and looked at Enboryay, who opened and closed his mouth, and then said, "Oh, really, can we just get on?" Which wasn't what you might call helpful.

I was going to have to deal with the captain at some point, if I wanted the guard on my – or rather Enthemmerlee's – side, but all I needed right now was for him and his troops not to start a riot.

At that point Selinecree leaned out of the window. "Captain Tantris," she said, her voice as silky as one of Laney's scarves. "I'm sure you can keep order, as you always do, without anything getting *out of hand.*"

"Ma'am," he said. "Right, you lot. Keep your eyes open, no jumping at shadows."

That was probably as good as it was going to get. I opened the door for Enthemmerlee, went up the ladder ahead of her and held out a hand which she didn't need. She climbed with swift grace, despite the cumbersome gown, and settled herself in the seat.

Then she was able, as was I, to get a proper look at the size of the crowd. I'd underestimated by at least a couple of hundred. I heard Enthemmerlee draw in a hard breath.

The driver pulled the steps up.

At a slow walk, the long scaly beasts swaying in front of us, we passed through the gate. The gate-guards gripped their weapons and bowed.

So many eyes. It seemed as though hardly anyone was breathing.

Then, like the wind passing through the trees, it started; *Itnunnacklish, Itnunnacklish, Itnunnacklish.*

Old men, bent over canes. Babies, pointing fat webbed fingers, wide-eyed.

Itnunnacklish, Itnunnacklish, Itnunnacklish.

Tails moving restlessly, the males' cranial crests flicking up and down. All ages; mostly in plain loose clothing, not new, carefully mended. Here and there the gleam of jewellery or a brightly coloured waistcoat. Enthemmerlee sat beside me, very upright, looking straight ahead.

They were five and ten deep, spread out along at least a mile of road, up to the point where it entered a rocky defile and there was nowhere for anyone to stand. Something, either rain or sweat, was trickling down my neck.

We were getting past them, at a slow, steady pace.

Itnunnacklish, Itnunnacklish, Itnunnacklish.

Someone cried out, a phrase I didn't know.

"What does that mean?" I muttered.

"They are asking, 'Is it true?'" the driver said.

Silence spread out from the words. Enthemmerlee turned to look for the speaker, but in the sea of faces, it was impossible to tell.

"You ask if it is true? I am what you see," Enthemmerlee said. "What that means, we must decide together."

A murmur, neither pleased nor angry. Considering.

And a movement.

I knew before I knew, my body acting alone, my shield leaping up. There was a loud *ponk* as whatever it was hit the shield, then one of the beasts jumped and gave a loud, hissing yawp. The carriage rocked and I heard Selinecree cry out in shock. "Get down!" I said.

"What..." Enthemmerlee's shoulder felt terribly fragile under my hand as I shoved her down against the swaying roof. She gasped, flinching, and I wondered if I'd hurt her.

The driver wrestled the reins, swearing under his breath, and I planted my feet. Shrieks from the crowd; a deep rising roar. Out of the corner of my eye, I saw the guard, shuffling, looking at their captain, who, belatedly, snapped an order. They clustered around the carriage, facing every which way, weapons bristling and eyes wide.

In the crowd, a converging motion. A hand flung up, a cry of pain.

"What's happening?" Enthemmerlee cried.

"It was a stone. They've got hold of someone."

"Wait!" she said. "Let me up!"

"Lady..."

"Let me up. Now."

"Yes, ma'am."

I kept the shield over as much of her as possible. She stared at the crowd, which surged and swayed. "Wait!" Enthemmerlee cried. "Stop!"

She had a remarkable voice, when she chose to use it. It flashed out over the crowd, bright and clear as an arrow.

Someone shouted out. "The Itnunnacklish speaks!"

Like ripples in reverse, silence narrowed in until it reached the scuffle. At its centre, a couple of young males, gripped in a dozen hands. One had his arms wrapped around his head; the other was staring straight at Enthemmerlee, a trickle of blood running down his forehead, dark against the pale creamy gloss of his scales.

"Please," Enthemmerlee said. "Why did you do that?"

The young man with his arms around his head lowered them just enough to let one eye be seen, fixed warily on the household guards. "I don't do nothing!" he said. "Just standing here and suddenly everyone is crazy!" He glanced up at Enthemmerlee. "I am not throwing no stones!" His crest flicked up and down.

"No. *I* was," the other male said. His crest was up, rigid as a blade, and he never took his green eyes off Enthemmerlee, only blinking the blood out of them.

Those around him swore, gripping harder.

"Why?" Enthemmerlee said.

"You are a lie," he said. "You are a trick." He hissed as someone yanked his arm up behind his back, those around him roaring disapproval.

"Let him speak," Enthemmerlee said, very clear over the noise. "Don't hurt him."

"Oh, I will speak," he said, his voice tight with pain. "Let these others stare and worship with their backs still bloody from Gudain whips; I know. *We* know."

"You think I am a trick," Enthemmerlee said. "But will you give me a chance to prove I am not?"

"Why should we? All these years of waiting and saying, maybe tomorrow, some justice, maybe tomorrow, you get to have what is yours. We will *take* what is ours. You cannot stop it."

Enthemmerlee leaned forward, gripping one of the metal ornaments with one hand, while I swore silently to myself and tried to keep her covered. "And if you take what is yours," she said, "by shedding blood; if you extract vengeance for every wrong, even against those who never harmed you, is that justice? Does that make things right? Or does that make you exactly like what you hate?" She gestured to herself. "This that I am now," she said, "is what *we* are. One people, united in hope. Do not give in to hate, to fear, to those things which would divide us. Only together can we mend our country, only together can we heal our wounds. You look at me and you see Gudain, but I am not Gudain." She raised her head and looked across the crowd. "I am not Gudain, and I am not Ikinchli. I am *Incandrese*."

A murmur rolled across them like the wind across corn.

"I am not here to create further division, further hatred. Of that, there has been enough."

There was another murmur. I kept my eye on the stone-flinger. I was pleased to see his captors showed no sign of letting him go. I tried to catch the captain's eye, but he was staring rigid-faced at nothing.

The beasts, disturbed, snorted and swayed their heads.

Enthemmerlee was smiling, but the hand on the ornament was white-knuckled.

"Captain! Captain..." I said, trying to remember the useless idiot's name.

"It's Captain Tantris," Enthemmerlee said, from the side of her mouth, still smiling at the crowd. "I don't want that boy hurt."

Boy! He was older than her by some years, if I was any judge. "Yes, well, if we leave him to the crowd, I think he will be." All right, I was more concerned with her safety than his, but I wasn't exactly lying, either.

"Very well." She leaned forward again. "You, what's your name?"

"Kankish."

"Kankish. And you, holding him. Thank you, but please, let him go."

Reluctantly, they did. He shrugged his shoulders, easing them. I watched his hands. Someone had taken his sling, but that didn't mean he hadn't something else about him.

"You have a choice, Kankish," Enthemmerlee said. "You can be part of this. You can begin to build, with us, a new country. Or you can walk away."

Surrounded as he was, he didn't have much choice, and knew it. He looked at her, his face unreadable. Then he stepped onto the road, and turned away, towards the border and Calanesk Port. He started to walk.

Most of the crowd didn't even turn to see him go. Of those that did, some hissed. A handful of mud splattered his shirt. He kept walking.

I saw Rikkinnet leaning out of the other carriage. I caught her eye.

She nodded, baring her teeth.

A would-be assassin, walking away. But without undermining Enthemmerlee's authority in front of this crowd, there was nothing either of us could do.

If that captain had the worth of his shabby uniform, he'd do something about it, but I wasn't making any bets.

"Enthemmerlee?" Selinecree's voice wavered up from the carriage. "What's happening? Are you all right? Do come back in, dear; you'll get dreadfully wet."

"In a moment, Aunt. I'm perfectly fine." Though in fact she was beginning to shake, and her always-pale skin was the colour of a cold dawn sky.

We moved on, slowly, Enthemmerlee holding herself upright, and smiling. The rain formed a thousand fine, tiny drops on her scales and skin, making her look jewelled.

"Did I hurt you?" I said, keeping my voice down.

"Hurt me?"

"Your shoulder. You made a noise – I'm sorry if I grabbed too hard."

"Oh, no!" She flushed. "I was just startled. We don't... I mean, Gudain don't... touch. Not in public."

Damn. I'd forgotten. "Sorry."

"I think actually it is more important to survive than to be always proper." She managed a smile, though it obviously cost her something. "And for me, it is already too late for being proper."

We passed into the defile. A few Ikinchli, mostly very young, were perched here and there on the rocks; but gradually, the whispering chorus faded behind us.

One of the guards, I couldn't see which, spat, deliberately.

Then, there was only the sound of the wheels, and the boots of the soldiers, and the padding feet of the beasts. I eased my aching shoulders and hoped we didn't have much farther to go.

CHAPTER
NINE

I PERSUADED ENTHEMMERLEE back inside the carriage before we got to Lincacheni.

The city seemed barely awake. Great houses and public buildings turned shuttered faces to the wide, sweeping streets. The rain called out subtle colours from the buildings, deep soft greens and plummy reds and blue-greys; the overall effect was oddly dreamlike. Yet it was an uneasy dream. Many of the stately old buildings had closed shutters, crumbling under beards of grey-green moss, and here and there small trees grew in the guttering.

There were smaller, more recent-looking buildings too, of pallid grey stone the rain did not flatter. These seemed to be inhabited mainly by Ikinchli; handsome, long-jawed faces watched from windows hung with ragged cloth. A few children scrambled about on the narrow unrailed stone stairs that ran up the sides of the buildings, stopping to stare at the coach with wide gold eyes. I'd got used to seeing them in Scalentine, but never so many at once. I was struck again by what a beautiful race they were. Their main scales varied from deep bronze to the green of ferns growing in shade, while the softer, smaller scales that covered throat and chest and belly were every blend of amber and cream.

The few people on the streets, too, were mostly Ikinchli. I saw a few Gudain, some with Ikinchli servants in tow, and one Gudain woman followed by a young Ikinchli girl laden with parcels. The girl caught sight of the symbol on the carriage and gasped, dropping one of the parcels and immediately falling to her knees to scrabble for it. The Gudain woman grabbed the girl by the back of her shirt, hauled her to her feet and slapped her, the sound sharp enough to be heard over the boots of the guard and the rumble of carriage-wheels.

The woman strode away, chin up. The girl trudged along behind her, eyes carefully on her parcels.

The other Ikinchli watched this with utterly expressionless faces, but you didn't need to read faces to see the number of crests that were up, the number of tails flicking. Some noticed the symbol on the coach; those who looked twice glanced away quickly. I wondered why, until I spotted the two Gudain in the bulky brown uniforms and low helmets, looking over the passing figures. Fenac. Otherwise known, though not aloud, as *guak*, or 'the shits.' They had a tough, narrow-eyed glare and a bullish stance, but their hands were hovering an inch from their hilts and their shoulders were hunched. Arrogant, but nervous. Not a good combination.

We went through what looked like a market area, where a few people were setting up trestles and benches in a space big enough for many more, and past one old building that, unlike many of its fellows, was in fine condition. Deep red spiralling pillars held up a roof tiled in red and green. The carved oxblood doors stood open. An old man, a Gudain, swept the forecourt with careful pride.

It wasn't until later I realised that he was the only Gudain I would see at any such task.

The rain was still falling, not cold, but persistent. The smell of damp and that odd alchemical taint clung to everything.

As we turned uphill, I caught a glimpse of the main road out of the other end of the town. A wide, straight, well-kept road; I could glimpse the tail end of a caravan train heading into the city. No way of telling what the cargo was from here.

I wondered where they stopped. There are usually places that cater for that sort of traffic, but with the Gudain being so suspicious of foreigners, maybe not.

Still, people who dislike foreigners are often amazingly willing to make money off them.

The buildings of the Ten Families were set high on a hill at the centre of the city. As we approached, we moved up away from the clatter of commerce into sculpted parkland. Thin, upright trees with silvery bark shivered with thousands of narrow leaves that whispered and hissed together in the breeze. Gravelled paths swept in elegant curves, streams chattered, tumbling among rocks thick with brilliantly-coloured mosses: scarlet, viridian, bright pale yellow.

Mansions stood among the trees. Elegant, no doubt, with their softly-coloured stone, but they looked oddly dumpy, to me. Their roofs, like flattened cones, were somehow too low and wide for the buildings. Admittedly, the Red Lantern would have fitted into most of them five or six times over.

Right at the top of the hill, dominating all the other buildings, was the Palace. Its long-gone architect had decided that the subtle tones of the local stonework were insufficient for the glory of the royals; they needed something more colourful to show them off.

They'd got it. Every single ashlar had been faced with marble. *Different* marble. Black marble swirled with white. Plum marble blotched with violet. Forest green marble. Butter yellow marble. Even in the rain, it looked like a giant gaming-board; in sunlight it probably hurt the eyes. Its wide, low roof swept up to points at intervals. The overall effect was somehow both squat and fussy, like a plump, overdressed child. Behind it was a slope of green hill, and at the top, a small, plain structure that was not much more than columns and a roof. That was where the Patinarai would take place.

Enthemmerlee's family home proved to have a wall, though only about a foot taller than I was, so not much of a defence.

It was pierced by a pair of rather fine wrought-iron gates, in a pattern of twining vines and little running lizards, but from the greenery growing lushly around the posts, it didn't look as though anyone had closed them for a long time. That would need dealing with. There was a small stone guard-house, and two Gudain standing either side of the gate. They peered at the carriage, nudging each other. Sloppy. That would need dealing with, too.

We passed onto a paved driveway of a soft rust colour; the large central building was of deep green stone, with a sprawling litter of outbuildings. Standing off by itself was a smaller version of the red-pillared, mosaic-roofed building down in the city where the old man had been sweeping.

"That is our family chapel, where we take *privaiya*," Selinecree said. "The oldest part of the estate, going back at least ten generations. The Entaire family was the first to have a private chapel, you know. Until then, we worshipped at the Palace with everyone else."

"Really?" I said, trying to sound suitably awestruck.

I was, in fact, more depressed than impressed. The place had enough outbuildings, statues, fountains and decorative shrubbery to hide a hundred assassins. And everywhere faces peered, mostly Ikinchli: the family servants, wanting to catch a glimpse of Enthemmerlee.

Several servants were heading towards us, following a middle-aged Ikinchli male with a little belly rounding the front of his dark-blue livery, who moved with a curious un-Ikinchli-like rigidity that made me wonder if he had something wrong with his spine.

"Thranishalak, we have one extra guest," Selinecree said, as he handed her out of the carriage. "This is Mr Fain, a very important gentleman from Scalentine. I hope you can find somewhere to suit him?"

"I believe the western suite is free, Madam," Thranishalak said.

"I hope you will find it adequate, Mr Fain."

"I'm sure I will," Fain said.

Enthemmerlee, stepping down behind me, smiled. "Thranishalak. Oh, it is good to be home!"

Thranishalak, seeing her for the first time, blinked. Once. Then he bowed, and said, "Welcome home, Ma'am."

He was good; his voice hardly wavered at all.

"Madam Steel I believe is next to me?" Enthemmerlee said. "And the honoured Scholar is across the corridor."

A flicker of movement out of the corner of my eye. My sword was out, my shield up, and I was staring at a Gudain girl-child, with the pearly, ethereal looks I remembered Enthemmerlee having before her transformation, who skittered to a halt, staring at me.

"Who are you?" she demanded. "And why are you hiding that person?"

"I'm here to protect her," I said. "In case anyone wants to hurt her." I hoped everyone was listening; I could feel the shocked looks.

The child, at least, seemed unbothered. "Oh. Where's my Aunt Emmlee?"

Enthemmerlee moved my shield out of the way. "Here, darling," she said. "It's me."

The girl looked at her, and said, "*You're* not my aunt."

"Yes, I am. I just look different now," Enthemmerlee said. "Selinecree. You were supposed to have warned her."

"I did," Selinecree said. "Chitherlee, sweet, I *told* you your aunt was going to be different when she came home. You remember."

Enthemmerlee knelt down on the stone pathway, and said, "Chitherlee, *itni*, it's me. Truly. Come and look close."

"*You're* not my *aunt!*" The girl's mouth drew down in a trembling bow. "I want my *Aunt Emmleeee!*"

"Now, now, that's no way to go on," Malleay said, striding forward. "That's not the way my sunshine girl behaves, is it?"

"Mally!" The girl sobbed in that unashamed, open-mouthed way of small children. "She in't Emmlee! She in't! Make her go away!"

Malleay knelt down and produced a handkerchief. "Come, come, shhhh."

He produced a necklace from his pocket and tried to get her to play with it, but did not put his arms around her. No one touched the child until an Ikinchli woman hurried up, scattering apologies, and scooped her into her arms. The girl buried her head in the curve of the woman's neck. The woman stroked and patted her back, with the unconscious automatic motions of someone who's spent her life looking after children, while she stared at Enthemmerlee.

"Ma'am?" she said, the word barely more than a whisper.

"Yes, Enkanet. It's me."

Enkanet kept soothing the child, but seemed to be shocked into immobility.

"You'd better take her," Enthemmerlee said. "We'll have to give her time."

"Oh! Yes, ma'am. Sorry, ma'am."

"Don't be sorry, Enkanet," Enthemmerlee said, with a strained smile. "We all have to get used to this, you know. Even me."

"Yes, ma'am," Enkanet said, and walked off, the child still sobbing into her neck.

Enboryay shook his head, went up to the beast that the stone had hit, and ran his hands along its flank, making hissing noises. "Sha, sha. There, beauty. This needs poulticing." He unhitched it from the carriage, and led it away, still muttering.

Enthemmerlee turned and strode swiftly towards the house. Thranishalak, who seemed to be some sort of head servant, struggled to stay ahead of her.

It should have been a relief to get out of the rain, but though it wasn't cold, the place struck chill. Grey rainlight failed to reach all the corners of the entrance hall; faded hangings in muddy colours hung limp against the wall. The ceiling was at least five feet above my head, but I felt as though it pressed on my shoulders.

We followed Enthemmerlee down long, empty corridors. All the doors were shut, and I didn't sense any movement behind them. How many empty rooms were there in this place?

Thranishalak opened the door on a pretty suite decorated in blue and white, uncluttered, but seeming overlarge for the slight, weary-looking girl who stood in the doorway. I gave it a quick check, with Bergast, to the obvious disapproval of Thranishalak, and found nothing that seemed threatening.

"Thank you," Enthemmerlee said. "Now please, go make yourselves comfortable. They will call us for a meal soon."

"But surely..." Bergast said.

I could hear the barely controlled shake in Enthemmerlee's voice. "Yes ma'am," I said. "We'll see to everything. You rest."

"Thank you." She closed the door. I gripped Bergast's shoulder and moved him away, ushering the others ahead of me.

Thranishalak opened a door opposite Enthemmerlee's suite. "Your rooms, sir," he said.

Bergast's glance swept the funereal purple-draped splendour before him. He nodded, and placed his pack on the bed as though afraid it might raise a cloud of dust, though the place looked clean enough to me. "Thank you."

My room was next to Enthemmerlee's, with a connecting door. Fern-coloured silk hangings, clothes chests the colour of pine forests, a bed draped in dark jade covers, two pale green couches, and a heavy, ornate washing set, in green marble with gilding. Rather like the bottom of a luxurious pond.

I gave the place a quick going-over. Nothing but a few abandoned bits of clothing lurking in the chests. "Now, Mr Thranishalak, you know why I'm here, and why the Scholar is here?"

"To protect the... the Lady Enthemmerlee."

"Yes. And am I right in thinking you are the head of the household?"

"I have the honour to be my Lord's seneschal." He had a way of staring just over my left shoulder which was like having a chilly draft run across my collarbone.

"Excellent. You'll know the running of the place better than anyone. I'll need to go over things with you, when you can give me a few moments. And perhaps you could spare someone to show us about?"

"That sort of thing would be the duty of the guard," he said.

"Oh, of course, for the more obvious things," I said. "But they won't be on such terms with the inner household as yourself."

"Certainly. If there is anything you wish to discuss, please call on me."

"And when would be a good time to do that?"

"After supper. You will find me in the Lower Quarters. One of the other servants will direct you."

"Before that, the gates."

"The gates?"

"They need to be shut. The main gates. The ones that are standing wide open for any passing assassin to wander in."

"I have received no such orders from the family," the seneschal said.

"The family may not have thought of it. I am responsible for the Lady Enthemmerlee's safety, and I *have* thought of it." I shrugged. "If you don't have the *authority*, of course..."

His tail twitched, once. "I will make arrangements." He bowed about half an inch, and left.

No sooner had he disappeared than Malleay, flushed green in the face and gesticulating wildly, appeared with Lobik at his side. Malleay had a pretty green and gold snake draped around his shoulders, which seemed to be placidly unbothered by his extravagant gestures. "Where's Enthemmerlee?"

"She's in there," I said. "She's tired."

"Oh. Oh, of course. The child upset her. But I must speak to her! I'm in the west wing near Fain, and Lobik and Rikkinnet have been shoved in the servants' quarters!"

"Ah," I said.

Malleay made for Enthemmerlee's door.

"No," Lobik said. "She is tired, and should rest, not be troubled with this."

"But you're being insulted!"

"Malleay, we have big battles. Maybe better to pick other fights than this."

"But whoever arranged the rooms..." Malleay said.

"The seneschal, I imagine. He is... *tic dricancai.*"

"What does that mean?" I said.

"*Tic dricancai?* It means having chains in the head." Lobik's mouth twisted. "He has been a servant all his life; for him, to be a good servant is the highest he can reach. He does not wish to see himself as Ikinchli, any more, but he cannot be Gudain."

"That's horrible," Malleay said.

"Do you think he's likely to be a threat?" I said.

"To Enthemmerlee?" Lobik frowned. "He lives by his loyalty to the family. He might wish things would return to the way they were, but I do not think he would hurt her to make it happen."

"How can he want that?" Malleay burst out. "How can he possibly want that?"

"Change is frightening, Malleay," Lobik said. "For you, no. You are young, you welcome it, you see a future you can take in your hands, and shape. But for someone like him... Imagine you are a poor carpenter, Malleay, scraping a living with the work of your hands. Perhaps you did not want to be a carpenter, but it was expected, or it was all there was. It is hard, and you have very little. Your one hope is to earn enough that when you can no longer work, you will have enough to keep you. And someone comes and says, soon, no one will need chairs any more. The first thing you will see is not, perhaps, that now you might be able to do something else with your life, that you are free, but instead, you think only that you will starve for lack of work.

"Once cannot force people to welcome change. One has to coax them into the net, like fish. No, that is a bad... what is the word? A bad metaphor. And also now I am hungry." He grinned, and I felt that stab of attraction again. It was, as much as anything, that smile; his was a face that had seen trouble, but his smile was joyous, life-embracing. "I think he may be difficult," Lobik went on. "He may make trouble in small ways. But an assassin? No."

"Good. Because it's not as though we need another one," I said.

"You don't think that one, what was his name, that Kankish, has gone," Lobik said.

"Maybe. But if he had the guts to risk his neck in that crowd, who'd have torn him apart if she hadn't given the word, maybe not. And maybe he'll find some friends. Either way, I'd rather know where he is. Any chance of sending someone after him?" I said.

"We can, at least, alert the Fenac. Or, rather..." Lobik shrugged. "His lordship can. If I go..."

Malleay said, "Even if they listen, they'll just arrest the first Ikinchli they find near the border."

"It was attempted murder," I said.

"It was attempted murder of the Itnunnacklish. Most of them would probably be happy to see her dead."

"On the other hand, it was attempted murder of a member of the Ten Families," Lobik said. "Put like that, perhaps..."

"I'll report it," Malleay said. "But it still doesn't mean they'll do anything. Now, the rooms."

"Rikkinnet needs to be here," I said. "I can't watch Enthemmerlee every minute, there have to be at least two of us."

"Well, I can watch her," Malleay said.

I was still trying to come up with a tactful way of telling him why that wasn't going to be good enough when Rikkinnet arrived, scowling.

"Rikkinnet!" I said, with relief. "Excellent. Will you have any objection to sharing my room? It's more than big enough."

"I do not object. Others will."

"Others will have to. I'm here to guard Enthemmerlee, not be a damn diplomat," I said. Although according to Fain, I was supposed to be doing both. And, of course, I needed to track down the blasted silk, if possible. But Enthemmerlee came first. Which meant I was going to have to have a word with Bergast, too.

MOVEMENT IN THE corridor had me rushing out again half-changed, to find servants with jugs of steaming water knocking on the doors. Enthemmerlee opened her door as I was confronting the nervous Ikinchli lass who stood in front of it.

The girl took one look at her changed mistress and nearly dropped the jug. Enthemmerlee smiled at her, and took it gently out of her hands.

"May I?" I said, following her into the room.

"Of course, please."

I shut the door behind us on the staring girl. "Would you hold off on using that water for a moment?" I said

"Certainly, but why?"

"Just a precaution. At least... Do you know if humans and Gudain can crossbreed?"

"I don't know. We don't... I don't know."

"It's just that species close enough to crossbreed are usually susceptible to a lot of the same poisons. And this" – I took out my jug, a tiny thing of pale blue opalescent stuff which held barely a thimbleful of liquid, and dripped a little of the washing water into it – "detects most of those poisons."

Enthemmerlee peered at it, fascinated as a child. "And if there is poison, what happens?"

"It turns red."

"What a wonderful device," she said. "So useful. Where did you come by it?"

"Don't know where it came from, originally; I got it as part payment for a job. I was transport security for a Farhiseer Kai tripart, dealing in precious metals."

"What is a Farhiseer Kai tripart?" Enthemmerlee said.

"They're actually three interdependent beings. Each of them performs part of the physical function for the whole, but they have separate identities."

"Oh, how strange! They gave it to you?"

"No. They tried to pay me in fake currency. I took it as compensation."

"You have seen so much," she said. "I must seem very ignorant."

"It's surprising how much you see when you're running away," I said. "I spent a lot of my life doing that. You could have done the same, but you didn't."

I realised I was still slightly mis-buttoned, and showing more cleavage than was probably acceptable. I buttoned up, and Enthemmerlee blushed.

"Sorry," I said. "I will try and stay within the code of dress, but when I heard people... your safety comes first, you know?"

"No, please," she said. She pressed her hands to her cheeks, as though she was trying to force the blush away. "Oh, this is very foolish! If you are not embarrassed, why should I be?"

I fiddled with the washstand for a moment, choosing my words carefully. "I'm used to a life with a lot of, well, skin in it. And where I came from, clothes are mostly ornament; it's a hot country. It's different here."

"Not for the Ikinchli. I am still... In that way, I am still very much Gudain." She indicated her robe. "The first time I put this on, I felt as though I were walking around naked. I wanted to find something that was a good compromise, between the way both races dress, but I do not think I have done very well.

The Gudain think I look outrageous, and to the Ikinchli I look no differently dressed than any other Gudain."

"I think your attempt is perhaps more successful than Malleay's."

"Neither of us is really successful," she said, sighing. "We look foolish. It is perhaps too trivial a matter to spend so much thought on."

"I'm not sure," I said. "I don't think you look foolish."

"But you think Malleay does?"

"No, no, just... He's not at ease in them."

"You are too polite to say, but I know you think... People underestimate him," she said. "He is a good man. He is perhaps a little impatient, and not always careful in what he says, but he is a good man, he wants to do what is right. I only wish..." She shook her head. "But now, I must wash."

I KNOCKED ON Bergast's door.

"Yes?"

"A word."

"Wha...?"

I walked towards him, until he had to back away or be walked over, and pulled the door shut behind me.

He had already changed into another expensive-looking robe, and redone his hair.

"Now, Scholar Bergast. I assume you've not done this before?"

"Done what?" He raised his hands in front of him, round-eyed. "Madam Steel..."

"Bodyguarding."

"Oh!" he said, with a relief that was, frankly, a little insulting. "Well, no, but..."

"I have. You're the magical expert here, but I've done a fair bit of this style of work. I need to have a quick word with you about the rules."

"Rules?" He gave me that high-nosed look. It tends to work better if you're taller than the person you're trying to look down at.

"Yes, rules," I said. "Now, I was glad to see you keeping your eyes open, down on the docks."

He blinked, and flushed a little. "Well..."

"But you walked off. You're all we've got on the magical side, and that means that you don't leave Enthemmerlee when we're out in public, see? Even for a minute. Even for a piss. Hold it in, until you know she's got someone else watching her."

High colour surged into his cheeks. "I don't believe I was told to take my orders from you."

I hauled back on my temper, hard. "I *believe* Darask Fain will tell you the same thing. I assume you'll be happy to take your orders from him?"

"Certainly, since he is the one who appointed me. As he did you, I believe."

I decided to ignore that.

"Now if you'll excuse me, I need to work."

"Of course," I said. "Setting wards and such."

"Yes," he said, "wards. And such."

I took a look around the grounds; or as much of them as I could in the time I had before the meal. It wasn't a vast estate, compared with some I'd seen; if the family owned farmland, it was elsewhere. There was a park, a small wood (growing too close to the wall, that would need watching), outbuildings. A rear gate, wooden, banded with iron, and locked. No guards. I boosted myself onto the wall and looked down. A rutted driveway led down the hill. I could see the roofs of the city below.

I dropped back, and made my way to what proved to be the stables, where they kept the carriage-beasts. The stables were solidly built – stone, not wood – and warmer than the house.

I poked around; a young Ikinchli boy in stained leather jerkin and loose trousers was dealing with one of the beasts, rubbing oil into its scales with a cloth, making a low hissing between his teeth. Either the beasts or the oil had a strange scent, like a mix of cream and metal.

"Hey," I said.

The boy looked up, and said, "Heya."

"Nice... er... What are they?"

He grinned, and started scratching just above the beast's brow-ridges. It stretched its neck and made a low groaning hiss. "You don't know? So what are you?"

"I'm a human. From Scalentine."

"Foreigner. Huh. You going to stay here?"

"Only for a while."

"These're disti. Best ones in the Ten Families."

"I'm sure."

"He's been sick. I'm looking after him."

"They get sick often?"

"No. I look after them good." He grinned, showing a couple of missing teeth. "My lord says I'm a natural. Also I pray to the ancestors."

"I'm sure that helps," I said, and left him to it.

There were a number of empty stables, and several old coaches that had been well kept up but didn't look as though they'd been used in Enthemmerlee's lifetime.

Not far from the stables was a long low building with a squat chimney, which gave out appealing smells of cooking. Near it was a neat but neglected-looking cottage. And further out in the grounds were a number of buildings of uncertain function and abandoned appearance. The Gudain habit of building in stone rather than wood meant most of them were still standing, but several had lost their roofs and held no more than a slew of wet leaves.

The little chapel was the best-kept of all the buildings; its pillars, a deep warm red, looked scrubbed, its pale stone walls gleamed, and not one of the small polished tiles was missing from the roof, so far as I could see. The little gravelled area around it, of green and cream-coloured stones that squeaked and chattered underfoot, was raked and weed-free. There was one door at the front, and a set of steps led down to another below ground level.

Both doors were locked; the one window closely shuttered. I tugged at the shutters, but they didn't move.

Not a god you just turned up and chatted to, then, the Great Artificer. But at least if they kept the building locked, it meant one less place for an assassin to hide. Probably.

Most of the buildings weren't worth a second look, and probably hadn't been worth a first, but it gave me a better idea of the danger areas. The main one being the fact that I hadn't seen a one of the so-called household guard apart from the scruffs on the gate. They certainly weren't patrolling the grounds.

CHAPTER
TEN

SERVANTS CAME TO call us to dinner a few minutes after I got back. By that time I could have eaten one of the disti, whole, raw, and with carriage and harness included. Unfortunately I'd not be eating yet.

The dining hall was a chilly low vault of a place. Enboryay, Selinecree, Fain and Chitherlee, seated around one end of a great long polished table that could have held thirty, looked like children playing at some grown-up game. Enthemmerlee took a seat partway down the table. Bergast hesitated, and Selinecree gestured him to the seat next to her.

There were at least three times more servants than masters, standing about like furniture. No guard, though. I stationed myself behind Enthemmerlee's chair.

Everyone had dressed for dinner. Enthemmerlee had on another of her half-way robes, this one in dark blue with lighter blue embroidery. The colour was good, but the shape – well, you couldn't exactly call it flattering.

The door opened. "Ah, Ambassador Dree, Lobik, Malleay," Enthemmerlee said. "Please join us."

Selinecree gasped. I heard indrawn hissing breaths from a few of the servants, too. Malleay went straight to the seat Enthemmerlee indicated. Both Lobik and Rikkinnet hesitated, then walked up to the table, as though afraid the floor might open beneath them.

Enboryay drew in a thick breath and said, "Enthemmerlee, do you think this... this is quite..."

Selinecree looked from her brother to her niece, a half-unfolded napkin in her fingers.

"Father," Enthemmerlee said, "This is, of course, your home. But it is also mine. Ambassador Dree is a guest of our house, and Lobik and Malleay are my husbands. If you do not wish us to dine with you, then we will go elsewhere."

"Now, my dears," Selinecree said, as bright and brittle as the glass she picked up with shaking fingers, "we have fresh blackfish tonight, with a green sauce; don't let us spoil it with serious talk! Enboryay, I ordered it especially for you."

"Blackfish? At this time of year?" Enboryay said. "Never."

"I have my sources, brother dear."

"What wine?"

"Thressalian, from the low hills. And a little treat to follow."

"Thressalian wine?" Fain said. "I must enquire into these sources of yours, madam."

I slipped Enthemmerlee the blue jug; a flicker of feeling darkened her face as she looked down at it, in the family hall where a privileged little girl had once had nothing on her mind but her supper.

I once attended a meal where the warlord I was working for gave his defeated enemy the choice of serving him his wine or being the main course. The enemy chose to serve wine, at which point his own retinue slaughtered him as a dishonourable coward and flung him on the fire to roast. I left shortly after, having lost my taste – as it were – for the company.

That first meal in Enthemmerlee's ancestral home, while less obviously lethal, was almost as uncomfortable.

The first course, some steaming savoury thing that arrived with six or seven different sauces, was carried in by a servant who was trembling so that the lid of the great dish chattered against the bowl, and it was a miracle any of the stuff ended up on the plates.

Thranishalak the seneschal entered with the wine, his bearing so rigid I wondered how he even managed to walk. He poured wine for everyone, until he got to Lobik, whereupon he looked at his master.

Enboryay, it seemed, was too busy adding a number of precisely measured amounts of different sauces to his portion to notice.

"Thranishalak," Enthemmerlee said, her voice quiet but extremely clear. "Why do you not pour for our guests? Surely we have not run out of wine?"

"Ma'am."

"How unfortunate," she said, choosing to hear "yes," even though it was perfectly obvious that that wasn't what was meant. "Lobik, take mine."

"There's no need," Lobik said.

Malleay opened his mouth, caught Enthemmerlee's look, and closed it again; he pushed his glass over to Lobik instead.

Lobik nodded his thanks, tilted half the wine into his own glass, and returned the rest to Malleay.

"If he can have some, I should have some," the child piped up.

"Chitherlee!" Selinecree said. "Hush."

"Why is everyone so cross? And why is that person sitting in my aunt's chair?"

"Now, now, *itni*," Malleay said. "You know you can't have wine, you're too young. And I told you, that lady is your Aunt Enthemmerlee."

The girl glowered. "Isn't."

"Yes, she is. It's like a costume, you see? You know how you wear your costume for the festivals? Well, it's like a costume you can't take off again, that's all."

"Don't like it."

"But it's a very pretty costume. And you're going to hurt her feelings if you don't like it."

"S'a costume?"

"*Like* a costume."

The girl got down from her chair, and came up and looked closely at Enthemmerlee. "All your hair's gone," she said.

"Yes, Chitherlee."

"Why do you have to wear this costume? It's *silly*."

"Because it will let me help people, darling."

"But you can't ever take it off?"

"No."

"Oh. Can I have some wine now?"

"No, you know you can't."

"Can I go play then?"

"You haven't eaten your supper yet, have you? Now sit down, there's a good girl."

The child looked up at me. "Why are you standing there?"

"So I can watch," I said.

"Aren't you hungry?"

My stomach answered for me, loudly, and the child laughed. Even that bright sound seemed to fall flat in the room's leaden atmosphere. Her Ikinchli nurse, stifling a grin, ushered her back to her chair.

"I hope our guests will excuse us in the morning. We must attend *privaiya*," Selinecree said. "Oh..." She looked at Enthemmerlee. "I mean..."

"Yes, Aunt, I will be attending."

"But you... I'm not sure... the priest..."

"It is written that only Gudain may attend *privaiya*. If I go, I go as the Itnunnacklish. And I will go to the public precinct."

"The public precinct?" Selinecree wailed. "Oh, dear, Enthemmerlee, no."

"Aunt, soon I will be seen everywhere in public."

"Yes, I know, but *please*, dear, can we have the family ceremony first? You're only just home."

Chitherlee said, "I don't want to go to *privaiya*. I don't like the smoke. It smells funny."

Enboryay leaned forward and winked at the child. "I don't like it either," he said. "Shall we go to the stables instead?"

"I said she wasn't to be taken to *privaiya*," Enthemmerlee said. "Selinecree?"

"But Enthemmerlee, it's *privaiya*. We have to go! The priest..."

"The priest says if we don't go we'll turn into animals," Chitherlee said. "I'd like to be an animal. I want to be a boom beetle." She filled her small chest and bellowed, "*Boom!*"

"Chitherlee," Enthemmerlee said. "Be good. Selinecree, I do not want Chitherlee to be taken to *privaiya*. The incense is not good for her. If he stops using it..."

"What animal would you like to be, Aunt Selinecree?"

"I don't think that's what the priest meant, dear," Selinecree said. "Enthemmerlee, please. Fodle is very old, and set in the old ways. He would never accept so radical a change."

"Then I will go, if it pleases you, but Chitherlee is not to. I do not wish to see her in the chapel again."

"But must you go to the public precinct?"

Enthemmerlee sighed. "How bad has it been, since you got back?"

Selinecree looked at her plate, twisting her napkin.

"What have they been saying?" Malleay said. "Oh, don't tell me, I can imagine."

"No, I don't think you can," Selinecree said. "I really don't."

"I'll go to the family chapel," Enthemmerlee said. "Tomorrow. Then... Well, then I shall be out where I can be seen, and people will say whatever they must."

I coughed behind my hand. Enthemmerlee looked around at me. "Oh, yes; Madam Steel and Scholar Bergast will also need to accompany me to the chapel, of course."

"But... Will that be allowed?" Selinecree said.

"The restriction is on Ikinchli, not on other... non-Gudain," Lobik said quietly.

"Besides, you really think poor old Fodle would notice?" Enboryay said. "Half the savages in the Perindi Empire could ride in on wild disti and he'd just mutter on."

"Enboryay, please, a little respect," Selinecree said.

"I shan't be attending," Malleay said. "And I can't for the life of me imagine why you would want to either."

"Malleay," Enthemmerlee said.

"You know what I think."

"Malleay, my love, *everyone* knows what you think when it comes to *privaiya*," Enthemmerlee said. "Now, *I* think we should discuss something else before we embarrass our guests."

Malleay blushed bright green and looked at his plate.

"But no, please," Fain said. "It is good to attend a family dinner, you know. Working as I do I so seldom have the opportunity. And all close families have these little disagreements; it makes me feel quite at home!"

"Ha!" Enboryay said. "So, Mr Fain, ever seen disti racing? Now there's a show worth betting on. Take you to look at my beasts tomorrow."

"I hear you have something of a reputation as a breeder?" Fain said.

"Oh, I've had some good results. I breed 'em for speed, you know. Some breed for looks, but I reckon it weakens the line."

Enboryay took up his glass, realised it was empty and waved to the seneschal. Thranishlak's face froze briefly, then he gestured to a lesser servant to fetch more wine.

This time around, Lobik shook his head before the seneschal could get to him, though I wondered if he wanted a drink as much as I did by that point. Rikkinnet glared at the seneschal, who poured her drink without, apparently, noticing her existence; as though the glass just happened to be there, requiring filling.

Fain, listening with apparent fascination to Enboryay chatting about Ikinchli jockeys, breaking harness, and the best bloodline of disti to race on soft ground, shook his head to wine. I wondered if he really did have a family; I found it hard to imagine him surrounded by happily squabbling relatives, or indeed by anyone at all.

Selinecree recovered herself enough to chatter brightly of trivialities.

Bergast, either tactful or blissfully oblivious, continued talking to Lobik about local religious customs, use of magic, and, from what I caught, languages. The boy seemed to have a bit of an obsession with them. "So there are still Andretic words in use among the Ikinchli?"

"Oh, yes, though it varies with the district, and of course, the meaning shifts. In the western valleys, you'll still hear, for example, *kitesta* used to mean cooked meat."

"Andretic for..." Bergast frowned. "For 'feast,' I believe."

"Indeed."

"And the Itnunnacklish? What does that mean?"

"*Itnun* is 'woman.'"

"*Itni* is 'girl,' in Andretic," Bergast said, nodding. He pulled out his notebook and reached for his quill, then remembered he was at the dinner table and that unless he dipped the thing in the gravy he had nothing to use for ink.

"Oddly, that word survives among the Gudain," Lobik said, "though the spread of Lithan has almost wiped out their native speech. You'll hear *itni* used as a term of affection, meaning 'little girl.' *Ack* is 'whole,' or 'complete.' And *li* is 'to calm' or 'soothe,' and *esh* is 'the world.'"

"Interesting. So it means... what, 'peacemaker'?"

"So we hope, Scholar Bergast, so we profoundly hope."

Eventually the conversation turned to business. "Trade's not so good," Enboryay said. "You know, Mr Fain, we could do with some investment from outside. We have the marble, but the Ikinchli, well, *they* don't seem to fancy the mine-work these days." He seemed to have forgotten the two Ikinchli sitting at his table, not to mention those still serving him. "They'd rather farm, or fish, or just walk away; maybe to Scalentine, eh?"

"And Gudain workers tend to insist on being paid," Enthemmerlee said quietly. "But they don't like the mines, either. They're dangerous. A family with only one child, as so many are now, is reluctant to risk them in such work. Only the desperate do it."

"We have to keep the roads open for the Empire trade route," Enboryay said, "but what good it does us, I don't know. Caravans come through" – I pricked up my ears – "but it's all from elsewhere. We used to export marble."

"And what else?" Fain said. "I am ashamed to admit I know little about your major trade here."

"Ah! Main course!" A positive stream of plates followed; the combined odours were strong enough to make my eyes water, although my stomach seemed to find them appealing enough.

"Fish," Lobik said to Fain. "Fresh and dried. And lichens, for use in dyes. In these, the land is generous."

Somehow all this chatter only seemed to emphasise an underlying silence. Cutlery clanged on the plates, and the whisper of rain against the windows haunted the room.

I LEFT RIKKINNET to watch Enthemmerlee, borrowed my jug back, and started towards the barracks. It wasn't hard to find them; there's something about the sound of a bunch of soldiers together.

It had some of the reek and roar of any barracks: cheap food, cheaper beer, weapon-oil, metal, sweat and ancient boots, intermixed with a wet-stone smell and the faint, unmistakable lemony aroma I associated with Ikinchli. Laughter and arguments, boasts and plain lies. But it was all in miniature. Empty tables were stacked at the back of the room, and the shouts bounced off the walls.

Two long tables. Gudain at one, Ikinchli at another. It was an Ikinchli guard who noticed me first; she tapped her companion on the arm and jerked her head in my direction.

The noise ebbed away. Before everyone in the room could stop eating and stare, I made my way to the hatch, where I saw people coming away with plates.

The smell of food was making my stomach growl like a chained dog. Behind the hatch was an Ikinchli woman, tunic splashed with what I really hoped was gravy. I almost leaned over and licked her to find out.

She looked at me, holding a ladle as though she were

considering whether to hit me with it.

"Any leftovers?" I said.

She gestured to a series of tureens. "Those, on the right," she said. "Those are Gudain. Left is for Ikinchli."

Damned either way. I chose the solution that matched my appetite. "Then I'll take a little of everything, please."

Silently, she ladled me scoops from each one. The stuff from the Gudain end was a bright scarlet mush, purplish leaves, and some sort of meat in a thick sauce, all powerfully scented. The Ikinchli end was fish, and dark green mush.

Now came the problem of sitting to eat it. I leaned against the wall and looked around. There were seats enough, at either table. But if I chose one, I would be seen to be choosing more than a place to sit, and I didn't want to do that. No one offered me a seat.

There was a chair about a foot to my left, back against the wall. I sat in it, only to discover it wobbled, which was probably why it had been pushed back. I managed to keep my balance – just – rested the plate on my knee, and, as subtly as possible, tested a little of everything with the jug. Nothing seemed poisonous, though the sauced meat made the tip of my finger tingle in a slightly worrying way.

The first mouthful of scarlet mush seemed to be made of crushed perfume. I gagged it down, and ate some of the green strands, which seemed not to taste of anything.

It only took me a couple of mouthfuls to realise that the Gudain liked more spice to their meat than I found palatable. In fact, the stuff was so powerfully flavoured that after eating some of the purplish leaves my mouth went numb for several seconds. The Ikinchli food was much more subtle; at the risk of offending the Gudain, but for the sake of my stomach (and my palate) I decided I'd stick with that.

I kept one careful eye on the guards.

A young Gudain with sticking-up hair was glowering at me as though I'd stepped on his toe. I could see the Gudain guards working up to something, with significant looks and whisperings, but they didn't touch each other. There were no nudges, no hands on shoulders.

The captain was nowhere to be seen.

A young Gudain male, a snake curled around his arm, got up and came over to me. "So," he said. "You been hired from outside."

"S'right," I said.

"You something special, then."

I shrugged.

"You going to teach us to be special, too?"

"For all I know, you're already special. What's your name?"

"Brodenay."

"Mine's Steel. Nice snake."

He glanced down at it. "Forest brown," he said. "He's a beauty, isn't he? Fancy a stroke?"

I bit back several of the more obvious responses. At least, they were obvious to me, but here, maybe not. I reached out a hand and paused. "Depends," I said. "He poisonous?"

"He's a *forest brown.* 'Course he's poisonous. But he's trained."

"Thanks all the same, but no. He doesn't know me. He might think I'm attacking you or something."

"Yeah, maybe," he said, grinning.

"So you all have poisonous snakes, then?"

"Do if you're a *man,*" he said, with a contemptuous glance at the Ikinchli table. "Scalys don't like 'em."

I looked around at the other Gudain males. Yes, they all had a snake.

Spiky-hair boy had a particularly fine specimen, a glossy black creature with a row of scarlet scales running down its back.

"You looking at Dentor's snake?"

"Yes, pretty thing."

"Pretty!" He laughed. "Don't get near it. That's a scarlet angel, that is. Deadliest snake in Incandress, and one wicked temper on it too. Dentor's the only one who can handle it." His eyes shone with admiration.

I caught sight of Captain Tantris out of the corner of my eye, leaning in the doorway, watching.

"I'll remember. You did well this morning," I said. "Could have been nasty. You all acted sensible."

"We weren't worried. Just a bunch of scaly peasants, what were they going to do? Here," the boy said, leaning forward, "is she really... you know. She some kind of... she's like their god, right? What's going on there, eh?"

He hadn't lowered his voice more than a token. I could feel every eye focused on us; the Ikinchli table especially.

"She's the person I was hired to guard," I said. "That's my job."

I finished my food and stood up. Standing, I was a good head taller than the boy. "She's of the family," I said. "So I guess guarding her's your job, too. Right?"

"If it's really her," someone said behind me. "And not some fucking scaly trick."

The Ikinchli table was already silent. Now, the silence took on a decidedly thickened quality.

"That's *enough*," the captain said, finally deciding to make his presence felt. "I want you, Bentathlay, and you, Esranay, on the gate. *Move*. And keep your eyes open. The rest of you, I'm *watching* you. You, Sticky."

"Sir." The Ikinchli he'd addressed stood up.

"You're on cleanup. Get to it."

"Sir." She was a rangy young female, tall for an Ikinchli, long-limbed and graceful. As she stepped past me heading for the kitchen, she gave me a quick but extremely thorough once-over, with eyes of an extraordinary shade of green, like sunlight through spring leaves.

"Ah, Captain Tantris," I said, as though I'd only just noticed him. "Could you spare me a moment? If you've eaten, that is."

"I've eaten. What did you want to talk to me about?"

Actually I could have told that from the fresh stains on his uniform, but it didn't seem politic to point them out. The smell of old wine hung around him.

I started to walk towards the door. He didn't move until the very last minute, when I was almost on top of him, and he was forced to back up, out of the barracks, into the soft, damp evening air.

"Ah, that's better," I said. "Bit of air after being cramped indoors. I don't know if you heard, but I thought you and your crew handled things very well this morning."

He grunted.

"I wanted to talk to you about how things were best dealt with. You know the layout, the family..."

"I do my job," he said. "How about you do yours, and I'll carry on doing mine?"

"Well now," I said. "That's going to be much easier if we work together, since my job is to guard the Lady Enthemmerlee, and so far as I know, so is yours."

"Yes."

"And just now, Lady Enthemmerlee is the most at risk."

"I know she is."

"So what can we do to help protect her?"

"You've seen the guard. Bunch of rag-ends and scrapings, and half of them scalys too useless even to bugger off to some other country, because no one would have 'em. But for now, they're *my* rag-ends and scrapings, and I'll thank you to leave us be."

He'd kept walking, and we'd reached the cottage. It had once been a neat little building, in the same soft-coloured stone as the main house. It even had a garden, or the remains of one. Some grey, hairy creeper type thing had sprawled over most of it, leaving vague lumps and hollows where perhaps once there had been flowerbeds. He put his hand on the door.

"Captain Tantris? The grounds aren't being patrolled. And even if that fella Kankish, the one on the road, really did keep walking, there will be others. And that wall couldn't even keep *me* out with a running start."

The door slammed.

CHAPTER
ELEVEN

I WALKED BACK towards the main building, leaned myself against a nice cool wall and let the rain patter my face with little soft hands. In the distance I could see a glow on the underside of the clouds, though it was long past sunset; a strange, low, unhealthy looking light.

"Heya, miss?"

It was the Ikinchli lass with the very green eyes.

"Hey," I said. "All right?"

"Yes. What to call you, please miss?"

"Oh. The name's Babylon Steel."

"I am Stikinisk."

"Stikinisk. Okay. How's it going?"

"Okay, I think. Can I talk with you, please?"

"Sure, of course."

"We walk a little, maybe?"

We moved out into the grounds. The rain still fell, that small sort of rain that doesn't feel like much but gets right in every chink and crease. The great trees of the park loomed like veiled ghosts.

The rain did not trouble Stikinisk at all; Ikinchli are a water-loving lot.

I prefer my water hot, in a bath, with soap, though I'm no paper doll to crumple under a little rain; I've stood guard, and fought, in worse. But this constant drizzle was beginning to depress me.

Unseen creatures creaked and chirruped in the darkness, and something gave a sudden loud *poom* that made me jump.

Stikinisk hissed laughter, then glanced at me apprehensively. "Sorry, miss. Madam Steel."

"Hey, don't worry about it. It's probably a frog or something, right?"

"Oh, no. It is Doronakaiken."

"Which is?"

"Gudain call it 'boom beetle.'"

"That's a *beetle?* How big is it?" I hate beetles.

"Oh, not so big." She held up a hand, the finger and thumb about an inch apart. "Dawn and dusk, they call out."

"So," I said. "What was it you wanted to talk to me about?"

"You here to look after the Itnunnacklish, yes? And Lobik Kraneel?"

"Well, mainly the Itnunnacklish. You think Lobik needs protecting, too?"

"He is a great man," she said, with fervour. "If a man could be the Itnunnacklish, it would have been him, I think. And a Gudain woman took him to be her husband. Yes, I think there are plenty who would like him dead."

"And Malleay?"

"Him I do not know so well." She shrugged. "He talks a lot."

"But you don't think anyone wants him dead?"

"I think if he is in the way, then, yes."

Poor old Malleay. Nothing but an obstacle to a would-be assassin.

"But us," Stikinisk said. "The guard, it is our job, too, to protect the Entaire family, and now, that is the Itnunnacklish and both her husbands. Only we are not so trained like we could be."

I wasn't sure what to say that wouldn't sound insulting, so I kept my mouth shut.

"Used to be more guard, better, ex-soldiers, some, but not now."

"I thought the family guard didn't *get* dismissed?" I said.

"Dismissed, no. But these last months; well, there was Hathlay, her daughter gets some trouble, she goes home to look to her. There was Bernak, he gets a chance to go to Scalentine, work with his brother. Prestallak, he has to take over the family farm when his parents die. And..." She broke off. "Some, one day, they just don't turn up."

"The loyalty doesn't work both ways, then?" Hire family isn't, I suppose, the same as birth family. I wouldn't know.

"Things here" – she looked around, and ran her long blue tongue out, a gesture that looked nervous – "they feel... things are changing. Some things for good. Some things, I don't know. People, they don't like change, you know? Even when it should be good."

"Yeah, I know."

"And some people, they are just bad poison, and don't need a reason to make everyone sick."

"You going to tell me who we're talking about?"

"Dentor. You see him? He wears the scarlet angel, his hair is..." She gestured above her head with long, elegant fingers, the webbing shimmering like smoke. "Hates Ikinchli. Hates the idea of the Itnunnacklish. Hates everyone, they look at him wrong. But he has those who follow him." She glanced at me, her eyes luminescent in the gloom. "You tell anyone I say this to you, I am going to have a very unlucky accident, maybe."

"I won't tell anyone."

"He tries to hurt her, what will happen to him?"

"If he tries something, I get between him and her. He might live through it."

"Might."

"My first priority is her; if I can only stop someone harming her by killing them, that's what I'll do."

She nodded, looking away into the misty night.

"I'd really rather not have to protect her from her own damn guard, though. And it's not as if it's only Gudain she has to watch out for."

Stikinisk's head whipped around. "What you mean?"

"Well, you must know, there are Ikinchli who think she's a fraud. Some kind of Gudain plot. We met one on the way here, and he's not the only one."

"You did?"

"Yeah. They missed. And she let them walk away. So, in the guard? Are there any? Come on, Stikinisk. You want to protect her, you need to tell me."

She sighed. "Not in the guard. That I know."

"All right. What about the captain?" I said.

"Captain mostly looks at us, sighs, goes away again." She shrugged. "He hears you are coming, he is not happy."

"I'm not planning to take his place. But he seems to think that the guard are going to be disbanded."

"Yes. We been hearing that, when lady Enthemmerlee become Patinate, she is meaning to send us all away, hire foreign guards in. She is all for change things, you know, breaking traditions, so maybe it is true."

"How would you feel about that?"

She looked at the ground. "Is okay here, you know? I mean, Dentor, he is not so fun, but is people like him anywhere. And I like the Lady Enthemmerlee. She always treat us decent. She doesn't think we are so good as guards, she is right, but maybe we can be better. So, I would like to stay. To guard the Itnunnacklish, that is something, yes?"

"You believe in her, then?"

She shrugged. "The priests say that she is the bringer of peace. This is good. Me, I don't want a war." There was the faintest emphasis on *me*, and I remembered what Fain had said.

"You think some do?"

She sighed. "For some people, fighting is the only way to solve anything." She glanced at me again. "I got to go."

"All right. Thanks for talking to me, Stikinisk. One thing, before you go. No one's patrolling the grounds. Now, I don't want to get you in trouble with your captain, but maybe if you know a couple of people who are trustworthy, you could set something up, hmm? Just walking about, looking, making sure no one's sneaked in over the wall, you know?"

She nodded. "I talk to some people, we get something going."

"Oh, one more thing," I said. "I don't suppose you know anything about the silk route, do you?"

"Goes through to the docks. Seen the caravans sometimes. Always lots of guards, lots of weapons."

Well, that was faintly comforting. "Thank you."

"You be careful, Lady Steel."

"I'm always careful," I said, as she hurried away.

Then I realised I was echoing the Chief, and it was as though the rain had made its way right inside me, chilling my bones. Suddenly I could feel every one of the miles between us.

The seneschal could wait. I had to talk to Fain.

ON MY WAY back, out of the corner of my eye, I saw movement over by the curtain wall.

A little late for gardening, and they didn't move like someone familiar with the ground. I drew, and moved up as quietly as I could.

Bergast, feeling his way along the wall and breathing like a man trying to push a cart stuck in the mud. He seemed to be sticking some kind of black threads to the stone, fragile stuff that clung like spiderweb, then dissolved. A faint smell of burning sugar hung in the air.

Eventually he straightened up, hands in the small of his back, panting, and saw me. "Oh, it's you."

"Yes. Wards?"

"Yes." He wiped his forehead.

"And the gates?" I said.

"Yes, I've warded the gates," he said. His expression was so exactly that of Jivrais being asked if he'd picked his laundry off the floor that I felt at once exasperated and desperately homesick. He didn't look as though it had been that easy, though; there were shadows under his eyes and his hands were shaking.

"They were shut?"

"Yes."

"Good. What do you make of the guard?"

"No worse than one would expect. I don't suppose it's a job requiring much intelligence."

Since it was a job I'd done, more than once, the remark got my back up somewhat.

"Well, I'll let you get on," I said.

"Thank you."

I watched him for a moment. I still wasn't sure about the lad, although there wasn't anything I could put my finger on other than that he irritated the hells out of me. And if that was a crime, half the people I'd ever met would be in gaol.

"AH, MADAM STEEL," Fain said. "Where have you been?"

"Getting some food," I said, fighting to keep a straight face. I'd found my way to Fain's room to discover him clothed in traditional Gudain costume, which even his looks and grace could not render anything other than absurd, especially when he sat down, looking like a cloth caterpillar bent at the middle.

"Well, we need to talk," he said. "This situation is ridiculous. I cannot possibly stay here, but at the moment it is proving impossible for me to leave. I tried earlier, to arrange transport back to the port, and a wheel came off the carriage. All my clothes are covered in mud."

"Ah," I said. "That explains... Right."

He gave me a supremely irritated look. "I'm glad you find this amusing."

"I don't," I said. "Really."

"*If* you remember, I don't happen to have any spares with me. Or much else."

"I know. I don't know how many more ways I can apologise," I said. "Look, I need to talk to you."

"About?"

"The attempted assassination, for a start."

"Ah, yes. Unfortunate."

"One word for it. It didn't even sharpen the guard up worth a damn, and she just let him walk off."

"You think she should have done otherwise?" Fain said, linking his fingers under his chin, and watching me.

"As her bodyguard? Bloody right I do. As a politician? You'd know better than I whether she made the right choice."

"I rather think she did. How naïve a choice it was remains to be seen."

"Depends whether or not he comes back, doesn't it?" I said, throwing myself into a chair so overstuffed I almost bounced straight back out.

"It depends whether she saw the small group of determined looking Ikinchli who started to walk in the same direction our murderous friend did. I do not think they were planning on patting him on the back."

"Oh. I missed that."

"You were, very sensibly, concentrating on your charge. They were heading away from her, not towards her."

Had Enthemmerlee noticed? If she had, and had done nothing... No. Not naïve, unless it was naïve to assume your supporters would do your dirty work for you.

I tried to think back; had she glanced behind us? Hesitated? I couldn't remember.

And it wasn't my place to ask. If she was less naïve than she sometimes seemed, then, frankly, it improved her chances of survival considerably.

I knew that from brutal experience.

"You think he's dead?" I said.

"I believe it is more than likely, unless he had the sense to run like the very hells as soon as he was out of sight."

"Didn't strike me as the type."

"No."

"Well, that's one less thing to worry about. I hope. Now, how quickly can we get a message back to Scalentine?"

"Normally it would take at least a day and a night, probably more."

"Well, you might have to resign yourself to another day here, then," I said. "It's all I can think of."

"You plan to send a message? Who to?"

"To Laney, asking her to come here and do whatever it is that has to be done to take off the oath. It'll dent our takings something rotten, but..."

"I hope you're not going to ask me to pay you more, considering that you're the one who put me in this absurd situation."

"No, I'm not. But I'm not going to send for her unless you do something for me."

"I am not in the mood for bargaining, Madam Steel. What exactly do you want from me?"

"I want you to tell me who you were talking to on the boat. And what's going on that involves the Chief."

His face went very still. "What were you doing, spying on me?"

"Oh, come on, Mr Fain. You *hired* me to spy. And I overheard you, purely by accident."

"Why do you want to know?"

"Look, Fain. I have enough of a situation here, without having my mind distracted by wondering what's happening back home."

"So you *are* involved with Bitternut."

"We don't shout it about, but yes. Don't tell me you didn't know."

"Not for certain, no."

"Fine, happy now? You've another card in your hand. I told you I was no strategist, Fain. I don't like these games. I just want to know what you think you're doing telling people to watch him as though he was up to something. If you don't know he's the straightest arrow ever shot, you're mad. Or maybe working for the Section distorts your way of thinking; you said as much to me once. But if he's in some kind of trouble, I want to know about it, and I've no intention of yanking Laney over here without having some idea of what the hells is going on."

"There are means by which I could get her here myself," he said.

"And when she finds out she's been deceived, I'll watch you try and deal with one pissed-off Fey with a *deal* of power, and you won't be in Scalentine, where it's damped. I'm pretty sure the oath will be the least of your worries, at that point." Not to mention, which I didn't, the fact that Laney might still be up to her neck in remorse and somewhat to the left of rational. "Besides, what were you planning to do with me while all this was going on? I can't exactly bodyguard Enthemmerlee if I'm in irons."

Fain shoved himself to his feet. "And if I cannot get back to Scalentine I can't keep an eye on a situation that may be at least as bad as the one here!"

"Meaning *what*, exactly?"

"Meaning I should be there. That is my *job*. And if it becomes known that I am *not* a businessman, it will do nothing to improve things here, either."

"You'll just have to be discreet, then, won't you? Tell me why you want the Chief watched."

"Whatever you think you heard, Madam Steel, I have the greatest respect for Chief Bitternut. He is an asset Scalentine can ill afford to lose, and I have every intention of trying to ensure that it does not."

"Fine. When you decide to tell me what's going on with the Chief, I'll send for Laney. Until then..." I turned to leave.

"Madam Steel."

"What?"

"I cannot force *you* to take a Fey oath, but I need a promise from you, that if I tell you, *you* will stay here, and complete the task – both the tasks – that have been asked of you."

I turned around. "How bad is it?"

"Do I have your promise?"

"What happens if I break it?"

"Then you break another promise. You said you would guard Enthemmerlee until after Patinarai. And it wasn't a promise made to me. You promised *her*."

I had, too. And having seen what passed for a household guard... Well, I wouldn't think too well of myself, if I left her safety to that scrow.

And what would the Chief think of me, if I went back now?

"All *right,* damn you, I'll stay. But you'd better tell me what the hells is going on, Fain."

He sighed. "You may have noticed an increase in... tensions, recently, between Scalentine's various citizens."

"The Builders?"

"Among others. There have been a number of murders."

"Yeah, I heard."

"Did you also hear that the murder victims have only one thing in common? They're all weres."

"They're all..." It hit me in the guts, and to stop myself falling I fumbled into the nearest chair, banging my hip hard on the arm. "You think the Chief..."

"I think if one of these groups is targeting weres, for whom they do seem to have a particular hatred, then the Chief is likely to be a tempting prize."

"But..." My throat locked. *Oh, Hargur. You must have known. And you didn't tell me.*

He wouldn't have missed it – not a connection like that. But I had. Like I'd missed whatever else had been worrying him.

Fain passed me a cup of water. I looked up when I took it, and thought I saw something showing through the usual smooth façade. He looked... stricken. But then there was nothing in his face but mild concern.

"You didn't tell me," I said. "You *knew* this, and you didn't tell me."

"I'm sorry."

"Are you?"

"Babylon..."

"I'd rather we went back to Madam Steel, if it's all the same to you, Mr Fain. *You didn't tell me.*"

"And what would you have done, if I had?"

"Stayed on Scalentine and watched his back, what do you think?"

"And who would have watched Enthemmerlee's?"

"You could have found another bodyguard."

"She wanted *you*. And so did I."

"Damn you to hells, Fain. *All* of them. So what will you do when you get back, since you're so concerned to protect him as an 'asset to Scalentine'?"

"I'll be honest with you," he said. I snarled, but he ignored me. "I don't know if I can protect him, but I do know I can try. And I can do things, or arrange for things to be done, that members of the Militia can't. You remember our conversation about Bergast? Before we left Scalentine?"

"No."

"I told you he wouldn't have been my first choice; though his qualifications are extremely good, he lacks experience. But our major specialist in defensive magics is currently assigned to Chief Bitternut."

"You... But magic strong enough to kill isn't usable on Scalentine."

"I considered it a reasonable precaution to take." Which gave me serious pause. Firstly it meant that Fain was taking the threat to Bitternut really seriously. Secondly, it meant that Fain, a man high up enough in the Diplomatic Section to know a deal more about how Scalentine worked than I did, thought that assassination by magic might, under the right circumstances, be possible, even there.

"So Bergast is your second best?" I didn't even know why I was asking, except that it gave me something to say while I tried to cope with the idea that Hargur – whose job, the All knows, was dangerous enough anyway – was now, possibly, the target of some nutter who wanted all weres, especially influential ones, dead.

"No," Fain said. "Another of our magicians was assigned to another non-human in a vulnerable position, in case weres were not the only ones in danger. Personally, I was not sure this was necessary, but I was overruled. And another was supposed to be returning from a mission, but her ship was delayed. So, it ended with Bergast."

Right now I didn't give much of a fart about Bergast. "A day and a night before a message will reach Laney," I said. "Another day and a night before she can get here. *If* there are ships going in the right direction. How much would it cost to hire a ship, just to carry a message? Is it even possible?"

"Not, perhaps, so long as that," he said.

"What do you mean? You were the one that said it."

"Yes, assuming you go by civilian means. However, there is an alternative. Considering the urgency of the situation."

I had no idea what he was talking about. I was trying not to let the churning panic in my stomach overwhelm me. I'd never felt this kind of fear in battle. I didn't think I'd *ever* felt this particular kind of fear. Except perhaps once, long ago, for a sweet-eyed gentle boy who'd been burned alive in front of me.

Don't think of that.

"Here." He held something in his hand. It was only a few inches across, and put me in mind of those armatures that sculptors use before they add the clay; a structure of wires that indicates a shape to come, set into a base covered in tiny cogs and dials no bigger than my thumbnail.

"What is it?" I said.

"It's a device for speaking between planes."

"Oh. That's what you were using in the cabin."

"Yes. It is fortunate that I had a chance to pick this up, at least, before my need to follow Enthemmerlee became overwhelming."

"Why didn't you ask for someone to be sent, then, to take off the oath?" I said.

"There are no Fey employed in the Section. They do not seem to find it conducive. Getting someone to find and persuade another Fey to come here would take days, and would risk exposing the situation."

"So you can send a message to Laney."

"Yes. Well, I can send a message to someone who has the other part of this device, and they can contact her by more standard means."

My brain hurt. "But if you could do this, why is it so vital for you to be in Scalentine? Surely you can tell people what to do from here?"

"My job consists of rather more than 'telling people what to do,' Madam Steel," he said, a little crisply. "And there are other factors. But for our purposes, this should be perfectly adequate."

"Show me," I said.

Using the device, or rather watching Fain use it, was an exercise in frustration. It had to be fidgeted and fadgeted with, twisting the dials the merest fraction this way and that way, edging a tiny handle down the smallest bit with a fingernail, and so on and so forth, until finally there was a kind of tingling crackle and a shiver of blue-purple light ran along one of the wires.

I got excited for a moment, but that wasn't it, either. After what felt like a decade or so of more fidgeting, there was another crackle, and one of the spaces between the wires seemed to catch hold of the blue-purple light and hold it in a wavering, shuddery shape that did funny things to my eyes.

Fain said, "Don't look directly at it."

"All right." I was quite glad to look at the wall instead, that wavering light made me queasy. Fain muttered a string of choppy syllables, and the light was suddenly, furiously bright, flinging our shadows stark on the wall, showing every crack and ripple in the ancient plaster.

Fain said; "*A swift rabbit isn't a hare but still leaps the moon.*"

"...the moon under water snares the unwary fox..."

Every hair on the back of my neck stood up straight as a soldier on parade. It was an ordinary voice, though faint and wavering in and out – the Scalentine accent was plain, I could even place it to within a few streets of King of Stone – but going through that device *did* something to it. It carried an uncanny freight, of all the distance it had been through; it had passed through realms of things that knew neither air nor light nor warmth, but lived. And they had heard it as it passed.

I was still staring at our shadows on the wall, thinking they looked too dark, too solid, but Fain was speaking, calm and clear. "A message to Laney at the Red Lantern in Goldencat Street. Babylon, speak, they'll pass it on."

I cleared my throat, which had locked cold. "Tell her... tell her the Mehrin brothers will have to wait. I need her here. And Enthemmerlee needs advice on her wardrobe."

Fain's eyebrows almost took off from the top of his head at that, but he said, "Did you get all that?"

The voice read the message back. The sound of my own words was somehow loathsome; I just wanted the voice to *stop talking*.

"Thank you," Fain said. "Is there any news from the Militia?"

No, it couldn't stop talking yet. I leaned close, looking away from that bruising light, not wanting to get near the thing, but desperate to hear.

"...all as before. Chief Bitternut" – my hands clenched – "arrested several of the Builders... bail was paid."

"Very well. Thank you." Fain flicked something on the base of the device. The light disappeared. The room sprang back into a much more comforting gloom, and Fain said, in an oddly tight voice, "Would you please let go?"

I hadn't even realised; I was gripping his shoulder so hard that my fingers creaked as I released him. "I'm sorry."

"I'm sure I'll be able to use it again eventually," he said, rotating the joint. He looked up at me. "I hope you are feeling reassured?"

"No."

"No, you're not, are you?" He looked at me keenly.

"What do you expect?" I said. "I'm not going to be reassured until whoever's killing weres is safely caught, until I can get home and see with my own eyes that Bitternut's all right."

"Is that all?"

"If you want to know the truth, no. That device of yours... It's..."

"It's what?"

"Where did it come from?"

"Does that matter? It's what, Babylon?"

"It's making me think I'll stick to messengers in future. There's something *wrong* about it."

"You're not the first to say so. But one would be foolish not to use such a useful tool, would one not?"

"Tools can turn in the hand, Mr Fain."

"True. Which is why one uses them with due caution. And for this, twice in such a short time is more than enough."

"Why?"

"One does feel somewhat fatigued afterwards."

I looked at it, a tight little bundle of dials and levers and a bare sketch of wires. It didn't look dangerous. But then, neither does poison, most of the time.

Neither does a competent assassin.

CHAPTER
TWELVE

I SHOULD HAVE gone to bed, Rikkinnet had the duty, but I was too unsettled and miserable even to try and sleep. I took a lantern and started to explore the house. I told myself I was checking for risks I might have missed, but really, I was just trying to distract myself.

Too many silent corridors, too many empty rooms. Dust motes dancing in my lantern's light. Hargur's lean face, the angle of his smile, the feel of his chest beneath my hand, his heart beating warm and strong.

Fain, that perennial chessmaster, was worried enough about Hargur to keep his best magical defender at his back, instead of bringing them to Incandress.

Or, at least, the best one he trusted. For a moment I almost felt sorry for Fain, surrounded as he was by those he couldn't trust; but then I cursed his name again. If it wasn't for him, I'd be there, with Hargur. No wonder my gut hadn't wanted me to leave.

My gut didn't like the device either. But if it could get a message to Hargur... What message, though? He already knew he was under threat, he already knew weres were being targeted.

There was really only one message I wanted to send him; and I doubted Fain would let me use the wretched device for it.

I love you. Stay alive, for the All's sake, until I can get home and tell you that.

I rubbed tears from my eyes and went outside to scout the yard; cursing whoever had decided that bushes and statuary were a good thing to have near the house, but glad to be out of all that emptiness, I worked my way around to the servants' quarters.

Voices, laughter, an arrhythmic thudding that might be dancing. Above, a few windows sent out gleams here and there under the low eaves; below, around the kitchens, every window was aglow, shutters thrown open, yellow light gleaming in the puddles like melted butter.

I poked my head in at the side door, to see a mass of bodies; it seemed as though every Ikinchli servant in the place, which was going on for forty of them, not counting those in the guard, were crammed into the kitchens and spilling into the hall, gabbling, drinking, dancing. Some were smoking long-handled, elaborately carved pipes, filling the air with a sweetish fug. Someone was playing an instrument, or at least I thought it was an instrument; it sounded to me like someone intermittently strangling a pig with a silver wire.

"*Itnunnacklish!*" someone yelled, high and exulting. "*Itnunnacklish!*"

Others took it up. "*Itnunnacklish!*" "*Itnunnacklish!*" "*Itnunnacklish!*" Pipes and mugs were waved in the air.

One of them noticed me, and waved his pipe. His third eyelids were half-up, which meant he was either sick or so dosed on something he was about to fall over. "Join our worship," he said.

"Worship, right. Thanks, but... I was just..."

"She doesn't want to join our worship," someone else said, and went off into a stream of Ikinchli.

A few more people had noticed my presence, and had stopped to look at me. They didn't look unfriendly, exactly; just watchful. The more sober of them, anyway.

Another, sitting on a low table, leaned in, the lower halves of his eyes also sheened with the pearl-coloured inner eyelid. "Don't have to believe in the Itnunnacklish," he said. "Don't have to believe in anything. Drink. Smoke. Tomorrow, everything be like it was, is just another party, okay? *Good* party."

"Is *everyone* here? How many of you are there?"

But he just belched and slid off the table in a heap, sending a handful of metal tankards clanging to the floor, to laughter and shouts.

If any of the servants weren't feeling like celebrating the arrival of the Itnunnacklish, it was impossible to tell. Enthemmerlee had, on my insistence, given me a list; but I didn't know all the faces. The only ones I could see were missing were a handful of the Ikinchli guard; I hoped they were on duty, and not tucked away plotting their mistress' demise.

Someone tried to thrust a tankard into my hand, but others were beginning to stare and mutter. Time I left, before they decided I was here to spy for their masters.

I smiled as best I could and backed out, straight into the seneschal, who was staring at the partiers. His face was expressionless, but you could have played his spine like the string on a lute. He hissed something at those nearest. They pretended not to hear.

"Madam Steel," he said, with a frigid little bow.

"Seneschal."

"I was looking for you."

"You were?"

"There is someone at the door who *insists* upon seeing you," he said.

"Wha?" My first, insane thought was Laney. But even Fey magic wouldn't transport her across the sea and through a portal at that speed. "Who is it?"

"He says his name is Mokraine."

I stared at the seneschal, so deeply confused it felt like being drunk. I wondered if he was lying, or up to something, but I couldn't imagine how he would even know of Mokraine's existence. But he made me twitchy; he had the look of someone wound so tight that if the wrong pressure was applied, he would spring apart, with little cogwheels and nasty pointy bits flying in all directions.

"Mokraine? Here?"

"That is what he says he is called."

I followed the seneschal's rigid back.

At the door was the guard, Brodenay, and one bedraggled warlock, with a miserable-looking familiar at his heels.

"Ah, Babylon," Mokraine said. "An interesting place. So much emotion in the air."

"Mokraine, what are you *doing* here?"

"Talking to this young man," he said. "This is a decaying culture, sadly lacking in magical history. I'm wet."

"Yes. Mokraine. Why are you here? And *how?*"

"I am here because..." For a moment he looked nothing more than an old man, confused, and at a loss. "Something drew me. A portal, I think."

"A portal? You mean Bealach?"

"No. Yes. I don't know. As to how..." He shrugged. "The usual way. A ship. Some sort of vehicle. That style of thing."

"But..." I didn't finish. You don't ask a warlock as powerful as Mokraine still possibly was, "Where the hells did you find the money?" At least, I didn't feel like risking it.

"You know him?" Brodenay said.

"I'm never quite sure about that, actually," I muttered. "Recognise him, yes. Well, he's here. Seneschal, any chance you could find him a room? Or something?"

"I cannot accept a guest without consulting the Family," the seneschal said. "It is late. I should not wish to disturb them."

The fella even *talked* like a Gudain. I wondered how hard he'd had to work to rid himself of the usual lilting Ikinchli susurration. I took him by the elbow and drew him – perhaps slightly more firmly than necessary – to one side.

"Look, chum," I said. "That gentleman may look as though he just wandered in off the street, but he is in fact an extremely powerful if somewhat *distracted* warlock and I really, really would advise you not to risk annoying him, do you follow me?"

"What is a warlock?"

"Oh, for..."

"Can I be of assistance?" a familiar and smooth-as-silk voice said behind me. "By the All, is that *Mokraine?*"

Even Fain sounded slightly startled; he gave us both a *What's going on?* stare, at which I shrugged and which I doubt Mokraine even noticed. He was staring at the seneschal with a disturbing intensity.

"You know him, sir?" the seneschal said, flicking his gaze away from Mokraine's stare.

"Why yes, a most respected magical practitioner. Who should *not* – may I make this very clear – should *not* be upset or annoyed. Or touched. At all."

The seneschal blinked his third eyelids, the first time I'd seen him make that particularly Ikinchli gesture. "I see," he said, backing away slightly. "Then please follow me, and I will find some accommodation for the gentleman." He looked at the familiar as it lurched after Mokraine. "That... Is it likely to... Should I have some straw fetched?"

"Oh, it doesn't excrete matter," Mokraine said, striding into the hall.

"It doesn't... What does it excrete?" I said.

"The sensation you feel when it brushes against you? I believe that may be its version of the eliminatory process."

"So when it touches you it sh... *eliminates* on your soul?"

Mokraine actually laughed. "Possibly. But I'm sure your soul can shrug off any such thing, Babylon."

I wasn't at all sure about that.

ONCE HE'D BEEN sent off with the seneschal, Fain said, "Was this your doing?"

"*Me?* No!"

"I really hope not. Introducing Mokraine into an already unstable situation would be an act of extraordinary foolishness."

"I didn't bring him here! I had no idea he was planning to come here, and neither, from the sound of it, did he."

"Do you have any idea of the current extent of his abilities?" Fain said.

"No. He's been on Scalentine as long as I've known him."

"That, of course, is part of the problem. He is no longer in Scalentine."

"I know he's no longer in Scalentine. If he was, we wouldn't be *having* this conversation," I said.

"Please endeavour to be serious. His power is no longer damped. This makes him, potentially, extremely dangerous."

"I know! What, exactly, do you suggest I do about it?"

"I suggest that you keep a careful eye on him and inform me if you notice any changes."

"Fain, I can't watch him *and* Enthemmerlee, *and* spy for you, *and*..." I managed, just, to stop myself mentioning the silk shipment. Which I had to do something about. Though what, I still had no idea.

"True. Then I will watch him myself."

"And what will you do if you think he's becoming a threat?" I said.

"I shall take whatever measures I deem necessary," Fain said.

"Are any of them likely to work?" I said. "Because if you attempt to restrain him in some way, and fail, I don't want to be you. Or anywhere near you, actually."

"I am aware of the risks. Now, unless you are on duty, I think you should try and get some sleep."

"Thank you, I'd never have thought of that," I said.

"Madam Steel..."

"Goodnight, Mr Fain."

I wasn't the only one up late; Bergast's light was burning. I heard him muttering behind his door. I couldn't make it out, but it sounded like the same set of phrases, over and over again, with occasional pauses for much more audible swearing.

I MANAGED TO grab a couple of hours of uneasy sleep, darkness woven through with voices and a sense that things were moving around me that I couldn't quite see. Then Rikkinnet was shaking my shoulder and telling me it was time to accompany the family to *privaiya*.

Bergast and I went into the little chapel to check it out; inside, it was low and dim, the eaves of the tiled roof hanging half over the windows. An elaborate brazier of some darkly gleaming ceramic stuff stood at the front, a stone table behind it. The priest was an elderly Gudain male, in multi-coloured robes whose internal ruff was square, making him look like a small, mobile building until you got close enough to see that inside the boxy outline he was so wispy and frail that a strong wind would send him drifting over the roof of his own chapel like a kite. "It's not quite ready," he said. He was setting out various bowls and implements on the table with slow care; shuffling back to a recess in the rear of the chapel to fetch more items, bringing them back and laying them out. He couldn't carry much at a time, and everything had its own place. A copper bowl, a knife, worn thin and shiny with use. Flint and tinder.

I checked out the recess: nothing more than a shelf-lined cupboard, too small for anyone to lurk in. "Please don't move anything!" the priest said.

I looked at him as he tottered up, hands held out in distress. He hadn't reacted to my non-Gudain appearance, or Bergast's for that matter, and as he turned yellowed eyes on me I realised he was nearly blind. He blinked slowly at me, looking vaguely puzzled. I had the right-shaped features, but was the wrong colour.

"I won't move anything," I said. "I'm a guest of the family. Just having a look about."

That seemed to satisfy him.

He took something else out, a lump of dark green stuff like mud, about the size of my fist. It smelled oversweet, sickly. Incense, probably. No wonder the child didn't like it; I wasn't looking forward to breathing that for long. He made his slow, painful way back to the table. That seemed to be the last thing. Bergast wandered about the chapel, making notes, his quill scritching like a mouse in the walls.

"Bergast?"

He looked at the stuff on the table, broke off a bit of the incense, and crumbled it under his nose.

"Bergast. Anything?"

"Oh, yes," he said. "It's very interesting. You know, there are some fascinating similarities..."

"I meant, any threat?"

He looked slightly miffed at being reminded of his actual purpose in being here. "Oh. No, nothing I can detect."

I nodded to the family waiting in the doorway. Enthemmerlee, Selinecree and Enboryay filed in, leaving Rikkinnet outside. Fain was nowhere to be seen, and I wondered, uneasily, what he was up to.

Empty benches, great old polished stone things too heavy to move easily, lined the chapel. The little family, huddled at the front, looked like flotsam washed up on some rocky, hostile shore.

The priest lit the brazier with agonising, arthritic slowness, and only after several tries and almost setting light to his own robe.

"Burn down the bloody chapel one of these days," Enboryay muttered, quite clearly, but the priest didn't seem to hear him. Selinecree made a faint distressed noise.

The priest hadn't seemed to notice Enthemmerlee, sitting a few feet from his nose. He muttered almost inaudibly, with occasional, apparently random, outbursts.

Soon the smoke began to rise, wavering towards the low ceiling, spreading out. A smell of tomb spices and dying lilies thickened the air.

"*Mumble mumble mutter* GREAT ARTificer *mumble mumble* CONTROL *mumble mutter mumble* UNTO his beLOVed CHILDren..."

I felt the smoke creep inside my nose and throat, and tried not to cough. My hair was going to stink of the stuff.

"*Mumble mutter* SACRIFICE *mutter* INNOCENT..."

Oh, that charming old story about the sacrifice maiden again. I wondered if the priest knew, or cared, how many Ikinchli had been beaten up or slaughtered because of a stupid myth. Mind you, being a priest, he might actually believe it himself.

At least standing here gave me a chance to think. I worked out what to do about the guards, if I could find the right lever. I also decided that to find out more about the silk route, I must use Fain's stance as a merchant to my advantage, *if* I could do it without letting him know my situation. Damned if I would give the man more advantage over me, he had plenty enough.

And he owed me.

Bergast surreptitiously scribbled in his notebook.

Eventually the priest became more consistently audible, as though his voice had needed time to warm up.

"Earthly PASSions burn and *mumble*. Great ARTificer stretches OUT his hand, and quenches the FLAME. *Mumble* so the smoke rises; all is calm, praise the name of the one who quiets the unRULy HEART."

"Praise the name," the family mumbled, as though they had caught inaudibility from the priest, apart from Selinecree, sitting very upright, whose voice rang out.

The priest raised his hands to shoulder height, palms down and fingers pointing towards his own chin, then dropped them, and came to a halt, blinking at his tiny congregation.

They all made the same gesture. Selinecree paused to speak to the priest, while the rest of us filed out.

Chitherlee, banned from *privaiya,* had curled up on one of the benches outside. Enthemmerlee stroked the girl's long pale hair. "Chitherlee, wake up."

Selinecree hissed, "Enthemmerlee!"

Chitherlee, blinking, righted herself. "Oh, I thought Enkanet was here."

"No, darling," Enthemmerlee said. "It was me."

Chitherlee slid off the bench, frowning. "So now you're different, will you hug me like Enkanet does?"

"Would you like me to hug you, Chitherlee?"

"Only servants *hug*," the child said, the jab quick and ugly, and ran off.

Enthemmerlee closed her eyes for a moment.

I caught sight of Stikinisk and another Ikinchli walking near the wall. They seemed to be patrolling. Good. Stikinisk looked different, though; I watched them, trying to work out what had changed. The other guard said something and she threw back her head, hissing laughter, then took a mock punch at him. As they moved on I watched their tails briefly twine around each other, and wondered if that was friendship, or more.

The thought passed across my mind with no more ripple than a leaf drifting on a lake.

Lobik and Fain, deep in conversation, waited for us outside the house. Lobik smiled at Enthemmerlee, but his smile seemed strangely dimmed. Fain watched us with his usual expression of impenetrable courtesy; he had his own clothes back, which must have pleased him. Normally it would please me, too; but his neat figure and handsome features were just that. Neat. Handsome.

I realised the dimness wasn't in them, it was in me. Not a flicker of lust, not a pinch of passion. What in the name of the All? I don't walk around in a permanent fever of desire – I'd never get anything done – but here I was, looking straight at Darask Fain, and I felt about as lustful as a loaf of bread.

I turned to look at Stikinisk; those slender, powerful hindquarters, that lithe grace. Nothing. Not a spark.

I felt a chill down to the bottom of my soul. What had happened? Had I been bespelled, poisoned, what?

Chitherlee was waiting for us, peering around the base of one of the statues. She was chewing a lock of her hair, and watching Enthemmerlee.

"Come here, Chitherlee. I want to talk to you." Enthemmerlee's voice was gentle, but implacable.

Chitherlee shook her head, but didn't move.

"Come here."

Chitherlee let go of the statue and shuffled forward, still chewing her hair.

"Chitherlee, you see me now," Enthemmerlee said, kneeling down, mud seeping into her gown. "What do you see?"

"You're different."

"Yes. I am the Itnunnacklish now. You know what that means?"

Chitherlee started to nod, then shook her head.

"It means I am part of your family, and I am also part of the people who have always served you, and dressed you, and hugged you. Everyone..." She sighed. "Everyone is just people, Chitherlee. Do you understand?"

"Are you part animal now?"

"No. I am part Ikinchli now. But I am still Enthemmerlee. Now," she said. "Will you hug me?"

Chitherlee put her arms around Enthemmerlee's shoulders and hugged her, quickly, as though afraid she would break. "There," she said, stepping back. "Can I go now?"

"Yes, go on," Enthemmerlee said, getting to her feet.

But Chitherlee didn't move. "You don't *feel* like an animal," she said.

And suddenly, I remembered what she had said at that horrible meal, about becoming an animal. And I knew what had happened.

It was the All-cursed smoke. Intended to damp the flames, to keep the Gudain's 'animal' natures under control.

I was furious. And more than a little frightened. What if it was permanent? I felt numb, crippled. The thought of feeling

Gaie Sebold

like this for the rest of my life... I tried to calm my racing heartbeat.

Lobik glanced at me. "Madam Steel? Is something wrong?"

I looked at him, desperate for that tingling jab of attraction. And there was, still, something. But it was cerebral, detached; I liked him, even more now for his concern, but my body was quiet as an empty house.

Enthemmerlee, overhearing, turned around. "Babylon?"

"The smoke," I said. "It..."

Selinecree had emerged from the chapel and overheard. "It affected you?" she said, her eyes widening. "But you're not – I mean, really?"

They knew what it did. Of course they knew. But it wasn't supposed to have an effect on Ikinchli, or on other barbarian races, like me.

"What about the smoke?" Bergast said.

"Is it permanent?" I said.

"Oh, no. At least, not for us – I mean, for Gudain," Enthemmerlee said. "Me, it seems, it no longer affects. I didn't think it would affect you either. I am dreadfully sorry, but it should wear off."

"Thank the All for that."

"Lunch!" Selinecree said. "Please, everyone, shall we?" Flushed bright green, she hastened away, and we all hurried after her.

"What does the smoke do?" Bergast hissed at me.

"By the All, Bergast, you're a healthy young lad, didn't you *notice?*"

"Notice what?"

"That you felt no desire. Unless it's just that no one here has any effect on you anyway. Fussy, eh?" I was babbling, mainly with relief that the effect wasn't, apparently, permanent.

He flushed. "Oh. Well. It was a chapel. I mean, one doesn't think of such things during an act of worship."

"One bloody does where I come from," I muttered.

Bergast blinked at me. "Really?"

"Yes, really."

"The ceremonies involve, ah..."

"Sex. Having of. Yes. Well, some of 'em."

"Fascinating. Could I ask..." He scrabbled in his pocket, and produced his notebook, a little bottle of ink, and a battered quill. "What language did you use? What plane was this?"

"No."

"But..."

"It is not something I care to discuss."

"But..."

"The fact that I am a whore by trade does not give you the right to interrogate me, Scholar."

"Oh." He looked down at his notebook, and closed it. "It's just I'm interested in language, particularly religious language. One finds the oddest things. Similarities. Links. It... Anyway."

"Well, go talk to the priest, then," I said.

He looked back at the chapel, and said, "I can talk to him. Whether I can *hear* him..." Then he looked at me. "Should I?"

"What?"

"Well, Enthemmerlee. Should I remain with her?"

At least he'd asked, this time, before rushing off.

"So far as I am aware no new threat has appeared. I'm sure we can manage without you for a few minutes."

"Thank you." He scurried back to the chapel, apparently unaware that he'd just treated me like his superior officer. He still had all the graceful tact of a muddy dog, but he was learning.

I HANDED OVER to Rikkinnet and walked across towards the guard quarters, only to see Mokraine wandering through the apparently eternal rain.

"Mokraine!"

"Ah, Babylon." Water dripped off the ends of his hair and ran down the deep creases of his face.

"How long have you been out here?"

"Some time. I am endeavouring not to put myself in temptation's way. There is a great deal of temptation here."

"You're trying... You're trying not to feed?"

"Yes. That little creature, the both-at-once, she requires harmony, does she not? Feeding near her might disturb that. A fascinating mind," he sighed. "Fascinating."

"Mokraine..." I was thrown enough by him turning up, and now this? "What's going on, Mokraine? Seriously."

"You are very troubled," he said.

"Damn right I am. And confused. And short of sleep. Please, Mokraine, tell me what you're doing here, and why you're having this sudden bout of conscience."

I immediately regretted my choice of words, but still... He set very few limits on his addiction. He didn't feed off children – but something he once mentioned suggested that it was only because their emotions were too simple, and he preferred something more complex. Other than that, he'd feed off anyone who was in an extreme emotional state who let him get close enough.

"Conscience?" he said. "Perhaps. But I think... I think that something has changed."

"What?"

"I do not know. But recently, after feeding... You know, *feeding* is really the wrong word, Babylon. It's a much more... *immersive* experience than simple chewing and swallowing. In any case, I spent several hours looking for a home that I never lived in, and a family that I do not have. I suppose I must have had a family, once; one does not drop fully formed out of the ether, after all. But not this family."

Sweet merciful All.

"You thought you were this person."

"I had their mind, for a little. Once free of its immediate troubles, it was a very mundane mind."

"You lost yourself."

"Yes. My mind is not what it was, I am aware. But I would prefer to keep what remains of it."

"But... How?"

"I intend to practise restraint."

I didn't know what to say. I've known more than a few addicts in my time; and whether it was drink, cloud, sex or any of the other myriad means the planes provide of running away inside your own head, I've never known one of them who found it easy to stop.

"You said last night," I said, carefully, "that you could feel the emotion in the air. But you hadn't fed."

"No. It appears to be another new aspect; I do not need to touch someone to be aware of their emotions. It is not the same as feeding. It is more like... the scent of a dish, instead of eating it. You, for example, are troubled. And... frightened? That, Babylon, is not like you. And there is something else, or has been..." He looked at me, his eyes in their deep wrinkled beds sharp as obsidian. "Or someone else."

"Please stay out of my head, Mokraine."

"I am not in it, Babylon. You are leaking."

"Thanks for that."

"My pleasure."

"I wasn't... Never mind." I'd just had a thought. "Mokraine?"

"Yes."

"I'd like to ask you a favour, but I don't know if it would be something you'd want to do. It might not help. Might not help you, I mean."

"Tell me."

"I'm heading to the guardhouse. It could be very useful if you would come with me and see what anyone might be... leaking. Not to feed, just to get whatever it is you're already getting. Only I don't know – would that be difficult for you? I mean would it..."

"Would it drive me mad with a desire to feed?" He turned that arrogant stare on me. "Babylon, I have been surrounded by a great many people in a state of high emotion for the past several hours and have not yet succumbed. I think I can manage to control myself."

"Well, er," I said. "Good. Marvellous."

"Will there be food? Actual food, I mean."

"Yes, there should be. I hope. I want some myself." At least I still had *that* appetite.

"Then let us go." If he was feeling mundane hunger, things had definitely changed; but I still didn't think that he was going to get rid of his addiction that easily.

The familiar lurched after us. The man on the door gave it a *what is that thing that is making my skin try to crawl off my bones* stare I knew well.

"It will stay outside," Mokraine said. He gestured at it and it crouched by the door. I wondered if its skin, if you could call it that, was actually paler and slimier-looking than usual, or if it was just the grey wet light.

CHAPTER
THIRTEEN

I'D TIMED IT right – the guard were at lunch. The shine coming off the Ikinchli almost blinded me. Though they weren't allowed swords, they had polished up every button and bit of braid until it gleamed; the leather thongs and cradles of their slings were oiled and their uniforms, be they never so worn, were mended and spotless. At the other end, spiky-haired Dentor and Brodenay, his hanger-on. Unshaven, unbuttoned, and crumpled. Their messiness looked too excessive to be anything but deliberate.

The captain was absent. Perhaps on purpose. After all, if he didn't *see* his men looking a mess, then he couldn't do anything about it. I wondered if he planned to remain absent until they were already on the way to the Palace, when it would be too late to tell them to smarten up.

I made a great show of fetching Mokraine's breakfast for him, seating him by himself a long way from the others, and waiting until he had started before beginning my own meal. Mokraine ate with his usual absent-minded haste. In my distraction, I took some of the Gudain food, a stew so outrageously peppery I almost spat it out.

I began to understand a bit about Gudain cooking. Everyone has to get their jollies somehow.

The guard watched; the Gudain males' snakes, dopey with food, curled about their arms or necks. I saw Dentor stroking the snake encircling his chunky upper arm. He gave me the kind of sneering glare intended to prove that he was only sitting there because he couldn't be bothered to come and give me the kicking I deserved.

I took our dishes back to the server and turned around, to see Mokraine wandering among the tables.

Crap. But he wasn't touching anyone, just meandering, smiling vaguely at the air. I saw a few of them looking at each other. Brodenay watched Dentor, not Mokraine; Dentor cleaned his nails with the tip of his knife, waited until Mokraine was close, then belched loudly.

I saw Mokraine pause; and closed my eyes briefly. I didn't have any time for Dentor, but there was still a chance that Mokraine, now he was outside Scalentine, might have both the inclination and the power to turn him into a pair of smoking boots. I didn't feel that would help matters much.

But Mokraine moved on, and, relief hollowing out my stomach, I followed him through the door.

"Fascinating," he muttered.

"Leakage?"

"What? Oh, yes. Leakage indeed. Fear and fury and hope and desire and hate. What a boiling pot of a place this is."

Among the quiet dripping trees we could hear the calm domestic sounds of a large household starting its day: orders and chatter, doors opening, water pouring, cooking-pot clatter, the snorting of beasts and the jingle of harness. And under it all, a boiling pot.

"So can you tell me who was leaking what?"

"Individually? Not in most cases. There was too much in the air, too many sources."

I felt myself slump. Damn. Too easy.

"I could go back, if you wish," he said. "But to be sure, I would need to touch them."

"I think that might cause trouble. Gudain have a strong taboo against touching in public."

"However, that rude young man who belched is hiding a

secret, to do with that snake he wears. He has a great deal of emotion connected to it."

"Really? What sort of emotion?"

"Shame. A sense of... something like powerlessness." A dark, unpleasant smile touched Mokraine's mouth. "Perhaps I could feel it so clearly because the sensation is one I am accustomed to these days."

I didn't know what to say to that.

"It *is* just a snake, I suppose?" I said. "Not some sort of demon, or device, or something?"

"So far as I could tell, it is just a snake."

"Anyone else that you got something specific from?"

"No. Oh, yes. That young Ikinchli female with the green eyes is lusting after you."

"Ah. Right."

"So are others, but any lust among the Gudain... They strangle it as best they can. As though it were some savage beast ready to devour them. My genitals do not trouble me greatly these days," Mokraine said, "but I do not fear them. What strange people these Gudain are."

"You're telling me," I said. "Thanks, Mokraine. I think that will help."

"Not at all." He started to wander off.

"Do you know where your rooms are?" I said.

"Oh, yes. Though I think I shall walk about a little first." The rain had turned the hair around his face to rat's tails; they shivered, shedding droplets.

"Mokraine, are you feeling all right?"

The lines either side of his mouth deepened. "No."

"Can I help?"

He managed a smile that looked hard-won. "Your particular comforts are not for me, Babylon."

"I didn't mean that. Unless it *would* help."

"I don't think so, but thank you." He raised a hand, then turned away, the familiar at his heels.

I went back to the rooms to check in with Rikkinnet. She was wearing a beautifully embroidered green and gold tunic and trousers, very smartly cut. She tugged at the high collar.

"Very smart," I said.

"For the ball. Is too tight. I am strangulating."

"You look magnificent. Very ambassadorial."

She shrugged. "To the Gudain, I will just be a jumped-up Ikinchli in pretty clothes."

"And what will you be to Rikkinnet?"

She gave a smile which was mostly teeth. "Sometimes also Rikkinnet feels like a jumped-up Ikinchli in pretty clothes."

"If it's any comfort, you'll *look* better than any of the Gudain."

"So? Is true anyway."

I had to laugh. "How's Enthemmerlee doing?"

"Okay. She is nervous, but hold up good. You?" She looked me up and down.

"As I can get." I was in my usual kit: toughened leather breast and backplate, bracers, greaves. A little decoration, nothing that stuck out to catch a blade. Over leather trousers and a silk shirt. I'd left it hanging on the bedpost, hoping the creases would drop, only to discover someone had come in and pressed it. Which was helpful, but a little unnerving. I'm out of the habit of being served.

"No, is good," she said. "Anyone want to make trouble, you make them think twice."

There was a knock on the door. I opened it to see Scholar Bergast. "Yes?"

"I heard..." He swallowed and glanced up and down the corridor as though he expected something to leap out at him. "It can't be true... Adept Mokraine arrived last night?"

"Yes."

"But what... I mean... Adept Mokraine? Is here? Who sent him?"

"Sent him? No one sends Mokraine anywhere. He just turned up."

"But why?"

"He's not sure."

"What do you mean, he isn't sure?"

"What I said. He said something drew him here."

"Who," Rikkinnet said, somewhat sharply, "is this Mokraine?"

In all the confusion I'd kind of forgotten to let her know. So then I had to explain. And then I had to explain some more.

Bergast listened, but kept shaking his head, as though he wasn't convinced by what he was hearing. Well, he'd meet Mokraine for himself eventually. "I have to go," he muttered, and skittered off towards his room as though his bowels were troubling him.

Rikkinnet looked less than pleased. Female Ikinchli have no crests, but her tail was twitching. "But why is he *here?*" she said. "I do not like this. You say he is, or was, a most powerful warlock. He is not in his right mind. This is not a good situation, no?"

"Believe me," I said, "I'm aware of that. But he's not *interested* in the things that interest other people, Rikkinnet. Politics and such just don't seem to enter his head. Besides, he's already been useful today. Look, trust me, he doesn't want to cause her any upset. Which is odd in itself, that that should even bother him, but there. I think you can believe he has no intention of harming her."

"I hope you are right," she said, glaring in the direction that Bergast had disappeared. "Her magical defender, he seems as much use as a holed net."

"Well, he was chosen by the Section... hmm. Yes. We'll just have to hope, won't we? Right now the main thing I'm worried about are those guards. They let Mokraine walk right in. I think I'm going to have to have a *word*."

"Good," Rikkinnet said. "I should like to come watch."

"Well, one of us should stay with Enthemmerlee. But can we get to talk to that cousin of yours? Insh... er."

"Inshinnik? You want him brought here before tomorrow?"

"Can you organise it?"

"For when?"

"As soon as possible. An hour?"

"Yes, I think."

DENTOR, HIS RUFF soiled, his hems coming down and his buttons dull with tarnish, was sitting surrounded by similarly scruffy cronies, telling a joke in which the word 'scaly' figured a lot.

The Ikinchli were studiously ignoring his little performance, though I could see a number of raised crests.

I walked over to them. "You're Dentor, right?"

"Yeah."

"I would like," I said, "a word. With you. In private."

Anywhere else, that sort of approach would have led to all sorts of comments. But this was Incandress, among the Gudain. Not a joke, not a nudge; though I heard one of the Ikinchli say something that contained several words I recognised. *You must think I have no taste.*

"Why?" Dentor said.

I let my eyes travel to the snake around his arm. "Scarlet angel, am I right? Deadliest snake on Incandress."

"S'right."

"Kill you in an instant if you didn't know how to handle it."

"Yeah."

"Man like you, can handle a scarlet angel, you got nothing to worry about having a few private words with me, now have you?"

He stuck his lower lip out like a pouting baby, and glanced around at his cronies, who were hanging on every word.

Dentor shrugged, and got up. "Come on, then."

I followed him out of the room, round to the back. "What d'you want?" he said, gracious as ever, running his snake-free hand through his hedgehog hair.

"Captain or no captain, I get the impression you're the one they follow, am I right? You've got influence."

He stuck his chest out. "Yeah, I do. I talk, they listen. Captain don't have a problem with it."

The captain, I thought, either hadn't noticed the way his guard was looking or had decided to ignore it until forced to do otherwise.

"Now, I noticed something in there. The Ikinchli, they look like they're going on parade; shined up to the last button. You boys... Well. Not so much. So, you want to tell me what that's about?"

"They want to get all in a lather for some scaly superstition, that's up to them, ain't it? Me and my crew, we don't put stock in that stuff. And anyway, you can't make a scaly look like a *guard*, don't matter what you dress 'em in."

"You don't think people might get the impression that maybe they're, I dunno, better disciplined, better guards, than you Gudain?"

"What, them? Don't make me laugh."

"And you don't think it might be seen as showing disrespect to the family?"

"The master's head of the family, no one else. He seen us, just this morning, and he didn't say nothing. Nor'd the captain. Seems like we look plenty smart enough for *him*."

Right, tact wasn't going to work. I leaned over him, close enough that he had to lean back to meet my eye.

"I want you to smarten up, *soldier*. Your boots are filthy, your uniform's disgusting, and you look like you've forgotten how to stand up straight. You're a disgrace. So sharpen the hell up *and* tell your friends to do likewise."

"Or what?" he said, grinning. "You ain't my captain, you can't tell me what to do."

I reached my hand out to the snake and it reared up, flickering its tongue at me. Fervently hoping I'd interpreted Mokraine correctly, I stroked its head with one finger. It hissed, but didn't bite. Yet.

"*Or...* your cronies find out about your angel," I said. "Drawn its venom sacs, haven't you? How brave will you look when they find out it's less, shall we say, *potent* than you'd like them to think?"

His eyes changed, and I had half a second to think, *Thank you, Mokraine, I owe you one*, before I saw his hand drop. I grabbed his wrist, hard enough to hurt. "Don't be a bloody fool."

"You can't hurt me!"

"What would you care to bet?" I said. True, I couldn't *kill* him, loathsome as he was; it might cause trouble for Enthemmerlee, and that was something I was here to prevent. Plus, however great the temptation, I'm no frigging murderer.

"Let go!"

"Listen to me. You are going to straighten up, and you're going to tell your chums to do the same. And you are going to act like *guards*. You are going to treat the Itnunnacklish's life as far more precious than your own, or the news about your little pet is going to get out."

"All right, all *right*."

"And I want you and the rest of the guard at the gate, in just under an hour. All of 'em."

I let him pull his wrist out of my grip. He was looking at me like a bad-tempered dog on a tight chain. A grudge would be held, no doubt about it; but then, it wasn't as though we were ever likely to be the best of chums.

He pulled his mates into a huddle, and I heard him telling them that they weren't going to let the Ikinchli get above themselves by trying to look smarter than Gudain.

It was a start. But without the captain actually acting like one, Dentor was still going to think he was in charge.

STIKINISK WAS HEADING back from her patrol of the grounds; she picked up her long easy stride to catch me. Her uniform was crisp, every button polished. Oh, those eyes. Delicious as fresh apples.

"Ready for the Palace tomorrow?" I said.

"Yes. We wait a long time for this. Hope we are good enough to keep her safe."

"Me too. That's our job."

"Maybe you give me some tips, hah? Train me up, private?"

Subtle, by some standards. And I was tempted. Oh, the relief, that I was, looking at her, seriously tempted. It was like walking into sunshine after too long in shadow. But now Mokraine had *told* me she was attracted to me, doing anything about it seemed somehow like cheating. Besides, I was on duty, and it might complicate things, which were complicated enough already.

"I don't think I'm going to have time for private lessons," I said, letting the regret show. "But maybe your captain will be willing to let me give the guards a bit of a sharpener. We'll see what can be done, eh?"

"Okay." She lidded those remarkable eyes briefly, and I felt a little pang.

"Have you been with the Guard long?" I said.

"A few years. Me and – a while."

"You and?"

"My brother, he used to be with the Guard."

"He left?"

She scuffed the ground, not looking at me. "Yes. You got family back home?"

"I have my crew. They're my family."

"Crew like ship?"

"No, I run a... business, with them."

"You get to choose who makes your family, then," she said.

"I suppose so," I said, looking at her. There was something in her voice; this conversation wasn't quite as casual as it seemed, but I was damned if I could work out what was going on. I'd probably know more if I took her to bed, but doing that just to try and dig out whatever she wasn't quite telling me... Well, that's getting into dodgy business. There's whoring, and there's whoring.

"Anyway, is good. You got people to look out for you," she said.

"And I look out for them."

She nodded.

"Stikinisk? There is something maybe you could help me with," I said. "Is there someone in the household the guards like? Someone you *all* see as a friend, or... heck, even an animal everyone's fond of?"

Her tail flicked. "What you going to do?"

"Oh, hey, nothing bad. I promise. No one – not even a snake – is going to get hurt. That's what I'm trying to prevent. I just need to know."

What I needed was leverage. There was Dentor, but I had a feeling Dentor was the kind of lever that might snap under the hand, leaving a nasty jagged edge.

"The little one. Chitherlee."

"Enthemmerlee's niece?"

"Her father, he died of a bad fever. Her mother she had it too, get very sick, too sick to look after Chitherlee. At least, that is what they say, only..."

"Only?"

Stikinisk shrugged. "Maybe I should not say."

"I won't pass it on, Stikinisk."

"The mother, she is not... She is like a little girl, in the head, you know? Not very smart. She go back to her family, leave the baby behind to grow up here. Chitherlee, she's smart. Lucky, yes?"

"Yes," I said.

"And she is everyone's baby, she come toddling around the guardhouse as soon as she can walk; everyone, Gudain and Ikinchli both, all like Chitherlee."

"Thank you, Stikinisk."

"Anything bad happen to her, you going to have big trouble."

"Trust me, I do not want anything bad to happen to her. Or anyone else." I just wished I could trust that nothing would. This whole situation reeked of bad. "I want the guard, all of them, to the gate, in just under an hour's time. I've told Dentor to bring his cronies, can you bring the rest?"

"I will try."

AS I HEADED for the gate, the seneschal hurried up to me with that odd, stiff-backed walk of his, and said, "I have arranged for the... the warlock Mokraine to have rooms. I spoke to Lady Selinecree. She has ordered that he be at the far end, near the kitchens. I hope this will be sufficient?"

"Why so far from the family rooms?"

"Oh, they are not servants' quarters," he said, hurriedly. "A good room, I assure you. I told her he seemed unwell, and might need care, and I believe she also spoke to Scholar Bergast. She thought it best he be near the servants, so that he can be easily looked after. Also, his meals will be taken to his rooms."

"I don't think he's that sick. Or at least, not sick in that way, precisely."

"The Lady Selinecree insisted."

"Well, thank her for her care." The woman might be a complete flibbertigibbet, but at least she tried to look after her guests, even the ones who turned up unannounced in the middle of the damn night.

And got let in.

AT THE GATEHOUSE, the guard were leaning on the wall, blinking at the rain, weapons loose in their hands. One Gudain, one Ikinchli; both young, male and bored.

After a few minutes, I saw an Ikinchli in purple and green

livery (Laney would have had a fit at the sight of it) coming towards them.

The guards nodded him straight through.

"Excuse me," I said, going up to the new arrival. "And you are?"

"I am Inshinnik," he said. "I come to speak to Rikkinnet. Is okay?" He blinked nervously at me.

"Yes, of course," I said. "Come with me."

I took him straight to Rikkinnet, keeping a very careful eye on him en route, and explained about the guard.

Rikkinnet swore, very quietly but for quite some time. "I have told her. I have told her and told her. This, though..."

Inshinnik looked anxiously from her to me and back. "I did wrong?"

"Not you, no," I said. "Where's Malleay?"

Rikkinnet snorted. "In his room, reading. We need another useless man?"

"Maybe not completely useless," I said, and went and told him what I wanted.

"You want what?"

"Look, it's important. Come and watch, if you need to. Can you get it?"

He protested, but eventually he disappeared, and came back, with one of the child's dolls clutched in his hand.

"It's not a favourite, is it?"

"No. But I don't see... What are you going to do?"

"Come and watch," I said. The doll was a fairly elaborate one, and looked not unlike Chitherlee. Good.

I went back to Inshinnik. "I think those guards need a little lesson, if you'd be willing to take part in it."

"Surely," he said, when I told him what I wanted. "But this livery, is quite tight, no? How do we do this?"

"Allow me," I said.

Under other circumstances, dressing him for the part would have been quite fun. He had a nice body under the appalling uniform, and no objection to being manhandled. In fact, he enjoyed it. Quite obviously, too. I eyed his emerging cocks with appreciation; Ikinchli penises are handsome things, to my eye, though a little startling to those not used to them.

Rikkinnet rolled her eyes. "Inshinnik. Babylon does not want to roll with you, okay?"

"Maybe I ask her, not you," Inshinnik said.

"I appreciate the thought, handsome, but there's no time. Try and think of something else, I don't want the guards to look more closely than usual."

"Hah. Gudain never look. Gudain pretend no one has body at all. Poor Gudain ladies," he sighed.

Malleay chose that moment to walk in, glanced down, spun away and stared at the wall, positively vibrating with embarrassment.

Poor Gudain ladies, indeed.

"I did warn you, this one keeps his brains under his tail," Rikkinnet said. "We ready now?"

"As we can be," I said, as Inshinnik, with some difficulty, laced his trousers.

Malleay, his blush only slowly fading, followed us as far as the gate.

Inshinnik walked through it. The guards watched him go, with the idle lack of interest of people lounging in a park. The rest of the guard had turned up: Dentor and his cronies in a bunch, a handful of Ikinchli with Stikinisk in their midst. The rest, the hoverers, in ones and twos. They eyed each other. The gate-guards looked at them, and at each other, and shrugged.

Rikkinnet and I withdrew to the trees, taking Malleay with us. "I really don't see..." he said.

"Just wait," I said.

Inshinnik strolled back in through the gate, calling out that he'd left his bag behind. The guards nodded him through.

Rikkinnet walked up to him and took his arm. "All right, lads?" I said to the gate-guards. "Now, come here."

They glanced at each other and did as I asked.

I grabbed a collar in each hand and drew their heads close. "I should crack your fucking skulls together right now," I said. "Maybe let in some daylight. What did you just do?" I pitched my voice loud enough for them all to hear.

"Here, what are you..." The Gudain boy tried to pull away and I tightened my hand. He clawed at my grip, and failed to break it. The Ikinchli, who seemed to have at least half a brain, stood very still.

The rest of the guard stirred and muttered.

"I'll tell you what you did," I said. "You just let someone walk in through this gate, that you are supposed to be *guarding*, because you've seen him before. And last night you let a total stranger in. A stranger who happens to be an extremely powerful warlock."

"But he..."

"One more word and I gut you. I do not care what he did, or what he said, or why the fuck you let him in. Now." I tightened my grip. "I want you all to watch this," I said, looking around at the rest of them. "I want you to watch this very closely."

Rikkinnet took Inshinnik by the shoulders and stood him in front of us. I tossed him the doll.

He turned up his hands, bowed, and drew a short, vicious knife from his sleeve, and cut off one of the doll's hands. He regarded his work, shrugged, and drew another knife, much longer, with a serrated edge that caught the light like shark's teeth, from under his coat. With this, he sawed off a leg. He tossed the knife onto the grass, drew out of his trousers (carefully) a fat-bladed dagger. Then a well-used short sword. Finally, from his coat, a small hatchet.

One weapon at a time, with a calm, almost studious expression on his face, he dismembered the doll. Stuffing drifted on the breeze. The two gate-guards watched, frozen. When the hatchet appeared, the Gudain drew a breath, which he seemed to have been holding all this time, and said, "Don't."

Inshinnik glanced at me.

"Why not?" I said. "It's a doll. It can't scream, or bleed, or choke on its tears while someone slices the life out of it."

"Just... fucking... stop," he said.

I let them go. The rest of the guard were watching, round-eyed, though Dentor still looked mostly sullen.

"Do you understand?" I said. "That could be the child. That could be Chitherlee. You *know* there will be people after the Lady Enthemmerlee the Itnunnacklish. They won't stop if any of her family get in the way, you know. Not even that little girl. I don't know what being a guard has meant to you up to now, maybe it's been a cushy post, nice easy work and three meals a day, but that is not what it means now. Now, it means you do not let *anyone,* you do not let an *ant,* through this gate without checking their identity and searching them for weapons.

"I don't care if it's your own grandma, I don't care if it's the Lord High Poobah of all creation, you stop them, you politely ask them their business, and you check them. If you do not do this, even *once,* and even if nothing happens, even if it doesn't mean everybody down to that little girl being found in their bed with their throat slit, even if *nothing* comes of it, I will personally skin you, by inches, and roll you in salt and leave you in the sun. Do not doubt that I can do this, and that I *will* do this. *Do you understand me?*" By this point I had the guard's face an inch from mine and was damn near screaming.

"Yes, ma'am."

"Say, 'I understand, no one gets through this gate without being checked.'"

"Yes..." – swallow – "ma'am. I understand. No one gets through this gate without being checked."

When we left, both guards were standing rigidly, hands on weapons, staring around as though assassins might leap out of the very grass. The rest of the guard dispersed, some muttering, others very quiet.

Malleay was looking at me as though he'd never seen me before.

"That was... thoroughly unpleasant."

"I know," I said, perhaps a little more snappishly than I should have. The sight of that stuffing floating on the breeze had given me the shudders.

"It worked, though," Malleay said. "You know, the third Palatine emperor had a very similar training method. Only he used several of the guard's own relatives."

"Really."

"Yes. Very effective, apparently."

"Oh, good."

CHAPTER
FOURTEEN

DARASK FAIN WAS waiting for me at the house. "An impressive demonstration."

"I didn't realise you were there. Let's see if it works. In the meantime, I've been thinking about my other task. There's usually at least one place in a city on a major route that caters to the caravans. I think I should go find it. Talk to some people, find out if there's been anything unexpected about what's going through."

"I see," he said. "Yes, that could be productive. When would you wish to go?"

"As soon as I've spoken to Rikkinnet's cousin. I can walk into the town from here. If you can, again, keep an eye on things."

"It really isn't as though I have a choice," he said.

If he was waiting for me to apologise, he was out of luck. I'd apologised all I was going to. If something happened to Hargur without me there, he'd be lucky if I didn't kill him.

INSHINNIK KNEW HIS stuff, all right, and obviously didn't keep all his brains under his tail, as he'd thought to bring drawings of the Palace. Bergast, Rikkinnet and I pored over them.

Fancy as the Palace was, it was based around something built as much for defence as for show. The inner keep was a solid block of stone. Unfortunately, over years of comparative peace, it had sprawled and spread, narrow defensive windows had been widened to let in the light, and more doors had been cut. There were dozens of places an assassin could sneak in, not to mention all the people who wanted Enthemmerlee dead who would be there quite legitimately.

"Where's the ball going to be held?" I said.

"Here." He tapped one of the drawings. "The Room of the Cousins. Two entrances; one for important peoples to come in, one for servants. Main entrance leads to vestibule here. Here is three doors, two go to outside, one to stables."

"That's all right, I'm only interested in these entrances right now. What does the servants' door open onto?"

"Corridor to kitchens, lots of doors off to pantries, store rooms, cellars."

"Windows?"

"Three windows, high up, all done with painted flowers, very pretty, not so easy to get in though. Need a ladder and need to be skinny like me."

"Who will be there?"

"The Patineshi, like the Lady Enthemmerlee. Those Advisors to the Crown, that is, those already Patinate, who have a relative who is Patineshi, next in line. The other Patinate, those without a young relative who is Patineshi, they do not need to be there. Only I think many of them will. Curiosity, yes?"

"I assume the attendees will include Tovanay Defraish and his mob?"

Inshinnik winced slightly, though he tried to hide it. "Tovanay Moth en Laslain Defraish, and his lady mother, yes."

"You know the Advisors to the Crown, Inshinnik. Any of them likely to want to harm the Itnunnacklish?"

He shrugged. "Want, perhaps. But to do? I do not know."

"I don't suppose there's some massive unbreakable taboo against killing in the Palace... is there?"

"No."

"I thought not." I'd been grabbing for a passing straw, and knew it. The closer we got to Enthemmerlee's first appearance, the twitchier I was getting. I might have got the household guard smartened up, but it didn't mean they were going to be any better at their job.

"So who else will be there? Guards, servants, and so forth?"

"Palace guard and servants, and individual escorts of each of Patinate. Guard usually wait outside."

"Not this time, they don't."

"Can bring them in, yes; will perhaps make a little gossip, but still. Then music, little bits of food on plates, drinks, all that."

I'd have to remind Enthemmerlee to use the jug.

"Then there's the ceremony in the Ancestor Caves, the..."

"The Enkantishak," Rikkinnet said. "And before you ask, every Ikinchli who can get there will be there. Thousands. All of the tribal leaders. Even if they do not believe, they will feel it politically necessary to be there."

"And then there's the Patinarai ceremony. Who'll be at that?"

"Representatives from all of the Ten Families, the other Patineshi and their families. Also guild leaders, local dignitaries and such."

"Significant individuals?"

"Enboryay, of course. The Patineshi is accompanied by the person who is handing over to them."

"Handing over?"

"Yes."

"So when Enthemmerlee becomes Patinate, her father isn't Patinate any longer? Even though he's still alive?"

"Yes. Can only be so many Advisors to the Crown at a time, you know?"

I remembered the conversation at that damned awkward dinner. "So she gains his political position *and* control over the household and the estate. What are the chances that papa is not too enthusiastic about that?"

"Patinate is a very old thing," Inshinnik said. "Big taboo against causing harm to the heir, big law, big tradition."

"Especially now," Rikkinnet said. "The old houses, they are dying out."

"I don't know," I said. "Some men find it hard enough to deal with their daughters growing up as it is, but she's done rather more than that. He may no longer regard her either as his daughter *or* as the legitimate heir."

"He has no choice," Rikkinnet said. "There is no other. There was a brother, but he died."

"They're not a fortunate family, are they?" I said. Then I wished I hadn't. An ugly echo seemed to hang around the words.

I CHANGED MY shirt and grabbed my heavy coat for the trip into town. It was too warm for the weather, but I didn't want to get soaked. Even the best-made armour starts to rub and gall when everything you're wearing under it is wet through.

The soft dripping silence as I walked towards the town made me twitchy, as though I were listening for something. This is why I prefer cities; there's always a distraction. The country's just too damn quiet.

Eventually I was in among people again. I had pulled my hood up, to try and stay slightly drier, but though it shaded my face a little, my height and the coat screamed 'foreigner,' and I was getting a few looks.

There were plenty of shops along the trade road, their windows large and fine, but almost empty. Now, there are shops that display only one or two items because their price fills up all the rest of the space, and there are shops that only display one or two items because that's all the shopkeeper can get. Most of these looked like the latter sort.

It didn't take me long to find the place that catered to the caravans. It was one of the few buildings with fresh paint and recent repairs, with a wide gate for big loads and a vast stableyard to cope with a lot of beasts. There were only a few at the moment; little dun-coloured Perindi workbeasts. They're like a stocky pony, but with a long floppy nose that hangs over their upper lip, legs like columns, wide flat feet, loud voices and the brains of a flea. They sat and looked at me, chewing.

Inside, the place felt welcoming: a cavernous room, with bunches of drying herbs and fat hard sausage hanging from the ceiling. The ceiling itself was pleasingly high after the louring Gudain buildings; I supposed they had to cater to taller races in a place like this. I was surprised to see some Gudain servers as well as Ikinchli. The people they were serving were a mix: Monishish with yellow, creased skins like old leather water-bottles, hanging in warty folds, and long snakelike necks which bent as they talked, gesturing with their long-fingered hands. A Thrail, and a couple of stocky, green-skinned, tusky types who looked like Gornack, the woman I'd seen in the fight Filchis and his crew had started. Several humans (we get everywhere).

For a second I felt so utterly, wrenchingly homesick for Scalentine I almost burst into tears. Instead, I went to the bar, and eyed their stock, which was wide and various, another advantage of being on the caravan route. They even had some half-decent golden. I ordered, with some regret, a glass of fokee juice.

One of the humans came up to the bar while I was waiting, a hard-muscled type with short, greying hair and a look of ex-soldier about him. The one he'd been sitting with was, by contrast, a skinny drink of water who sat staring mournfully into his beer.

Grey-hair nodded at me. I nodded back. "Hey. What's the food like in this place?"

"Not so bad," he said, "but I'd stay away from the Gudain dishes if you want to be able to taste anything else for a week. Oh, and don't bother asking for bread, or dumplings. They don't do 'em."

"Grain doesn't seem to be a big thing here," I said. Something about that struck me as odd, but I put it aside.

"No."

"Good travelling?" I said.

"Fair. Apart from the fever, been quiet as a virgin's bedroom, the whole trip."

"Fever?"

"Me and my mate got sick, they dumped us off. We were going to hang around until they came back, only..." He gave a glance around. "You been here a while?"

"Few days."

"I think we might wait somewhere else," he said. "It's got that *bad times* smell, you know?"

"I do. All too well."

"You with one of the caravans?" he said.

"No, I'm working local, but the job finishes in a couple of days, I thought I'd scout round for some guard work. So what was your cargo?" I said.

"Why'd you want to know?"

"Just curious."

"Well, they're two days ahead of us now, so I don't suppose it matters," he said, eyeing me sidelong. "Besides, if you *were* planning on robbing it, you'd need help. Never seen so many damn guards on one caravan, we were jostling each other out of the road. You stick that many guards on a load you're pretty much yelling that it's worth a touch, am I right?"

"Point," I said.

"And Tesserane drivers. I *mean*."

Tesserane. That was it. Our silk, I'd bet money on it. Of course, I already had, though not willingly. "Might as well light a beacon."

"Well, they'll be coming into port in Scalentine in three days, if someone doesn't knock 'em over." He grinned, and I did my best to grin back. I just hoped he was right. We must have been damn close to passing the load on our way into Incandress. I thought of the empty landscape we'd travelled, and peopled it with bandits behind every bush; I thought of the sea, and imagined storms, and wrecks, and the worth of the Lantern and everything in it sinking to the ocean floor, of sharks trailing scarves of Tesserane from their fins as they swam heedlessly away.

Well, there wasn't a damn thing I could do about it now. For all I knew, the stuff was already in Scalentine.

Where warehouse fires weren't exactly unknown, either...

Stop it, Babylon.

I bid my new friend farewell and headed out, but realised as I left that I wasn't going to make it back up the hill without a stop. The privies were around back, and – perhaps in tribute to Gudain modesty – were actual wooden cubicles, with latches, instead of a bench and a row of buckets. The latch on the one I chose was so new the wood still bled sap, and stiff as an old woman's knees. I spent some time ramming it into place before I could get down to business.

I was lacing up when I heard the next stall open and close. "They're going to think we've come in here for a poke," muttered someone who sounded a lot like my friend from the bar.

"Why would you care?" said a second voice.

"And it stinks."

"Shut up complaining. That woman. You think she was law?"

"So she sounded like Scalentine. Doesn't mean anything."

By this time I had my ear pressed so hard against the adjoining partition I was getting splinters.

"I don't like it. What'd you have to go and tell her about the cargo for?"

"I was checking her out, donkey-brain. She was looking for work, like she said. Look, even if she was law, what's she going to do? It's all sorted. Into the warehouse, out of the warehouse, neat as you like. It's all *planned*."

"And we'll get our cut."

"You bet your arse, or someone else'll get *cut*."

I'd heard enough. I hit the latch with the heel of my hand.

It squeaked, but wouldn't move.

Shit.

I wrestled with the bloody thing, but they'd heard the movement; there was the sound of running feet, and by the time I got out, they were long gone.

There was no sign of them in the bar, of course.

I WAS DUE back on duty and couldn't even find Fain before I had to stand guard through another excruciating formal dinner.

I had to fight to concentrate. What I'd overheard had been enough to tell me that somebody had plans for that silk when it hit the warehouse, and I didn't think they involved legitimate trade.

What the hells was I going to do? Even if I told Fain, he couldn't do anything from here, not in the time. And he'd want to know why I was interested, which would give him information I wasn't comfortable with him having.

I watched the servants come and go. The main dish this time was some kind of yellow vegetable so powerfully spiced that my eyes watered, surrounded with a flotilla of tiny dishes of this, that and t'other; colours of cinnabar and jade, sunsets and seascapes. I wondered if the spices did that, or whether they just liked their food exotically coloured.

I leaned close to Enthemmerlee's ear. "Jug?" I whispered.

She nodded, and gave a small sigh, as she spooned a fragment of the first dish into the jug as surreptitiously as she could.

Selinecree scattered bright, pleasant chatter like sequins, Fain made himself pleasant without being remotely flirtatious. Enthemmerlee was gracious. Lobik and Bergast talked about magic and ritual. Rikkinnet had declined dinner, saying she needed to sleep. The room hummed with all that wasn't being said.

I forgot my own troubles long enough to tense when the seneschal came in with the wine, as did everyone else. He walked around the table, serving people one by one, until he came to Lobik. He stopped. He looked at Enboryay.

Enboryay glared. Then he flicked his hand.

The seneschal poured.

So many held breaths were released it was a wonder the lamps didn't get blown out.

The dinner seemed to take several million years. I kept my eyes open and half an ear to the conversations; Lobik mentioned that he had recently seen a disti race, which engaged Enboryay's enthusiastic attention. Discussing pace, stride, and ground, he seemed to forget he was talking to an Ikinchli. But then all his stablehands were Ikinchli, so this sort of conversation probably felt quite natural. Selinecree quizzed Bergast about magic. "So fascinating. You probably know, we don't have much here; you have a great deal more on Scalentine."

"Only so much. Lethal magics are damped."

"Really? How intriguing! How does that happen?"

"Well," Bergast said, knowingly, "it's terribly complicated."

I caught Fain's look; it was no more than the most fractionally lifted of brows, but still, I had a hard time not grinning. Bergast, in magical terms, was just out of the egg. The damping effect of Scalentine still baffled the greatest of warlocks.

The lengths a man will go to to impress a woman, even one he hasn't the slightest hope of bedding, often amuse me.

Then I remembered about the silk, and my mood dropped right through my boots.

I glanced at Fain again, but he had turned to talk to Malleay. I couldn't tell him.

But... The thought snuck into my mind, like a finger tapping on a window. Maybe he could be of use. Or at least, his device could.

My stomach clenched, but it was probably hunger; I hadn't eaten since the morning, and I was ravenous.

How could I keep him away from his room long enough to use it?

Probably by making no obvious effort to do so. He was a suspicious beggar, and if I tried too hard to engage his attention elsewhere, he'd know something was up.

My stomach clanged harder. Damn, I was hungry.

The family withdrew to the main hall, another ill-proportioned, gloomy room with dark, clumsy furniture. It was, like the dining room, like the whole house, far too big for the people it contained.

I shuffled and twitched until Rikkinnet appeared, and handed over to her with barely a word. She gave me a narrow look as I hurried off, but I ignored it. Now the thought of using the device was in my mind I couldn't get it out.

Fain hadn't locked his room, but then, he hadn't brought much with him to be stolen. I hesitated with my hand still on the door. What if he'd kept the device on him? It wasn't that big... Well, there was no harm in looking.

What are you doing, Babylon? What is Fain going to think if he comes back and finds you here, or catches you using the device? Never mind think, *what's he going to do? He's not a man to cross, you know this, and you've already caused him trouble...* But these thoughts fled when a glimmer of blue-purple light showed me that the device was indeed there, sitting on the ornately carved dresser.

I opened the door the rest of the way and slipped inside, shutting the door behind me. If Fain turned up, I'd just pretend I'd arrived with seduction on my mind. Surely he'd believe that?

My stomach ground out a protest. *Shut up, I'll feed you later.*

I took hold of the device, trying to remember what Fain had done. A movement of *this* little copper wheel... that tiny lever down, the smallest fraction... and... *there*.

I remembered, just, to look away when the wavering shape of liquid-shuddering light formed between the wires, and turned hard and bright.

Shadows scuttled up the walls. Something somewhere was shrieking; some night-hunting bird, perhaps.

I leaned in close. *"A swift rabbit isn't a hare but still leaps the moon,"* I said.

Silence, with things in it that hissed and crawled.

I had a moment's fear that they might have changed the passwords, but the voice came back: *"The moon under water snares the unwary fox.* Mr Fain?" The same female voice I'd heard before.

"No. It's Babylon Steel. I need to get a message to the Lantern."

"I can't do that, without the express order of a member of the Section. Where is Mr Fain?"

"Elsewhere. Charming his hostess, probably. Dammit! All right, can you get one to the Militia?"

"Not without..."

"Look, it's a legal matter! A robbery, or about to be. There's a cargo of silk coming in, and I overheard plans to get to it at the warehouse." I thought furiously. "If it's taken, the Section will lose the tax revenue on it."

Silence. The silence went on too long; it was too full of whispers that seemed on the verge of becoming articulate.

"I need more detail."

"A cargo of Tesserane silk, coming in via Scalentine, due in about two days."

"And the nature of the crime?"

"Robbery! I told you!"

"Look," the voice said, suddenly friendlier, perhaps because my desperation had been audible. "I can't do this officially, but I can get one of the clerks to drop a word in someone's ear. I'll send Suli over to the barracks, all right? It's as much as I can do. And if anyone asks, I didn't."

"Thank you! Tell them it's me, they'll know I wouldn't waste their time."

"I will."

The quality of the silence changed, and I realised she had turned off her end of the device. *Suli,* I thought. I'd heard that name before, somewhere. A client? A...

"Babylon. Oh, Babylon, that is very unwise."

I jerked backwards away from the machine, and Mokraine reached past me, and flicked at the base of the device.

The light died, and the shadows on the wall collapsed in the warm, sane glow of the lantern in Mokraine's hand.

"These are not toys for the unlearned to play with," he said.

What had I been doing? My arms were pebbled with goosebumps. My stomach roiled and rolled. It wasn't hunger, it was my gut. It had been shrieking at me, and I had ignored it. Why in the name of the All had I used that thing?

Mokraine leaned forward, holding up the lantern and peering at me.

"What is it?" I said.

"I do not know. Perhaps nothing. Come away."

"Gladly."

I stumbled after him, feeling doped and utterly confused. "Mokraine? What were you doing there?"

"I felt something. Something in the structure..." He stared into the flame of the lantern for a moment. "I know I am mad," he said. "But also I know that I feel the portals, now. I feel the tug and pull, the net of thought that laces the All. The gates and passages through which things pass. I think that is why I am here. And that device is part of it. But... I do not know. In any event, you should not use it again."

"I don't plan to! I don't know why I did. Except I was desperate."

"Yes."

"But I hated the thing. When Fain first showed it to me I didn't trust it. I can't believe I did that."

"Perhaps something wanted you to," Mokraine said.

That was a thought I could have lived without.

CHAPTER
FIFTEEN

I TRIED TO shake it off. I had done something foolish, but I felt perfectly fine, now. Nothing had happened. And I'd sent a message. Hargur would send some guards, at least.

Fain had to chant. You didn't. And he had to fidget with the thing for minutes, you found the right position for all those little wheels and levers without even thinking...

Perhaps something wanted you to...

"Oh shut up," I muttered. "Nothing *happened*." Nonetheless, I wouldn't be using the Section's little toy again.

My gut, possibly still annoyed at being ignored earlier, pointed out that it hadn't had supper and would like some, now, please.

It's a bit much when your own bloody insides take against you. I made my way towards the barracks to get some food.

And while I was there, or rather, after I'd eaten, I'd see what I could make of the captain. At least that would take my mind off my own idiocy.

Yelling at him, I knew, would only make him even more resentful, and this wasn't a case for seduction, except of a very specialised sort. I was going to try telling him a story, based on something I remembered, from long ago. Storytelling is part of my job, one way and another. Usually specifically for erotic effect, but I've used it to rally soldiery, too.

Standing in front of the overgrown mess that had once been a garden in front of the captain's cottage, rubbing at the scar on my jaw, I wondered if I should have chosen something else. Or if I should just give up, and try and persuade Enthemmerlee to, if not sack her damn guard, just stop using them; or hire in a decent officer, and see what they could do. But I didn't think she would. I pushed a hand through my damp hair, feeling my fingers catch and pull in the tangle. How had I got myself in such a mess? I was never going to get anywhere with this. Even if Stikinisk was being straight with me, she was just one, half-trained, with whatever supporters among the guard she could scrape together. The rest were probably, in the way of people, waiting to see which way the wind blew; which wouldn't do Enthemmerlee any good if they were still making up their minds when someone attacked.

Once, I could have bound them to me with a word, forced their obedience with lust in their hearts and joy in their steps. I remembered what it was like, and for a moment I longed for the powers I'd once had. I felt a tickling buzz, like something pressing on the back of my skull, and whipped around. But there was nothing there, except the rainy night.

Nerves, perhaps a windblown leaf tangling in my hair. And reluctance for the task ahead of me. How easy it would have been, once, to convince the captain of the virtue of his task, to turn him into someone not only effective but furiously loyal, with nothing more than words.

That tickling buzz strengthened, became words inside my head. *You could do it again, Avatar that was.*

That voice. I knew that voice. I'd heard it last on Tiresana.

Babaska. Not a mere Avatar like me, but the Goddess Herself.

The voice was distant but clear; a far lantern in a night wood. I shuddered with a mix of fear and fury.

"Get out of my head," I whispered into the night. "I did what you wanted, leave me be!" How had she found me? How had she made the connection with me, here, uncountable miles from Tiresana, on another plane?

I can help you, Babylon. I can give you back the voice that raises the sword to your command – a little, unexpected flicker of humour at the double meaning – *you know I can.*

Yes, I believed she could, even so far removed from her home plane and mine.

"No. I'm done with it. That power was stolen."

But it was mine, and I offer it. You cannot steal what is given.

"And what would you ask in return?"

...

"There's something, isn't there?"

Perhaps. For now, only that the door should be left open.

"No."

Ebi that was, Avatar that was; I can help you.

"No!" I shouted, and slammed... something, shut.

The light was gone. The buzzing at the back of my skull was gone.

I stood alone in the whispering night.

There was a muffled thump from the cottage, and a voice said, "Who's there? Who's out there?"

"It's Babylon Steel. The bodyguard. Could I speak with you?" My voice sounded calm, but my hands were shaking. I clenched the fingers and released them, glared at them until they held steady. *I have a fight to fight. Everything else can wait.*

There was a grumbled response I decided to take as a 'yes.' I pushed the door open. Didn't anyone lock anything around here?

Something clinked against my foot.

A wine-bottle; full. I hefted it. Well, I'd brought some anyway. He must have left it outside, forgotten it, perhaps.

Inside the cottage it seemed colder than outside, and almost as damp. I followed the glimmer of lamplight.

The lamp stood on a table with a single plate holding the remains of a meal. There was a slumped shape in a low chair. Tantris, or so I assumed. He turned his head towards me. He had a mug in his hand and a blurred look, and there was an alcohol tang in the air. Apart from that, the place smelled like dust and emptiness.

"I'm here about the thing at the Palace. Tomorrow, right?"

He didn't answer, just glared at me.

I held up the bottle I'd brought, and put the other one on the table. "Found this outside. This one, I brought with me. I don't know about you, but I could do with a drink." I looked at him, trying to keep my face calmly expectant, like that of an old friend who'd dropped in, and was just waiting for him to fetch my usual tankard.

Eventually, when I didn't move or change expression, he grunted and got to his feet. From his movements, he wasn't that far gone; he didn't have the exaggerated carefulness of someone fighting a swaying floor.

The tankard he brought in was tarnished, but without any of the wear or dents of use. He'd gone to the trouble of wiping most of the dust out of it.

I poured him a slug of wine and a swallow for me and perched myself on the only other seat, an upright wooden chair that creaked in protest, or possibly shock at actually being used.

"I need your advice," I said. "Obviously you and the guard will be there, but you know the place far better than I do, and I'd like to know if there's anything in particular you think is a danger."

"Anything in particular? The place will be full of people who want her dead," he said. He drank, knocking it back. Lucky I hadn't brought the *good* wine.

"And what do you plan to do about that?"

"I plan to do my job, best I can with what I've got." He gave me a brief, red-tinged glare.

"Rag-ends and scrapings."

"That's right."

"You've been with the family long?"

"Long enough."

"What do you call that vine out front?" I said.

"What?"

"That vine, growing all over the front. Hairy thing."

"Creeping garrotte."

"Creeping *garrotte?*"

"Strangles everything."

"Oh."

"What's that got to do with anything?"

"I just wondered," I said. "Looked like there was a garden out there."

"I don't have time to keep it up," he said.

No. You're too busy sitting here in the dark feeling sorry for yourself.

"Back where I come from," I said, pouring more wine, "it's desert country." I felt my hand start to shake and put the bottle down, harder than I meant, but Tantris didn't notice. Oh, I wished I'd chosen another story, this was no time to be talking about my past. But I couldn't think of another. This one I knew well enough to tell almost without thinking. I took a breath to steady myself, and carried on. "Hard land; hard to grow anything much. But they love their gardens. If you've access to water and enough people to work it, you can make glorious gardens. Some people made places that were so green and scented and quiet you'd think you were in a dream. Rich people, of course. And the temples. No shortage of workers, and they could get water most of the time.

"But there was a lady who lived nearby where I grew up. She didn't have much. She made her living weaving; not even fancy stuff, just plain cloth. She had this tiny patch of sun-blasted ground in front of her place, with soil like dust.

"And over the years, she worked that patch of ground. She collected dung, she dug in all sorts of things, begged or scavenged around the city. It was barely bigger than that table, her garden, but she loved it. And she fed the ground, and watered it with her washing-water. And one spring I walked past and this tiny patch was like a piece of embroidery; little bright flowers, everywhere.

"By summer, she had flowers that were the envy of the city. Not many. There wasn't room. But what she had was better and brighter and more highly scented than the best of what grew in the temples.

"She was a quiet, nervy scrap of a thing, like a little brown bird. I was there the day some high-nosed priest, sweeping down the street in robes worth more than the house she lived in, stopped and looked. He knocked on her door. I remember her face. She was terrified. But as they talked, and he asked her how she'd made her garden, she started to stand up straighter, she smiled. She told him everything she could.

"Word got about. The priests and priestesses started to summon her to the temples for advice, and she went.

"They still couldn't grow flowers like hers. Some offered her gold, some offered her a high position in the temple to come make their gardens, but she wouldn't go. She'd have had to leave her own garden, and she loved it too much. I suppose because she'd done it all herself, from nothing. And they kept coming to her for advice, and they paid her for it. She'd *take* gold, but she'd rather have seeds, or cuttings. She never moved from that house. And everyone stopped and looked at her garden. Avayana, her name was. She bred a new kind of lily, and they named it after her; a little gold-flecked flower with a scent like an angel's dream. It grows in the harshest places, where nothing else will."

His head had nodded down to his chest, and I wondered whether all I'd managed was to send him to sleep, but his hand went out to his cup again, and lifted it.

After a few minutes, I put down my own barely used mug, and stood up. "Well, I'd best be off. And if your lot are as hopeless as you say, maybe I *should* just advise the Lady Enthemmerlee to hire guards in. She wasn't going to – she seems to think they were worth keeping – but you're the one who knows them, and you don't agree. I saw you've a training-ground behind the barracks; I'll be checking it over tomorrow, just after sunrise."

He was still slumped in his chair when I left. Probably a waste of half-decent wine and a better story, but the best I knew to do.

On the way back, I kept my ears open, both inner and outer, and heard nothing but rain, the shift of the beasts in their stables and the subtle scrabblings of small creatures going about their overnight business in the wet leafmould.

Halfway back to the house, it hit me properly. *Babaska*. She had found me, and she wanted something. I didn't know what, I didn't know if I could go on keeping her out, I didn't even know how I'd managed to shut her out this time. My hands and feet went to ice, and I shook like rat in a dog's jaws. I wrapped my arms around myself, and waited for it to be over. When the shivering finally let go, I felt as leaden-weary as though I'd been fighting for days.

At least now I knew why my gut had been unhappy about leaving Scalentine. It seemed disease and powerful magic weren't the only things the portals blocked. And perhaps my use of the device had opened a door that might otherwise have stayed shut, even outside Scalentine.

"WHAT IS IT?" Fain said, snatching the door open. "Is something... No. It can't be something wrong with Enthemmerlee, can it, or I wouldn't be standing here. You know, I'm somewhat weary of feeling like a damn weathercock."

"A weathercock?"

"Twitching with every breeze that might bring a threat. It's hardly restful."

He did look tired; his beautifully curved cheekbones were more prominent, and shadows had been brushed under his eyes with an artful hand. It was the sort of look that would make the susceptible long to soothe away whatever troubled him.

"You look tired," he said, startling me.

"I was about to say the same."

"Well, we both have our troubles."

"That's what I wanted to talk to you about."

"Then I suppose you'd best come in." He gestured me towards a chair, and paused. "You appear to need a towel."

There were some of the house towels, embroidered with the reaching lizard, done in scarlet. They were thick, velvety things, almost as good as the ones we had at home. The ones back in my room were mostly slung over the backs of furniture. I'm not naturally tidy. Fain, on the other hand... if he hadn't been standing there, holding out one of the towels, you wouldn't have known the room was inhabited, there was so little sign of him scattered about.

"Thank you," I said, and took the towel. "Has there been any news?"

"News?" Fain went to the window and ran the curtain through his fingers, frowning at the faded cloth.

"From home." I coughed. "Through that loathsome device of yours."

"You really do dislike it, don't you?" I watched him carefully, but there was no extra weight to his voice. If he knew I'd used the thing in his absence, he gave no sign.

Of course, the next time he used it himself, the woman on the other end would no doubt tell him. Then I'd be up to my knees in shit.

What had I been thinking?

Perhaps something wanted you to...

"Yes," I said, meaning it. "I do dislike it. A lot. But I admit it's a very useful thing, and I just hoped..."

"No. There's been nothing. We do not use the device casually, but if there had been anything of importance, someone would have contacted me."

I didn't know whether or not to feel relieved.

"Now," Fain said. "Since you're here. The ball. There will be outsiders, according to what the family were telling me earlier.

And I would be grateful if you could mingle with the crowd. Keep your ears open."

"For what, exactly?"

"Chatter about grain prices. Chatter about trade, and borders, and so forth. Merchants' chatter."

"Oh, yes. I wanted to talk to you about that. You noticed anything about the food?"

"The Gudain cuisine is quite lively."

"That's one way of putting it. But they don't have bread."

"No? Well, one can live without it. Why?"

"Mr Fain, they don't have *grain*. They don't grow it. They don't eat it. It's not part of their diet. So why would someone be stockpiling it and planning to try to sell it to them?"

He laced his fingers under his chin. "Hmm. Interesting. Then perhaps something else is going on."

"You were talking to Lobik. He didn't have any ideas?"

"No, although his grasp of the politics of the situation is astute. Remarkably so, considering that he was deprived of any real education until adulthood. A most extraordinary man."

"Enthemmerlee's lucky to have him, then."

"Indeed. So long as the Gudain do not see her as too heavily influenced by an Ikinchli; that, too, is a danger he is aware of, but there is little he can do except not make it obvious when he is giving her advice."

I shuddered. "Politics."

"Indeed."

"So," I said. "Do you still want me to listen to people talk about stuff I don't understand and which, quite frankly, will bore me so much I doubt I'll be able to remember a word of it?"

"Yes."

"I was afraid you'd say that."

"Something *is* going on, Babylon. Something someone with influence in the Section doesn't want me to find out. This makes me *exceptionally* eager to find out what, in fact, it is, and who is behind it."

His eyes glittered darkly, and I wondered if whoever it was realised just what they'd taken on when they decided to mess with Darask Fain. *Including me*, I thought with something of a chill, although messing with him hadn't been my original intention.

"So long as I can still watch Enthemmerlee," I said.

"Since I will be there, it can be assumed that that damned oath of yours will ensure that I fling myself between her and any potential assassin."

I didn't think it would improve matters if I pointed out that some weapons can go through two people almost as easily as one.

"What will you be doing?" I said. "Apart from any flinging that may be required."

"I am going to be attending as Darask Fain, potential investor. I, too, will be listening to the chatter, but I may be seen as a possible rival. People might be less cautious about what they say in your hearing."

"You think they might try and seduce me with exciting talk of crops and trade percentages?"

"I doubt they will try and seduce anyone at all. Not at the Gudain court."

It was time I took over from Rikkinnet. I wasn't looking forward to standing outside Enthemmerlee's door all night; too damn much time to think.

RIKKINNET GAVE ME an unnervingly sharp once-over. "Trouble?"

I shook my head. "Nothing to do with this, no." At least, I hoped not. "Rikkinnet, do you know the servants here?"

"No, I do not," she said. "You think because I follow Enthemmerlee I am a servant?"

"Dammit, no! I just thought you might know the household, that's all. Last night the servants were partying, because of Enthemmerlee; I couldn't tell if anyone was missing. If they didn't think it was something to celebrate, they might be a threat. Or a potential threat."

"I think that Dentor is a much more obvious threat."

I gritted my teeth. "It isn't always the obvious threat that bites your arse."

"One Ikinchli with a badly aimed stone is not all Ikinchli."

"It wasn't..." I looked at the dent in my shield, and was suddenly overwhelmed with a sort of weary anger. "Never mind. I'm just trying to do my job. If you think I'm the wrong person for it, you persuade them to send me home. Right now, I'd damn well thank you for it."

At that moment Enthemmerlee's door opened. "Madam Steel? May I speak with you?"

"Of course," I said, with some relief.

"Rikkinnet, please, go; you haven't eaten."

She looked at the two of us with an expression I couldn't read, nodded, and walked off.

"And you, have you eaten?" Enthemmerlee said.

"Yes, ma'am."

Enthemmerlee gestured for me to sit down. She remained standing herself, fidgeting with a lamp, adjusting the wick, turning it down low. The room, like all the ones in this damned house, was too low in the ceiling for its height. It was too large, and too full of oversized, elaborate furniture; turning down the lamp should have made it cosy, but it simply allowed shadows to leap from the walls and cluster around the big, empty bed. I shuddered, hard, but fortunately Enthemmerlee wasn't looking.

"I understand we have another guest?" Enthemmerlee said.

"Oh, yes, Mokraine. I'm sorry about that."

"Sorry? Why?"

"Well, it might complicate things. I had no idea he planned to follow me here... Well, I don't think he was following me, actually. I don't know why he's here. Neither does he." Well, not in a way I could understand, anyway.

"He doesn't know?"

"No. He gets confused. A lot."

"And he is a warlock? I know almost nothing about those who use magic. We have so little here."

"He is. He was very powerful, once. I don't think he'd damage anyone on purpose, but he should be treated with caution."

"Poor man. Is there anything we can do to help him?"

"I don't know. Him being here... I've no idea if that's a good sign or a bad one, and I don't know what drew him any more than he does. He might actually be useful, but he is, potentially, dangerous."

"Should we perhaps provide him with transport home?"

"I think it might be advantageous to keep him around a bit, if you've no objection. There are things he can do, even in his present state, that might be useful."

"Then I will be guided by you on this. But if it seems he may become a threat, your advice will be required on how to deal with him."

"Of course." What advice I could give, I didn't know. Apart from knocking him out when he was distracted, I really wasn't sure how to deal with a (possibly) very powerful and (definitely) less than sane warlock. Fain had claimed to have a plan; I wondered if he really did.

"Is it right that he is able to read minds?"

"Not precisely. Who..."

"Oh, Scholar Bergast mentioned something."

"Well, he's got it wrong. Mokraine can pick up powerful emotions, occasional individual images, but not complex thoughts. He couldn't snatch the words you're about to say out of your head. He might have some idea about how you felt at the time, but that's all. And maybe if you had a very clear mental image of something, he might get that. At least, I think that's how it works."

"I see."

"Was it Mokraine you wanted to talk to me about?"

"No. I... Madam Steel... I... Oh, this is very difficult. I hope you will forgive me."

I wondered, with unseemly hope, if I was about to be fired.

"I need..." Enthemmerlee moved her hands in a gesture of graceful helplessness. "I need your advice."

"Oh, right."

"Please, sit. I..."

I sat down. Her cheeks glowed with that soft green blush, and she stared anywhere but at me. I began to get an inkling.

"Lady Enthemmerlee? This advice, are you asking me because of my profession? Not the soldiering, I mean."

"I hope... Yes. I don't mean to, I know you are here as a bodyguard, and I don't wish to have you think that I see you as..."

"A whore?" I said, as gently as I could.

"Is that..."

"One word for it. There are others. I don't know if you can understand this, I know things are very different for you. But it's what I do, Lady Enthemmerlee, and I'm not ashamed of it. I'm very good at it. I trained to do it. I make people happy. If I get it right, they go back to their lives feeling better about themselves and the world around them. So you won't offend me by calling me what I am. Please, ask me anything you want, I'll try to help."

"For us," she said, still staring at her hands, "I mean, for the Gudain... We do not talk of it. It is like, well, urination. Necessary, but not something one thinks about much, or for polite conversation. Or any conversation, except to speak to a healer, if things go wrong. One does it when it is necessary."

"But what about desire?" I said. "People can make all the rules they like, but lust happens."

"Did you notice anything about the streets of the town, as we drove through?" she said.

"It looked rather empty," I said.

"Did you notice *who* was on the streets?"

I thought back. "Ikinchli, in the main. Servants. A few Gudain."

"Yes." She stood up, and went to the window, and drew the curtain back a little; I nipped up alongside her, hoping those damn guards on the gate were still doing their job.

"Lady, it would ease my mind a deal if you wouldn't stand in the window with the light behind you."

"Oh, of course." She sighed, and moved away, letting the heavy curtain fall back. "I do not know what I expected to see." She turned to me, her gold eyes lambent in the soft light of the lamp. "There are more Ikinchli than Gudain. Many more. The trend has been increasing for several generations. We – *Gudain* – no longer breed well."

"The smoke," I said, without thinking.

If she was shocked at what I'd said, she gave no sign. "The *privaiya* smoke. It affected you, which is proof of something I have suspected for a long time. The smoke is called the gift of the Great Artificer, given only to Gudain, so that they may control their animal lusts, and concentrate instead upon the higher purposes for which they were created. But you are not Gudain; and that to me says that it is no tool of any Great Artificer, but a drug and a curse."

"But you attended," I said.

"Oh, yes. To do so was, well, politic. I suspected it might no longer affect me, and I was right." She clenched her hands. "Yet if I campaign to ban its use, as part of *privaiya* worship, I will be seen as campaigning against the Great Artificer, as introducing animalistic Ikinchli ways... The Gudain need no further reason to fear and mistrust me. Yet they are wiping themselves out. The Ten Families, particularly: they bear fewer children every year.

"You must have noticed how these halls echo; this house is meant for a family, not this sad remnant. And once it would have been full. But our servants outnumber us ten to one. And this creates another problem. Selinecree... There were no men

of the appropriate class for Selinecree to marry when she came
of age, and she would not consider marrying outside the Ten
Families. Many others are the same. I don't know if you have
worked with beasts, you have had such an interesting life..."

"I'm not sure what you mean, like herdbeasts?" I said. "Not
since I was very young. Mainly, in latter years, I've just acted as
a guard when they were being driven across bad country, that
sort of thing. Why?"

"If the flock is too small, and the beasts are bred too close,
there are consequences. Unhealthy ones."

"Oh. I know what you mean. I've seen it in court circles,
and in isolated villages." I could remember more than one
place where the majority of the inhabitants all had disturbingly
similar features... Not to mention a few other things about
them that were disturbing.

"Chitherlee's mother. She is weak. Both physically and... She
would never have been able to look after Chitherlee. And she
is not the only one."

She rested her hands on the table, opening and closing
her fingers so the delicate webbing between them stretched,
relaxed, stretched again. "The Gift of the Artificer. Perhaps it
is. Perhaps the Great Artificer did not like his own creation
very much."

She pushed herself away from the table, and started to pace
the room, shadows passing over her as she moved. "I have
read histories. And I have learned this. Being outnumbered,
especially in a time when resources are scarce, makes any group
more defensive, more determined to attack any threat before it
even exists. I believe this imbalance in the population is a large
part of why treatment of the Ikinchli has worsened, and more
severe laws have been passed, even in my own lifetime. I wonder
sometimes if it is merely a just reward for the folly and arrogance
of my... *former* race. That perhaps it would be better this way;
that eventually the Ikinchli, with no help from me, would be
freed from their oppression, because there will be no Gudain

left to oppress them. But foully as the Gudain have behaved, I cannot stand by and witness this. And even if I did, they will cling to power for more generations, during which more children will be born like Chitherlee's mother and more Ikinchli will suffer. And it is not just the smoke. The smoke is only one of the Gudain's attempts to separate ourselves from desire, to prove how very unlike the Ikinchli we are. Even without the smoke, we are crippled by this. So, I need your help."

I stared at her. "What exactly do you want of me, Lady Enthemmerlee? I'm not a herb-wife or a healer; I certainly don't know how to make people more fertile. Any expertise I have tends in the other direction, to be blunt."

"No. It's your... other profession, that I think... I mean, I hope..." She tugged at one of the curtains so hard that a section of it tore away from its mountings, and she looked at it helplessly as it sagged. "I'm sorry, this is very difficult for me. But my entire race is out of the habit, the practice of desire. It is destroying us."

Oh, boy. "I'm a good whore, my lady, but I think getting a whole *species* primed for wick-dippage is more than I could manage." *Not when you were the Avatar of Babaska,* memory muttered. I shoved it aside.

Enthemmerlee looked bemused. "Wick...?"

Oops. People who never talk about nookie aren't going to have a lot of metaphors for it. "Sex," I said.

"Oh, no," she said. "If you could, from your experience, advise me, yes, I would be grateful. But I was merely explaining the background."

Well, it isn't unusual to have a client walk a mile around the thing they want to say before they say it.

"Background to what?" I said.

She sat down. "When my marriage took place," she said, "I thought I was prepared. I knew the basics. I knew that once it was over, the transformation would begin, that it would be painful, perhaps fatal. I did not know that even making the attempt would be so difficult for me. It was not necessary for me to admit to, even to *feel* desire. Malleay had to."

I nodded. He had to feel desire, or the essential aspect of the marriage, Enthemmerlee's transformation, couldn't have taken place. Gudain and human anatomy were that alike, at any rate.

"If it had not been for Lobik," Enthemmerlee went on, "I think we would have failed. He was so kind. So understanding. With me, and with Malleay. He understood that... He knew, and he..."

I waited.

"He knew I felt desire. For him. And he was not disgusted. He was happy." She realised she was crying, and wiped impatiently at her eyes. "I did not know... I did not realise it was possible. There was even pleasure. Not much, that first time, but it was there. But poor Malleay... He tries to think like a revolutionary, but he is still a Gudain. He felt desire, but this disturbed him; greatly." She paused.

"He stopped attending *privaiya*, didn't he?" I said. "Now he's not taking the smoke, he gets lustful."

"Yes. And I hoped that would... But..." She got up, and messed with the lamp again, so she wouldn't have to look at me. "I disgust him now," she said, softly. "He flinches away from me. It is not necessary, of course, that he desire me; there is no need for us ever to be together again, in that way, if he does not wish it. But he is unhappy. I want him to be happy. And also... This is vile, but it is politics. His disgust is visible. It is damaging, for others to see him flinch when I am close. You have seen it?"

I nodded.

She sighed, and sat back down, turning out her hands in a helpless, beautiful gesture. "I do not know what to do," she said.

"Do you feel desire for him?" I said. "For Malleay?"

She hooded her eyes. "I did," she said. "His mind – there, he is very passionate. He always has been. Since we were children, we have talked about how the world should be changed. I loved him, I think. I still do. But desire? I do not know."

Desire is a powerful thing. Powerful enough to change lives, to punch through city walls. But it's fragile, too. If it's constantly rejected, it can wither like a flower out of water; and sometimes, it can't be revived.

"I can talk to him, if you wish. Just to find out what's going on."

"Would you? Please?"

"Of course. But how would you feel if the discussion took a more practical turn?"

She just looked at me.

"I mean," I said, "if I decided the only way was to get him between the sheets, and see where we went from there, how would you feel about that? Because I can talk with the best of 'em, but if I really want to know someone, well, that's where I find out the most. This is assuming he can be persuaded."

"If you can help him to be happier," Enthemmerlee said, "I would only be grateful."

Not so much as a hesitation. I wasn't sure whether to be glad about that, to be honest. On the one hand, it made things easier – but on the other, it meant that she had no jealousy about Malleay. I don't like jealousy, I think it's a waste of emotion, but it can be a useful indicator of where someone's passion lies. And if Malleay had managed to completely kill hers, it might not be capable of resurrection. But it wasn't her desire, it was Malleay's that was my immediate problem.

And I didn't think he liked me that much.

But that was for later. "I need to ask you," I said. "Would you be willing to talk to me about what pleases you? Because if I can get him back to your bed, there's not a lot of point if he's not going to make you happy in it."

"Oh. Oh!" She flushed again, even darker. "I... Is that important? So long as *he* is happy..."

"Well, you can just put up with someone in bed, yes. I've done it, often enough. But I'm trained to make them think they've pleased me. You're not trained like that, and people know. He'd pick up on it, trust me. People do, when they care about the person they're bedding." The memory of my last conversation with Hargur caught at my throat, and I had to push myself on. "You don't have to *show* me. Just tell me. When you're with Lobik... What does he do, that you like? What makes you tingle?"

She held her hands to her face, and looked at me, eyes huge. "I don't think I can."

To make it easier for her, I tucked my legs up on the bed and turned so I wasn't looking at her, though I kept an eye on the door and window. "Well, shall I talk about things I like?" I said. "Then you can tell me if it's the same for you. I don't know how different our bodies are. Now, breasts." I knew she had those, I'd seen when the sea breeze blew her gown against her on the trip over. Although if she'd been wearing full Gudain costume I never would have.

She made a faint noise, that might have contained a question.

"I like it when they're touched," I said. "Not too rough. Nothing worse than someone acting like they're milking a cow. Or that thing when they pull on your nipples like they're trying to get a cork out of a bottle."

I heard a stifled squeak, and risked a glance. She still had her hands over her mouth, but her eyes were squinched up with amusement. "People do that?"

"Oh, yeah. Much nicer when they just stroke. Or kiss. Or lick. You?"

Barely above a whisper, she said, "Kissing. Kissing is nice."

"Where?"

"On... on the breasts."

"You like his tongue? I've an Ikinchli friend," (at least, I hoped I still did; if things here went badly, I might never again be able to drink in Kittack's bar – or do any of the other things I enjoyed doing with him). "He's amazing with his tongue."

"You have done... this... with an Ikinchli?"

"Oh, yes. Very much so and quite often." I sighed. I was feeling a bit deprived, one way and another. I tried to get back to the matter in hand. "Other places than the breasts? Thighs, maybe? Having your thighs stroked or kissed?"

"That's nice, too."

"How about between them? What do you like there?"

There was a long silence. I didn't look at her, but stared at the hangings. Dark blue lilies, done too large, heavy heads bent as though in sorrow.

"When he strokes... There's a place where I join, that is very sensitive. And stroked the right way, that is very pleasant." Her voice had strengthened a little; she sounded more, now, as though she were discussing what to have for dinner. If that was how she felt easiest talking, then I wasn't going to stop her.

Sounded like our anatomies had some similarity, too, though I wasn't sure about the 'join' part. "Slow, fast?"

"Slow. Then fast."

"What about when he's inside you? What do you like him to do?"

Silence.

"Once he is inside me, I don't care," she said, finally. "The feel of him, the feel of him, oh, Great Artificer, I love him so much."

Well, that wasn't going to help poor Malleay.

"But you do *notice* how he feels?"

She gave a little choke of laughter. "Yes. He feels wonderful. Either side."

"Oh, right, of course. Well, Ikinchli are usually pretty symmetrical. But you enjoy the actual sensation."

"A little more so in one than the other. It seems I am not so symmetrical."

I wondered for a moment if we were talking about back door play, but then it struck me. "You have two," I said.

"Yes."

Ikinchli males have two penises. Why wouldn't Gudain women have two vaginas? And she must have had them before her transformation. 'Mated at the same time to both a Gudain and an Ikinchli' obviously meant *exactly* that.

It also made sense of the Gudain men and their snakes. Their Great Artificer was having a bit of a laugh, if you ask me.

"Right, well. If you like things in one more than the other, then I'd suggest you guide the gentleman to the one which works better for you. You don't have to *say* anything, if you find that difficult; just use your hands. Now, generally I like things to start off slowly in there, and get faster, which is convenient because that works for most of the men I bed. What about you? I know you like it, and that's good, but there must be some things that feel particularly pleasant?"

"If he... if he touches my breast... while he's..."

"Good."

And so the conversation went on, until I had enough, at least, to give Malleay some idea. If he was willing to listen, of course. Enthemmerlee had relaxed a little, though she still found it easier to talk if I wasn't looking at her.

At the end, I couldn't resist asking. "So with both of them... that must have taken some arranging," I said. "The first time I tried that I fell out of the bed. Twice."

She gave a hitch of laughter. "Yes, so did I! It was most embarrassing."

"You need a bigger bed, then."

"You think the three of us... Oh, I don't know if..."

"You've done it once, my dear. If you all *want* to do it again, I see no good reason why you shouldn't." Oops, the 'my dear' was a bit of a slip – she was my employer, after all. But she didn't seem to notice. "If you do, don't be surprised if the boys discover they enjoy each other, too, though."

"This happens?"

"You know, you really need to come to Scalentine for longer next time. It happens. It happens with women, too. It happens with people of any gender, including those who are more than one."

"I had no idea. How fascinating."

"I would have thought it would be mentioned in the Moral Statutes," I said. "Places that have lots of rules about sex often have a problem with it, I've never really been sure why."

"I don't think the people who created the Statutes had any idea that such things were possible," she said. "There is in fact no Statute against what we did. The idea that a Gudain woman would *voluntarily* bed with an Ikinchli is simply not considered."

"I'll eat my hat if you're the only one who's ever done it," I said.

"You do not have a hat," she said. "You think so?"

"Well, if they've managed to avoid the *privaiya* smoke for long enough," I said.

CHAPTER
SIXTEEN

I RETREATED TO my own room to change my shirt, which had suffered slightly from my hasty supper. Rikkinnet gave me a frosty look as she left. That was a bridge that needed mending, but right now I didn't have any more tact left in me.

I'd barely got my clean shirt on when someone bashed on the door.

I opened it, sword in hand, to see Captain Tantris, two of the guard, Rikkinnet, and the seneschal. Again. "What is it?"

Captain Tantris stood with his mouth open, as did his two guards, as though they'd been frozen in mid-explanation. Tantris was flushing a dark, unhealthy green. Rikkinnet hissed, "Is maybe a little trouble. Out by the gate."

"Right, I'll be there. Captain?" Neither he nor his guards had moved; he was staring very hard at a point somewhere to the left of my ear. The guards... weren't.

Honestly. Gudain are mammals, and not *that* different from humans. I knew this lot had seen breasts at some point in their lives, however long ago. I did my shirt up, slung on the nearest bits of armour, and shouldered past them. "If you're that easily distracted, better hope that no assassins turn up naked," I said.

They weren't assassins. They were just... Ikinchli. Some sat outside the gate, patient, quiet, with babies clinging to their shoulders, impervious to the constant slow drizzle. Some came walking up through the darkness, left something by the gate, and walked away again. Fish. A root vegetable. A piece of parchment scrawled with words.

Standing there in the night, the rain whispering down all around, falling sparkling through the soft lamplight from the gatehouse, I remembered a temple with the sound of the sea coming through the doorway. A young girl laying out her basket of pitiful treasures at the feet of what she thought was a goddess.

A sudden brutal shudder took me, all my flesh clenching tight to my bones.

"Babylon?" Rikkinnet said.

"Nothing. I don't see a threat here." If there was a threat to Enthemmerlee, surely Fain would have been aware of it. Mind, Fey oaths are twisty, they seldom work in the way you might expect.

"What if one of them decides to climb the fence? Eh?" Tantris growled.

"They're not stupid," I said. I walked up to the fence. "Hey. Anyone here planning to cause trouble?"

"Like they'd *tell* you," Tantris said.

A few of the Ikinchli exchanged glances, then looked at me. Rikkinnet snapped out a stream of liquid-hissing Ikinchli phrases.

An older male pushed himself to his feet, and walked up to the gate. He limped badly, and even in the flickering firelight I could see long twisting scars on his back and legs. The gate-guard moved forward. The Ikinchli stopped a few feet away, and said something to Rikkinnet.

She said, "They are hoping to see the Itnunnacklish, that is all."

"They really think she'd be wandering about out here this time of night?" Tantris said. "So Ikinchli aren't stupid, eh?"

"Captain Tantris?" I said.

"What?"

"Insulting a large number of people who can certainly understand you, even if they don't always choose to speak

Lithan, and who up until now have been behaving perfectly peaceably, is not necessarily wise. Nor is insulting the Ikinchli Ambassador to Scalentine, who is standing next to you, in case anyone had failed to inform you of the fact."

"The wha..." Tantris turned to look at Rikkinnet, who was examining the tip of her knife with every appearance of unconcern except for her tail, which was ticking back and forth like that of a cat about to pounce. "She's the... You're the..."

"I am, yes." She turned away, towards the gates, and raised her voice so the watching Ikinchli could hear her. "And as the Ambassador to Scalentine, I tell you, the Itnunnacklish is sleeping now. If you cause no trouble, no one will drive you away..."

I looked at the guards, hard. They glanced at Tantris, who scowled.

"...but she will not come out tonight," Rikkinnet went on.

"It doesn't matter," a young voice said in the darkness. "We watch with her. We hold her in our hearts. We ask the ancestors that they should watch over her and keep her safe. We bear witness."

"You don't think she is safe, here among her family?" I said.

"Surrounded by Gudain, guarded by Gudain?" someone else said. "No, we do not think she is safe. We do not know if she is even alive."

"Not all of us are Gudain," Rikkinnet said.

"No, we're not, thank you," I said.

"And who are you to guard the most precious Itnunnacklish?"

"My name's Babylon Steel. I am here as her bodyguard, and her friend."

Their eyes went back to Rikkinnet. She gave me a long look, then said something else in Ikinchli. There were a few rustles of laughter in the dark. I recognised a couple of words, and grinned. Funny how the obscene ones are the ones you learn first in any language; after, 'a drink, please.' Fine by me if knowing what I did meant they felt better about me.

"No trouble?" Rikkinnet said.

"No."

Whispers, a rising chorus of pleas and declarations.

"No trouble."

"We don't want trouble, we just want to watch over her."

"To be near her."

"*Drican Thelash.*"

"She is the one promised."

"Itnunnacklish."

They quieted; the pupils of their eyes, brilliant yellow with the glow of the fire, fixed on the house where their hope lay sleeping.

As we walked back, I glanced at Rikkinnet. She caught my look. "What?"

"If I offended you, I'm sorry."

She shrugged. "You are not Ikinchli."

"No, I'm not. And I can't know how it's been for you. I hope... I hope it gets better."

"Yes." It seemed like that was all I was getting. But I hoped I'd rebuilt enough of a bridge to walk on.

WE SWAPPED GUARD partway through the night, and I managed a little sleep. I woke to grey light to find my worries had woken up before me, and were waiting around the bed.

I had told Captain Tantris that I would be on the practice ground at daybreak; well, since I wasn't going to get any more sleep, I might as well go straight there.

Rikkinnet took one look at me and said, "Training?"

"Yeah. But..." I glanced at Enthemmerlee's door. "You need to sleep. Damn those guards. We need someone else we can trust."

"For now, we have to make do."

So I went to Bergast's door. I raised my hand to knock, and heard him muttering. Dreaming, or already awake? "Bergast?"

"What? Wait, who is it?"

"It's Babylon."

"Just a moment!"

He sounded embarrassed, almost panicked.

"You've nothing I haven't seen before, Bergast," I said. "If you're human. You *are* human, are you?" Acting on some half-felt suspicion, I shoved at the door, which opened to reveal Bergast, fully dressed, frantically shoving books and papers into a pile. The candle in his lantern had burned to a stub.

"Do you always burst in that way?" he said. He picked up a shirt that was lying on the bed and dropped it on top of some other papers. "I must ask about laundry."

Funny, that shirt had looked perfectly clean, and crisply folded, to me. Now, though, it did need the laundry; a brown stain of ink was blooming on one cuff as I watched.

Suddenly I didn't want to leave him to watch Enthemmerlee. Not without someone else to keep an eye on him. "Your turn on watch," I said, and left before he could do more than blink.

Fain was sleeping nearby. If anything threatened Enthemmerlee, perhaps the oath would drag him awake, but it wasn't something I wanted to put my trust in. I went to his room, instead.

He opened his door on the first knock. He was, sadly, also fully dressed. Hadn't *anyone* slept tonight? "Trouble?" he said.

"Can you watch Enthemmerlee for a bit? I have to deal with the guard, and Rikkinnet needs to sleep."

"Where is Bergast?"

"Bergast is there, and he may be effective with magic, but if someone comes screaming down the corridor with an axe in each hand, I'd rather bet on you."

"I am flattered. Very well." He picked up his swordbelt and strapped it on as we walked. It had the effect of giving the Gudain robe a waist, and Fain an oddly religious look. I left him with Bergast, who was looking bewildered and somewhat grumpy, and headed out.

I passed the seneschal on my way, scolding one of the servants, who was carrying a breakfast tray. "I will hear no more foolishness. The gentleman is a distinguished visitor. He is to eat in his rooms and you are to take his food to him."

"But that beast. And he looks at me as though..." The maid dropped into Ikinchli and the seneschal stiffened.

"The lady Selinecree has given these orders. Do you wish to go and tell her that you plan to refuse them?"

I butted in. "Seneschal?"

"Madam. Please excuse this display."

I looked at the maid, and tried for a reassuring smile. "Is it Adept Mokraine that you're taking food to?"

She made an odd bobbing motion, somewhere between a curtsey and a flinch.

"He's all right. He's a bit strange, but he won't hurt you. Just don't let that beast brush against you. It's not dangerous if it does" – well, so far as I knew, it wasn't – "it's just unpleasant. And don't worry if he doesn't eat much of what you bring him, he never does."

"Yes, miss. Thank you, miss." She scuttled off, not looking much happier.

"Lady Selinecree suggested he had food taken to his rooms?"

"Yes. She thought it would be more comfortable."

For him, or for everyone else, I wondered? Still, it might be easier on him than dealing with the undercurrents of the dining room. Though, if he actually fed, he'd probably enjoy them.

THE TRAINING-GROUND WAS deserted in the dim predawn light. The ground was soft after all the rain. I ran through some basic warm-up moves, then went into my standard training set, as best I could without someone to train against. Unfortunately doing it by myself didn't distract my mind as much as I'd have hoped. I pushed harder, trying to concentrate on footwork, on speed and motion and breath; to get into that state of mind that feels mindless, where everything is focused on the motion of the body.

I saw movement from the edge of my eye. Didn't break the routine, slowed to a halt only at the end of the set. Tantris was watching, arms folded. "Morning," I said.

He nodded. He looked a little pouchy about the eyes, but he'd shaved, and his head was slightly higher than the last time I'd seen him. "So," he said. "Can you turn my rabble into a bunch of gilded lilies, then? In time for the ceremony?"

Sweet All, that was almost humour.

"No," I said. "I can't. There isn't time, and it's not my job. I'm still thinking about hiring in."

"You'll get nothing," he said. "Not now. There's a lot of nervous people out there. They've been hiring everything there is to hire, including foreigners, at twice the normal rates."

So to a populace already bubbling with tension had now been added a whole bunch of mercenaries. Now, I'm not one to make assumptions about mercenaries. I don't have to; I've been one. There are a handful of decent people who end up selling sword for one reason or another, but too many of the ones I've met are little more than enthusiastic killers with the morals of a vulture in a famine.

Just what Incandress needed.

Some of my thought must have shown on my face. Tantris was watching me with a twisted smile.

"Well," I said. "Up to you, then, isn't it?" And I walked away.

It was a gamble. But I thought, or hoped, that he had some pride to salvage.

"Wait!"

I stopped, and turned around.

"Last night," he said. If he was about to make some comment about my state of dress, I was more than ready to slap him, but that didn't seem to be it. He had his helmet clutched in his hands, and was twisting the chin-strap.

"There wasn't any trouble overnight, was there?" I said.

"No. It's just... It's real, isn't it? At least, they believe it is."

"You didn't."

"I..." He looked down at his helmet. "I don't know if I do, still. But if they believe it, there's going to be lots who do, aren't there? Sca... Ikinchli and Gudain both."

"Yes."

He rubbed a hand over his neck and looked at me; his eyes were frightened. "I've been in a few scraps," he said. "Got sent to fight in the border wars. It's not like I've never seen action. But that was twenty-some years ago. And this, this is different. I've heard the guard. Had to pull two of 'em apart last night. Thought the whole lot of 'em were going to go at it for a minute. Never had that sort of trouble, never."

Or if you did, you pretended it wasn't happening, I thought.

"What are you asking of me, Captain?"

"Advice, I suppose. I don't know what to do for the best."

Your bloody job, I managed – just – not to say. "All right. The ones you had to pull apart, where are they?"

"I put them in lockup."

"Good. Who else do you know is hard-line, one way or the other?"

"I *don't*," he nearly wailed. "It's never come up before!"

"What do you fear, Captain?"

"What?"

"What do you fear? What is the worst that could happen?"

"The worst? There's a riot, someone in the family gets hurt, or killed..."

"And why does that matter? To you. You don't care one way or the other for the Itnunnacklish, so why do you care at all?"

"It's my *job!*" He looked down again and muttered, "It's what I've got."

"Then do it. Dammit all, man, I used Chitherlee's name to work them up, and I found out what she meant to them before I'd been here two days! How long have you been captaining this lot? You've got to know what they fear, what they'll fight for."

"Well, the child, yes. They're all fond of the child."

"But it's not enough. Chitherlee's not joining us for the ball or the other ceremonies, is she? We need 'em roused, Captain."

"Oh, they're roused all right. Boiling like a pot of soup, they are."

"You *know* that's not what I meant."

"I'm a waste," Tantris said, his shoulders slumping. "You were right, I could have made something of them. Now it's too late."

"You really think this is a time for self-pity?" That got me a glare. Good. "All right. I'll talk to them. But you'd better bloody well be prepared to back me to the hilt, or I'll see you gutted. You got any plans for the layout today?"

"Bowmen on both the carriages, and in with the spears. Standard point and rear-guard."

"Who's best with a bow?" I said.

"Dentor. But he's in lockup."

"Oh."

"I put them through target practice yesterday. That Sticky, she pulled a sling, got the target neat as you like. I've put her on top of the second carriage. She won't have the distance of an archer, but she's fast." He looked apologetic. "Can't give her a bow, see; weapons laws. Scalys... Ikinchli ain't allowed edged weapons."

"Oh, that's helpful. Right. Get 'em out here, Captain."

"What are you going to say to them?"

"You'll find out. Go."

He went.

What *was* I going to say to them?

The Avatar of Babaska; goddess of love and war, could turn a rabble into an army, could take a terrified sixteen-year-old who'd never held a sword and turn him into a battle-leader worthy of the name.

But I wasn't the Avatar of Babaska, not any more. I could still fight, and I could still seduce; but without the stolen powers I'd once had, how could I turn this squabbling, ill-led mess into something that would protect Enthemmerlee?

I rubbed the scar on my jaw. It was itching. *Moon's fattening,* I thought randomly.

The moon fattens, the planes dance. It is not syzygy, but the ways are open, Ebi that was, Avatar that was.

And there was that tickle at the back of my brain.

"Oh, no, you don't," I muttered.

By ones and twos, they arrived. They did look smarter. No match for the Palace guard, but better than they had been. Even Dentor's cronies were looking trimmed up.

But there were still a lot of sulky faces, a lot of eyes flickering from side to side, a lot of hands gripping weapons too tight. There was more yanking their tails than Dentor and a captain who'd let the reins slacken.

"All right!" Tantris barked. "Going to get some expert advice here. You'd better listen."

Not the most elaborate introduction, but it would serve. I hoped.

I ran through the standard precautions, told them what to look out for; kept it short and simple and hoped at least some of it went in.

"All right," I said. "Any questions?"

One of the Ikinchli raised a hand. "If we are attacked by Gudain, what then?"

"What do you mean, what then?" I said. "You defend the Lady Enthemmerlee. What else would you do?"

"If an Ikinchli harms a Gudain, is death."

"What? Surely not if you're defending your sworn family? Tantris?"

The captain shrugged. "They wouldn't use the laws that way. Wouldn't make any sense."

I wasn't sure about that; laws aren't always about sense. But it wasn't as if I could get 'em changed. And guards who can't actually risk bruising anyone are no damn use. "If you are defending your family," I said, "I am sure people will see reason. I don't want anyone overreacting, mind. No jumping at shadows.

"We're here to protect the family. I will do my job. I trust you to do yours. If you fail because you couldn't stop something, but you tried, that's one thing. Try, and fail, and I'll be the last to blame you."

I leaned forward, and pinned the sulkiest-looking, one by one, with my gaze.

"Fail because you don't believe this job is worth your time, because you were lazy, or careless, or more interested in some private quarrel, and you will discover there are much worse things than being confined to barracks. Lots worse. And one of them is me."

There was a flicker, then. In me, and in them, as though something had run through us all, a shudder of something bright-dark and molten.

No, I thought. *Back off. I don't want you.*

But whatever it was had gone; might not even have been anything but my own unease. A few of them looked shaken, yes, but that was what I'd been aiming for.

"Right," I said. "Do your job, get the family through this, and I will personally buy every single one of you enough drink to drown in as soon as Patinarai is over. Any questions?"

There weren't.

"Form up," I said.

Running through basic drill, most of them weren't *entirely* terrible. Just sloppy, out of practice, undertrained and ill-disciplined. Some took the opportunity to slack off the minute my eye was off them, while others kept going by themselves, Stikinisk among them. What she'd said about private lessons gave me an idea.

I drew Tantris to the side. "I want four of them, two Ikinchli, two Gudain. I think I know which ones, but I need you to tell me if any of them are inclined to be a problem." I pointed out the four I'd picked.

"When you say 'problem,'" he said, "what sort of problem?"

"Any sort. Especially if they have funny ideas about the Itnunnacklish."

Tantris sighed. "You've got to understand something," he said. "They're *bonded*. A family guard... This lot may not be much, but they're in a contract. The guard is loyal to the family, and the family to the guard."

"And they no longer see the Itnunnacklish as family?"

"If there hadn't been this talk of her having them... us... turned out, then, well, I'm not saying all of them would be happy about it, but there wouldn't be so much bad feeling."

"Who started this talk?"

He shrugged. "Dunno. Just started hearing it, and then it was everywhere before you could blink."

"Have any of you actually *asked* the Itnunnacklish?"

"Speak direct to a member of the Family?" His face went slack with horror. "That's not *done*."

Oh for... "All right. So which of them can I rely on?" I said.

Relieved to have the subject changed, Tantris looked at the ones I'd picked. "That Stikinisk, she's no trouble. And she's fast. The other scaly, Vasik, yes, well, I don't know him so well, but he's all right. Vorenay, yes. Bassin..." He hesitated, and his gaze shifted away from mine.

"One of Dentor's crew?"

He shrugged.

"Not him, then," I said. "The chunky lad, with the broad shoulders. Him."

"Koverey."

"He'll do."

"What are you planning?"

"You'll see. You," I said, pointing to Stikinisk. "Over here." She stepped out.

"And you" – I pointed to the chunky lad – "Koverey. And you" – the Ikinchli male, slight but whip-quick – "Vasik?"

"Yes."

"Right. We're making you the core. You come with me."

I ran them through a series of scenarios, using each in turn as a stand-in for Enthemmerlee. I worked them hard, and praised them loudly, while Tantris carried on with the rest.

I worked them hard enough to feel it but not so hard they'd be useless this afternoon, then dismissed them. With extra praise and a nip out of my flask for the core.

Then I went over the forthcoming occasions with Tantris. Of course he didn't know the layout of the Ancestor Caves, but we could work out basic strategy. It's always the same, in any case; get and stay between the target and any trouble, and if the trouble gets more than you can deal with, get the target away, whatever else is going on behind you.

In some ways, the Enkantishak ceremony was the most worrying in security terms. A huge cave, with only one entrance or exit. A good thing for stopping the dodgy getting in. A decidedly bad thing if the dodgy were already there and you wanted to get your client out safe.

The ceremony sounded simple enough: prayers to the ancestors, then something called the *Ipash Dok,* which was a ceremonial gift, a sort of box, which Enthemmerlee would lay on an altar, and open. It was supposed to contain the hopes of the supplicant, or something.

A box with hope in it sounded like a good thing, but for some silly reason it gave me a little chill, as though it reminded me of something I'd rather forget.

On my way back, I saw Dentor slouching among the outbuildings. There was something about the way he was walking that gave me pause. His usual thug's stride had a furtive slither about it. Besides, he was supposed to be in lockup.

I decided it wouldn't hurt any to see where he was going. I had an itchy feeling about Dentor. First I'd knocked him off his perch, then Tantris had started taking back some authority, and Dentor struck me as the sort who might get spiteful.

A barn, still relatively sturdy, stood by itself, being slowly strangled by those same hairy grey vines that grew all over the captain's garden. These, perhaps getting more sun, had broken out in unwholesome-looking fleshy pink and yellow flowers, as big as my hand and none the prettier for it. They put me in mind of wounds that were going bad.

I saw a flicker of pale blue inside the barn: someone there, waiting. Dentor took a last look around, and stepped inside.

I edged around until I was under the nearest trees; I couldn't get any closer without giving myself away. All I could hear was a faint murmur of voices. Dammit. The place might have been specifically chosen with an eye to its lack of cover.

Dentor hadn't struck me as that sharp. Maybe I'd misjudged him. Or maybe he wasn't the one who'd chosen it.

Then I heard a laugh... a female laugh, in that low register that, done right, is like a well-placed touch. It's a talent, a laugh like that; I've never quite managed it.

Seduction. And Dentor, of all people.

Well, so much for that. The rain had gone from misty to damn near solid so I trudged off before I could drown where I stood, feeling somewhat foolish.

CHAPTER
SEVENTEEN

LATER THAT AFTERNOON I changed, again – Bergast wasn't the only one who needed some laundry done – and lined up with the others by the main doors, all in our finery; well, everyone else was, and I'd given my gear as much of a shine as I could. Fain had managed to get his clothes cleaned and had obtained, from somewhere, a very fancy embroidered cloak with a high ruff collar; unlike the rest of Gudain clothing, it suited him. I had no idea where Mokraine had wandered off to.

I could hear the tramp of feet outside; the guard. I bit my lip, wondering what state they'd be in.

The seneschal opened the doors.

For a wonder, it had stopped raining. Low light flooded the courtyard, and the guard, and dazzled back from button, boot and helm.

On closer inspection, the spit-and-polish job was pretty hasty, but all things considered, it wasn't bad. The captain himself was in what I assumed was his seldom-used kept-for-best uniform; around the middle the buttons were straining so hard that if the thread gave way they'd be making holes in passers-by, but at least they were shiny.

"Why, how splendid you all look!" Enthemmerlee said. "I am very fortunate to have such fine soldiers to accompany me."

"Present arms!" Tantris shouted, and with only a little fumbling, they did.

* * *

I WATCHED THE two great heavy coaches with the lizard symbol on the roof leave, past the Ikinchli waiting outside the gate, drawn back either side of the roadway: a crush of dun and green and brilliantly embroidered waistcoats sewn with fragments of shell and bone and glass, some in the livery of the great houses. I even saw some of the Palace purple. They held little ones up on their shoulders, straining for a glimpse.

Itnunnacklish, Itnunnacklish.

Guard uniforms around the coaches.

"Right," I said. "Everyone ready?"

An old trick. The fancy coaches sent off empty, escorted by a few of the guard, and some house servants in guard uniforms. The actual party going out the back way, in plain old coaches.

Mokraine opened the door of the coach and settled himself next to Enthemmerlee. "Mokraine? You're joining us?" I said.

He gave a weary smile. "The young lady was kind enough to invite me." Someone had lent him a clean robe. It was Gudain design, though perhaps an old-fashioned one, since the ruff beneath the cloth was only a few inches wide. Oddly, it gave Mokraine an impressive look, like an ancient king.

Selinecree opened the door of the coach. "Oh, you're here. Good," she said, and hurried off to one of the others.

Bergast, a moment later, opened the door, took one look, and said, "Ah, well, since you're here, Madam Steel, I'd better be in the other coach."

"What?" I said. But he had scuttled away. Mokraine opened one eye, sniffed, and closed it again.

"I do not like this," Enthemmerlee said, as we rolled away. "I hate to deceive them."

"I know they want to see you. I know you want to show them that you're here, that you exist. But they're not all your friends. You know this." I turned my shield so she could see the dent, where the stone had hit. "Remember him?"

She sighed. "Kankish. Yes."

"And we still have to get there, so please, stay inside the coach. It can protect you from an arrow better than I can."

As we headed up the hill to the Palace, the air thickened. That strange alchemical tang became stronger, tainted with rotten eggs. In the grounds themselves was a thing I'd never seen before: a lake of mud, steaming and bubbling like a giant stew, the bubbles as big around as plates. They struggled up slowly, expanded, and broke with *pops* and *gloops*. I could feel the heat coming off it.

The Palace's garish patchwork of marble jarred even more in the sunlight, but quickly became background. I was watching for shapes, for movement, out of place. The swarms of people were only that: swarms, vague undifferentiated shapes, unless one of them moved contrary to the flow.

Ikinchli waited patiently in the courtyard; the Palace guard lined up by the inner gates. They looked impressive, certainly. Their uniforms were so black they seemed to cut a hole in the colours that surrounded them. Enthemmerlee stepped out of the carriage, and a whisper shifted across the crowd. Her father stepped down, an order was shouted, and the Palace guard snapped their spears to the salute, slamming the butts as one against the marble floor.

Other carriages drew up. That slamming salute was repeated as each of the members of the Ten Families appeared. The disti didn't like the salutes, tossing their heads and whipping their great muscular tails every time those spearbutts hit the floor.

Every window looking down on the court was crammed with faces, both Ikinchli and Gudain, though seldom at the same window.

Enthemmerlee took her father's arm. His face was held in a kind of frozen haughtiness; hers was calm, though pale.

More whispering. I caught a few words of spiteful nastiness from some pudding-faced Gudain. I thought Enthemmerlee heard; I know one of the guard did, I saw him smirk.

I watched for the quick or unforeseen move, the flicker of metal, a hand raised.

Into the main doorway. Heavy perfumes and lamp-oil, and the pounding of booted feet in the low flat rooms. And warm; steamy-warm. The citrus tang of Ikinchli sweat, the heavier, more metallic smell of Gudain. Scented braziers and crisply-dressed servants, a high archway carved with lilies.

Plenty of space, for all that it was a major social occasion. These rooms, too, were built for more people than now filled them. People chattering in little groups. As we entered the conversation faltered; then it rose again, mixed with a deal of whispering and sidelong glances.

A servant walked up with a tray of savouries, made to look like tiny birds and frogs and flowers. Enthemmerlee smiled and took one. A flicker of blue at her cuff. Good girl, she remembered the jug.

A cluster of foreign dignitaries; most of the crowd Gudain. Lobik stood alone, until Malleay went up to him and started talking, ignoring the cupped hands, the looks and whispers. I clung to Enthemmerlee's side, as did the core. Bergast stayed close. Good.

"I heard it was some sickness that deformed her." A voice, not low enough. Enthemmerlee must have heard, but she didn't show any sign. "Terribly sad, really. But why such a charade?"

"A charade? You don't think there's any truth in the idea, then?" A new voice.

"Oh, don't be absurd. It's a disgusting idea."

"Not everyone thinks so."

"Oh, well, if you will side with these *revolutionaries*. You know half of them don't even attend *privaiya*?"

"It's a big world out there, my dear. We're in danger of looking like throwbacks."

"And since when did you care about the opinions of the outside world?"

"As an outsider, I would say, it is always worth being careful of the opinions of others. One never knows when they may be of use." Fain. Playing the charming merchant for all he's worth.

"Well I think it's *unnatural*."

I let the words flow around me.

A few of the curious strolled up, watching Enthemmerlee with bright, avid eyes. Others did their best to pretend she didn't exist, that there was a sort of smudge in the air where she was standing.

The crowd made me uneasy. The Gudain carried themselves so rigidly, it was like being surrounded by crudely animated chess-pieces. And I kept seeing the same sets of features repeated, with slight variations, on different faces, male and female. As though someone had made four or five woodcuts, and used them hurriedly, over and over, but the wood was soft, and with each stamp grew blurrier. Odd projections, a lump where an ear should be, slurred speech. A grown man who giggled then suddenly flung a cake away from him and bawled like a furious child, a watchful Ikinchli male always at his side, occasionally wiping his chin. There were no actual children at all.

"Babylon?" Fain said. "Over there. And yes, I will stay with Enthemmerlee, I can hardly do otherwise, remember?"

I could see the little cluster of foreigners. I motioned to Rikkinnet. She nodded.

I slipped away, found a room where I could take off the helmet and attempt to smooth my hair. I slipped on a plain tabard of blue silk, which I'd brought with me, over my armour. I frowned at the colour, something tickling my memory, but it wouldn't come. I went back out, to mingle and listen, still keeping one eye on Enthemmerlee.

I moved around, edging my way towards the foreigners. Picking up fragments like a magpie.

"...hear she had to hire a *foreign* bodyguard because her own guard wouldn't take the job."

"They're here, aren't they?"

"I wonder what they bribed them with..."

"...that the foreigner? Funny, if it wasn't for the colour, she could almost be one of us..."

Presumably they thought I should be flattered. Or was deaf.

"...my own daughter. It's impossible to talk to her. She's fallen under the influence of these agitators. She won't come to *privaiya*..."

"...lose all sense of proper behaviour..."

"But surely the Moral Statutes..."

"Well of course, if they were ever caught at it. But I heard only the other day..."

"*I* heard it's something the scalys are putting in the water."

"Oh, what nonsense you talk, Mansenay. Putting something in the water indeed! If people are behaving differently, maybe it's because they've had the sense to stop doping themselves with *privaiya* smoke."

"That's disgusting talk. I suppose you think being an agitator is *fashionable*. Just because the young people are doing it."

"First I'm an agitator for wanting justice and now I'm only doing it because it's *fashionable*?"

"Well if you're happy with people inciting riots, just don't expect me to pick up your corpse."

"Indeed, the Fenac seem to be far better at inciting a riot than stopping one."

"The Fenac protect the public!"

"Protect that bit of the public who happen to be the right shape, you mean."

"...calling a dressed-up Ikinchli 'Ambassador.' Whatever do the Scalentines take us for?"

"Oh, of course it will never hold. *That* can never be considered one of the Advisors to the Crown."

"Enboryay has obviously decided the opposite."

"Well, what choice has he, unless he wants to be exiled to one of the family farms?"

"Really, they can't..."

"Oh, they can. There is nothing in the Statutes that says otherwise. She is of age and in her right mind."

"If what I hear is true... and after all, she has officially *wed* them both... she is most certainly *not*. She couldn't be."

A brief, appalled silence, and a sudden frantic chatter of irrelevancies.

I was glad to reach the other end of the room, and the silence surrounding the three foreigners.

There was an Empire delegate – you could tell by the brilliant scarlet and purple sash they wore over the elaborate layered robe that was the current fashion in the Empire court. I didn't know the species, or the gender; only a nose and mouth and a few inches of skin, patterned with rich brown whorls (tattoos or natural, I couldn't tell) were visible between the collar and the elaborate headdress. I wondered what the delegate was doing there; judging by what Malleay had said, the Empire didn't want to get involved in this particular local difficulty, but presumably they thought the situation worth keeping an eye on.

There was also a Monishish and a tall Dithanion.

"May a favourable wind fill your sails," I said, bowing. "Babylon Steel."

The Empire delegate nodded. "And may all your ships come safe to harbour. Kinesitra dahana Oristin."

The Monishish interrupted his conversation to wave at me. "Bententen Ententen Enthasa Enthasik." Which might have been his name, with luck. His long, fragile-looking fingers glimmered with rings.

The Dithanion tipped her long bony head. I knew the Dithanion had some exquisitely complex greeting rituals, none of which I could remember, but as a trader among barbarians, she had presumably got used to such ignorance; she fluttered

her mouth-fringes at me, and said, "Greetings, Babylon Steel."
Her voice was flutelike in the upswing, with a sort of moan in
the lower register, like a mournful fiddle. She told me her name,
a short but complex piece of music, and completely beyond
my ability to pronounce. "You are here to see the Patinarai
ceremonies?"

"I'm providing security," I said. I didn't say who I was
providing it for.

"Ah. A much-needed service, at this time, I think," the
Monishish said.

"Indeed. Did you bring your own security?"

"Always," they said together, and looked at each other with
amusement.

"One was not expecting," the Dithanion said, "to require
such a degree of it. Next time I think I shall take a different
route."

"I must admit, I was surprised to see any foreign visitors still
here," I said. "Under the circumstances..."

The Dithanion pursed her fringed lips, her version of a shrug.
"My business brought me in this direction, and I admit I was
curious; I wanted to see the Itnunnacklish everyone speaks of.
But as to actual trade, no, I think not, not now. I shall regard
this as a brief and interesting diversion."

The Monishish folded his long fingers in on themselves. "A
pity. They have some superb hardwoods here, and the marble,
of course, but everyone is waiting on the outcome of this
current situation." He swung his long-necked, warty-skinned
head towards the Empire delegate. "Are they not?"

The delegate managed, elegantly, to be at that very moment
looking elsewhere – at some long-lost acquaintance, perhaps –
and thus able to ignore the question without appearing rude.
The Monishish turned back to me. "Should things resolve
themselves, so that supplies and labour can be relied upon, we
may be looking at potential trade."

"Are there other traders still here?" I said.

"Not that I have met. Had we not been somewhat delayed, we would not be either." He opened his fingers, fanlike. "There is another foreigner, though. From Scalentine, I believe."

I tried not to let anything show on my face. "Oh, really? But not here to trade?"

"He seems to be here mostly in order to talk," the Dithanion fluted. "Of which he does a great deal, to little point."

The delegate excused him – or her – self and moved away. The Monishish made a gesture at their departing back. "In disgrace, I think," he said. "I wonder why?"

"Who knows?" the Dithanion said. "The Empire being what it is, the delegate could simply have displayed the wrong décor at a reception."

"In disgrace? What do you mean?" I said.

"A civilian delegate in high regard would not be found in a country of little power, on the verge of civil war, in which the Empire has shown absolutely no interest of late," said the Monishish.

"Unless the Empire is playing a double game," said the Dithanion. "Or did not realise that the situation was, in fact, as unstable as it appears."

The two of them began an extended examination of current Empire politics; a subject about which I knew little and cared less. I extracted myself politely and moved off.

Scalentine? Someone here from Scalentine? They couldn't mean Fain – he'd not been out, except to the Palace. Who the hells could it be? Maybe this was the clue Fain had been waiting for. I had to find out.

I didn't have to wait long. "Well, of course, this sort of situation is inevitable when too much power gets into the wrong hands."

I *knew* that voice. I turned.

Black hair, chunky build, several chins.

Oh, dragonfarts.

Angrifon Filchis. Angrifon bloody Filchis. What in the name of everything sane was he doing here?

Fain was deep in conversation with a group of Gudain; I moved over to him and waited. He caught my eye, eventually.

"What is it?" he said.

"Don't look round. There's someone here from Scalentine. You might want to keep your head down."

"Who?"

Filchis was standing with his hands clasped behind him, his chest (or rather, the upper part of his not inconsiderable stomach) thrust out, and an air of trying to look down his nose at everything.

"Oh, yes," I heard him say to the Gudain male standing at his side. "Of course, you know, humans and Gudain must be of the same line, one can always tell a superior species."

"Angrifon Filchis. Leader of the Builders."

"*Here?*"

"Yeah. As if things weren't bad enough..."

"Go talk to him."

"He might recognise me," I said.

"A client?"

"Oh, please. I'd sooner bed a maggot."

"We need to know why he's here."

"Fain..."

"It is what I hired you for, Madam Steel."

"*I don't want to talk to him,*" I said. "If I talk to him I may not be able to stop myself breaking his neck."

"Ah. The threat to the Chief?"

"Among other things, yes."

"If you were to break his neck, apart from causing a diplomatic incident, it might make it much more difficult to find out who is involved in the were murders."

"If you already know *he's* involved, why the hells isn't he under arrest?"

"Because we don't, for sure. And can you imagine the Chief arresting anyone without evidence?"

"No. The Section, on the other hand..." I said.

"You make assumptions."

"Yes."

"Madam Steel, if we have left him running around loose, perhaps we have our reasons. Now, if you please…"

"Oh, all *right*. I'll try."

"Find out anything you can."

Find out anything… I looked around.

Mokraine, oblivious to the concerns of foolish mortals as always, was talking with one of the Ikinchli servants. The servant scurried off as I approached.

"Ah, Babylon." Mokraine looked ghastly; not so much an ancient king as the revenant of one. And he was shivering, slightly but constantly.

"Oh, Mokraine."

"So much emotion, so tangled. So… close. I am a starving man at a banquet." He laughed, a sound so cracked and horrible that several people looked around.

"Would you rather leave? I can get someone to escort you…"

"No. You want something."

"No. No, Mokraine. You should go, you look dreadful."

"There is nowhere to go. Who do you want me to listen to?"

"The… You called it 'leakage.' It doesn't satisfy, does it?"

"No. It makes the hunger worse. It is the scent of a meal, it is not the meal. But I will not eat. I will not lose the last of myself."

If he was getting bombarded by emotions from others without even trying, I wondered just how long he could hold on to the last of himself in any case. "Mokraine, I won't ask you. Please, get out of here. Go somewhere quiet."

"The world is full of noise," Mokraine said. "Except for Darask Fain. He is quiet. So is the Scholar. They have taught him little else, but at least they have taught him to be quiet."

"They have?"

"Oh yes. Fain has a thoroughly defended mind."

"Defended how?"

"It appears to be his nature. The Scholar, on the other hand; he struggles to maintain his walls. A weak mind. Weak and arrogant and mundane."

"Walls? I don't understand."

"He has built defences against me." Mokraine smiled. If I'd been Bergast, that smile would have had me on the next boat back to Scalentine.

"I see," I said. "I think. Well, perhaps he's not comfortable with the idea of you picking up what he's feeling." Although I wondered.

"I could break his walls in a moment, if I wished." He shrugged. "I do not." The hunger in his eyes betrayed him. "I *will* not."

"Oh, Mokraine."

"Do not pity me, Babylon. Everything I am is the result of what I chose. I remember little, but I remember that. I can choose to be other, and I will." His eyes were glittering cinders in his wrecked face; his will, the only thing holding him upright, flared off him like heat.

I couldn't use him, not in his current state. I'd have to sound out Filchis alone. "Take care of yourself. Eat something, at least."

He smiled, again, and this one had some genuine humour in it. "Babylon. You are not old enough to be my mother."

"Well, I feel it," I muttered. I started to move away, only to find he was following me.

"Who is it?"

"No, Mokraine, it's not fair on you."

His thin hand, veined and trembling, clamped on my wrist, icy. "We are not on Scalentine now, Babylon Steel. Do not presume to tell me what I will do."

"Fine, all right!" I extracted my wrist, too easily, from his grip. "It's the tubby bugger over there, the one who looks as though he's just stepped in dogshit and is wondering what the smell is. But he has a disgusting little mind, don't blame me if it gives you indigestion."

"You're angry."

"Yes." The idea that the smug, ugly-minded creature might be involved in a threat to Hargur filled my stomach and throat like a bad meal.

"Now, Mr Filchis," someone asked him. "What is your feeling on the Ikinchli question?"

"Ah, well, if you saw how things were in Scalentine. It's all become so mixed. No one knows where they stand any more. It's hardly fair; one sees so many people who are simply not capable of the offices to which they've been raised, and the fact is, they will be as grateful as anyone once things are returned to their proper order."

"You see a change coming, then?"

"Oh, it is inevitable that natural superiority will assert itself. Here, of course, you have the disadvantage of sheer numbers. These lower races so often breed like rats. Of course they don't care for their children the way we do, having so many of them."

I bit my tongue, hard, unclenched my fists, arranged my face into a simper, fluffed my hair and walked so as to make the tabard sway and swirl about my hips.

"Excuse me, but are you from Scalentine?" I fluted.

"Why, yes, madam." He bowed, looking slightly puzzled.

"I *thought* I recognised the accent. How *charming*. Do tell me, is it true, one can buy things there from the farthest planes? Even Dofrenish perfume?"

"Well, we do have a great deal of passing trade, yes, but I'm no expert on perfumes, I fear."

"What do you trade in?"

"I'm not a trader. I'm here as a representative of certain interests on Scalentine, keeping an eye on developments, you might say."

"But how *intriguing*. What interests? Do tell!"

"Ah, well." He tapped the side of his nose. "One must remain discreet, you know." He reached out a hand. "Angrifon Filchis. Charmed to make your acquaintance, madam...?"

I couldn't avoid taking his hand, not without seeming rude. It was plump and dry.

"Angrifon Filchis?" I fluttered. "Well, I'm sure that's a name I should remember. I expect I shall be hearing it in *very important* circles. Not that I know the slightest *thing* about politics, but I have been known to spot a man with a future, you know. And it seems I'm not the only one. *Someone* thought a great deal of you, to send you into such a situation; I must say, with things so very..." – I looked around, but my chatter had driven off other listeners, for the moment – "so very *tense*, I'm not sure I should be able to keep my head and *observe*."

"Well, I hope that I shall be able to fulfil the trust of my sponsor. And yourself? How did you come to be here, with things as unsettled as they are?"

I waved a hand. "This is what happens when one leaves one's travel arrangements to others. Your sponsor... Perhaps, if I am fortunate enough to visit Scalentine, you could effect an introduction? It's always so useful to know people of influence, when arranging *parties* and so on."

"I'm sure that could be arranged," he said. "Charming ladies are always a welcome new acquaintance, after all. Tell me, where are you from?"

"Oh, a tiny little place you'd never have heard of," I said, which was probably true. "Tell me, this mentor of yours, he's a politician? Don't they have some *strange* arrangement on Scalentine? I've heard that..." – I looked round as though fearful of being overheard – "even someone who isn't, you know, *of the right sort* can achieve office there. It must make things so difficult."

"Well, there are those of us who think it could be better regulated," Filchis said. "But you can be assured that it will be. Quite soon, perhaps. And then" – he smiled – "a lady such as yourself need feel no qualms about visiting."

I have seldom in my life wanted so badly to plant my fist in someone's smile.

I kept my eye on Mokraine as I wittered brainlessly, and when he started to drift away, I extracted myself with a few more phrases of admiration and astonishment, and followed him.

Mokraine staggered, and I got a hand under his arm. "Right, that's it. I'm getting someone to take you back to the house."

"Nonsense," he rasped. "Well, that was quite a performance, Babylon."

"Me or him?"

"You. Very convincingly foolish."

"Thank you."

"As for the little wasp of a fellow..."

"Wasp?"

"A bee, without honey. All swollen fat with poison. Not an incapable mind, but one wrapped about with fear, and resentment; a conviction that someone, somewhere, is robbing him of what he deserves."

"Unfortunately that doesn't tell me what he was doing here."

"Exactly what he said, so far as I could tell. He has been sent here, certainly. I can tell you what he feels about the one who sent him. Mistrust. A grudging admiration, an unhappy sense of obligation, fiercely denied."

"Anything at all about his paymaster?"

"Eyes like coins. A currency he suspects is false."

"No actual *name*, I suppose?"

"No. I do not know if he even knows it."

"So whoever it is who sent him here managed to do so without giving anything away. I wonder what they promised him?"

"He sees it, as a cold traveller sees the light of a glowing fire. A time when he will have everything he wants, when all who have ever insulted him will be destroyed, when he will wallow in his triumph while others grovel. How this will be attained, I cannot tell you. I need to sit down."

I propped him in a chair, motioned a servant to bring him some food and drink, and went back to Fain, keeping out of Filchis' line of sight. Unobservant he might be, but there was no sense being too damn obvious.

I told Fain what I'd heard, trying at the same time to keep an eye on both Mokraine and Enthemmerlee. I felt stretched like a bowstring.

"Interesting," Fain said. "So he's here at someone else's behest. Yet why him?"

"Well, yes, that's the question. Do you know anything about him?"

"His family had money, once; no longer. Poor investments, I believe."

"Why did you let him set up the Builders?"

"It is not the place of the Section to allow, or disallow, the expression of opinions. And sometimes one must provide people with rope, in the hope that eventually they will make themselves a noose of it."

"So what are we going to do about him?"

"What can we do? He is doing nothing illegal."

"He's making the worst element of Gudain society think there are those on Scalentine who will back any play they make."

"There are. Our Mr Filchis has been sent here to spy out the land. But by whom, and why, remains to be seen."

"Maybe they couldn't stand the man and simply wanted him somewhere else," I muttered.

"That, also, is possible," Fain said. "For now, let us make sure he is nowhere near the Itnunnacklish."

"I don't think he'd try anything," I said. "He doesn't strike me as the type to risk his *own* skin. Well, except by pontificating in a public place, and even then, someone just threw fruit at him. A waste of fruit, if you ask me."

"But he is here for a reason, one we must discover. Did you hear anything else of interest?" Fain said. "Before Mr Filchis turned up and provided distraction."

I dragged up what I could remember about my conversation with the two traders, and the Empire delegate. "None of it sounded as though they were doing anything other than watching, with one foot out the door."

"It would be interesting to talk to them myself. I may try to do so, later, if this blasted oath permits." He frowned. "Time is passing. I assume your Fey friend got the message?"

"If your messenger was reliable, and gave it to either Laney herself, or Flower, or Ireq... I hope they didn't give it to Jivrais."

Fain's gaze sharpened. "Why not?"

"Because the irritating little f... *faun* is likely to forget it, remember it wrong, or decide it sounds so interesting he wants to come too. Or instead."

"That would *not* be helpful," Fain said.

"You're bloody telling me. Especially since he's grown horns. Half these Gudain would probably think he's a demon. Is it any good my apologising again?"

"You can hardly be held responsible for Jivrais."

"I mean for the oath."

Fain looked at me gravely. "Babylon, if anything that I could have prevented happens because I am here, rather than on Scalentine, I know that your regret will be far greater than mine. Apology is rather beside the point, don't you think?"

Then I spotted Tovanay, the rejected suitor, making his way through the crowd with determination. I set my feet to his charge.

He made that sideways Gudain bow. The snake on his arm shifted its coils, raised its head. "Enthemmerlee. Or should I say Madam Patineshi Defarlane Lathrit en Scona Entaire the Itnunnacklish?"

The words were loaded with ice. The crowd hushed, and turned to look.

"Tovanay, I am glad to see you here," Enthemmerlee said.

"I regret that I do not share your gladness. You desired this more than an alliance with my house. I will not stand in the way of your triumph, such as it is." He gestured at her, the great puffed sleeve seeming to move slowly, a sail bellying in the wind. I was already between them; his hands moved, and I grabbed for his arm, but not fast enough, because it wasn't Enthemmerlee he was going for.

He pinched the back of the snake's neck, and it sank its teeth into his wrist, inches from my fingers.

He stayed smiling, calm, even as he buckled, a sudden weight against my hands.

Enthemmerlee said, "Tovanay."

I let go, let him fall, got back in front of her. He hit the floor, shuddered, and his eyes rolled back.

The snake dropped to the floor. People shrieked, leaping out of the way, and it whipped away between skittering feet, lost. Some of the household guard were around us now, a rank of blue backs, holding off the crowd.

I didn't look at Enthemmerlee. I kept watching, every face, every movement. A Gudain woman running towards us; my shield went up, but she wasn't even looking at Enthemmerlee. She fell on her knees beside Tovanay, calling his name.

The resemblance was clear, even in this place with too many faces that looked alike. His mother.

Even now, she didn't touch him. Her son lay blue and rigid on the cold marble, and she only said his name, over and over, like a spell or a prayer.

EIGHTEEN

THE WHOLE ROOM was focused on this pathetic little tableau, silent, staring. Enthemmerlee moved forward. "Daryellee. Daryellee, I am so sorry."

"Sorry?" The woman's head snapped round as fast as a striking snake; her eyes flared with hatred. "My son is dead. My line is dead, because of you, because you chose a scaly myth over your own people. And you, you are *sorry?*"

She got up, tripping over her gown. I moved in front of Enthemmerlee. Daryellee looked at me. "Another foreigner. Will *you* bed her next?"

Shock slapped through the watchers. Daryellee turned and walked away.

"I must go after her," Enthemmerlee said.

"Lady Enthemmerlee!" I said. "I don't think that's wise."

"I agree," Lobik said.

"She blames you," Malleay said. "Em..."

"And so she should," Enthemmerlee said, her voice dead. "Who is responsible, if I am not?"

"How about bloody Tovanay?" Malleay said.

I couldn't help agreeing with the boy, for once.

"She has lost her *son!*" Enthemmerlee's voice cracked. "This is not... I never meant..." She pressed her fingers to her mouth and shook her head.

Lobik glanced around. People were looking, so he leaned close, to hide the gesture, before taking her hand and pressing her fingers to his lips. "My love," he whispered. "My brave one, my *itna*. He made his choice, as you did, as we all do. You cannot take responsibility for it."

Malleay looked away, saying, "Maybe we should..."

Fain moved with almost inhuman speed, his arm flicking upwards. There was a *crack*.

My shield went up, but Fain had got there before me; deflecting whatever it was. He was swearing, supporting his arm with his right hand.

There was an odd, gulping sound. Lobik, looking puzzled, had his hand to his throat.

"Lobik?" Enthemmerlee said. "Lobik!"

The tall Ikinchli's chest heaved. His hand fell away, and he crumpled to his knees. His throat was the wrong shape; there was no blood, only an awful, obscene dent.

"Lobik." Enthemmerlee fell to her knees beside him, took him in her arms. "Help him, please!"

I couldn't. I had to guard her. I didn't know where the missile had come from. It lay on the floor; a grey lump of stone. The household guard clustered around, looking every which way; a couple of them dragged the others into position around Enthemmerlee.

Fain fell to his knees beside Lobik, digging into his pockets one-handed, cursing. "Has anyone a pipe? A quill? Something hollow!"

Bergast thrust a quill at him. "Hold it steady." Fain sliced off the feathered end, then held the knife, point first, to Lobik's throat.

"What are you doing? No!" Enthemmerlee grabbed for the knife. Fain elbowed her aside, with no ceremony.

"His windpipe's crushed," Fain said. "He needs air, and this is the only way he'll get it. Give me room."

Lobik's chest pulsed, his hand flailed, knocking the knife away. He convulsed upwards, his hands clutching at the air, then he fell back, his head hitting the floor with a dreadful solidity. His eyes rolled up; the third eyelid slid over them.

Fain pressed the tip of the knife to the hollow at the base of Lobik's throat, and pushed. The knife slid in; there was no gush of blood, only a small bubbling of fluid. A little air wheezed out.

Fain slid the quill into the cut. "Please," Enthemmerlee said. "Please." She took Lobik's hand.

Malleay dropped down beside her. "Lobik?"

Lobik lay unmoving.

Fain put his lips to the quill and breathed. Breathed. Breathed.

It was one of the most extraordinary pieces of field surgery I've ever seen.

People tried to crowd round, peering over each other's shoulders; I snarled at them. The assassin could still be among them, weapon hidden, face innocent.

Finally, Fain sat back, cradling his wounded arm to his chest, and shook his head.

The crowd let out its breath, and shifted, and there was Daryellee, the dead boy's mother, standing only feet away from me. She had an Ikinchli sling in her hand. She hadn't even thought to hide it.

I wondered, for a moment, where she had got it, and where she had learned to use such a thing. Perhaps from a nurse, or a stableboy. From some Ikinchli who had brought her up with love, and care. And this is what she had given them.

Of course, it hadn't been meant for Lobik; she'd probably hardly realised he was there.

Now she looked bewildered, the lethal thing hanging limply from slackening fingers.

Enthemmerlee didn't notice when I moved. Daryellee didn't even try to run, though she gasped when I grabbed her wrist and held up her hand, with the sling. A murmur ran through the watchers.

"You?" I said.

Daryellee shook her head, but it wasn't a denial. "I didn't... Is he dead?"

"Did you do this?"

She looked down at the sling; its cradle empty and slack. "Yes," she said.

"Lobik," Enthemmerlee said, her voice barely a breath. She hadn't even looked up.

"He can't..." Malleay said. His hand moved out, towards hers, but dropped back to his side, as though it were simply too heavy.

ENTHEMMERLEE DID NOT weep. She did not scream. She stood up, silent and pale, and turned, and saw Daryellee, and the sling.

She nodded. Then she turned to walk out as though none of us were there. "Guard! Stay with her!" Tantris snapped.

I shot a glance at Fain, who said, "Go with her." His normally warm-coloured skin was wax-yellow, with blue shadows under the eyes. Abruptly, his knees folded, and he slid down the wall.

"Fain!"

"Arm. Broken, I think."

"Guard!" I snapped.

Enboryay burst through the crowd, choleric and yelling. "What's going on? What..."

I thrust Daryellee at him. "She killed Lobik. It was meant for your daughter. Do something with her."

Enthemmerlee walked down the steps as though in a dream. The guard hovered around her, at a loss.

"Lady Enthemmerlee. Enthemmerlee," I said. "Come this way. I'll take you home."

She was crying now, but she didn't seem aware of it; the tears spilled, unnoticed, down her still, pallid face. I manoeuvred her towards the waiting carriages, opened the door, helped her in. "Stikinisk, Vorenay, Koverey, get in with her. Vasik, you're on the roof, with me." We climbed up beside the driver.

"They threw her out?" he said. "I knew it."

"Oh, no," I said. "Lobik... Lobik's dead." Grief, sharp and mostly unexpected, clawed at me. I'd hardly had time to get to know the man, but what I knew, I liked a great deal. And he was gone: stupidly, pointlessly dead. And poor Enthemmerlee... I hadn't liked the way she looked, climbing into the carriage. I hadn't liked it at all.

"Lobik?" The driver looked at me. "Lobik Kraneel? What... No. You joke me."

"I don't joke you, mate. I wish I did."

"Ah, *guak*," he said. "*Guak*. Fuck. Bastard. Fuck."

"All of that," I said.

Guilt assaulted me, that sick hollow ache curling in the back of my thighs.

It was the oath; the oath I'd forced Fain to take. He had acted without thought, without awareness, when he deflected the stone. The oath had used him to protect Enthemmerlee, and in doing so, it had killed the man she loved.

I felt as guilty as if I'd slung the stone myself.

THE SENESCHAL THRANISHALAK must have been watching. The sight of a single coach brought him scuttling down the driveway as fast as his stiff-backed gait allowed.

He was too well trained to ask what had happened, but glanced up at me before he opened the door of the coach. I just shook my head.

Enthemmerlee got out, moving as though she were half-frozen.

"Miss?" He said.

"She killed him, Thran." She made a terrible, ugly noise, as though her insides were being torn out, and bent over, clutching her arms across herself.

Thranishalak looked up at me again. "Lobik," I said.

The skin of Thranishalak's face quivered; his crest flicked up, once. Then his feelings, whatever they were, disappeared under the mask of the perfect servant. And he put his arms around Enthemmelee, holding her, rocking her against him as she wailed. "There, Miss. There. Hush now."

I heard the driver hiss with surprise.

Thranishalak picked Enthemmerlee up, like a child, her arms around his neck. She was so small; so frail. He carried her into the house. I followed.

We put her to bed in the blue and white room. Thranishalak had hushed conversations at the door, and a few minutes later there were mugs on a tray, steaming. He put one in her hands, folded her cold little fingers around it.

He offered the other to me. I took it. It smelled of sweet syrup, sleepy and comforting. I put it aside.

Enthemmerlee had stopped that dreadful wailing, but now, holding the mug, not drinking, she stared at the faded hangings.

I knew she wasn't seeing them. I thought I knew what she was seeing instead.

I got up. "I need to stand guard."

"I'll stay with her," the seneschal said.

"I'll be outside the door." Guilt and pity clogged my mouth. "Enthemmerlee. I'm... I'm so sorry."

"Thank you," she said, in a distant little voice.

Don't thank me. For the love of the All, don't thank me.

I stood there until the others returned. I stood there while her father went in, and sat, silently, on the end of the bed, and came out again, shaking his head.

I stood there while Selinecree fluttered in, and said, "Oh, Enthemmerlee." She pulled at a curtain, fussed with the covers. "Have you had anything to eat? You should probably eat something."

"No, thank you, Aunt."

I stood there while Malleay came to the door, his eyes raw with tears, and said, "Em. I'll... if you want anything." He stood there for a minute, and she said, in that same distant voice, "Thank you, Malleay."

He went away. I stayed.

Eventually Rikkinnet stood in front of me and said, "Go."

"I..."

"Go. Sleep." She spat the words out like small stones, everything about her tight and furious.

"I can't."

"You must."

"I should have..."

"No." She swallowed, and I saw, for just a moment, the grief and guilt smear across her face like a dirty rag, before she pulled herself back to rigid control. "Do not say it. It does no good. We cannot save him. We still have her to watch, and to watch, you must sleep."

IT WAS SOME time before Malleay answered my knock; when he did so, he looked dreadful, his green flush faded to a pallid grey.

"Oh," he said. "Is something wrong? Is it Enthemmerlee?"

"Well, yes and no," I said. "Rikkinnet is on guard."

"Oh. I mean, that's good. Did you want me for something?"

"May I come in?"

"Oh, of course," he said. "How rude of me. Please." He waved me past him. "I'm sorry it's such a state. I don't like to let the servants clean it, but they keep trying. I tell them I can do it myself, but..." He moved about, jerky as a badly handled marionette, lighting another lamp, making ineffective attempts at tidying the piles of books that rustled and teetered on every available surface. "I'm studying Hodrinka. But every reference I find turns up six more, and there are so many books that are impossible to get. Or they take months, and then when they arrive they're not what you ordered. That was one thing about Scalentine. I wish I'd had longer to get to know the book dealers. They had some magnificent stock. Please, sit down."

"Hodrinka?" I said, seating myself in the only chair no longer acting as a library.

"One of the founding thinkers of political philosophy in the civilised planes. But so little is known about him. Or her. It's thought there were many more writings, but even those fragments we have, one could build a civilisation on them." His eyes lit with fervour and I suddenly got what it was Enthemmerlee had first seen in him. He glanced at me, and the smile dropped away. "It was Lobik who told me about Hodrinka, you know."

"He was a good man."

"A good man? He was a *great* one," Malleay said. "And... he was..." He turned away.

"He was a friend, too, wasn't he?"

"Yes."

"Malleay, would you like a drink?"

"A drink?"

"Alcohol."

"Oh, I don't... Oh, yes, why not?" He rubbed his face, as though he had only just realised how tired he was. He was shadow-eyed and too thin. The brightly coloured Ikinchli-style shirt he wore only emphasised his pallor.

He slumped in a chair, and took the flask, though he didn't drink. Instead, he turned it in his fingers, staring at nothing.

"If you're not going to drink that," I said, "give it here."

"Sorry." He took a slug, looked startled, and handed back the flask. "What is that?"

"Golden." Damn good golden, too. But I wasn't going to drink it myself; I was still on duty.

"Oh."

I sat back. "It's so sad. You know, I've been thinking about it, and considering everything you had to overcome, I'm truly astonished that you actually succeeded in doing what was necessary for Enthemmerlee's transformation. It must have taken great courage, to do what you did. The political pressure, the rules you've always lived by, the consequences of failure... Really, you're to be congratulated."

"Congratulated?" His voice rang like a lead coin.

"Why, yes."

"I've always loved her, you know. Since we were children."

I nodded.

"When we found out what she was, and she asked me to be one of her husbands – oh, you can't imagine. To be trusted to stand with her at the heart of history, to be given the chance to change everything... but I... You see, it wasn't..."

I waited.

"It was a great moment, you understand? And I was – I stopped even *thinking*." He remembered he was holding the flask, and took a deep drink, which made him cough. "I didn't... To be in that room, with them both... and knowing that what I did would change her, and that it would *hurt* her; and I was still able to do it." His fingers tightened on the flask. "It wasn't for all the reasons we'd talked about, for the country, for the people. I could do it because..."

"Because you wanted her."

He looked at me then, and his eyes were hollow and haunted. "You... you guessed? I did, and I was able to do that. To hurt her. I was a beast."

"*Did* it hurt her?"

"She said not. But she's always kind. And she made a noise, and I... It *must* have hurt her. I mean, two of us..."

"Do you think Lobik was cruel?"

"Cruel?" He looked horrified. "Lobik? No, he's... he *was*... the kindest, gentlest... *and* brilliant. Do you know he could recite the entire Ebarneren Saga? He knew more about political history... And he never even saw a book until he was ten years old."

"But you think he was cruel."

"No!"

"But you both did exactly the same thing, and you think *you're* cruel."

"I..." He stopped.

"Are you disgusted by her?" I said. "Now she's changed."

"What? No! She's beautiful. Even more beautiful. Every time I look at her I... My heart... it shakes. As though something in my chest were trying to get out."

"So why do you flinch?"

"I don't... do I?"

"You twitch away from her as though you found her loathsome."

He chewed his lip, and took another drink. I waited.

"Every time she gets close to me," he whispered, "I remember. I remember how I hurt her, and I don't know how she can bear me."

"Do you think Lobik hurt her?"

"He'd never hurt her. Not on purpose."

"Would you?"

"Of course not. But I did, didn't I?"

"Do you feel desire?"

"Yes," he whispered.

"But you've been told, all your life, it's shameful. Do you think that's right?"

"I don't know."

"You don't attend *privaiya* any more."

"No. And since I stopped... I stopped going because I don't believe in the things we're told, and because I think the smoke controls us, I don't want to be in the control of something else. But since I stopped, I'm out of control anyway. I feel... I can't even say it."

"Malleay, you're not out of control. If you were out of control, you'd take what you wanted whether the other person desired you or not. To feel desire and not exercise it? That *is* control. Look, if your desire hurt someone, then it would be right not to exercise it." I heard Cruel and Unusual protest in the back of my head, but shoved them away. This wasn't the time to take Malleay on a tour of the wider ranges of passion. "But what if the thing that hurts is to believe that someone you care for finds you ugly, and disgusting?"

"You mean Enthemmerlee? Is *that* what she thinks?"

"You flinch from her. What's she supposed to think?"

"But I love her. I just can't... What I did, it hurt her. Once she started to change, you could see it."

"But it was what you all wanted, what *she* wanted, for her to change. It was what was meant to happen."

"I didn't know it would hurt her so much," Malleay whispered.

"It doesn't hurt her now."

"But I did that to her."

"Yes. So did Lobik, and so did she. You all decided on this course of action. After what she's been through, do you want her to think that she disgusts you now?"

He shook his head.

"Malleay. The act itself, did it hurt *you*?"

"No."

"It's not supposed to. And sometimes, yes, there is pain, especially the first time. But it's also about pleasure, Malleay. It's *supposed* to be about pleasure. My first time... Well. It wasn't as good as it was later, but I wanted the other person so much that it was still very pleasing."

"But it wasn't the same. You weren't going to change, to have something terrible happen that might kill you. Besides, you're..." He stopped.

"One isn't *born* a whore, you know. I was just a girl, back then."

"But it's different for you. We're not the same race."

"Malleay. Enthemmerlee is the *Itnunnacklish*. What does that mean?"

He looked confused.

"Do the Ikinchli women hate sex? Do they avoid it? Do they turn their men away with cries of disgust?"

"No." He blushed again. "I haven't... But they seem to like it quite a lot, actually. So do the men."

"And Enthemmerlee is part Ikinchli. She *always has been*. So, in fact, are you. Isn't that the whole point? Isn't that what her very existence proves?"

"What are you saying?"

"That you're part Ikinchli, too. That this whole fear of passion that you've been taught, it's a con. It's a dirty trick. It's just another way of trying to say the Gudain and the Ikinchli are different. And it's a lie. It always was. And it's destroying your people, Malleay. They're dying."

"Yes. I know."

"Of course you do, you're not stupid. But you've had generations of this evil, ugly nonsense and it's hard to change the way you think overnight."

"I know. I do know. But this doesn't help Enthemmerlee, does it?"

"It could. Because she is grieving, and lonely. First of all, don't let her turn you away. Stay with her. Just *be* with her. Hold her hand. Hug her. So people will mutter. Who cares? They mutter already. One more scandal can't possibly make any difference."

"You think she wants me to?"

"I think she needs you to, whether or not she knows she wants it. And you can prove to her that she is a force of life and joy, Malleay, but you need to get back into her bed. I bet it feels pretty bloody empty right now."

"How will that help?"

"Warmth. Comfort. Another warm body. Just *hold* her, man; you can do that, can't you?"

"Of course I can."

"And you could probably do with it too, am I right?"

He closed his eyes, and nodded, tears spilling from under his lids. I moved over and sat on the arm of his chair, and, very lightly, stroked his hair.

The sobs came all at once, shaking him. Half-formed words tumbled out. I put my arm around his shoulders, and he clutched at me, his head pressed against my ribs. His tears soaked through my shirt. I felt, suddenly, stupidly, like crying myself. He was so young, a boy trying so terribly hard to be a man. I murmured comforting, meaningless phrases and waited.

When his sobs finally tailed off, he let go as though I'd suddenly got hot enough to burn him. "I'm sorry."

"Don't worry about it."

He scrambled out a scrap of ink-stained cotton, and blew his nose.

"Malleay. Would you like to know how to please Enthemmerlee? How to make her happy?"

"Of course I would!"

"I mean, between the sheets. When the time is right, to take it beyond comfort, to something else. Because I can show you. If you would like."

A deep green blush flooded up his neck, as though he were sinking into water. "Do you think... But surely..."

"You love her, don't you?"

"Yes."

"Then just be aware, and you'll know, when she's ready to ask more than comfort from you. It might be sooner than you think." Sex, done right and with the right person (and hells, even, occasionally, with the absolutely wrong person, so long as you *know* that) is a great healer. I wasn't just here for Enthemmerlee, or for Malleay. I was here for me, too.

I couldn't bring Lobik back, I couldn't unhappen what had happened. But maybe I could make Enthemmerlee's future a little less bleak. And maybe I could, at least for a couple of hours, shut my damned mind up about everything that was wrong.

"But you're not... I mean... How would you know?"

I wasn't going to confess my little chat with Enthemmerlee. People can be funny about that sort of thing. "I'm not that different, Malleay. And neither are you." Considering some of the beings with whom I've spent sheet-time, he was so close to human any differences were barely noticeable. "It's your choice, of course."

"Why would you do this?" he said. His voice shook a little.

"Because I like Enthemmerlee, and I want her to be happy. And because you're cute, and I've never had a Gudain." He looked up, startled, eyes wide. I wasn't lying, either. He was cute.

"Lock the door?" he said.

*   *   *

ONCE OUT OF the dreadful clothes, his body was pleasing; his pale green skin luminous in the warm gloom, like a pearl found far under water. I slid under the sheets, not wanting to loom over the poor boy; the sight of the knife I kept strapped to my thigh had made him widen his eyes enough, even though I took it off. He was shivering, his cock curled against his own thigh as though it was trying to hide.

He began to babble. "Do you... do you do this? Often? Teach... this?"

"It's been known. I was taught, myself, so..."

"Really? How does one teach..."

"Sometimes, by telling the pupil to shut up and listen."

"Oh. Sorry."

I took his head in my hands. "Shh. Now, look at me," I said. "Do you find me pleasing?"

He looked. After a few moments, he nodded. I was pleased to see that his cock agreed with him; it began to unfurl, shyly, like a fern.

"Then say it."

He swallowed. "Say what?"

"Tell me something you like about what you're looking at. A lady likes to hear these things."

He looked at me pleadingly. "I can't..."

"Yes, you can. No one else has to hear; only the person you're with. Shall I start?" I ran a finger down his cheek. "You have lovely skin." Then I ran my finger down his stiffening penis. "And a very nice cock." He jolted at the use of the word, but it didn't do his erection any harm. "Your turn."

"You... ah... your hair is pretty."

"Thank you," I said, and smiled, and waited.

"And your b... breasts... are... very nice."

"I would like it if you touched them."

"Would you?"

"Yes."

He reached out, and hesitated. I took his hand, and ran it over my breast, showed him how to tease the nipple with his fingers.

He was extremely gentle; he kept glancing at me, as though afraid I would suddenly faint or scream. Compared to Enthemmerlee I must have seemed hulking, but he treated me like the fragile flower I am very much not.

But I was happy to let him. Too raucous an approach probably wouldn't do for Enthemmerlee. And, knowing something about her encounters with Lobik, I didn't want Malleay to end up a poor imitation of him. Lobik's ghost would already haunt their bed; there was no sense making things worse.

He must have been holding himself back for a long time; and, of course, he was young. A few minutes of breast-play and getting his cock caught in the sheets, and he clutched my arms, his breathing steepened, and he came, convulsive and silent.

"I'm sorry," he said, as soon as he got his breath back. "I'm sorry."

"What are you sorry for? I'm flattered."

"Flattered?"

"You found being with me so exciting that you came before I'd barely touched you. Don't you think I should be flattered?"

He looked shocked, then thoughtful. "Well... But that can't have been very, you know. For you."

"Seeing that happen to you *is* exciting for me. And besides, it's not as though we've finished."

"We haven't? Oh, no, I don't suppose we have."

"We're not here for *you* to have a good time," I said, grinning.

"Sorry," he said, with the beginnings of a smile, "I'm afraid I already have." The smile dropped away. "It seems wrong," he said. "I mean, with what's happened."

"You think we're being disrespectful?"

"Not that, exactly. I don't really know, it just seems we shouldn't be doing this."

"We should be grieving."

"Yes."

"We are. And we're doing this, too. Do you think he wouldn't want this, for both of you? That he would want you to both to be miserable?"

"No."

"I know you grieve for him. I know you will miss him." My guilt tried to surge up again, and I forced it away. "But this" – I ran my hand down his thigh – "this is what people do. We are alive. We feel sorrow, and we celebrate life, both at once. Yes?"

"Yes," he said, tears glimmering again. "Yes."

"Now, where were we? Ah yes. Breasts. One's tongue is not just for talking with, you know."

"Oh. Oh!" he said. And set to.

Tongues and hands. Fingers and legs and lips and hair and skin, the sweet and complex multiplicity of textures. Oh, how I'd missed this, needed this. How wonderful it was to be a body, with a body; a communication more straightforward yet more subtle than I could ever manage with words.

Of course, some words were needed.

I put his fingers to my cunny and said, "Is it the same?" (A tricky moment – I didn't actually want to mention Enthemmerlee, although she was the one all this was in aid of, in case it put him off.)

I had to bite my lip at his look of studious concentration, as though he were studying a difficult text.

"Not quite," he said. "But here..."

"Oh, yes," I said.

"Like that?"

"Oh, yes. Gently now... Oh, hells, yes."

Of course, one night's lessons wasn't going to change everything; I wasn't *that* good a whore, now I was only human again. But it would do to begin with. The rest was up to him, and Enthemmerlee.

Afterwards, he fell asleep smiling, and looking so young he put me painfully in mind of my first love.

That made me think of the Chief, and I felt a sudden loneliness so deep it hurt. I couldn't bear to stay there; he was cute, yes, but it was Hargur I wanted.

I managed to leave without waking him, and shut the door behind me. The place was so utterly quiet it seemed as though everyone had simply vanished away, but I felt eyes on me all the same.

I turned, but if anyone had been watching, they were gone. Somewhere, a door closed softly.

SELINECREE CAME TO Enthemmerlee's room as I was taking over from Rikkinnet; she had something in her hands. A small box, oval, set with so many bits of glimmering shell and polished stones one could barely see the wood. "Is she awake?" Selinecree said. "Only... Well. One of the maids found this, clearing out the room that the... that her... that Mr Kraneel was staying in, and I thought perhaps she would like to have it." A bright yellow thread had caught in the ornamentation of the box, wavering like seaweed in the air of the corridor. Nervously, Selinecree tugged it free and let it float away.

"What is it?"

"It is an *Ipash Dok*," Rikkinnet said. "At any ancestor ceremony the suppliant places this on the altar." Her face stiffened as she looked at it. "It must have been meant for the Enkantishak."

Enthemmerlee opened the door. "Is something wrong?" She looked like the ghost of a dryad, a wisp of green pallor. Then she saw the box.

"This was in Mr Kraneel's room, dear," Selinecree said. "I thought I should bring it to you. Perhaps I shouldn't have, but..."

"No, Aunt. Thank you." Enthemmerlee took it, and turned it over in her hands. Selinecree twisted her own together. "It's... it's all right, is it? It won't open, or anything."

"No, it won't. They only open when they're placed on the altar," Enthemmerlee said, in a flat, distant voice. "It's probably the heat. I shall take it. I shall take it and put it on the altar with mine, where it should be. Thank you, Aunt."

"Well, since I'm not coming myself... You will be all right, will you? I mean, your father's going..."

"I'll be fine, Aunt Selinecree. Thank you."

She shut the door again, quietly but firmly. Selinecree let out a shaky sigh, shook her head, and walked away.

Rikkinnet made an odd huffing noise.

"What is it?" I said.

"I always thought Lobik had better taste," she said, blinking hard. "That is like the ones they sell to travellers. The primitive art of savage Ikinchli. Hah." I realised her eyes were glittering with tears, and that she didn't want me to see. I looked away.

RIKKINNET HAD JUST reappeared, not looking as though the shift break had brought her much rest, when we heard shouting from outside. We looked at each other. "I will go," she said.

I could hear Enthemmerlee moving about in her room; I wondered if she'd slept. I moved over to the window; I could make out the gate-guard, and beyond the gate, the baggy brown uniforms of the Fenac. Five of them.

Whatever this was, it looked like trouble, but (assuming the uniform wearers actually were Fenac, and there weren't five Fenac bodies naked in a ditch somewhere) it looked like *official* trouble.

That didn't mean it wasn't of the killing sort.

I went back to Enthemmerlee's door, loosened my sword in its scabbard and waited.

I didn't have to wait long.

Rikkinnet came belting along the corridor. "They've come to arrest you."

"Me? What for?"

She hissed. "Moral Statutes."

"What?"

"What is it?" Enthemmerlee said, opening the door. She was freshly dressed, but by the look of her, no, she hadn't slept. The shadows around her eyes hurt my heart.

"The Fenac are here to arrest Babylon for violation of the Moral Statutes."

Enthemmerlee rubbed her hands over her face. "I don't understand."

"Nor do I," I said. Of course, there'd been the previous night... but how the hells would anyone have found out? I didn't think Malleay would have blabbed.

The seneschal came up the corridor; his face was expressionless as ever, but he radiated worry with every rigid step. "Madam Steel? Your presence is requested in the main hall."

"Thranishalak, do you know what's happening?" Enthemmerlee said.

"The Fenac have a warrant for the arrest of Madam Steel," he said.

"They're in the house? I'll skin those fucking guards," I said.

"Lady Selinecree came to the gate, and told the guards 'not to be silly,' Madam," Thranishalak said.

Ah.

"I will come with you," Enthemmerlee said. "There must be a mistake."

Malleay, Enboryay and the Fenac were already gathered in the main hall. Malleay looked up as we arrived and his face flooded with colour; if anyone had been looking for a guilty party, he shone out like a hilltop beacon. Fortunately none of the Fenac were looking at him.

The only Ikinchli stared fixedly at some point in mid-air, while two of the Gudain were looking round with an air of intense discomfort, as though afraid they would dirty the furniture just by getting close to it, and another was practising his sneer. The commander, in a tall helmet, with a chunk of silver attached to it in the shape of a hook, was talking to a flushed and distinctly unimpressed Enboryay.

"Behaviour likely to corrupt the public morals?" he sputtered. "Nonsense. What are you talking about?"

"Will somebody explain, please?" Enthemmerlee said.

The Fenac commander glanced at her with barely hidden contempt.

"What are your grounds for this accusation?" Malleay said. "And who is the accuser? You are required to inform us of these things."

The Fenac smiled, unpleasantly, and said, in the tones of one who had been coached: "This accusation has been brought under the Moral Statutes and the identity of the accuser is therefore protected."

"And the grounds?"

The Fenac commander looked him up and down, and his unpleasant smile widened in a way that made me want to put my fist through it. "You're Malleay Devinclane Solit en Scona Mariess? Well," he said, "I've *got* the papers with me. I *can* read them out. You know. Here. Or the foreigner can come with me, nice and quiet."

Malleay glanced at me, and colour raced up his neck and face again, but he stood his ground. "You are required..."

"Firstly," the Fenac said. "That the accused did appear in public dressed in such a manner as to corrupt the morals of those present..."

"Now hang on," I said. "Who?"

"Members of the household of Enboryay DeLanso Lathrit en Scona Entaire, presently Advisor to the Crown of the House of Entaire."

"I have never seen this person other than, ah, respectably covered," Enboryay said.

"Well, sir, seems someone did. *Several* people."

I knew damn well that Malleay wasn't the one who'd brought the accusation. I was pretty sure I hadn't been sleepwalking.

And I hadn't been up to anything with anyone else – there'd been little time and less temptation... Speaking of which, where was Fain?

Nowhere to be seen, dammit. What was he up to? Distancing himself from any association with me? And did it mean the Fey oath was wearing off? Without that and without a trained bodyguard, I didn't like to imagine the situation Enthemmerlee would be left in.

"And that the accused did engage in corrupt practices with another person outside of the marital state..."

"No," Enthemmerlee said. "No. This is outrageous behaviour towards a citizen of another country. The Statutes only apply to Gudain!"

"The Statutes apply to all who are capable of being restrained by them," the Fenac said. "Whether or not they're a *foreigner*."

I was beginning to feel fairly annoyed. And the way the little sleazelet was looking at me wasn't helping. But I didn't think battering my way through them was going to help Enthemmerlee.

"It's fine," I said. "I'm sure everything can be sorted out. Just tell me where I'm supposed to have been improperly dressed."

"When answering the door to members of the household," he said. "Now let's have any weapons you're carrying, please."

It must have been the night the Ikinchli had turned up, and Captain Tantris had come to fetch me. Had he been spreading the word? Or one of the guards who'd been with him? The guard, what was I going to do about the guard?

They wouldn't be able to look after Enthemmerlee. They were better, but they weren't *good,* and with someone deliberately getting me out of the way...

"Wait," Enboryay said.

"I remind your lordship that under the Moral Statutes I am empowered to arrest any member of a household who attempts to obstruct or impede me in the performance of my duties," he said. Gosh, he was proud of all those big words; I wondered who'd taught them to him.

"Lady Enthemmerlee," I said.

She looked at me, eyes wide with distress, but her voice was calm and clear. "Madam Steel," she said. "This is a disgrace, for which I apologise for my countrymen. You must think us quite barbaric. I assure you every effort will be made to sort out this *misunderstanding*."

The Fenac commander gave a snort of contempt. I calmed myself by planning the exact pattern of bruising I was going to leave on his slimy little hide, the minute I got the chance. "Lady Enthemmerlee, I think I'm going to have to go along with this... person. Please take care of yourself." I thought as fast as I could. "Rikkinnet, you've ambassadorial privileges. Talk to Fain. Maybe, between you, you can do something to get me out. But in the meantime, Enthemmerlee is your first priority. I've been locked up before, I'll survive."

Bergast, who I'd forgotten about in the confusion, was standing with his mouth open. "Scholar Bergast!"

"Yes?" He was round-eyed as a child. I wondered if his briefing had covered the possibility of being thrown in stir. Maybe he thought it didn't happen to people like him.

"Just do your job, Bergast."

"I..."

The Fenac, who was obviously getting annoyed at being ignored, drew his sword. He hadn't had it out until now; sloppy. More used to dealing with intimidated Ikinchli who weren't allowed edged weapons, presumably. Good.

"Enough chat," he said. "Let's have those weapons. All of 'em."

"Very well."

I unslung my shield, and handed it to Rikkinnet, followed by my sword and dagger, and the arm-knife.

"Now, you can't give them to her," the Fenac said. "Scalys don't get to carry edged weapons."

"*She* is the Ikinchli Ambassador to Scalentine, and I am a citizen of Scalentine," I said. "I am trusting the Ambassador with the property of a Scalentine citizen, to be returned through the proper diplomatic channels. I don't know if you know Scalentine, but they have *very* strong ideas about property. They get extremely touchy if they think their citizens are being robbed." I was bullshitting for all I was worth, hoping that the thought of annoying a neighbouring country might get him worried – or, at least, confused.

"Quite right," Fain said, *finally* appearing in the doorway. He was still pale, and his arm was in a sling. "After all, who will trade with a country where the property of any passing foreigner may be appropriated at any moment?"

The Fenac commander became aware that he was in danger of treading on the toes of the rich and powerful. He waved a hand. "Well, don't blame me if she goes off and murders someone with 'em."

"I should also mention," Fain said, "that Scalentine feels very strongly about the treatment of its citizens while in custody. Very strongly indeed. If Madam Steel should happen to suffer any accident, I fear there will be *consequences*." He let a little bit of the real Darask Fain show through then; well, one of them, anyway. The commander dropped back a step. That was probably all the help the Diplomatic Section was going to be able to give me, but it was better than nothing.

"Right. Hands," the commander said.

"What exactly do you want me to do with them?" I said.

"Hold 'em out and don't try and be funny."

I held out my hands, and he bound a chain around them. I felt my skin shrink from the touch of it as he led me away, to the coach waiting in the courtyard.

CHAPTER
NINETEEN

PRISONS ARE NEVER pleasant. The type of stink varies a little depending on which species get put in the cells most, and how often the buckets or the straw are changed. This one was better than some I've been in, maybe because it was in the base of the Advisory Hall and they didn't want the stink rising to disturb the nostrils of government. Talk about keeping your friends close and your enemies closer.

It looked as though it had once been a set of cellars. I wondered if they'd kept wine in them; I couldn't half have done with a glass. After all, I was off duty. Possibly permanently. The cells, barred cages that had been set into the alcoves, were full of Ikinchli, some of them no more than children. Their eyes glowed in the dim light, watching, as I was marched past them.

There were five or six miserable-looking Gudain in a cage by themselves. No sign of Daryellee. Members of the Ten Families perhaps got a special cell, upstairs; or maybe she had been sent home with a stern word, if that.

I found it hard to care. It was the chains. How I hated the chains. The cold weight made me shudder.

The Fenac gave me a cage to myself. I don't think they knew what else to do with me.

"Hey," I said. "The chains?" I didn't like the way my voice sounded, weak. But it was the feel of them, of being bound that way. My skin seemed to shrink around me in anticipation of pain.

"The chains?" one of them said. "Oh, you don't like the chains, eh?"

"Come on," I said, trying not to let my voice shake. Almost succeeding. "Please. What am I going to do?" At that moment I didn't know myself. I could hardly think straight. *This is not Tiresana. There is no pillar of adamant for them to bind you to; Shakanti is not waiting for the moon to rise so she can play with your pain.*

But my skin was unconvinced.

They didn't take them off. They searched me in the most perfunctory fashion, without actually touching my flesh at any point. I still had a knife on my thigh, my modesty – such as it was – and not a lot else.

Tired, smoke-coloured light drizzled in through the high window slits. Two Fenac I didn't remember seeing before sat at a table, pushing counters about, occasionally glancing over at the cages. The other prisoners shifted and whispered.

I shuffled some straw into a pile as best I could with my feet, and sat down. Things skittered in the corners. I hoped they were rats, not beetles.

"Hey," one of the prisoners whispered. "Hey, you the one who was with the Itnunnacklish?"

"Who wants to know?"

"You think she's real?"

"For what it's worth, I think she is."

"'Course that one think she's real," someone else hissed. "Get paid, hey?"

"I get paid to use my sword, not to lie about what I think," I said, and yawned helplessly. I hadn't slept much the last few days. In fact, it felt as though I hadn't slept much for weeks. Despite the crawling sensation the chains gave me, suddenly I wanted nothing more than to lie down, whatever was lurking in the straw.

"You think she's the Itnunnacklish, you supposed to guard her, but you get yourself arrested. Maybe you Gudain after all, not give half a shit."

"I give," I said. "I give plenty of shit." I yawned again. "Trust me."

If whoever it was answered, I didn't hear. Sleep grabbed me like a drowning man, and took me under.

I WOKE CLUTCHING for balance, utterly confused, certain I was falling. I couldn't get hold of anything, my hands were still chained.

I sat up and tried to ease the stiffness out of my joints. The tiny window was black; it was night. How long had I slept? The Ikinchli in the cages either side watched me, some warily, some with interest, some just with the blank gaze of people with nothing else to look at and nowhere else to go. A lot of them were bruised.

"Hey, Curves," one of the Ikinchli males said. He was a chunky sort, with wide, muscular shoulders. There were stains on his face I realised were probably dried blood, and his grin showed a missing tooth.

"Hey, Muscles. Do we get fed in this place?"

"Once a day." He tilted his head. "You missed it. Terrible *guak*. You wouldn't like. Next time I eat it for you."

"Generous of you," I said.

I desperately needed a piss, and realised that there was, actually, a degree of privacy; a curve of wall with a bucket behind it. The wall was high enough to conceal me from the shoulders down. Gudain ideas of modesty again, I supposed.

"Hey," I said. "Hey, mister."

"What?"

"I need..." I jerked my head towards the wall. "And I can't, you know, with these things on." I turned my back, shook my chained wrists, looked at them over my shoulder. I'm not great at winsome, but I made a stab at it. "Come on, give a girl a break, what do you say?"

The Fenac looked at each other.

"All right," one of them growled. "But don't do anything stupid."

I don't know what they'd been told about me, but they were pretty cautious; and of course, they were on edge. The Ikinchli weren't the only ones with bruises, and one of the Fenac had had a clump of hair torn out, leaving an ugly, crusting wound.

Five of them came in, one dealt with the chains, and the others held sharp objects close to bits of me I didn't want punctured.

They waited while I used the bucket. I checked my thigh-knife, but left it where it was.

At least they rechained my hands in front of me. I wondered what the hells had made them so nervous; none of the other prisoners were chained as well as locked up. Maybe my reputation had preceded me. It was obviously a more impressive one than I realised. Three I could have handled – maybe. But five, with another three waiting outside and on the alert for trouble, not to mention the guards upstairs... No.

I wondered what they planned for me. A trial? To make me disappear? That might prove awkward, Fain having made it clear that eyes were being kept on me.

Not impossible, though. Just awkward.

So I sat, and thought, and watched the Fenac. Those baggy brown uniforms had a bit of stiffening around the neck, like the internal ruff of Gudain fashion, but smaller. It probably meant the throat was fairly well protected. Couldn't tell if they were wearing groin-guards – the material was too loose and puffy. They had helmets, low and round with a small brim, held on with a chinstrap. No noseguard – hmm. Short, efficient-looking swords. They were still playing their game, but they glanced up every now and then. They looked alert. And they were both Gudain. The chances of using a few wiles to persuade either of them to get close enough to give me an advantage was pretty minimal; even when they'd been 'searching' me, they hadn't taken the opportunity for fondling, though that might just mean they had more sense than first appeared.

The Ikinchli ceremony, the Enkantishak, was the following day. Would Enthemmerlee take the Household Guard with her? Better them than nothing, but All preserve us, that could go so very wrong.

Now I'd slept, and had nothing to do *but* think, my mind began to pick through the last few days like a bird fossicking in the undergrowth, turning over every leaf and twig.

Because my gut was yelling at me again. Something was up, something was wrong, something much more than my being locked up.

I'd missed something. I knew it.

I stared at the Fenac, until one of them clocked and glared at me in that gaoler's *stop looking at me or I'll come over there and make you regret it* way. Funny, the way you can feel someone's look on the back of your neck.

I'd felt it leaving Malleay's room. Someone had been watching. The person who'd accused me of breaking the Moral Statutes? Whoever they were, they wanted me out of the way.

The captain? He'd certainly seen me in a state of undress, but it seemed unlikely he'd know about Malleay. In fact, the only person other than Malleay who could possibly have any idea was whoever had been watching that night.

The nearest room was Selinecree's. But... Selinecree? She didn't seem likely. The mere fact that someone in her household had been accused, surely, would be an embarrassment. More scandal, more gossip...

Fain? Could he have wanted me out of the way? Why?

All I could think was that when Laney turned up, if I wasn't there, he'd have a better chance of persuading her to take off the oath – or so he might think. But he wanted Enthemmerlee alive, and she had a slightly better chance of that with me around. Fey oaths... Well, they're not infallible, from what I understand. They'll do their best to be fulfilled, but in the end all they really do is tip the odds.

And for all I knew, Laney had already turned up. It was more than time. She could already have undone the oath. If she knew where I was, she'd probably come racing in to sort everything out... but she'd be walking into a bunch of Gudain not only immune to her seductions, but with an automatic prejudice against foreigners. And in a building full of iron.

She'd be weak as a kitten and probably end up in the cell next to me. If they chained her, she'd be in agony.

One of the Fenac was writing something, the scritching of the pen just audible over the sighs and mutterings of the prisoners. He had his tongue pressed against his upper lip, and squinted at the page as though afraid it might leap up and bite his nose off.

That made me think of Bergast.

There was something going on with Bergast, I was convinced of it. The constant muttering of spells, the way he'd dropped his shirt over the papers in his room, the twitchiness around Mokraine... He was hiding something. Was he working for whoever wanted Enthemmerlee gone? Was he part of whatever was going on inside the Section? Had his been the eyes I'd felt?

I stared at the lampflame on the Fenac's table. Yellow flame, glinting on the coins as they half-heartedly shoved counters about in some game.

A yellow thread, wavering in the light, plucked away and gone. It bothered me, that thread. Why did it bother me?

Yellow and blue, blue and yellow. Something, thin as a thread, wavering. Refusing to be grasped and woven into a pattern.

Blue. Blue cloth. Blue cloth glimpsed in the rain, the sound of a laugh.

Selinecree had been wearing blue, that day I'd seen Dentor sneaking off to the ruined building.

But Selinecree? Seducing *Dentor?* That had been my assumption; but then, I was thinking like me, not like a

Gudain. They didn't *seduce*. And she attended *privaiya* regularly, which meant she couldn't feel desire even if she wanted to.

I felt a tingling in my hands. Maybe desire wasn't the point. Maybe the point was to get to the guard. To cause trouble. To weaken their ability to protect Enthemmerlee. Which had started even before I got there. Rumours that the guard were to be disbanded – who had started them? No one knew. But it was a good way to make them unsettled, to thin an already uneasy loyalty to one *many* of them would regard with suspicion, maybe even fear.

A bottle by the captain's doorstep. Who had put it there? I'd assumed Tantris had forgotten it, but what serious drinker *forgets* a full bottle? Keeping him oiled would certainly reduce his effectiveness.

It didn't even have to be her who put it there. If she was in cahoots with Dentor, or more of the guard, she just needed to get one of them to leave it for her. And if the guard in question would rather the captain kept to his old slobby ways and left them to their own devices, instead of getting them to buck up, they'd be happy enough to do it.

My brain was racing now, thoughts tumbling over each other, like the fall of pebbles that heralds a rockslide.

She was the one who'd told the guard to let the Fenac in, wasn't she? I'd thought she was just being an idiot, but maybe she wasn't the idiot I thought.

The Statutes apply to all who are capable of being restrained by them. I'd been affected by the smoke. Which, twisted the right way, meant I was capable of being morally restrained. And who had been there, who had been startled, by my response to the smoke?

Selinecree.

I stared at the hanging lamp, the flame trembling with my quickened heartbeat. Yellow. Yellow. Why yellow?

The thread attached to the *Ipash Dok*. The little decorated box, intended to be laid on the altar, where some natural action of the heat would make it open.

I'd never seen Lobik wearing yellow. But I'd seen Selinecree carrying a small parcel at the docks. A small parcel tied with bright yellow ribbon.

And Rikkinnet had said the *Ipash Dok* didn't look like something Lobik would have chosen. It looked like something sold to travellers.

Something that would make a perfect vessel for... What?

Nothing good. I knew that. Nothing good at all. It would be opened at the Enkantishak; tomorrow, or – I glanced at the dark window – maybe today. I didn't know how long I'd slept. But when it was opened, something bad would happen.

I had to get out of here.

How?

I pushed myself to my feet and looked around.

The bars were solidly set in the stone. The door, any cage's vulnerable point, had hinges as thick as my arm and no evidence of hasty construction. There was a big, thick, ironbound and solidly locked door at the top of the stairs, with, if I remembered rightly, two Fenac standing in front of it.

If you keep your prisoners right beneath your seat of government, I guess you *really* don't want them getting out.

"Hey. Hey," I said.

"What d'you want? Need another piss, do you?" said the one with the torn scalp.

"No, I just... I realised something. Something dangerous to the family. The Entaire family. They need to know this."

"Yeah, I'm sure they do." The Fenac yawned. "I'm sure they want a message from a criminal."

"Look, there's a ceremony tomorrow, they'll be there, something bad's going to happen. They need to be told. I'm not asking you to let me out, for the All's sake, I just want to give them a warning!"

"So what's this bad thing, then?"

"I..." *Shit*. "I don't know, exactly. But they've been given something, an *Ipash Dok,* and there's something wrong with it. Something bad inside it."

The Fenac snorted. "Nice try," he said, and turned away.

"I'm serious! Dammit..." But they ignored me, moving right to the other end of the room.

"Hey, Curves," the muscular Ikinchli hissed. "This is the Enkantishak, the welcoming of the Itnunnacklish. You say the *Ipash Dok* has something in it that will harm her?"

"Yes! And she doesn't know!"

He turned and said something to those behind him.

There were suddenly a lot of Ikinchli eyes on me.

"This is true?" someone said.

"Yes, it's true. I need to get a warning to her, *something.*"

"They will not take," Muscles said. "Most of the Fenac, they *want* her to disappear. Don't care if she dies."

"Well, I bloody do," I said. "Do you?"

"Yes."

"Then help me!"

"How?" Muscles said. "If I could make the bars melt, would have done it by now."

He had a point.

I gripped the bars, looking at the damned Fenac with their card game and their letters home and their weapons.

Place looked a lot like a barracks.

The Fenac looked a lot like soldiers.

I *can't believe you're thinking this, Babylon.*

I'm not. I can't think it. There has to be another way.

Eight Fenac. Fifty or so Ikinchli, behind bars.

I sat down on the straw, leaned my head against the wall, and closed my eyes.

"You going back to sleep? Much help for the Itnunnacklish, that."

"Shut up, all right?" I said.

But the harder I thought, the further I was from seeing any kind of solution.

The sound of footsteps on the stairs, and a familiar, human voice should have made me feel better.

Except the voice sounded a lot like that of Angrifon Filchis. I opened my eyes, and there he was, standing at the base of the steps, holding onto the railing.

"Here, here, what are you doing here?" said the Fenac commander.

"Come to visit the prisoner," Filchis said.

"At this hour?"

"Got to check in on one's fellow citizens, you know," Filchis said, grinning like a dead carp. "Oh, yes, another citizen of Scalentine. You thought I wouldn't find out" – he waved a finger at me – "you thought I wouldn't remember, but I did."

"What do *you* want?" I said.

"To make sure you're not creating trouble for our hosts, of course. Though it seems you've created *quite* enough already."

"She's been quiet," the Fenac said. "Now, if you don't mind..."

"Violated the Moral Statutes, I understand. Well, of course it's hardly surprising. Lax attitudes, you see. I hope you're keeping your men well out of her way."

The Fenac bristled. "I hope you're not suggesting my men are corruptible," he snapped.

"Not at all, not at all; only I know her type, you see. Lax attitudes, as I said. Mixing with all and sundry. Getting up to who knows what."

I realised suddenly that he wasn't just holding onto the bannister for show.

"You're drunk," I said.

"Oh, no. Not at all."

"You want us to throw him out, Commander?" said one of the other Fenac.

"Now, now," Filchis said, raising his finger. "I'm here as an envoy from powerful forces in Scalentine, you know. If you want people on your side in the struggle against *undesirable elements*" – he waved at the Ikinchli in their cages – "you've got to recognise your friends when you see them. I just want a little word with the prisoner, that's all."

I saw the Fenac commander glance up the stairs, as though checking for who might be standing behind Filchis. "Make it quick, then," he said. "And no passing anything through the bars, right? I'll be watching."

"Oh, don't worry, I have no intention of passing anything."

"Wind, maybe," I said. "Go away, Filchis."

He came up to the bars, too far away to grab, close enough for me to smell the wine on his breath. He put his hands behind him and swayed, looking at me.

The grin had gone. Now he looked like a stray dog that hopes for a scrap and will turn nasty if it doesn't get it.

"What do you know?" he said.

"About what?"

"You were asking questions, earlier. Questions about why I'd been sent here." He leaned closer. "*I want to know what you know.*"

"I don't know what you're talking about, Filchis."

"Maybe it was just... *someone's* way of keeping an eye on me. Is that it? He doesn't think I can be trusted. He'd rather tell *her* all his secrets. *I* know."

"Well," I said. "*I* don't. You're not making any sense."

"'Get to Incandress,' he said. 'And then, just listen, and watch. After the barbarians have their ceremony,' he said, 'everything will be settled.' But you know..." Filchis leaned back, and out came the finger again, wavering a few inches from my nose. "I don't think I believe him."

I felt my back hairs start to creep. "What do you know about the ceremony, Filchis? What's supposed to happen?"

"He told me Scalentine will be just what I always wanted. A place that can no longer be corrupted by outside influences. But you know what? You know what? I think he favours her. And I don't think he's telling me everything."

"Favours who?"

"The blonde. That silly woman. All very well if you need someone to stir up a crowd, but I don't think he should be telling her important things that he's concealing from *me*."

My head hurt, and I fervently wished for Mokraine. I couldn't make head or tail of what this fool was babbling about.

"'After the Enkantishak, Scalentine will be free of outside influences?' What does *that* mean?" I said.

"You're claiming you don't know."

"I *don't*."

How could a religious ceremony to acknowledge the Itnunnacklish *possibly* affect Scalentine?

But whoever had sent Filchis here believed it. And Filchis believed something was being hidden from him. He believed it enough that he'd sought me out, he'd come down to this stinking hole to try and get it out of me.

I stared at him. He stared back, his full-fleshed, smooth, politician's face flushed with drink and suspicion.

"Commander," he said, still looking at me. "I believe this woman is concealing important information. Information that may be of importance to Incandress. I think perhaps she should be *questioned*. Closely."

"She's here for violation of the Moral Statutes," the commander said.

"Which is enough to tell you that she is a person of questionable integrity," Filchis said, every sign of drink smoothed away. Sounding reasonable. Sounding *plausible*. "Now, we both know the situation here is dangerous. You have been dealing with it with great effectiveness, so far. But should something happen, and it turns out that she is responsible, and that if she had been carefully questioned, that something could have been prevented..."

Sweat began to prickle in my hair.

The Fenac commander looked us both over, rubbing his thumb over the hilt of his mace.

He'd heard Fain's warning about anything happening to me. But Fain was a foreigner, he wasn't here, and he'd been very careful that his reputation should *not* precede him.

I tried, anyway. "The Scalentine government will not be happy if one of its citizens is subject to..."

"Shut up," the commander said. He looked at Filchis. "You really think she knows something."

"I think it's more than likely. And as for being a citizen of Scalentine; things are changing there. The time when anyone and everyone can be considered a *citizen* is coming to an end."

Shit. Shit. Shit.

"She's up to something," the commander said. "She was trying to get a message taken, just before you arrived."

"Aha. Something intended for her co-conspirators, no doubt," Filchis said. "There are others involved, then. Perhaps names can be... extracted. Imagine if you could uncover an entire *nest* of conspirators, commander."

"Don't let him fool you," I said, trying, desperately, to sound calm. "He's not on your side, commander. He's not on anyone's side but his own."

"If that's true, if you're innocent of conspiracy," Filchis said, "why are you sweating?"

I'm sweating because you're talking about torture. You know it, I know it, the Fenac commander knows it. Everyone in this room knows it.

Fear was pulsing through me with every rapid heartbeat, throwing me off, making it hard to think. In a fight, I'm brave enough, because I'm good at what I do, and because there's something I *can* do.

Torture isn't a fight; there's nothing to reach for, no mates at your side, no enemy to defeat except the pain, which can't be defeated, except by dying.

This time, at least I'd be able to escape into death. That hadn't been true before.

No. I will not *think that way. I will* not.

I gripped those too-solid bars, and bowed my head.

"Considering your options?" Filchis said. "I do hope you will come to a sensible conclusion."

Oh, I was considering my options, all right. And I was pretty certain I only had the one. My mind raced like an animal in a cage, seeking exits where there were none.

The darkness in my head. I thought, for some reason, of the painful light of the device, shadows crawling on the wall.

Lady, if you're out there... I need you now. Babaska...

Long ago, ceremonies had been performed before me as Babaska's avatar. If I tried, I could remember many of them word for word. I had a good memory. Having a good memory isn't always a pleasant thing.

Think.

Lots of words, but words of summoning hadn't been among them. They hadn't *wanted* the real gods back...

Babaska, goddess of whores and soldiers. Babaska, goddess of helping your mates out in a tight spot, of seduction and death, of help to calm an angry client and help to... dammit, think, *Babylon...*

Something? Perhaps.

I called out into the void, and there was... something. That little shiver at the nape of the neck, that sense of being watched.

There was something there, but it felt different. It felt... cold.

Babaska?

The cold intensified, and suddenly, I felt stripped bone-naked, as though some brute, dreadful light had been turned on me, and then it was gone.

Babaska?

Silence. Darkness.

And up from my past there came a simple soldier's prayer.

Be the shield at my back, be the sword at my side, be the dust in my enemy's eyes.

A prayer to remember in the lines, under the unforgiving sun, waiting for the shock of onset and the meatcleaver punch of metal into flesh.

Be the shield at my back, be the sword at my side, be the dust in my enemy's eyes.

Be the shield at my back...

Hello, child.

Yes. I knew the feel of her instantly. A tingle like heat. Whatever else I'd felt was gone; the aftermath of the device, or of fear. Not that I wasn't afraid now.

Have you changed your mind, little avatar?

I have no choice. Help me.

Silence. Not empty, but considering.

I know there's a price, I thought. *Gods don't give away anything for nothing.*

You do not trust me, then.

I didn't answer that. I reckoned she already knew.

For a moment, nothing.

And then, something.

Heat. Light. Lust. Power. Joy. It clenched my hands on the bars and braced my feet and set my face in a grin.

Was it the power I'd had as an Avatar? No. No roaring orgasmic flame, no sense I could eat suns and spit worlds. But it was there.

"Now, Mr Filchis," I said. "There's no need to be unreasonable. I'm sure we can come to some... arrangement."

I raised my head and looked him in the eyes and smiled.

Filchis moved closer to the bars.

I reached through them and ran one finger over his forehead. "You have the face for command," I said. "You haven't had your dues, have you?" My voice, not quite my own. Dressed in silk and drenched in syrup. "Treated like a footsoldier in the great struggle, when you're obviously the one who should be general. Talk to me, Angrifon. Tell me what you desire."

He started to pant. "I desire... I desire... They'll kneel before me. They will. All of them."

"Yes," I said. "Yes."

"Here," the commander said. "What are you doing?"

"Commander!" I shook my head at him. "What are *you* doing? Here are you and your men, stuck underground, when there are enemies to be fought!"

A murmur from the men. The Ikinchli were utterly silent; nothing but a glitter of eyes. The Gudain prisoners clutched their bars and watched.

"What enemies?" the commander said.

Careful, Babylon. Careful. Don't want the slaughter of civilians on your conscience.

"I can show you. But not here."

The man was a gaoler to his bones. He looked at the keys in his hand and frowned.

"Come on, commander!" one of the Fenac said. "Let's get out there!"

Eager. The ugly eagerness of someone who wants an excuse. But it was what I needed.

"I can show you," I said, looking at the commander, loading it with promise. *I can show you.* It can mean many things, that. *I can show you where the enemy is. I can show you the blazing heart of desire. I can show you a good time, honeysweet, just let me out of this... fucking... cage...*

"Move aside," the commander said.

Reluctantly, still watching me, Filchis did so. His face was flushed and shining and his prick was pressing out the front of his breeches.

The commander opened the cell door, and beckoned me forwards; he was still frowning, as though he wasn't sure whether he was dreaming.

I stepped forward, chained hands in front of me.

Hurry. The link is weak, and there is something here... something that fights me.

Smoke, I thought back. With the Gudain's bodies rendered nearly incapable of passion, half Babaska's armoury was crippled.

Of course, the Ikinchli were feeling the effects of the goddess, too. Noticeably. Some of them had already lost interest in what was going on and were far more concerned with each other.

"Muscles," I said, not taking my eyes off the commander, hoping that Muscles wasn't already sinking himself into some eager companion.

"Who are you?" He was breathing fast, but he could answer. Good.

"I am the opening," I said, and a number of meanings swooped and hummed around the word. "You want to pass?"

"Yes." I hoped that meant he'd got it.

"Straighten up, commander," I said. I looked at the rest of the Fenac. I felt Babaska's smile on my face; hard, bright, loving, deadly. "Form up. Show some mettle. What, will you have them say you crouched here underground, when there was glory to be won?"

"No!" they shouted, as one. *Great, if that doesn't bring the bloody guards down from upstairs nothing will.*

"Then face about, gentlemen, and let's see how you're looking. Back up, and straighten up... that's right..."

The commander looked from his men, backing eagerly towards the cages, chins high, to me, standing in front of him with my wrists chained. "What –" he said, and reached for the chain.

I looped it around his hand, bent my knees and yanked my wrists down hard. His arm came with them, hauling him down, and I drove up, the top of my head cracking against his chin. I heard his jaw go, and felt the warm spatter of blood as he bit his tongue. His body arced backwards; I let myself go with it, both of us falling against another Fenac, slamming him back against the bars of the Ikinchli cell.

The commander and I fell to the floor, the commander under me, gargling and choking.

I looked up.

The Fenac were looking bemused. Suddenly they didn't know whose side they were on.

The Ikinchli did. Battle-lust and vengeance worked in my favour. They grabbed the Fenac through the bars by arms, clothes and hair and swiftly relieved them of weapons, keys and, in two cases, consciousness.

"Don't kill 'em!" I yelled.

I could hardly blame them for wanting to, but... Well. Like I said. Not a frigging murderer, even by proxy. If I can help it. Though the sight of Filchis, foggy as he was with lust and confusion, tempted me a lot.

Babylon. Hurry.

I'm trying, lady.

A weird, slipping sensation, a sudden flutter of images. A crack in stone; a huge wall holding back a river, with a tiny hole through which water was trickling; a strange room, as though someone had built inside a tunnel, brighter than daylight, things and people flying through the air, screaming... I blinked, and it was gone.

And so was she.

Shit.

She could have hung around another minute, dammit.

Muscles was gaping at me. He wasn't the only one. "Here," I said, holding my chained wrists out to him. "Be useful."

He unwrapped them, still staring. I tucked the chains into my belt. Now, they were a weapon; that felt a lot better.

"What are you?" Filchis said, somewhere behind me. "What are you?"

"Busy," I muttered. "All of you, *not* you, Filchis" – I grabbed him by the collar – "get the weapons. You'll need 'em." There was enough aftereffect that most of them listened to me. I was amazed that we hadn't already had half the building's guard and any stray Fenac down here wondering what the commotion was, but perhaps the big thick door had muffled any noise.

I took a handful of Filchis' coat. "You, chum, are coming with me."

"You can't..."

"Don't try my patience, there's none left." I looked at the remaining Fenac, either unconscious or backed into corners. "Right," I said. "Let's get 'em in there." They all fitted in the cage with plenty more room than their prisoners had enjoyed; I thought they'd been done pretty well by. The commander was awake, rubbing his head and still spitting bloody saliva, but he'd live.

None of them seemed at all sure what had happened. The few Gudain prisoners looked almost equally bemused.

"Let us out?" one of them said.

"What are you in for?" I said.

"Does it matter? You're letting the bloody scalys out!"

"For that, you get to stay where you are."

"How we going to get out?" one of the Ikinchli said.

Another held up a long, heavy key.

"Wait," I said. "Anyone know which way the doors open? I can't remember. Inwards or out?"

"In," someone said.

A chorus of agreement, and I realised I *did* remember, I'd just been so upset by the chains I hadn't been able to think. "Right. Damn. Okay, we're going to have to do this carefully."

I looked at the Fenac in the cage.

I looked down at myself.

Sometimes being this tall is a huge pain. If I put on one of these uniforms I'd look like an adolescent outgrowing their clothes. It might just be enough to trigger the guards' instincts.

Filchis, on the other hand...

I undid my trousers, removed my thigh knife, and did them back up. Muscles looked disappointed.

*   *   *

FILCHIS SHUFFLED UP the stairs. The uniform, baggy as it was, a little snug over his paunch. With my knife in his back. "One wrong move, one funny look, one word out of place, and I'll drive this into your spine. Even if they kill us all, *you'll* never walk another step. Smooth?"

"Smooth."

"Tilt your head down so they can't see your face."

"When we get back..."

"Shut up."

He did.

We got the doors open.

The guards saw only a Fenac officer's uniform coming out of the darkness. It was the depth of the night; a good time for an unexpected attack, especially when all their attention was focused outwards, on the watch for another riot.

We rolled right over them, through the hallway, slamming back the bolts and out of the heavy doors.

A couple of the guard tried to halt things, but they, too, were confused. For a few moments the courtyard was a seething mass of bodies. There were screams, the horribly familiar sound of blades meeting flesh. Muscles swung his stolen mace at a guard's head, connected with a wet *crunch*.

I wondered, briefly, what he'd been in for. But at this point I couldn't afford to care. He was big and he was strong and I needed him.

"Ram the gate!" I gestured to one of the benches.

He grabbed one side of it. Others saw what we were doing, and hands reached and lifted. *Run.*

The shock of impact. The gates clanged and bowed.

Back, heave, run. The hinges snapped, unevenly, the gates sagged outwards. People poured through the gap in a scramble; the guards roared and swung, and then everyone was in the street, scattering, hauling wounded comrades with them, disappearing down unlit alleyways among the crumbling, silent buildings.

I glanced behind me, saw the guard rounding up stragglers. An Ikinchli who'd fallen badly with his foot caught in the gate. I hesitated.

But then I heard it, above the cries and running feet.

Poom.

Boom beetle. *Dawn and dusk, they call out.* Dawn was coming.

I *had* to get to the house, and warn them.

I started to run, dragging Filchis, who flailed and swore. Damn, what was I going to do with him? He would attract attention and slow me down, but he knew things, and I needed to find them out. I didn't dare let him go.

Several Ikinchli followed me, Muscles included.

"What are you doing?" I said.

"The Itnnunnacklish must not be harmed. We will come with you. We will help."

"You really want to help? Draw off the bloody Fenac, so I can get there and warn her without being arrested again!"

They looked at each other, hesitated. Then most of them were running in different directions, away from me, shouting and yelling and drawing attention like good 'uns.

They may have been criminals – *if* they were criminals – but they still loved their Itnunnacklish.

A couple more simply faded away down sidestreets, still watching me. I could hardly blame them; they had no real reason to trust me.

"I might have known," said a familiar voice, wearily.

"*Fain!* What the hells are you doing here?"

"I was coming to negotiate your release. You appear to have rendered that unnecessary. Did you have to make quite such a mess?"

"Never mind that. Where's Enthemmerlee?"

"She is on her way to the Enkantishak."

"Already? Shit." I started on again, as fast as I could, hauling a protesting Filchis.

"This woman's insane! And a witch!" Filchis croaked. "Do something! I'm a citizen of Scalentine!"

"Shut up," Fain and I said, together. He looked at both our faces and, probably wisely, did so.

"Why aren't you with her?" I said.

"Certain constraints no longer apply." Fain fell neatly into step beside me.

"Laney? She's here?"

"Yes."

"Where is she?"

"With the others. Fortunately, since we seem to have lost Bergast."

"What?"

"Bergast has disappeared. I persuaded Laney to go in his stead."

"We have to get after them. We have to stop them."

"What is it?"

"The *Ipash Dok* that Selinecree said she found in Lobik's room. She didn't. She provided it herself, and... Look, I'll explain as we go, but we have to *go.*"

"Very well."

"Is Mokraine with them?" Laney obviously hadn't spotted anything wrong with the *Ipash Dok*, but then she didn't know to look for it. Mokraine just might have picked something up.

"Mokraine has collapsed."

"Oh, fuck."

Filchis made another effort to leave. "Filchis?" I said. "You come along quiet and cooperative and *fast* as your little legs will carry you, or I knock you out and leave you for the Fenac to find. I bet they'll be *very* interested in your explanation of how you just happened to be totally innocent of assisting in a massive prison break. You were trying to persuade them to torture me. You think they won't do it to you, *citizen of Scalentine?*"

"Did I hear that correctly?" Fain said. "He tried..."

"She's lying!" Filchis said.

"No, she isn't," Fain said.

I didn't even see his hand move. Filchis folded up like a paper flower in the rain, sagging to his knees, retching.

Then Fain's hand moved again and Filchis fell over on his side, eyes wide and fixed. I thought for a moment Fain had killed him.

"What..."

"Carrying him will be quicker," Fain said. "I assume there was a reason you were bringing him with you?"

"Yes. He knows things."

"Then let us move."

Still more than a little bemused by what had just happened, I put one arm around Filchis' back, Fain used the one arm that still worked (and with which he was remarkably efficient) and between us we hauled him off like a drunk at the end of a long night. Only faster.

Fortunately for us, the Fenac were concentrating on the Ikinchli rather than the random foreigners, Ikinchli being automatically guilty of *something*. The shouts faded behind us.

We slugged up the road towards the Entaire house. With what breath I had over, I explained to Fain what I'd realised about Selinecree.

"Tell me about Filchis," he said, when I finished.

"Oh, he thought I must know something, about what his mentor was up to; that's what he wanted to get out of me. Fain, why did you..."

"Tell me exactly what he said." It wasn't a tone that brooked argument.

"I can't remember word for word, and he was going on about some blonde woman he thinks his mentor favours, but after the Enkantishak he said his mentor had told him that – wait – 'Scalentine would no longer be corrupted by outside influences.'"

Fain was silent for some time except for his steepening breath. The boom beetles were all around now, as the sky lightened.

Boom. Boom. BOOM. Overlapping each other. *Boboom. BoBoom* BOOM BOOM.

The walls of the house came into view.

"So do *you* know what he meant?" I said.

"I think so," he said. His voice... I realised Fain was afraid. *Fain.* My guts went to melting ice.

"What is it?"

He sped up. Filchis' toes dragged and bounced on the ruts.

"Fain? Fain!"

"We need to get to the stables," he said.

"What..."

"Enboryay breeds racing disti. We have to take the fastest mounts we can find."

"Can you *ride* a disti?"

"Not yet."

CHAPTER
TWENTY

WE DIDN'T DARE go in by the gate; anyone who saw us might tell Selinecree.

We sneaked around to the place where I'd noticed the trees grew close enough to the wall to make good cover for an intruder, and then stopped.

"Wards. Bugger," I said. "What do we do about the wards?"

"A good ward should be specific; it should work against those with evil intent."

"You think Bergast's good?"

"You don't?"

"I don't know what Bergast is," I snapped. "Especially now he's bloody disappeared." What with one thing and another I was feeling a little edgy.

"Either his wards will work against us or they won't. There is only one way to find out."

"Then let's chuck Filchis over first and see what happens."

Slightly to my surprise, Fain agreed.

We got him into a tree, rolled him along a branch and let him drop.

There was a faint crackle – presumably the wards – and a thud.

It was followed by a groan, so whatever had happened to him wasn't fatal. And I couldn't smell burning.

I started to edge along the branch after him, and paused. "Are you going to tell me what you know?" I said.

"Let us deal with Filchis and get under way. Then we can talk."

Oh, we were going to talk, one way or another.

Assuming we survived the next few minutes.

I edged forward until I could see Filchis' shape on the ground. He was moving.

I held my breath and inched out over the wall. I felt the magic itch and crackle on my skin, but it didn't hurt.

Then I dropped in on the right side of the wall.

Fain followed – cat-neat, of course.

We worked our way along, dragging Filchis, until we were close to the stables, the metal-and-cream smell of the disti thick in the air. I could hear the hissing of the beasts and someone humming a string of whiny, nasal notes that was probably supposed to be a tune. The *clunk* and squeal of a pump, water drumming into a wooden pail.

I realised I was desperately thirsty.

Filchis was moaning and holding his head.

"Shut up, or you'll get it again," I said. He shut up.

"What did you do to him, anyway?" I whispered to Fain.

"Allow me a few trade secrets, Babylon."

I thought about asking him why, when he could simply have knocked Filchis out, he had gutpunched him first, but I had the feeling he wouldn't answer.

Besides, this didn't feel like the time for that conversation. I was a lot more concerned about the fear I'd heard in his voice.

"So what are we going to do with him now?"

"Find somewhere he can be confined until we return. I need to question him further."

There were empty buildings enough; we found one with enough of it left to hold him, stuffed rags in his mouth, and bound him with my chains.

"Pray we succeed," I told him. "Otherwise they'll find what's left of you in spring."

"If we fail," Fain said, "being forgotten will cease to concern him rather quicker than that, I think."

Filchis' eyes widened and he whimpered through his gag. My heart, already chilled, froze a little more.

"HEY, YOU GOT that upside down. She won't like that."

I swallowed my heart back down, turned around slowly and smiled at the stableboy. "Can you show me how to do it right?"

"Oh, surely. But you not taking her out, eh? She's carrying. No riding for her."

Damn.

"Show me the two best, please."

"Best for what?"

"A long fast ride," Fain said, appearing at the door of the stable. "Over rough ground."

I winced.

"Okay." The boy had two disti saddled and bridled in moments. He asked no questions, only patted his charges, gave us each bags of feed to sling from their saddles, told us they would need watering every ten *focat* (whatever those were) if we were riding them hard, and saw us off with a sunny, unconcerned grin.

"What's a *focat*?" I muttered, trying to act as though I knew what I was doing as the beast's unfamiliar swaying movement and the narrow, hard saddle told me I was in for a very unpleasant time even if I succeeded in staying on. I had already drunk about a gallon of water from the pump, and it was sloshing unpleasantly in my stomach.

"A unit of measurement, I imagine."

"Yes, Mr Fain, I gathered that. But what: feet? Yards? Miles?"

"I should imagine it is one of those dialect words Bergast is so interested in. When we find him, we can ask him."

"If the beasts collapse from lack of water before we do so I'm not going to be able to ask him."

"Then let us water them as soon as they show signs of fatigue." He stared at the approaching wall, and crouched down in the saddle.

So did I, though what I thought would happen next, I wasn't sure.

A cry came from behind us. "Heya!"

I stiffened up; I didn't want to hurt the boy, but if he was going to try and stop us...

I turned around to see him bouncing up to us on another disti, a big-boned ugly beast even by disti standards, so much too big for him that he seemed to have been stuck on its back like an afterthought. "No one else here, right? Everyone is gone. I let his lordship's guests go out with no one to show them the right things, he will be very angry. So, I am come with you."

"Good!" I said. "Marvellous. Show me how to make this beast jump over the wall."

"Oh, is easy," he said. "Hold on tight with the knees and go *yoka-ki!*"

His beast swayed its neck, and started to run, its stride lengthening as it approached the wall, until on the last its feet simply didn't come down again. It almost seemed to *flow* over the wall, the boy on its back laughing and barely bothering with the reins.

Fain and I looked at each other, and shrugged.

"*Yoka-ki!*"

The saddle slammed into me in places used to better treatment and I gripped with my knees like a nervous bride. The ground dropped away and reappeared with a jolt that went all the way to the top of my skull.

I hoped we wouldn't have to do too many of those.

Fain landed right beside me and muttered something under his breath, possibly obscene.

"Where we going?" the boy said.

"To the sacred mountain," said Fain.

"You going to the Enkantishak?"

"Yes."

"Good."

"We need to go very fast," Fain said.

"*Very* good. *Ki-tai!*"

We shot forward into the trees at a speed I found thoroughly disconcerting, especially with so many branches that looked ready to sweep me right off. I leaned flat to the beast's neck.

On through the trees, the green gloom lightening, giving way to open parkland; then the disti really started to run, their massive muscular legs propelling them in long smooth bounds, the landscape flowing past like water. We passed fine houses set far apart, some of them empty, disintegrating, flickers of pale sky showing through the broken walls.

The houses became fewer and fewer, and more of them looked abandoned, crumbling down like bad teeth.

Fields, either side. A single house, smaller, still occupied, a curl of smoke rising from a thin chimney.

Eventually the boy called a halt by a stream, to water the beasts. We were right out in the country now, surrounded by wide, flat fields, full of some silvery-brown crop that grew to waist-height and showed a tinge of pink when the wind disturbed it. Beyond the fields, hills rose, their sides washed green and purple and streaked with the white of hurrying cascades. Here and there I could see the deep grey, distinctively cup-topped shape of a volcano.

I walked over to where Fain stood by his beast, stretching his back muscles. I sympathised. My legs and arse were already sore; they'd be yelling by tomorrow.

"So are you going to tell me?" I said.

"Tell you... Oh."

"Yes."

Fain glanced at the stableboy, but he was downstream, stroking his mount and singing tunelessly to it.

Fain looked me in the eyes. "This goes no further, Babylon. Ever. Already you know far more than I am comfortable with."

"I am capable of discretion, though you might not believe it."

"Selinecree was on Scalentine. I think that she met with Filchis' mentor. I think he arranged for her to collect the *Ipash*

Dok." He laid his hand on the disti's smooth hide, as though drawing reassurance from it. "How much do you know about the portals, Babylon?"

"I don't. They open, they close, every time I go through one I get sick. They're known to drive people mad. So are people who don't give straight answers."

"I am attempting to give you a straight answer. The portals of Scalentine are unique. We know there are others, many others, throughout the planes. But none have been found that we know of that have all the same qualities. And there are writings in the Section's libraries that are very old, and talk of some other qualities the portals have, which no one now alive has seen in operation."

He fell silent, staring at the rippling crops. The hiss of wind, the gurgle of the stream, the sucking and splashing of the disti drinking their fill, the boy's tuneless singing.

"The portals of Scalentine are not exactly alive, and not exactly intelligent. But their function is, at least, twofold. To provide passage, and to prevent passage. If there is a sufficient threat, an *extreme* threat, they will close."

"Close? What, actually *close*? Even the permanent ones, like Bealach?"

"Yes."

"How long for?"

"Until the threat is considered to have passed."

"Who decides?"

"They do."

"What, the *portals*? But they... What?"

"Filchis' mentor, whoever it is, wants the portals to close. They have reason to believe something will happen at the Enkantishak ceremony which will provide a sufficient threat to Scalentine to *make* the portals close."

"All the way from here?"

"Yes."

"Merciful All."

"Let us hope so."

*   *   *

THE CROPS THINNED out; the land became rockier, silvery with pools and lakes. Lichen and moss grew everywhere, emerald and ochre and the rich red-brown of good leather. I saw a plume of what looked like smoke, or steam, coming up from the ground, and the air smelled like hot metal and gone-over eggs.

We saw no one on the road, not a single Ikinchli coming late to the ceremony. Had it already begun?

I had gone over the ceremony with Rikkinnet. The Itnunnacklish and her two husbands were gowned and garlanded. I'd worried about that, before; now, I had the dreadful thought that if someone did assassinate Enthemmerlee, it would probably stop the ceremony and prevent the opening of the *Ipash Dok*.

What was in that small glittering shell?

After the gowning – of course, now, there was only one husband to dress, dammit, even less time – there were words from the priests, an offering of fish to the ancestors, then the laying of the *Ipash Dok* on the altar.

I urged the disti on. It moaned. The stableboy, infected by our mood, had stopped singing as he rode and now crouched anxiously on his beast's neck, glancing over at us every now and again, but asking no questions.

I felt bad for the boy; but if whatever was in that thing was powerful enough to threaten Scalentine, an ocean away, telling him to ride like hells in the other direction probably wasn't going to do him much good.

Ahead, a great clump of hills, shaggy and brilliant with growth, and shrouded with mist. The road thinned, and steepened, and finally petered out into a narrow, muddy path, rising between banks lush with growth. The disti slowed, placing their great clawed feet carefully.

A small bird, of an extraordinary, heart-achingly brilliant shade of blue with a bright yellow throat, landed on a branch, scattering drops that fell like burning diamonds through the rays of the setting sun. It tilted its head, watching us with a bright orange eye.

We drove on up the path, while around us the landscape shimmered and hummed.

Suddenly the path flattened off, and there before us was a cliff-face, deep red, hung with vines. A set of steps cut into the rock led to a cave gaping dark among the green. All around us grew tall, flowering plants with trumpet flowers of a blazing, triumphant orange streaked with white, each bloom as long as my forearm. They gave off a richly honeyed scent, which drowned out the smell of decaying eggs.

We leapt down, and ran up the steps; red stone, a smooth shining dent worn in the centre of each by uncounted thousands of feet over who knew how many centuries.

The colour of the stone made the entrance to the cave, high and wide enough for two carriages, look uncomfortably like a mouth. The sun was behind the mountain; I could see glimmers of light in the darkness within. My spine itched, and my hand tightened on my knife. I missed my shield, wondered if Rikkinnet still had it

We stepped forward.

"Who goes there?"

Tantris, and a handful of the guard, flanked by Ikinchli.

"You! What..."

"No time. Let us in."

"Who are these people?" Two of the Ikinchli, hard-muscled and alert, stepped forward. "What do you want here?"

"Enthemmerlee!" I yelled.

"Babylon. Please." Fain bowed. "We are here to protect the Itnunnacklish."

"The captain knows me," I said. "Please. If you won't let us in, just tell them, they mustn't put the *Ipash Dok* on the altar! If it opens..."

They looked at each other, and in that moment I dived past them.

Heat, steamy as a laundry, smelling of eggs and greenness and packed bodies and something rich and sweet. The murmurous sigh of a huge crowd.

Beyond the glow of daylight falling through the cave-mouth, showing a floor of polished red stone, the place was a vast hollow, packed like a jewel-chest with lamps and candles and thousands upon thousands of glowing eyes.

It seemed as though the whole of the inside of the mountain had been carved out. The walls were a deep and bloody red, porphyry polished smooth as glass. Translucent slices and folds of agate hung here and there, like swathes of fantastic fabrics in shades of gold and copper and umber and flesh. Piled in mounds here and there, sometimes spreading up the walls, was what I thought, for one confused moment, was snow; but it was rock, smooth white stuff that glimmered where the light hit it as though a billion tiny stars were caught in its substance.

And crowded into this fantastical natural palace were thousands of Ikinchli. Every age, from tiny squirming infants to rheumy-eyed silvery ancients, sitting on low stools, on cushions, on rocks, on the floor. Perched in niches in the walls.

To the left was a great slab of that glimmering white stone, four feet high, six deep, and ten wide.

The altar. Mounds of incense were piled on its surface, sending sweet blue smoke up into the darkness. In front of it, Enthemmerlee and Malleay, tiny and doll-like in gowns of fantastic splendour; so covered with beads and stones and mirror-fragments as to render the fabric invisible. The gap where Lobik should have been was as shocking as a missing limb. In front of them, several Ikinchli priests, in elaborately embroidered gowns. Enboryay. Next to him a tumble of blonde curls, a shimmering gown: *Laney*.

The core of the guard at Enthemmerlee's back. Stikinisk, the others, couldn't remember their names, wouldn't matter in a moment.

"Enthemmerlee!" My voice was sucked away into the huge empty space, the murmuring crowd. I started to run.

Faces turning to look, shocked.

"Enthemmerlee!"

Cave was too damn big, acoustics shitty, she'd never hear me.

The priests could see me now, but they carried on, ignoring the disruption. They'd probably expected something like this.

More of the guard, seeing someone running, raising weapons, realising who it was, confused, uncertain.

Good. If they'd had proper training I wouldn't get within feet of her.

I jinked to the side without thinking. Something slapped my cheek, the side of my face went numb, I stumbled, kept running.

Stikinisk saw me, and her mouth opened. Malleay saw me, and suddenly there was a blade in his hand. *What, you think after all the trouble I've been to I want to finish her off?*

Someone hit me in the back, knocking me off my feet. I heaved them off, got up, kept running. "Enthemmerlee!"

Someone else slammed into me, and as I went over I saw Laney, wide eyed and furious, lifting her hand.

"No, Laney! It's the *Ipash Dok*, the gift, don't let it go on the altar!"

Finally, Enthemmerlee turned. I could see an *Ipash Dok* glittering in her hand; another – her own, I hoped – was already on the altar.

She held the thing up, looking at it, puzzled.

Then an awful lot of people landed on me.

"GET OFF HER!" Laney, never one for ceremony, marched through the crowd, throwing off sparks.

You don't need to have met Fey before to realise that you don't stand in the way of one when she's pissed off. The various people holding me down – some guards but mostly Ikinchli – got up, though several of them still held onto me.

"Babylon, you're bleeding."

I was also pretty sore, and still trying to get my breath back. Someone had landed on my stomach and knocked the wind out of me. "Laney," I wheezed. "That thing Enthemmerlee's holding, there's something very bad in it. Very... *huuhh*... bad indeed."

"Oh. Well, I'd better take a look at it then."

Enthemmerlee still stood by the altar, looking at me, as did Malleay. I hadn't been stared at by this many people at once since the *last* time I'd been at the centre of a religious ceremony.

Enthemmerlee said, "I hope that you will forgive us for the insult of this disruption, but it seems there may be a problem."

"Indeed there is," Fain said. "I apologise profoundly for this, but we had no choice."

"Please," I said, "let Laney look."

Enthemmerlee frowned at me, then looked at the small, glittering oval in her hand. "This."

"Yes."

"Surely you don't think *Lobik*..."

"No. Not Lobik. Please, trust me, it's dangerous."

I saw her fingers tighten, and I drew a breath. Her eyebrows went up, and, still slowly, she handed it to Laney.

"Don't try and open it," I said.

"Really, Babylon, I'm not an idiot." Laney frowned, running her fingers over the glitter and fragments. "It's... Oh."

"What is it?"

"A *very* clever ward," Laney said. "A ward made to not look like a ward. If I hadn't been looking for something, I'd never have found it."

Everyone was looking at us now. "What is it? How did you know?" Enthemmerlee said.

"Later. Please." I didn't think she needed the news of her aunt's betrayal right now. "It should be safe, for the moment. Laney?"

"Oh, yes. I'll deal with it." She looked up at the surrounding faces; the guards, the hundreds of watching Ikinchli, Enthemmerlee, the priests, and waved a hand. "Go on, then, carry on. I thought you had a ceremony to do?"

* * *

I<small>T WAS ALL</small> very solemn, and involved singing, but fortunately it wasn't very long.

The Ikinchli seemed pleased, and roared their pleasure when Enthemmerlee was declared the Itnunnacklish; I felt a little ashamed of myself for thinking that a trifle redundant.

A<small>FTER THE CEREMONY</small> Laney rushed over to me and enveloped me in a scented hug. "Babylon, darling, I'm so sorry it took me just the *longest* time to get here, honestly, what with one thing and another..." She looked closely at me. "Darling, you look quite dreadful, has it been ghastly? No, I can tell it has. I *knew* I should have come with you." Tears glittered in her eyes. "I'm so sorry."

"Don't be silly, love, I told you not to come. Laney, is everyone well? Are things bad, back home?"

"Oh, well, there have been a few silly squabbles, but nothing dreadful. And that nice little herbalist on Freshwater Street got burned down, can you imagine? *So* annoying, now I'll have to find someone else. Which reminds me, you're going to bruise, I'll put something on that when..."

"And Hargur?"

"Last I heard he was fine. It was him you meant, wasn't it? In your first message? About 'our dear Millie'?"

In everything that had happened, I'd completely forgotten about the message I'd sent from the docks when we arrived. "You got it?"

"Well, I wouldn't know what it said if I hadn't, darling, would I? Honestly, Babylon."

"Sorry. It's been a long few days."

"Yes, I can tell. Anyway, I did send a message to Hargur, saying that you thought Fain was watching him."

"Did he say anything?"

"Oh, you know the Chief, darling. He sent a message saying, 'I know.' That was it! And then I got your other one, and I spent *forever* trying to get passage. Two *days* in dockside offices!" Laney rolled her eyes. "I was beginning to think I'd been ill-wished."

Two days, plus the time it had taken to get here. Anything could have happened. Though even on the docks, surely, she'd have heard...

"Oh, and did you find out anything about the silk?" Laney said.

I groaned. I'd forgotten about the bloody silk. "Well, it was on its way to Scalentine, last I heard. But someone planned to rob the warehouse."

Her face fell. "Oh, no, that's awful! We must get home and stop it!"

"It should be all right. I got a message back, to warn the Militia. If they have time to deal with it, that is."

"Oh, well." Laney's face brightened again. "That's all right, then."

I hoped she was right. It was so good to see her I couldn't really stay annoyed with her, anyway; having her there was like a little slice of home.

Still not as good as the real thing, though.

"Have you found out what was in the *Ipash Dok*?"

"So far as I can tell, it's a disease. A very, very nasty one; some sort of plague. Without taking it to someone who specialises in these things, all I know is it would probably kill most things within a bee's flight of human. So, certainly Ikinchli *and* Gudain and you, and probably me, too. And very, very infectious. But I daren't look any closer."

"It has to have been made outside Scalentine, then."

"Well, I don't know, darling," Laney said.

"What do you mean? I thought the portals stopped diseases getting through."

"They stop them coming in from the outside, but I don't know if they stop them getting *out*. People going the other way don't usually *have* anything infectious."

Fain would probably know, and in the meantime, it wasn't my problem. "Can you make it harmless?"

"I already did. Well, I've *locked* it. It needs destroying, really, but I don't think I'm that good. I need Mokraine."

"What happened to him?"

"Oh, it was terribly shocking, darling; I mean I haven't seen him for so long, I had no idea he was that ill. And that creature of his was looking even more disgusting than usual. I've seen prettier slugs."

"I've seen prettier *turds* than that thing."

"Darling, ugh. Anyway, I was talking to Mokraine and I heard this scraping noise, and the familiar was lying on the floor, and well, you know it doesn't *breathe,* but it looked as though if it did, it would be struggling to, and Mokraine got down on his knees, and I asked if it was sick, and he said he thought it was dying."

"Did he catch something from it?"

"I don't know, he just collapsed. I did what I could, had him put to bed in his room, but I'm not sure what's wrong. I mean, this is Mokraine. He doesn't even get *sick* like other people."

"So who else was left behind?"

"A handful of servants," Laney said, "some rather horrid little guard with hair like a greased hedgehog..."

"Dentor."

"Well, anyway, I didn't like him, a few other guards, and the seneschal, of course. Honestly, I don't think you could get him out of the place unless you put a fireball up his bottom."

"I hope you weren't thinking of trying that."

"Now you know I wouldn't. By the way, that Captain Tantris is rather sweet, isn't he? Is he with anyone who'd *mind?*"

"Ah. Laney, I need to tell you about the Moral Statutes..."

WE HEADED BACK to the Entaire household. On the way, I had the less-than-delightful task of telling Enthemmerlee about her aunt.

I saw the muscles of her jaw tighten. Poor child. As though she hadn't had enough grief.

Then I saw Malleay put his hand over hers, and clasp it, and I felt a little better.

"I was an idiot," I said. "I should have seen it much earlier."

"How could you have?" Enthemmerlee said. "I never saw it."

"I made a stupid assumption. When I realised she was having a secret meeting with Dentor, I thought they were having an affair."

"An affair?"

"I thought she was bedding him."

"Bedding... Oh. Oh! You thought... *Selinecree?* And a *guard? Bedding?*"

"Yeah. Sorry. And when she realised what Mokraine could do, she had him shoved into a room as far from her as possible and kept from meals, so there was no chance he'd bump into her and get what was going on in her head. I actually saw her run from the carriage he was in, and it never occurred to me why."

There was another silence. The pinkish crops bent their heads. It had started to rain again.

"Papa would have died too," Enthemmerlee said. "She didn't try to stop him coming to the ceremony."

"No. And if I'm right, with both of you out of the way, the estate would be hers to manage as she pleased; and she'd be the victim of a terrible tragedy which nonetheless managed to remove a dreadful embarrassment. And she'd have Chitherlee to bring up, properly, in the old ways."

"Yes." Her voice was cold.

"What will you do?" I said.

"I will do what is necessary."

CHAPTER
TWENTY-ONE

WE PAUSED JUST out of sight of the house. It was dusk; smoke curled into the damp blue air. "We have to assume Selinecree's still at the house," I said. "If she sees this lot coming back, she'll know things didn't work the way they were meant to and probably make a run for it. I suppose a few of us are going to have to go in the way Fain and I came out."

Enboryay spoke for the first time since Enthemmerlee had told him the situation. He had ridden in scowling silence all the way from the ceremony, his face paling and darkening by turns. Now it was locked in a flushed glare.

"Stupid," he said.

"Papa?"

"Me. Bloody old fool I've been. You." He turned his glare on me. "That was a good bit of riding, though watching you on the way back, your seat's dreadful. No wonder you're sore. Got some ointment that'll help. Meantime, you come with me. I'll show you a better way in, get closer to the house." He looked at Tantris. "You too. And if you ever hear any bloody silly rumours about being turned away, talk to my daughter. As though either of us would ever turn out our guard. You should be ashamed, the lot of you."

"Sir," Tantris said, flushing furiously, and flushing more furiously when he caught Laney smiling at him. Perhaps he hadn't been attending *privaiya* recently.

"Papa?"

"What is it, child?"

"Be careful," Enthemmerlee said, clutching Malleay's hand. *"Please."*

Enboryay looked at his daughter, and nodded. "I will. Think I'm going to leave you with nothing but this sprig of a boy to help you run the estate? Hah. Come on then," he said, and we mounted up, in my case with considerable protest from my abused nethers.

We nipped over the wall at a point where it was only yards from the main servants' entrance.

The seneschal opened the door, letting only the briefest flicker of puzzlement pass over his face before he bowed. "My lord. Was the ceremony successful?"

"For us, yes. Where's my sister?"

"In the chapel, my lord."

We opened the gates, and got the chapel surrounded.

I'd got my arms back from Rikkinnet, and had them with me. Having misjudged Selinecree so appallingly, I didn't trust her not to have another trick up her oversized sleeves.

But there were no guards, no bully-boys, no signs of magic. We pushed open the door of the chapel to see her seated on the low bench, Chitherlee at her side. The old priest shuffled out from his cubbyhole, and didn't even seem to notice us. Dusky smoke curled from several burners, thick and sweet-smelling; I held my breath. Chitherlee turned as the door creaked open.

"Hello, Aunt Emlee. Is it finished?"

Then Selinecree turned around. She looked simply puzzled, at first, and then her face twisted into a sullen fury that made her look like a distorted child.

"Chitherlee, come out," Enthemmerlee said.

Chitherlee slid off the bench, and Selinecree grabbed her gown. The girl squawked. "No," Selinecree said. "No. You've taken everything else. You shan't take her! You shan't!" She pulled the child towards her by handfuls of material, backing along the bench. The priest, his back to us, oblivious, fidgeted with his bowls and rods.

"Selinecree. There's nowhere to go," Enthemmerlee said, her voice calm and clear and very, very cold.

"Let *go*, you're *hurting* me!" Chitherlee wailed, and pulled.

There was a low ripping, and part of the girl's gown pulled away from the ruff, revealing the armature, a stark ugly thing of wood and wire, like a cage. Chitherlee ran up the aisle, leaving a long strip of cloth in her great-aunt's hand.

"It's torn," Selinecree said. "Chitherlee, you bad girl, look what you've done."

THE PATINARAI CEREMONY was in less than six hours, and we still had Selinecree to deal with. I hurried along towards the main hall with Laney.

"Laney, what was going on, to keep you in the docks?"

"Well, I was the oddest thing. There was this ship, the *Lovely Aurette*, and she seemed nice and was going the right way, so I booked a passage, and as I was coming away there was this man, he looked sort of familiar, he said was I going to Incandress. I told him yes and he said, did I have friends there, because it was a bad situation and I said, that was why I was going. So I asked him if he'd heard anything, because, well, you know, I'd had your message and I was worried. The person who passed it on wouldn't tell me anything else except what you'd said."

"That's the Section for you. So what did this man say?"

"Only that he'd heard it was bad there, and he'd really advise me not to go. He must have been there to book his own passage and changed his mind, I saw him talking to the captain."

"Wait a minute. He asked if you were going to Incandress?"

"Yes."

"But the ships don't go to Incandress. Incandress is landlocked. The ships come into Calanesk. You can go anywhere in the

Flame Republic and half the Empire from there. So why did he assume you were going to Incandress?"

"You know, I've no idea," Laney said, wandering around the room, tugging at a frayed curtain. "Oh, this place needs so much doing to it. Really, some decent hangings, a good muralist... and these windows should all be enlarged, and the ceilings moved up. It's so *grim*."

"Laney... did you recognise him? The man who asked you about Incandress?"

"I've seen him about. Some dreadfully tedious dinner, I think. Oh, I remember; the Guild of Grain Merchants and Seed Dealers. Such a ghastly evening, I had to play little games with the client under the table just to get him to leave early." She smiled.

"Do you know his name?"

"Well, no, darling, I don't think we were ever introduced. I'd know him again, though. His hair was the oddest shade of red, I'm almost certain it was dyed."

"And what happened after that?" I said.

"I couldn't get a ship for love nor money, and I did try both. The captains either told me there was no room, or they couldn't go where I wanted. I ended up on a *tiny* little ship out of some place I'd never heard of, *and* I had to persuade them to go off their course, *and* I had to dim the whole ship; honestly, I was *exhausted*."

"You had to dim the ship?"

"Well someone was trying to stop me leaving, darling, it was quite obvious, so I had to be sneaky. Only we nearly got hit by another ship as we were coming out of the harbour, because they couldn't see us. The captain *wasn't* pleased. I had to spend ages making her feel better."

"Wait, we'd best talk to Fain."

He was in his room, shaking out a shirt. "Did you want something?"

"I've been talking to Laney," I said. "Someone on the docks found out she was going to Incandress, and I think they were doing something, bribery, intimidation maybe, to stop any of the captains taking her."

"Did she know this gentleman?"

"No, but she'd recognise him again, she said. Dyed red hair, and she'd seen him at a grain merchants' guild function. What is all this business with grain? Incandress doesn't even *have* any."

"Oh, no, it makes perfect sense," Fain said.

"What do you mean, it makes sense?"

"Someone planned to tip the balance, as I thought – but not in the way I thought."

"But who? And why?"

"A grain merchant."

"And the why?"

"A disease like the one contained within that spell would certainly be enough of a threat to force the portals to close. And if someone had built up vast stocks of grain, and became the only source of grain... Why, while the portals were closed, that someone would become very, very rich, and very, very powerful."

"That's why bread's been going up so much. Someone's been buying up all the grain," I said.

"Yes."

"Someone was prepared to kill thousands, maybe millions of people for this?"

Fain sighed. "It is not the first time such things have been done for money, or for power. It won't be the last."

"So is the redhead our man?"

"A subordinate, I think. It sounds as though he was planted at the docks to keep an eye open for Laney, or anyone else trying to book passage to Incandress, in order to provide... discouragement. If we can find him, he may lead us to the one in charge. That's who I need to find, and quickly. Before they realise their hand has been tipped. And *someone* in the Section is involved. You didn't trust Bergast from the start. While I think you were unfair in that, since I suspect him of nothing more than incompetence, I do believe that his being made available was deliberate. What better than to send to Incandress a Scholar incapable of detecting so lethal a spell?"

"You plan to question him?"

"When we find him, yes."

I STARTED TO search the grounds for Bergast, but instead found a wandering warlock. He looked dreadful, like a gargoyle on a frosty day, but he was alive.

"Mokraine! How are you?" I said. "What happened?"

"Oh, a folly. I had simply failed to take something into account. It seems I cannot yet rid myself of this troublesome need of mine." He looked down at the creature that hopped and dragged after him. "When I feed, it feeds. If I decline, it starves. Unfortunately, it seems our spirits are tied together, and if it dies, I die. I have not yet decided that I desire to do so." He gave a horrible, twisted smile.

"I'm sorry," I said.

"I know. Did you know there is a man tied up in one of those buildings?"

"Oh, yes, Filchis," I said. "I almost forgot about him."

"Yes," Mokraine said. "You have an... *occupied* mind, do you not, Babylon? Interesting."

"What?" I said.

"I think, perhaps, we should have a conversation," he said.

"Maybe later." I didn't know what he wanted, but I didn't like the look of mingled fascination and concern on his face.

Having freed a by now somewhat smelly and subdued Filchis, I decided to try the rest of the house, starting with Bergast's room. Mokraine came with me. Fain joined us. "Ah, First Adept," he said.

"Mr Fain."

We were in there turning over piles of papers when Bergast opened his door with his elbows, since he was using his hands to hold his head. He looked like the aftermath of three days in one of King of Stone's worse bars.

He looked up and saw the three of us. His face froze, mouth dropping and eyes widening. He turned to run and I grabbed his forearms, slammed the door shut with my foot and pushed him against it with his hands against his chest.

"What...? Get off me!"

"Don't try my patience, Bergast. I hope you never gamble, because guilt was written all over your face the second you walked in here."

"But I haven't... I didn't... Let go... I'll make you!" Blue fire flickered over his hands and I felt an unpleasant slippery tingle in my fingers.

"Really?" I said. "You have *met* First Adept Mokraine, have you? Or, for that matter, me?"

The fire went out, the slippery sensation dissipated. Bergast slumped. "All right. All *right*. Can you please let go? You're breaking my hands!"

"I'm not, my lad. If I were, you'd know it. Let's have those hands behind you." I bound his wrists together.

"First, where have you been?" Fain said.

"I fell asleep," Bergast said sullenly.

"You fell *asleep*."

"Yes! I was talking to Lady Selinecree about some of the work I'd been doing on the language – oh, I need to tell you about that – and she gave me a drink and I fell asleep."

"For an entire day?"

"Yes. I woke up a few minutes ago out in the grounds."

"Lucky," I said.

"Lucky? I got soaked through!"

"You're lucky that Selinecree either couldn't find, or didn't bother using, a lethal potion instead of one that merely knocked you out. Considering what she was planning."

"What do you mean? What was she planning?"

Fain told him. Bergast's mouth opened and shut a few

times as he considered the implications. "You thought I was involved?" he said.

"You've been hiding *something*," I said. "Right from the beginning. From me, from Mokraine..."

Bergast flicked a glance at Mokraine, then looked away, as though afraid it would burn him to look longer. There was hot colour in his cheeks, and a sulky set to his mouth. He looked like a boy about to be scolded for breaking a window.

"Guilt," Mokraine said. He moved closer to Bergast; a horrible eagerness beginning to dawn in his eyes. "Resentment." He reached out one thin hand, and traced a line across Bergast's flushed cheek with one cold white finger. Bergast flinched and shuddered. "I could see more... and I could take all this fear and shame and anger, and make it gone... at least for a little while."

"Mokraine..." I said, and he shot me a murderous glare. I shut up.

"I could," he said, looking into Bergast's wide brown eyes, cupping his face with his clawlike hand. "I could..."

"It would be helpful if we could question him afterwards," Fain said calmly. "Time, after all, is short."

Mokraine turned away, and I caught, for the briefest moment, the brute effort of that denial written on his face. Then he looked at me, calm and smiling. "Resentment, shame, and books. Piles of books. That's all, Babylon." He walked away and stood with his back to us; I saw him rest his hand against the cold plaster.

"Books?" I said. "Wait a minute. On the boat. You were studying... You looked embarrassed. I remember I couldn't work out why. I thought you might... Never mind. What have you been studying, Scholar Bergast? What are you up to? If you're dabbling in something you shouldn't be..."

"All *right!*" he shouted. "The first stage of the exams. I was... There was so much, and I was *tired,* and I've always been good, I knew I could make it up, and plenty of people do it. So what?"

"Tell me what you're talking about," I said, grabbing the front of his robe, "or suffer the consequences."

"The exams. I had a bit of help."

"The *what?* You *what?*"

"It's not cheating," Bergast protested, somewhat breathlessly. "I just got someone to help me with the sections on detecting hidden magic. They needed the money. I was helping *them*."

"Oh for the love of the All," I said, dropping him. He fell back against the door. "And I was wasting time on you."

"Am I right," Fain said, "in understanding that you cheated on your exams?"

"It wasn't..."

"Scholar," Fain said quietly. "Language is a precise instrument. As a magician, this is something of which you should be particularly aware. Cheating is precisely what it was. For such behaviour there are consequences. Because you cheated, you were considered adequate for this mission, which you were not. If it were not for the fact that we had a much more able practitioner turn up, your incompetence could have resulted in thousands, perhaps millions, of deaths. You understand?"

White-faced, Bergast nodded.

"On our way back to Scalentine, you are going to go over with me, in minute detail, the process by which you achieved this post. Who was your supervisor, who dealt with your paperwork, everything you can remember. And strive to be precise, and clear, and honest..." – he paused, and Bergast's pallor disappeared under an ugly flush – "and you *may* avoid the most extreme consequences of your behaviour. In the meantime, you will strive to make up for your idiocy."

"Yes!" Bergast nodded, eagerly. "I was going to tell you! I realised. The whole thing about the sacrifice maiden, it's a mistranslation!" He nodded at his notebook.

I opened it, and peered. "I can't make head or tail of this."

"Look." He pointed with his chin. "Oh, look, *please* untie me, I'm sorry, but this is really important."

"Fain?" I said.

"Yes, untie him. I am sure we would all find it enlightening and entertaining should he try and run away."

"What do you mean about a mistranslation?" I said.

"*Itni*," Bergast said. "It's still used by the Gudain for 'girl,' or 'little girl.' But in Old Andretic, *acliss* means 'sacrifice.' I think as the language changed, when Ikinchli talked about the maiden who calms the world, what the Gudain *heard* was 'the maiden who is sacrificed.' See?"

"And why did you think this was sufficiently important that you spent time on it instead of on the job you were hired to do?" Fain said.

"I..." Bergast shrugged. "Well, I thought if people *knew*, they'd stop, you know, believing it. That would be good, wouldn't it? I mean, for the Ikinchli."

"I am charmed by your belief in the healing power of etymology," Fain said. "Or would be, if I believed it. I suspect you hoped this discovery would bring you academic honours, and the respect of your peers. A not unreasonable aim, and at least in *this* case you would have earned it. However, it is not what you were appointed for."

Bergast looked away.

"Let me see," Mokraine said. He took the notebook from my hand. "Old Andretic. Of course, this is the right area..." He pored over the pages, his ancient eyes alight with interest. "I have not studied Ikinchli dialect. Interesting. *Itnun,* 'maiden,' yes; *ack* – what is that word? Your handwriting is a disgrace, Scholar."

"*Ack* is 'whole,' or 'both,'" Bergast said.

"The One who is Both," I said. "I've heard her referred to that way, too."

"And *li* is 'to calm' or 'soothe,' and *esh* is 'the world,'" Mokraine went on.

"It's a contraction," Bergast said.

"Yes, Scholar, that is obvious even to my mean intelligence."
Bergast swallowed.

"You think people will listen?" I said. "They've got other
things than language on their minds right now."

Fain was looking thoughtful. "The right words, at the
right time, can be powerful even when people are terrified or
starving. Perhaps especially then. But first, we must deal with
Selinecree, and find out what she knows."

"Oh, and Filchis," I said.

"Oh, yes, Filchis. What a tedious little man he is."

"I WILL ASK the Ten Families to consider exile," Enthemmerlee
said.

"Exile?" Selinecree's face drained of all colour. "No! No, you
can't!"

"Aunt, the choice will be exile or execution." Enthemmerlee
closed her eyes for a moment, weariness dragging at her face.
"Do you have *any* conception of what you did?"

"It didn't work," Selinecree said. "So I didn't do *anything*."

"If it had worked, you would be dead in about three days. So
would almost everyone else in Incandress," Laney said.

"It was only supposed to kill whoever was in the cave, close
to it," Selinecree said. "That was all."

"Your own brother. The family guard, who we are sworn
to," Enthemmerlee said. "And who knows how many innocent
Ikinchli. All to get me out of the way?"

"You've ruined everything, you stupid, stubborn child! And
Enboryay is as bad, all he cares for is those wretched disti. Do
you know, any of you, the trouble I've gone to, to maintain our
position? And you don't care, none of you care a bit. I did it all
for Chitherlee, so she'd have a future, but you don't even care
about her!"

"Yes, I do," Enthemmerlee said. "I care about all our futures."

"You only care about the wretched scalys. They won't thank you!"

"I don't want their thanks," Enthemmerlee said. "Selinecree..."

"What?"

"Who was it?"

"Who was what?"

"You know. Who sold you the spell?"

"No one *sold* it to me. I was sent a message saying a friend had heard of my troubles, and wanted to help. They told me where to collect it, and how it worked; that it would get rid of anyone standing close. That's when I decided how to use it."

"At the ceremony," Enthemmerlee said.

"Well, of course. Not here, with Chitherlee here!"

"So you just accepted it? You didn't question it?" Enthemmerlee said.

"Well, anyone in their right mind could understand my position!" Selinecree said. "I thought, perhaps, that one of the other families had arranged it. They've shown me a great deal of sympathy, you know."

"I think you may find that is no longer the case," Fain said. "Guards? Would you be kind enough to bring in Mr Filchis?"

Filchis had been given a plain Gudain gown to replace his Fenac uniform, which by the time we got him out of the hut was more than a little soiled. We hadn't yet told him about the *Ipash Dok*.

"Do you know this man?" Fain said.

"What? No," Selinecree said. "Him? Wasn't he at one of those ceremonies? He was talking to me about something, I don't remember what."

"I feared that was too easy," Fain said. "Babylon?"

"You're all going to regret this," Filchis said. "And you, *Madam Steel*, you should be in jail!"

"And you should be upside down in a privy, you little scrote. Tell me, do you know the name Mokraine? First Adept Mokraine?"

"No," Filchis said. "Why should I?"

"First," Fain said, "a few questions. Mr Filchis? Who sent you here?"

"No one sent me. I came of my own will."

"Indeed. Then who *suggested* you come?"

"A friend."

"A friend. And yet, he sent you here to die."

"What?"

"You see, it was planned that most of the population of Incandress would die, and you with them, Mr Filchis. You know who was behind it. You had to be got out of the way. Are you going to tell us who sent you?"

"I don't know his name, he never told me."

"Then," Fain said, leaning close, "you will tell me what you do know."

"You can't force me to anything! I'm a citizen of Scalentine!"

"Something you are eager to claim for yourself and deny to others."

I opened the door. Mokraine walked in. The familiar dragged itself after him as he walked, with painful slowness, towards the chair where Selinecree sat. She had twisted around to look at him.

"You can't do anything," she said. "I've told them everything. They know it all, so do your worst."

"My worst..." he said thoughtfully. "You poor creature. You haven't the faintest conception of my worst."

"What is all this?" Filchis said. "What's going on? I demand you tell me what's going on!"

"Oh, do shut up, you vile little man," Laney said. "Or I'll turn you into even more of a toad than you are already."

"You can't talk to me like..."

She flicked her fingers at him. There was a slippery blue-pink tingle, and Filchis' jaw shut with a snap.

"Be quiet," Laney said, "or I'll fill your mouth with worms."

"Well?" Mokraine said.

Enthemmerlee looked from him to Selinecree, and nodded.

"I can't promise I will find anything of use," Mokraine said.

"And afterwards?" Enthemmerlee said.

"Afterwards... Peace. For a little."

Enthemmerlee glanced to her left. Where Lobik had always stood. Then she looked at Mokraine. "Do it," she said.

The familiar leaned against Selinecree's gown. She made a disgusted face and tried to move her leg away; while she was looking down, Mokraine put his hand on her shoulder.

The change in him was immediate, shocking. It flowed into him like new wine, straightening his back, putting colour in his cheeks. Even the familiar's loathsome hide gained a faint sheen.

"Oh, what a moiling," Mokraine said. "What self-pity, what resentment! Even now she feels no guilt. See how everyone has sinned against her! And a spark, a little spark, of genuine affection for someone... the child... but even that, how thickly twined with what she wanted for herself. Oh, what a dark carnival you are, my dear." He patted Selinecree, almost affectionately, on the head. "But nothing useful, I'm afraid," Mokraine said. "She barely sees anyone who isn't herself. Most people are nothing but shadows or mirrors to her."

Selinecree's face went utterly slack, as free of any personality or thought as a mound of dough.

"Mmmm! *MMMMM!*" Filchis was writhing, his jaw still locked.

"Oh," Laney said, and snapped her fingers again.

"I'll tell you," Filchis said, staring at Selinecree. "Only don't let him do that to me. I'll tell you. I'll tell you."

"Who sent you?" Fain said.

Filchis, sweating, said, "I don't know his name, but he has offices on Little Copper Lane. I can show you. I followed him, after our meeting."

"So, you didn't trust him, either. Interesting," Fain said.

"And the woman?" I said.

"What woman?"

"The blonde woman. The one you think he favours. Her name?"

Filchis sneered. "He always called her *opio*. My little *opio*."

"Opio." Scalentine pidgin for *key*. Well, that was little or no help.

"That will do," Fain said. "At least for now. Tie him up. I'll take him back to Scalentine with me. And the woman... Exile?"

"Exile," Enthemmerlee said.

"No," Selinecree said. "You *can't*."

Filchis gaped at her. "But you... but she..."

"Oh, were you under the impression the effect was permanent?" Mokraine said. "Really, what sort of creature do you think I am?"

Selinecree said, "Where will I go?"

"Anywhere but Scalentine," Fain said. "I regret to say that you would *not* be welcome."

"There are plenty of people who would welcome me! I met a number of perfectly *charming* people, even if they were barbarians. It seems they'd treat me better than my own family!"

"Really? Who were these people?" Fain said, studying his nails with a weary air.

"Oh, a merchant, he was quite charming, really, for a barbarian, and some sort of soldier fellow, I think, and well, it was weeks ago, but I'm certain they'd offer me hospitality in a moment once they heard what I've been put through!"

"I don't suppose you remember any names?" Fain said.

"Names? Oh, no, I can't pronounce barbarian names," Selinecree said. "Besides, they all knew mine."

A small silence followed this.

"Are you *sure* you don't want her dead?" Laney said. "Because I've only known her a day, and *I* do."

"Even if I did, it is unlikely that the Ten Families will condone the execution of one of their own," Enthemmerlee said.

"Will you ask for it?" Malleay said.

"Ask? No," Enthemmerlee said. "Has there not been enough death?"

Fain looked at her. "She is, of course, family," he said. "But do you really think she still deserves your kindness?"

"Kindness?" Selinecree shrieked, half-rising from her chair. The guards either side of her, as one, put their hands on her shoulders. "How can you call it kind, to drive me from my home, from everyone... You can't take me from Chitherlee, you can't!"

"Alone? No, I can't. But the Ten Families will."

"They won't! They'll never accept it, never! They'll never accept *you!* You... you *monster!*"

"Selinecree," Enthemmerlee said, "there is only one monster here."

CHAPTER
TWENTY-TWO

THE DAY OF the Patinarai ceremony. I'd heard the noise as I was getting ready; the low sea-murmur of a great many people.

As we came out of the door, Enthemmerlee gasped.

Not only the area outside the Entaire grounds, but the entire top of the hill was covered in people. Thousands of them. Gudain and Ikinchli, nobles and shopkeepers. The crowd in the Ancestor Caves had been contained; this was not. The slope behind the Palace, where the actual ceremony would take place, was seething with them. The path we would walk up the slope and the area around the little temple were separated from the crowd only by massed ranks of Palace guard and Fenac. I wondered what had happened about the prison break. Laney had put a deglamour on me, so that the eye and mind would slide over me as someone of no importance, since being rearrested would be damned inconvenient.

Laney and I took the coach with Enthemmerlee and Malleay. I'd put Stikinisk on the roof.

The discovery of Selinecree's treachery had had one salutary effect, at least: the household guard were starting to look something like a unit, tight, contained, and wary as deer at a waterhole.

"You have done a remarkable job with the guard, Babylon," Enthemmerlee said. "I would like to thank you."

"It wasn't all my doing," I said, and suppressed a shudder. I didn't want anyone knowing quite how true that might be.

"No one likes realising that someone will throw their lives away without a thought."

"Indeed," Enthemmerlee said. "Now they have a common enemy."

She was so pale she was almost transparent. Malleay hesitantly put his arm around her shoulder and hugged her, as though she might snap, and she smiled at him gratefully. He smiled back. "You'll do splendidly, Em."

"Thank you, Malleay. I just wish..."

"Yes," he said. "Me too. But we're doing this for him, too, remember."

"Yes."

She was dressed in a pearl-coloured gown that was still of the Gudain style, but somehow hung in elegant folds and moved with her as she walked. The sleeves, instead of being absurd, gigantic puffs, were soft falls of cloth like folded wings.

I leaned over to Laney and muttered, "The gown?"

"Oh, I had to do *something*. I mean, you saw what she was wearing before."

We passed the mud pool; Laney stared, fascinated, but wrinkled her nose. A few flecks of rain pocked its surface as it glooped and belched and sent out jets of smelly steam.

THE CARRIAGE DREW to a halt, and the Palace guard thumped down their spears. We got out.

The rest of the Patineshi, with their families, arrived one by one. I eyed the crowd, eyed the guard, felt my nerves buzz and sing. There were the usual shifts and shufflings of any crowd waiting for something to happen; nothing untoward that I could see... yet.

Eventually everyone important had arrived. With the efficiency of long practice, we were manoeuvred around the Palace, in order, and up the slope.

The officiant was waiting for us at the temple. Like Enthemmerlee's family priest, he wore a four-cornered ruff beneath his elaborately embroidered gown; in front of him was a small altar covered with a scarlet and gold embroidered cloth. At least they weren't burning incense. He held up a bronze bowl and struck it with a small rod. "Let the first of the Patineshi come forth."

A young Gudain was prodded to the front. He looked nervous to the point of nausea.

"Who claims their role among the Advisors to the Crown?"

The boy watched him with anxious concentration, and after slight hesitation, replied, "I, Pranthrow en Laslain Degarth." His voice was odd, uninflected and somewhat high pitched.

"Do you take on the burden of government in truth and fairness, turning always towards the honest path, considering at all times what is best for Incandress in Reputation, in Commerce, in Faith, and in Art?"

Pause, consider. "This I do undertake." That same flat voice. I realised the boy was nearly, or totally, deaf.

"I ask now, do you understand the gravity of what you undertake?"

"This I understand."

"Do you have anything you wish to say before you become Patinate?"

"I will undertake my duties to the best of my ability, considering always what is best for Incandress."

The officiant touched the boy on each shoulder with the rod, and he bowed, and moved back, his face streaming with sweat.

"Let the second of the Patineshi come forth."

I felt Enthemmerlee breathe in, and then she moved.

The crowd had been merely watching, until now. When Enthemmerlee stepped out, they leaned forward, all together, like corn under the wind. The murmuring deepened.

"Who claims their role among the Advisors to the Crown?"

"I, Enthemmerlee Defarlane Lathrit en Scona Entaire the Itnunnacklish."

The noise increased. "You're not her! You've no right!" a woman shrieked.

"Shut up, bitch."

"How dare you, you scaly bastard!"

The Palace guard stepped up, planting their spears. The Fenac put their hands to their maces.

"Please settle yourselves," the officiant said. "We will continue."

"Oh, surely not!" said a large, double-chinned Gudain man in a truly appalling tube-robe of muddy yellow and red, that made him look like something I'd tell a client to take to the doctor sharpish. "This just shows how impossible it is that the House of Entaire should put forward its candidate. Such an action will only encourage such disruptions."

"Enthemmerlee Defarlane Lathrit en Scona Entaire is an acknowledged candidate for *Patinarai*," the officiant said. "Objections were filed and dealt with at the proper time. Please respect the ceremony."

"That *thing* is not Enthemmerlee Entaire!" someone in the crowd yelled.

"That *thing* is not the Itnunnacklish!"

Something flew through the air, and I stepped in front of Enthemmerlee. The officiant looked at me, shocked. The missile hit and rolled off the edge of the altar with a flat *thud*. A shoe. A wooden-soled, ugly, bright blue Gudain shoe.

"No," Enthemmerlee said.

"What?" the officiant said.

Enthemmerlee moved forward, hitched her gown, put her hand on the officiant's shoulder and with sudden, utterly Ikinchli-like grace, was standing on the altar.

I could see the faint blue shimmer of Laney's ward around her, but it wouldn't stop a missile. I scrambled after her with considerably less grace, though I was tall enough not to need to use the shocked officiant as a stepladder. I couldn't hold my shield in front of her if she was three feet above me.

She held out her arms to the crowd. "Listen to me," she said. Her voice cut across the crowd; strong and true.

"There is something I must tell you," Enthemmerlee said. "A great shame and dishonour, a terrible deception."

You could feel the crowd draw in its breath, as though they expected her then and there to remove her mask, to expose herself as a fraud.

Instead, she told them about Selinecree, and about the *Ipash Dok*.

"To take something sacred, and turn it into a means of vengeance and destruction," she said, "this is a dreadful evil. There are those among you who have sought to do this with the meaning of the Itnunnacklish."

A number of Ikinchli in the crowd looked at each other, and dropped their gaze.

"Yet Selinecree did not act alone. She did not even act knowingly. She was manipulated by one outside Incandress, who cared nothing for our lives; for Gudain, for Ikinchli. Someone willing to destroy us without thought, because to them *we do not matter*. To them, we are all, equally, worthless. And they knew that they could destroy us all, without once setting foot on the soil of our land. And why did they know that?"

She clenched her fists, and glared at the crowd. "Why did they believe that we would fall for so stupid and vicious a trick? *Because we let them.* Because in mutual fear and hatred, we allowed it." She looked down a moment, and swallowed. "A very good man once said to me, 'If we see only the scars of our past, the future will slip away while we lick over old wounds.' We nearly lost our future, *all* our future.

"Had we not been divided as we are, had we seen ourselves as one nation, instead of Gudain and Ikinchli, then this threat would never have come upon us.

"And how many more will there be? We are a small country. Can we look to the Perindi Empire to protect us? No. They can afford us only as much protection as will keep the trade routes open. We are alone, and we must stand alone.

"We must look to ourselves. And only if we are no longer Gudain and Ikinchli, only if we are one and all Incandrese, can we survive in a world to which, otherwise, we are *nothing*.

"By tradition and law I have the right to become Patinate, but without your will, that too means nothing.

"I tell you only this. If you join with me, if you will give me the chance to prove what I can do, I will strive with every last breath of my body, with every last shred of my spirit, to make Incandress what it can be. For I am not a daughter of the Ten Families, nor am I the Itnunnacklish, but first, and most, I am *Incandrese*. I ask you now: what are you?"

There was a moment's silence, the wind hissing across the hill, the soft taps of rain on cloak and skin and helm.

"Incandrese!" A high, exultant yell. I couldn't see who it was, or what species they were.

It didn't matter. The cry was taken up, by one after another after another after another, until they rolled together into a great roar.

"Incandrese! Incandrese! Incandrese!"

And Enthemmerlee stood holding out her hands, and smiling, and weeping, and Malleay looked at her with his heart in his eyes.

Seeing a movement near him, I happened to glance at Fain. He looked extremely thoughtful.

ONCE THE CROWD had calmed, the ceremony was concluded by a somewhat overwhelmed officiant; Enthemmerlee's acceptance set off another roar. There were only two other Patineshi, and both of them, looking more than a little shaken, gabbled through their responses, and jumped like deer when the crowd, obviously in a generous mood, decided to cheer them too.

It would have been nice to be caught up on the tide of it. But glad though I was that things were going Enthemmerlee's way, I knew that a crowd's love is fickle as the spring weather, and that among those cheering her to the echo today there were those who'd be looking to pull her down tomorrow.

Still, that part was politics, and not my business. I would be heading home.

And more than glad to do so. Filchis' shadowy mentor was looming in the back of my mind, murderous and still unknown; and we had to get home before the news could reach him that his plans had gone awry.

ENTHEMMERLEE, MALLEAY, RIKKINNET, and Enboryay stood in the hall.

Enthemmerlee turned to Darask Fain. "Mr Fain. Thank you for your help. I hope we will not need to call on you again."

"Madam Enthemmerlee." They bowed, not taking their eyes off each other. They put me in mind of cats, calculating whose territory ended where.

Then she turned to me.

I bowed. They bowed back. Malleay gave me a small, secret smile. Enthemmerlee reached out, still a little hesitant, and took my hand. "Thank you. You have done so much."

"I only wish... Well, you know what I wish."

"Yes." For a moment, grief shadowed her face again. "But we must deal with things as they are, not as we would wish them to be."

"Indeed. Good luck, my lady."

"Thank you. You too. Since we could not persuade Mr Fain that the one responsible should be given over to us... What will you do, when you find him?"

"Whatever's necessary," I said.

"Yes."

"Ancestors go with you," Rikkinnet said, rather unexpectedly.

I wasn't going to tell her that I bloody hoped not. I didn't need any more disembodied beings in my life.

"Luck, Rikkinnet. I hope we see you in Scalentine."

"Luck, Babylon." She tilted her head. "Oh, you will see me."

"Good."

Two carriages were waiting, the disti shifting and snorting with impatience to be off. Fain. Mokraine. Bergast, still somewhat subdued.

"Where's Laney?"

"Talking to someone," Fain said.

Captain Tantris stood a little to one side, with the guard. Both he and they looked harder, smarter, and taller than they had.

"Captain," I said.

"Madam Steel. Me and the guard, we... Well." He held something out to me.

It was a sling; an Ikinchli sling. Simple, lethal: leather thongs, a cupped cradle. "It's the real thing," he said. "Got ancestors on it, and everything." I could see them, cut into the leather. He handed me a leather bag. I could feel the smooth weight of the stones. "I'm having 'em all trained in it."

I cast an eye over the guard. Yes, they all carried a sling on their belts. "Can't defend against a weapon you can't use," Tantris said.

"Good point." I noticed a few scabbards among the Ikinchli, too. "Edged weapons?"

"No law against Ikinchli carrying them on private property," Tantris said. "I checked. And if it happens that we're not on private property, well, maybe they were taking 'em for sharpening at my request, something like that, eh?"

"You're pretty sharp yourself. Luck, Tantris."

"Luck."

Stikinisk stood very straight, her new sword gleaming in its polished sheath. "Stikinisk."

"Heya."

"Drop in on us some time, all right? If you ever decide to go travelling."

She smiled, not quite happily. "Okay. I will do that."

"I mean it," I said. "I'd like to see you, jewel-eyes."

This time, her smile was a little more genuine.

At that moment Laney came around the corner, chattering merrily, pointing up at windows and sketching things with her arms – curtains, perhaps.

Beside her, actually smiling, was the seneschal. As Laney scrambled into the carriage next to me, he gave her a shy little wave.

"Laney... did you seduce the seneschal?"

She giggled. "I've never met a man so happy to talk about décor." She leaned out and blew him a kiss. "And really quite surprising in bed, once you got him to relax. I can see why you like Ikinchli so much." She sat back, with a sigh.

I leaned out of the window as we drew away. At the top of the steps stood Enthemmerlee, with Malleay on one side and Rikkinnet on the other. They raised their hands, and I did likewise.

The guard thumped the butts of their spears against the ground, and we pulled away.

Fain glanced at the other carriage. "You think putting Mokraine in with Bergast and Filchis was wise?"

"I think it will mean both Filchis and Bergast will mind their manners, and it will keep Mokraine amused."

I leaned back, and stroked the sling.

"That's pretty," Laney said.

"Yes, it is. Lethal, too, if you know how to use it."

"Do you?"

"I haven't used one in *years*. I did, briefly." I ran my fingers over the figures on the leather. "Looks like I'm taking the ancestors with me after all." And what else? Well, that remained to be seen. I'd heard nothing, felt nothing since the gaol, but that didn't mean Babaska was done with me. I didn't want to think about it too much, in case it gave her a way in, but it was hard not to.

I still didn't know what I was going to tell the crew. And, oh, sweet All, what was I going to tell Hargur?

He was honest. It was as much a part of him as his spine. I couldn't go on concealing things from him. But if I told him...

"Do you think it will work?" Laney said. "All of this?"

"I don't know. They've a long way to go."

"So have we. I hope it's a fast ship."

"I'm still not sure..."

"Sweetie," Laney said. "You've *done* what you can."

"She roused the crowd. But there's tomorrow."

"And the day after that, and the month after that, and the year after that. Were you going to stay here forever?"

"No. By the All, no. I want to go home."

"Besides, I doubt Selinecree will prove a problem," Fain said.

"You think she'll go happily into exile?" I said.

"Not at all. Which is why I was glad you advised Enthemmerlee which guards should accompany her. The one called Dentor and two of his friends, I believe. A shame they never shaped up very well, as guards. I hear there are terrible bandit problems in the area she will be travelling through."

"Really. You heard that."

"Oh, yes, I listened very carefully to her route."

I wondered whether a message was already on its way, a bag of coin passing hands in some anonymous inn.

A carriage on a distant road. A handful of incompetent guards, and the swift silent approach of masked figures over the rocks.

A black snake, marked with red, slipping away in the bloody dust, to find a warm place to hide until the sun came up again.

* * *

Soon Laney dozed off in her corner of the coach, no doubt worn out from her discussions of décor with the seneschal.

"An interesting speech," Fain said, softly.

"Enthemmerlee's? Did the job, didn't it? I just hope the effect lasts more than five minutes."

"Yes. You weren't insulted?" Fain said.

"Insulted? Why?"

"Your part in things was not mentioned. You did, after all, prevent a disaster."

"Hah. Remind me never to go to another ceremony involving altars in any way, would you?"

He looked bemused. So he *didn't* know all the details about Tiresana. That was a relief. "Anyway, you think I was up there expecting the grateful thanks of the populace?" I grinned. "I was deglamoured, if you remember. And for good reason. If anyone had noticed I was there, they'd have slammed me back in gaol."

"Despite you deserving the... ah... grateful thanks of the populace?"

"Well, maybe not. Hardly worth the risk, though, was it?"

"I think that Enthemmerlee omitted your name quite deliberately, Babylon. I knew she was clever, but she is rather more of a politician than even I realised. And she was more than happy to wave farewell to two obvious foreigners" – he glanced at Laney – "your pardon, *three* obvious foreigners as soon as possible."

"You're getting at something, Mr Fain. What are you getting at?"

"Turning the Incandrese against outsiders, *all* outsiders, while a valid strategy in the circumstances, may have unfortunate consequences. Nationalism is a dangerous beast that can quickly turn ugly, as we have seen."

"The Builders."

"Yes."

"It would be a pity," I said. "But the Gudain were like that already."

"So, surely, were the Ikinchli."

"Well, yes, a bit, but they had better reason. And the ones who come to Scalentine seem to settle in all right."

"Scalentine is good at that," Fain said.

"It's a shame, though," I said.

"A shame?"

"If you're right..." I sighed. "Enthemmerlee's lost her innocence. Maybe it was losing Lobik. But there was something about her that was, I don't know. A kind of fire."

"Idealism. Yes. It is a tender plant, Babylon, and seldom survives long in the harsh soil of politics."

"I hate politics."

"I know."

I glanced at him and he was smiling. I smiled back, and he looked away, out at the passing landscape and the rain.

I looked out of my own window, listening to the *dap-dap-dap* of the disti's feet, the rumble of the wheels. It was getting dark; the low clouds hid any sign of moons or stars. I leant my head back, and tried to doze.

Eventually we reached Calanesk Port. Like ports everywhere, it was as lively by night as it was by day. Torches hissed and crackled, lanterns glowed, stevedores sweated and swore, roped cargo creaked and swung, on board or off.

Laney woke chilled and grumbling and fussed about getting her gear on board the ship; we had already booked passage, under false names. Fain walked off to speak to the owner of the shop where Selinecree had picked up the lethal *Ipash Dok*, but it was empty, the owner long gone, presumably with a handsome profit in hand.

I fidgeted on the quay, then once we boarded, I fidgeted on the deck. The closer we were to home, the faster I wanted to get there. I didn't know what was happening. And we still had some clues, but no *name*.

Fain strolled back along the quay, and walked up the gangway, exchanged a few words with the captain, and joined me at the rail.

"At least I didn't have to run up a rope this time," he said.

"Hmm?" I stared at the deep blue sky; there was a band of chilly pale green along the horizon, marking where the sun had disappeared.

"Babylon. Really. You missed an opportunity to remember my moment of extreme humiliation?"

"What? Sorry?"

"Never mind, I was being foolish. What's bothering you?"

"Everything. Now all *that's* behind us, I can't help wishing we had more. I mean, what are we going to do?"

"I am going to follow up what information we *do* have as best we can."

"I wish we had a name."

"Yes."

"We've *nothing*, Fain."

"Not so. We know he has offices on Little Copper Lane."

"Unless he *knew* Filchis was following him and deceived him on purpose."

"We know he is, or is connected with, a grain merchant, and that among his followers is a man with dyed red hair and a blonde woman he seems to favour."

"A blonde woman whose name bloody useless Filchis didn't know. How many blondes are there in Scalentine, anyway? At least we know she's human, or he wouldn't..." I stopped as something yanked at me. I stared at the fading remnants of the sunset. Deep blue, pale green.

The blonde woman had worn a dark blue cloak, with pale green lining.

I'd seen her. I'd seen her in the crowd around Filchis, when someone had thrown a piece of fruit at him.

I'd seen her at the Red Lantern. Asking if we had any weres on the staff.

And I'd seen her trying to pawn a piece of jewellery, and walking off on the arm of one Thasado Heimarl, merchant. Who'd asked her about the stain on her cloak. A fruit stain.

"What if she was a plant in that crowd, throwing the fruit to rile up Filchis's supporters?"

"Who, Babylon?" Fain was leaning forward, fixing me with those dark eyes, but I hardly noticed.

"The blonde woman. I've *seen* her. And I think I know who our grain merchant is," I said. "His name's Thasado Heimarl."

"What?" Fain said.

"Yes, listen! She came to the Lantern, she was asking about weres, pretending that was her thing. She was in the crowd around Filchis, and buggered off sharpish when things got nasty. And I saw her with Thasado Heimarl. He said something about getting justice. 'We'll get our justice.' And he was talking to me at the Roundhouse Tower, trying to get me to give away confidential information from my clients."

"That may be less than proper, but it is hardly proof, Babylon. Even if it is the same woman, there's no evidence he knows what she is involved in, is there? But certainly, we can question him."

Mokraine had wandered up on deck and now propped his arms on the railing and stared out over the water. The familiar gleamed at his heel like a lump of wet clay half-formed into some child's nightmare.

"Well it's suggestive, isn't it?" I said. "And at least I know her name, now. First name, anyway. He called her Suli."

"Suli. Suli. Now that name I *have* heard," Fain said.

"You know, I thought that..." I said.

"There's a woman," Fain said, slowly. "A blonde woman who works as a clerk in the Section. Her name is Suli."

And it came crashing through me. Mokraine lifted his head and looked at me, his hair drifting about his face.

"Oh, fuck," I said.

"What?" said Fain.

"I... Shit."

"Profanity is not information, Babylon."

"I used the device, Fain. I used the device to send a message, and the woman on the other end said she'd send it with Suli."

Fain looked at me. "What message?"

"That there was going to be a robbery at the silk warehouses. I heard it at the inn, on Incandress."

"And why did you feel this was urgent enough that you would use the device, which you are unauthorised to do and which you clearly disliked?"

"Because it's our silk," Laney said, coming up behind him. "I bought it, you see, as an investment, only I shouldn't have, and if it gets stolen everyone's going to be fearfully angry and lose all their money. Or the other way around, I suppose."

"That's not all," I said. "They're targeting weres. The Builders are targeting weres. Look. Maybe Heimarl thinks the Chief suspects something. Heimarl was at the party at the Roundhouse Tower. Hargur said, later, that someone had been sounding him out. Heimarl sounded *me* out at the same party. Maybe he was seeing if he could get the Chief on side, and then when he realised he couldn't, he decided that he'd be better off with him out of the way. And people know how the Builders feel about weres, suspicion's going to fall on *them* if the Chief..." – I could hardly get the words out – "if the Chief's murdered. That's why Heimarl was so determined to get Filchis out of the way, too. Because Filchis can identify him. He might not know his *name* but he knows what he looks like.

"And this woman, Suli. She knows about me and the Chief, she knows he'll trust information if he thinks it comes from me. And she's in the Section.

"She'll find some way to make sure he checks it out himself. And that means the Builders will know he's going there. They'll know where he'll be. Fain, we've got to use the device, we've got to warn him!"

"I'd advise against it," Mokraine said.

"What? Why?"

"Firstly, because it has been used too frequently of late, when things are already unstable."

"What things?" Fain said sharply.

"Everything," Mokraine said. "The matter of being, the All. Such devices as yours create cracks. They weaken the structure."

"It... What?" Fain looked as though someone had jerked the ground from under his feet. "But we've had it for years..."

"Does anyone know who made it?"

"No."

"Are there many such items of power in the Section's archives?"

"I am not at liberty to tell you that."

Mokraine looked at him. "No, you are not, are you?" he said. "I would advise you that any such things should be treated with extreme caution."

"Excuse me," I said, "if the All that Is isn't in danger of coming to an end right this *minute*, can we *please* get back to the matter in hand?"

"The matter in hand... ah, yes," Mokraine said. "Even if Mr Fain should be foolish enough to use the device again so soon, and so close to the place it was last used, *you* should not be anywhere near it, Babylon. And when I say nowhere near it, I mean that another plane would be preferable. Certainly not within the confined space of this boat."

"But..."

"At the moment, your mind is your own," Mokraine said. "I assume you would like it to remain that way?"

I stared at him. "Laney?" I said, when I found my voice. "Can you do anything? Get us there any faster?"

"No. Not if you mean mess with the weather, Babylon, and... No."

"Babylon." Fain took me by the shoulders. "Babylon. We are going as fast as we can. And I have people watching him, remember?"

But I could barely hear him. All I could do was clutch the railing and stare, begging the sky for the first light of Bealach portal on the horizon.

CHAPTER
TWENTY-THREE

WHEN MY HANDS cramped from clutching the rail, I practised with the sling, using whatever I could find for missiles, saving the stones in their leather bag for the real thing.

Mokraine came up to me as I swung and loosed, swung and loosed, his eyes following a collection of trivial objects on their journey over the water. They didn't usually get very far before they landed.

"Mokraine," I said.

"Babylon. Try to calm down. I can feel your anxiety all the way to the lower deck. There are probably creatures in the far depths wondering why they are becoming unaccountably anxious."

"Sorry. Mokraine?" Load. "Why did you come to Incandress?" Loose.

"I am a weathercock, Babylon."

Fain had used the same term. "How do you mean?" Load.

"I mean that what I did, when I created a portal all those years ago, has tied me to them in some way. And if their state is threatened with change, it pulls me in. I am at the mercy of something other than myself. I object to this, Babylon, I object to it strongly."

"I know the feeling." Loose.

"Yes, I know you do."

"You... Oh." Load.

"Beware of making openings," Mokraine said. "And beware

of widening them. One does not know" – he glanced down at the familiar – "what may come through them."

I shuddered, hard, almost dropping the sling into the sea.

"I'm sorry, Babylon," Mokraine said.

"I'm sorry, too. I'm sorry you couldn't... Well."

Mokraine shrugged. "I have not yet given up. There may be other methods."

"Yeah."

I wondered if there were methods of shutting the door on a god, too, once one has let them in.

But mostly, as I sent shot after shot over the empty ocean, apple cores and bits of wood and anything I could scrounge, I wondered about my crew, and about Hargur, and whether the watchdogs that Fain had set on him were keeping him safe.

I WAS STILL clinging to the rail and retching from the portal as we were pulling into the harbour. When I straightened up, Fain was standing beside me. He passed me a cup of water from the barrel.

"Don't you ever bloody get sick?" I said.

"Seldom."

"Lucky."

"I suppose I am."

Looking along the quay, I saw a bright red uniform, and for a moment my heart leaped. But it wasn't the Chief. Just a Militiaman, chatting to someone, dock patrol, checking things out.

It meant nothing. If the Chief... if something had happened to Hargur, things would keep rolling, at least for a while. He had a firm hand and good lieutenants.

"Oh come *on*, why do these things take so damn long to dock!"

Finally, *finally*, we bumped the quay and I was down the gangplank almost before it hit the ground.

"Where's this bloody silk warehouse?" I knew there were at least two hundred warehouses of various sizes around the dock.

"The harbourmaster will know," Fain said.

The harbourmaster was a big, red-faced, slightly pig-like sort who was gabbing in rapid pidgin to several flustered people about – surprise – grain. I didn't care about grain. Or silk. I cared about Hargur.

He flipped a dismissive hand at us. Fain went up and whispered into one of his large, pointed ears.

Some of the red left his face. He and Fain had several more whispered exchanges, and he spat out a stream of instructions. I couldn't follow them, but Fain strode off confidently.

"What about *him?*" Laney sniffed, gesturing at Filchis.

I looked around for the Militiaman I'd seen earlier, but he'd disappeared. "Bring him, bring him. There's no *time.*"

Bergast, grumbling, hauled Filchis along after him. Filchis moaned and fussed.

"It's daylight. Surely robbers aren't likely to go about their business in broad day," Laney said.

"It's not the robbers I'm worried about. It's Heimarl and his Builder friends."

Filchis glared and panted as we hurried after Fain. "I have done nothing, nothing. Once this gets to the proper authorities..."

"I *am* the 'proper authorities,'" Fain said. "Oh, and I think incitement to murder is something."

"You can't prove it!"

"No? I think you will have a long and interesting time in prison. Where you will find yourself surrounded by those you have so often described as violent and mindless."

"You can't! I'm a citizen of Scalentine!"

"Citizens are required to act like citizens," Fain said. "And they are subject to the laws that govern citizens. However. If you are willing to point out your mentor, in front of witnesses, as the man who financed the establishment of the Builders..." – he glanced at Filchis – "yes, I thought so... and as the man who sent you to Incandress, then perhaps arrangements can be made."

"Arrangements?"

There were guards on the door of the silk warehouse, of course. "Has the Chief been here? Hargur, City Militia?" Fain said.

"Who wants to know?" one of the guards said.

I slammed him against the wall. "Me. I want to know. Now."

"Yes! Yes, he was! Leggo!"

I was vaguely aware of Fain dealing with the other guard.

"He's not now?" I said.

"No!"

"Then where is he?"

"His friends came for him."

"His friends."

"Yes, they came and he went with them!"

I struggled to get the words out. "When? And where did they go?"

"No more than a minute or so before you got here, and they went that way!" He jerked a trembling thumb to his left, towards a narrow alley between two grain warehouses. "Please..."

I let him go, and ran.

"Babylon, dammit!" I heard Fain yell.

Halfway down the passage something caught my eye. A scrap of red.

Militia red. Woollen thread, caught on the wood of a small door.

I stood and tried to calm my breathing. If I went charging in, I could get Hargur killed.

The others caught up to me.

"There?" Fain said quietly.

I pointed to the thread.

He nodded.

"Mr Filchis," he said. "You will be absolutely quiet, until I require you to speak. You understand?"

Filchis opened his mouth, and Fain's knife was at his throat. He shut his mouth. "Good," Fain said. "I hope I do not have to tell anyone else? Babylon. Try not to kill anyone. We need witnesses. Excellent. Shall we?"

Mokraine had wandered off, to examine something of interest down the other end of the alley. We left him to it, and crept in like mice after the grain. There were a pair of big, trollish thugs just inside the door; Fain, despite still being one-handed, managed to take one out. Laney did that mouth-seal trick on the other that she'd used on Filchis, and I took him down. Bergast looked down at his own glowing hands, all magicked up and nowhere to go, and made a face; I saw, clear as day, his realisation that he was going to have to learn to be a damn sight faster than that.

Filchis stared down at the unconscious trolls.

Inside the warehouse was a vast, chilly, echoing place. The grain was stored in huge wooden bins, with steps running up the side of each to a small platform, and a hatch in the base for the grain to be spilled out.

It smelled of dust and chaff and slightly of mice. A cat slipped quietly in and out of the shadows. We crept among the bins. I could see a small figure standing on one of the platforms; as we got closer, I realised it was Heimarl. I heard Laney gasp, and glanced around. She was glaring and clenching her hands. Heimarl turned and looked down, but not at us. We kept to the shadows, creeping from bin to bin, until we were directly below him. I peered around and saw what he had been looking at.

Hargur. Leaning against the wall, his arms folded.

Either side of him were two cloaked figures. Insignificant, dull, irrelevant figures. My eye kept sliding off them. Deglamoured.

It didn't stop me seeing the blades they were holding to his throat and gut.

I drew back, and exchanged looks with Laney. One wrong move, and Hargur could be dead. I tried not to think of Lobik, collapsing and dying before my eyes. I readied the sling, waiting for a chance, however slim.

"You do realise," Hargur said, "that people know where I am."

"It would be irresponsible for the Chief of the Militia *not* to let people know," Heimarl said. "Of course, it was rather irresponsible for you to come alone, but then, you had a personal interest in the fate of that silk, did you not? And a dislike for anyone knowing your business. With which I sympathise."

"What do you want?"

"Oh, Chief Bitternut, I want many things. Firstly, I want to know what you have heard from Incandress."

"Why should I have heard anything from Incandress?"

"Don't play the fool with me."

"I'm not in the habit of playing the fool, Mr Heimarl. I'll answer your question if you'll answer mine. Why do you want me dead?"

"It's nothing personal. I simply prefer a Chief I can work with. We could still come to an arrangement."

"An arrangement? Like the one *we* had?" Filchis said, his fury overcoming his fear of Fain's knife. Fain, grimacing, slid back into the shadows before Heimarl's gaze could find him, leaving Filchis to stagger out into view, his hands still tied.

"*Filchis?*" Heimarl said.

"Why did you send me to Incandress?" Filchis said, looking up.

I couldn't see Heimarl's face, but I could hear the warm, entirely false smile he had plastered on. "Why, Angrifon! Because I trusted you. Tell me, how do you come to be here?"

"You mean, how do I come to not be dead?" Filchis jerked his head at the troll lying by the door. "A brute. In your employ! You lied to me. You *lied* to me. You told me you believed in our cause, but you didn't, did you? You sent me to Incandress to die. For *this*." Filchis kicked out at the hatch at the bottom of the bin. It couldn't have been very firmly fastened; the hinges creaked, and the door fell open. Grain began to pour out in a whispering rush.

It was enough to distract one of the figures guarding Hargur. I managed, more by luck than accuracy, to catch his shoulder with a slingstone, and his blade spun away. Hargur dropped and rolled; I saw the flash of a blade, dulled suddenly with blood. *His* blood. *Hargur.*

I drew steel. The first man went for his dropped sword, but a flicker of pink around his feet made him stumble to his knees. Laney, good girl. I slammed my hilt against his head as I went past and faced up to the next. He was slight, but damn fast; I felt a sting across my leg.

Fighting a deglamoured opponent is nasty. It messes with your concentration. I missed a couple of easy hits and got another blow to the shoulder before the deglamour suddenly lifted, and I found myself facing a pasty sort with hair of an unnatural red and a shorter reach than I'd thought; I got under it, caught his blade with mine, and punched him in the gut with my other hand.

He folded.

I whipped his blade away and kicked him in the head, just to be sure. 'Disable anyone you're going to turn your back on' is a good rule.

I spun round. Hargur was on the floor, breathing hard, Laney next to him.

Running footsteps. More of Heimarl's men, appearing around the bins. Ten or so, some human, some not.

"I really wouldn't advise that," Fain said.

"No, I don't suppose you would," Heimarl said. "Kill them."

"Boss..." His men looked at each other. Then they looked at Laney. She was concentrating on Hargur, but she glanced up and glared. Those nearest her backed off.

Bergast raised his hands. "Come on then!" he said, blue-green light flickering around his fingers. More of the men backed away.

"Magic can't kill you here, you fools!" Heimarl said.

"I can, though," I said. "Over here, boys."

Two more ran for it, out the door we'd come in.

The rest took the challenge. I found myself back to back with Fain. I tried to concentrate, not to glance over at Hargur. Downstroke opened one across the chest, sent him staggering back against the one behind him. Bergast behind me; a green flare and one of the men squealed and stumbled, briefly blinded. Got him with a straight kick, and he went down wheezing and gurgling.

Filchis, trying to run, hands still tied, skidding on the loose grain, going down hard.

Heimarl, looking down, exasperated, turning to come down the steps.

We were on the docks. If he got away, he could go anywhere.

"Fain, cover me!"

The smooth weight of the stone in my hand, slipping it in the cup, aim. Loose.

It clipped his shoulder. I heard the crack, and he yelled, and slipped, overbalancing the low rim of the bin, and disappeared.

Dammit. Well, it would take him a minute to scramble out.

The rest gone or down.

"Hargur." I dropped beside him. He was pale and panting. Laney had her hands pressed to his side, pink glimmer around her fingers, her cloak trailing in his blood.

"Scratch," he panted. "Get Heimarl."

"I've got him," Laney said. "Go catch my *yrrkennish* client."

"Your...? Never mind."

I ran up the stairs alongside the grain bin.

The dust of the corn filled my nose and mouth; the grains had dipped in the middle as they ran out through the hatch, and there he was, Thasado Heimarl, only his head and arms still visible. His expensively-cut hair oddly blond with dust and spiked with grains, his face and desperately reaching hands dusted yellow, grains stuck to the sweat. "Help... me..." he wheezed. The weight of it was crushing the breath out of him.

"Help you. Help *you?*"

"Help..."

"You were willing to murder millions of people, and you want me to help you?"

A retching groan, his eyes beginning to bulge. *"Huuh..."*

Oh, I wanted to let him choke. But unlike some, I'm no fucking murderer.

And Hargur, not to mention Fain, would be furious if he escaped questioning. I hooked an arm around the rail, and reached out.

But I couldn't reach. He was too deep. His waving, sweating hand didn't even brush my fingers. I pushed myself further out, horribly aware of the rushing sound of the grain still pattering out on the floor over the shouts and yells and sounds of the law being enthusiastically enforced. If I slipped, I'd follow him down.

The grain was up to his chin, then over it.

His mouth was open, taking shallow, gasping breaths; the grain crested, poured in.

I felt my hand slipping on the rail, and someone grabbed my belt.

The last glimpse I had of Thasado Heimarl was his hand, that soft merchant's hand, reaching and grasping above the choking mass. Then it was gone.

I scrabbled my way back onto the platform.

Fain let go of me and stood back. "Well," he said, looking down.

"Is it?" I stood up and brushed myself off as best I could.

I didn't hear his answer; a cry from below went through me like a spear. "Hargur!"

I almost broke my neck getting down the steps.

The place was full of Militia. They were lifting him onto a stretcher.

I pushed through them. "Hey," I said.

"Heimarl?" he said, and coughed, which obviously hurt.

"Fell in the corn. Dead. Stop talking."

"Babylon..." His mouth was tight at the corners. Pain, or something else. He met my eyes briefly, looked away; not like him.

"Sssh. Let them stitch you up, then we'll talk."

"We'll look after him," one of the Millies said.

"You'd better," I said. They carried him away.

"Where'd all the Millies come from?" I said.

"I sent a message by the harbourmaster," Fain said.

"Oh. Right." I stared at the cobbles. Grains lay scattered between them. "I didn't know you could drown in corn," I said. The remaining Millies were still trying to get Heimarl's body out of the grain bin. The others had taken Filchis off with them, as he gabbled names and details with a kind of furious fervour. How useful any of it would be, I didn't know; I just hoped they put the little scrote in a cell with a couple of pissed-off weres and an Ikinchli or two.

"It was Filchis kicking open the hatch that did it," Bergast said. "If the corn hadn't been running out, it wouldn't have happened." He looked up at the astonished faces. "I grew up on a farm, all right?"

"Ah," I said. "Well, you made a decent show in there."

He flushed. "What should I do now?"

"You should go home," Fain said. "And write out for me a list of everyone with whom you have had a connection. Everyone who might have had an interest in getting you sent to Incandress, everyone you have ever met who had any awareness whatsoever that you were interested in joining the Diplomatic Section, and anyone at the Section you have ever spoken to, and what was said. You will discuss this with no one. You will go nowhere. You will wait for me. You understand?"

"But..." Bergast said.

"Excuse me?"

"Yes, sir."

"And Scholar?" Mokraine said.

"Yes, First Adept?"

"When Mr Fain has finished with you, you will bring what is left to the old chapel on the corner of Fishpond Alley."

"Wh..."

"The existence of such an incompetent in the Noble Arts offends my soul. If you wish to learn, if you wish to leave the rank of Scholar behind, you will come to me."

If Bergast's mouth had opened any wider, he would have fallen into himself and disappeared. Once he managed to re-hinge his jaw, he said, "Yes, First Adept. Thank you, First Adept."

"Don't thank me. I have taught you nothing yet." Mokraine walked away, leaving Bergast staring.

"Don't you think you'd better get started?" Fain said.

"Oh, yes, I will, right away!" He scurried off.

"Laney, you recognised Heimarl, didn't you?" I said.

"Oh, yes. Remember I had a new client, just before you left?"

"Not really."

"Well, I did. That was him. I was talking to him about the new curtains and *he* was the one who advised me to buy the silk!"

"Oh." I'd forgotten about the silk, again. "Crap, the silk. I hope it's still there."

"Don't worry," Fain said. "I sent a message by the harbourmaster about that, too. If it is still there, it will be very well guarded."

"Thank you," I said, vaguely feeling more was required but not able to dredge it up. "Laney, did Heimarl suggest some of the people you should borrow from, by any chance?"

"Well, yes."

"He really didn't like being turned down, then," I said.

"I *didn't* turn him down!"

"No, but I did."

"It seems you have good instincts," Fain said.

"Bollocks. I'm an idiot. I almost got Hargur..." I had to stop.

"Come on," Laney said, grabbing my hands. "I'm taking you home. Mr Fain, will you join us for a meal?"

Fain bowed. "I don't think so, Lady Lanetherai. I have to deal with that woman, Suli. The little *opio*. A key, indeed. A key to the Section. I really *must* examine our hiring procedures." He bowed over her hand. "Thank you all the same." He stood in front of me, took my hand, bowed. Briefly, he pressed my fingers. "He will be fine, Babylon. Hargur is exceptionally tough." He turned away.

"Hey, Fain."

"Yes?" He didn't quite turn back.

"Thanks."

He touched his hand to his brow, and walked on.

We walked back along the familiar streets, with their noise and their colour and their dozen different races and their smells and their sheer, furious life.

I thought about going to The Swamp, to see Kittack; but I'd leave it a while. Let things settle out. I felt a small hollow in my chest at the thought they might not, a bigger one at the thought of Hargur.

We turned into Goldencat Street to see someone lounging in the doorway of the Lantern, talking to Jivrais, who beamed and waved.

"I know you, don't I?" I looked at the stocky, tusky female with the polished skin who was standing just inside the door, with a slightly embarrassed grin.

"This is Gornack," Jivrais said. "She's looking for work. She wants to be a doorguard. Say yes, do!"

"I've seen you somewhere before," I said.

"There was a bit of trouble, by the gardens," she said. "Some scrote who wanted to kick out half the city for being the wrong shape. Anyway. Heard you were looking for someone. I could do with some work, only I'd need to bring my lad with me. He's no trouble. Well. Not much."

"Your lad."

"Yeah."

"How old is he?"

"Seven."

"You know what sort of place this is?"

"Yeah. He knows, too. He heard about you. He wants you to teach him." She looked at my face and roared laughter. "*Fighting*. He wants you to teach him fighting."

"What, he can't learn that from you?" I said, looking at her rippling muscles and extremely well-used looking weaponry.

"I'm his *mother*. He doesn't think I know anything worth knowing." She rolled her eyes.

"I don't know if we can hire," I said. "We may be broke. But come eat, anyway," I said. "Flower?"

Flower poked his head out of the kitchen. "Hello, Babylon."

"We got enough food for one more?"

"Oh, I think I can manage that."

I fell into bed after I'd eaten. I was so exhausted I could barely see, but still I couldn't sleep. The thought of Hargur, injured because I'd been stupid. Because I'd used Fain's damned device even though my gut had been yelling at me not to. The hells with the silk; the stuff was bad luck from beginning to end. The way Hargur had looked at me, or rather, not looked. Eventually I fell into a thick, dream-riddled doze, in which over and over I saw the blade go dull with Hargur's blood. Familiar faces, drowning in grain. Heimarl. Kittack. Laney. Hargur. Me.

CHAPTER
TWENTY-FOUR

GORNACK YELLED UP the stairs, "Babylon! Visitor!" Damn, she had a voice like someone cleaning a well with a brick.

Still half-asleep, I dragged on a robe and staggered to the top of the stairs. "You still here? I'm not taking clients today..."

Hargur was standing in the doorway. He looked tired and I could see the bulge of bandages under his shirt. "Hey."

"What are you doing here?" I said. "I mean, I thought... How are you?"

"Not as bad as I looked, clearly," he said, smiling slightly. He took off his helmet. "Can I come in?"

"Oh, of course!" I hovered at the foot of the stairs. I didn't want to take him into the parlour, and the bedroom seemed... wrong. He didn't look as though that was what he was here for, even if he was up to it.

But he started walking up the stairs, and perforce, I followed.

"Oh, your silk thieves were caught," he said. "In time."

"Oh, good."

"You should do well out of that."

"I suppose so," I said, wondering if that was the only reason he was here.

He went into my room, and I shut the door behind us.

"So," he said, looking out of the window. "How was it? Incandress?"

"A long story. Hargur, please sit down, you look... tired."

He folded himself into the chair by the window, not looking at me, fidgeting with the helmet he held in his hands. "Hargur?"

"Babylon, look. I just wanted..."

"Hargur, I need to..."

We both stopped. I felt a dreadful emptiness waiting to open in my chest. *I messed up. I messed up, and I almost got you killed, and you've had enough.* "Go on," I said. *Get it over. Please.*

"I just wanted to say that if you're unhappy, with this, then I understand. You don't have to dance around it."

I must have looked very stupid. I *felt* very stupid. "I don't. I mean, I thought... Wait. Hargur?"

He looked up, and I realised he looked utterly miserable. It hurt. It actually hurt, to see him look like that. I went over and knelt by the chair, and took the helmet away, and held his hands. "Hargur, what is it? What made you think that?"

"Well, you know."

"I *don't.*"

"Before I left, something was wrong. And then you went off to Incandress. I wondered if you'd gone because of something I *said,* because I never meant... Oh, this is idiotic," he growled, suddenly sounding more like himself. "I don't *do* this."

I took a very deep breath. "Well, maybe we should." I looked down at his hands, stroked the hard calluses with my fingers.

"When you got that message, why did you go yourself?"

"Because they told me it came from Incandress, via the Section, so I knew it was something to do with you. I knew you wouldn't hand me a lead coin."

"But you went alone."

"You're joking, aren't you? I took young Roflet. But he got diverted by a weeping woman. Boy's too susceptible."

"Blonde, by any chance? In a dark blue cloak?"

"How did you know?"

"She's the one who passed on the message. She's mixed up with Heimarl's lot."

"Yes. Well, the Section's dealing with her, now."

"They caught her."

"*We* caught her," he growled.

"Is Roflet all right?"

"Sore head and injured pride. Why are we talking about Roflet, anyway?"

"I don't know. Hargur, there are things I haven't told you. About me. About who I was, and what that means. There's stuff even I don't know what it means, yet. And you need to know them."

"I put you in danger..." He started to protest and I put my finger to his lips. "Wait. Please. I put you in danger and I was stupid. I thought that was the end of us, and I wouldn't have blamed you. But that's not all.

"There's this goddess, and she's sort of got access to my head. I don't know if she can reach me on Scalentine. It's to do with what I was, a long time ago. But it's my fault she's there. I sent that message... Oh, never mind. But that was how she got in first. And then..." I seemed to run out of breath, and took another one, hard. "Filchis tried to get them to... to do things, to make me talk. I don't even know if they'd have done it, but it's been done to me before, and I... Well. I let her in. I was afraid, and it was all I could think of." I tried to smile. Hargur was looking so grim I felt a little frightened.

"Let me understand this. You mean Filchis tried to get them to torture you?"

"Yes."

His hands clenched hard on mine. "I see. And it's happened to you before?"

"Yes."

"Good thing I didn't know," he said. "Don't look like that. I mean, it's a good thing I didn't know about Filchis. If I had, I'd have broken the little scrote's neck. With or without a sword in my ribs."

"You..."

"So, this goddess of yours. What's she like?"

"Well, she was a goddess of soldiers, and of sex. I suppose she still is, but I don't know where she's doing her goddessing these days. Except, you know, in my head. And I don't really *know* what she's like, except she wants something. I've only spoken to her about three times in my life."

"But you know she's about fighting and sex. So, she's you, only more so?"

"Um…"

"Because frankly, that doesn't sound too bad. Considering that for three days a month I'm a mindless thing that can't be around you in case I try and tear your head off."

"Ah."

"Honestly, Babylon. Did you really think that would be enough to put me off? I'm a were, *and* there's the job. I see scarier things than you at morning lineup."

"There is something else," I said. This was the hardest thing, strangely. I couldn't even look at him.

"Tell me," he said, gently.

"Because I was an Avatar, see, well, I can't have children. Not ever. I don't even know if it matters to you, if I've any right to think it might, but…"

Before I could finish he pulled me up into a fierce hug, awkwardly, across his knees, and I heard him gasp with pain.

"Hargur!" I stood up.

"I'm all right," he growled.

"Get on the bed, let me look."

He lay down, and I checked, but the bandages were firm and no blood seeped around them. "Idiot."

"So're you. Come here," he said, pulling me down and wrapping his arms around me. I put my head on his chest, hearing his heartbeat, strong and steady. "I'm glad you told me," he said. "Is that enough? For now?"

"Yes."

"You're shaking," he said.

"I'm frightened."

"Of what?"

"Of this, maybe. Of us."

He pulled back and looked at me, brushing my hair out of my face. "Why?"

"I..." *The past,* I wanted to say. *I have too much of it, and it keeps coming back.* But I remembered Lobik, and Enthemmerlee. *The future will slip away while we lick over old wounds.*

Lobik was gone. He and Enthemmerlee had been robbed of their particular future. And the same might happen to us. But did that mean I had to waste what we had, worrying? "Oh, sod it," I said. "Give us a kiss, Chief."

"Gladly," he said. And he did.

THE END

ABOUT THE AUTHOR

GAIE SEBOLD WAS born in the US to an American father and English mother, and has lived in the UK most of her life. She now resides in leafy suburbia with her partner, writer David Gullen; a daft cat, and a lot of plants and books.

She began writing shortly after learning to read, and has produced a large number of words, many of them different.

She has worked as a cleaner, secretary, till-monkey, stage-tour-manager, editor, and charity administrator; she now writes full time and runs occasional writing workshops.

She is an obsessive reader, enthusiastically inefficient gardener and occasional poet.

Find out more at
www.gaiesebold.com

ACKNOWLEDGEMENTS

THANKS TO THE guys at Solaris for endless patience, catching all the stuff I should have caught, and helping me in my struggle with semicolon addiction.

Thanks also to the ever generous T Party Writers, to almost all of whom I now owe critiques…sorry, guys. Soon. Honest.

And to the staff of the RSA, especially the Fellowship department, who, during the years I worked there, generously put up with my: obsession with apostrophe placement; hatred of exclamation marks; discussion of disembowellings before coffee and moaning about the arguments I was having with the voices in my head. Without calling the men in white coats even once. Thank you.

'Ingenious, gripping, and full of pleasures on every level. Exceptional.'
- Mike Carey, NYT Bestselling author of The Unwritten

BABYLON STEEL

GAIE SEBOLD

UK ISBN: 978 1 907992 37 7 • US ISBN: 978 1 907992 38 4 • £7.99/$8.99

Babylon Steel, ex-sword-for-hire, ex... other things, runs The Red Lantern, the best brothel in the city. She's got elves using sex magic upstairs, S&M in the basement and a large green troll cooking breakfast in the kitchen. She'd love you to visit, except...

She's not having a good week. The Vessels of Purity are protesting against brothels, girls are disappearing, and if she can't pay her taxes, Babylon's going to lose the Lantern. She'd given up the mercenary life, but when the mysterious Darask Fain pays her to find a missing heiress, she has to take the job. And then her past starts to catch up with her in other, more dangerous ways.

Witty and fresh, Sebold delivers the most exciting fantasy debut in years.